THE CHOICE

THE CHOICE

MICHAEL ARDITTI

First published in Great Britain in 2023 by
Arcadia Books

An imprint of Quercus Editions Limited
Carmelite House
50 Victoria Embankment
London EC4Y 0DZ

An Hachette UK company

A CIP catalogue record for this book is available
from the British Library.

ISBN (HB) 978 1 52942 575 8
ISBN (Ebook) 978 1 52942 577 2

1 3 5 7 9 10 8 6 4 2

Typeset by MacGuru Ltd in Minion
Printed and bound in Great Britain by Clays Ltd, Elcograf S.p.A.

Papers used by Quercus Books are from well-managed
forests and other responsible sources.

For James Kent and Rodger Winn

'Sooner murder an infant in its cradle than nurse unacted desires'

William Blake

'No gown worse becomes a woman than the desire to be wise'

Martin Luther

'But I suffer not a woman to teach, nor to
usurp authority over the man, but to be in silence'

1 Timothy 1:12

'Painting is the grandchild of nature. It is related to God'

Rembrandt van Rijn

ONE

2019

One

Clarissa walked past the tower and gazed into paradise. It was an image that she'd seen almost every day for the past five years. The symmetrical intimacy of the figures in the foreground had formed the backdrop to her prayers and sermons. The heavily laden bough, which traced the arch of the panel, hung down before her as she elevated the Host. She'd expounded on the wolves and lambs frolicking in the meadow to children at Sunday Group who, unlike their parents, were not disturbed by the artless self-absorption of the two youthful lovers. She'd wearily corrected visitors, who questioned the authenticity of the quinces clustered tantalisingly above the couple's heads. She'd defended the scriptural snake in discussions with colleagues and scholars, as much from loyalty to Seward Wemlock as from theological conviction. She'd been filmed describing how in 1987, as a young radio producer, she had herself interviewed the artist as he worked on the decorative scheme for the body of the church. But she could not recall the last time she'd stood quietly at the west wall and gloried in Seward's singular, provocative yet compelling vision.

She well remembered his impassioned defence of his Eden: the choice of colours, the mauve, red and blue of the knobbled tree trunk and the orange and purple of the grass, so confusing to villagers who looked for a more realistic depiction of the natural world; the choice of fruit, the bright yellow quince, an affront to traditionalists who claimed that the forbidden fruit was an apple; the choice of two fifteen-year-old models, one his own daughter, as Adam and Eve. Asserting both their agelessness and innocence, he'd nevertheless taken pains to avoid offending those who would have had them ashamed of their nakedness before they'd even tasted the fruit. Adam knelt, straight-backed, his thighs at a perfect right angle to his calves, his arms hugging Eve and covering her breasts as she sat, legs crossed, pressed against him, poised to receive his kiss. Yet, while it was true that there was no overt display of their budding bodies, their pose was imbued with a sensuousness that made even sophisticated viewers uneasy, along with a purity that challenged their unease.

Most contentious of all had been the portrayal of the serpent: not wrapped around the tree or lurking in the undergrowth, as in conventional iconography, but deep in the background, on what, from the distance of the altar or the pulpit, looked to be a rocky landscape but which, from where she stood now, was without question a crumpled scroll. Moreover, what had seemed to be cliffs and crevices in the preparatory drawings was seen to be Hebrew script, several words concealed in the folds but still discernible as the Genesis verses in which, confronted by God, Adam blamed his disobedience on Eve, who in turn blamed it on the serpent, who coiled above his Hebrew appellation, שָׂרָ֣ב, like a blot on the scroll.

Clarissa surveyed the rest of the church. Above the arcades, flights of angels, their skin, wings and robes a lustrous white, with flecks of gold in their aureoles and sporting strikingly incongruous footwear, led the saved souls heavenwards, as fondly as the children who gathered their mothers to the altar on Mothering Sunday. The eight figures, one for each spandrel, had been chosen by Seward to reflect the diverse parishioners, both the old farming families and the incomers who had revivified the village. With no hint of mortality, the models were instantly recognisable: Lucy Dutton, last in a venerable line of Tapley cheesemakers; Dickon Yates, whose forebears had cultivated watercress on the wetland for almost as long; Hugh Clifton, who had set up a conservatory factory in his grandfather's barn; Stanley Furness, headmaster of the now defunct grammar school; Heather Fenn, long-serving barmaid at the Wemlock Arms; Bob Goodfellow, lock-keeper on the nearby Llangollen canal; Penny Harkinson, founder of the Tapley museum; and, in what some took to be a stumble but the subject himself insisted was a genuflection, Clarissa's predecessor, Vincent Slater, wearing a cassock and biretta which had dated him even then.

Four of the models were dead and, she prayed, enjoying the bliss prefigured for them in the paintings, one was in residential care and another refused to enter a church tainted by her presence at the altar. Two, however, remained regular congregants: Heather, who, after forty years of breathing in tobacco fumes, sat at the back, away from the asthma-inducing thrusts of the thurible; Bob, now in his eighties, who sat directly beneath his middle-aged self, affirming 'the resurrection of the body' in the Creed with a confidence that Clarissa could only envy. While less intense than the furore over Eden, there had been discord over the spandrels, with some would-be models suggesting that the choice should not be left to Seward but decided by lot. Clarissa couldn't help thinking that Daisy Quantock, the most vocal objector to the entire scheme, might have been mollified had Seward featured the headmistress of the primary school rather than the headmaster of the grammar.

The final panel hung above the chancel arch, depicting Christ in glory, with Adam on his left and Eve on his right. The presence of the primal couple had caused further dissension, but Seward justified their inclusion both artistically and theologically. His was a God of forgiveness, not judgement.

For all the responsibility of their custodianship and the wounds that were reopened whenever the panels came under discussion at the parochial church council, Clarissa gave thanks every day that God had sent her to a church with what experts described as *the most richly painted interior of the past fifty years*. Her husband, Marcus, attributed it to chance and her mother, Julia, to the enduring respect for her father in his former diocese, but Clarissa herself saw the hand of providence in her return to a parish with whose fortunes she had once been closely connected. Besides, although nothing had been said, she was convinced that it was the art which had secured Marcus's support for her move. While he'd long since renounced the faith that had brought them together, he attended services more often than at St Cuthbert's, where the chief visual attraction had been Lucy Skinner, the choir's buttery soprano. Clarissa was well accustomed to the Lord's mysterious ways, but how wonderful it would be if Seward's pictures proved to be responsible, even in part, for reviving her marriage!

After locking the door and setting the alarm, a requirement that always depressed her, she made her way through the churchyard. Opening the lychgate, she stared back at the ancient tower, a constant concern to one entrusted with the care of bricks and mortar as well as souls. The church was the heart of the village, even for those who rarely set foot inside. Attesting to six centuries of sustained devotion, its walls were as hallowed as the words spoken within them. The tower itself had suffered three lightning strikes during the last century alone, the only casualty being one of its twin clockfaces, whose hands had stopped twenty or so years earlier at 10.25. This had created a perennial diversion for the village children, who watched for the moment when the two sets of hands concurred, as eagerly as she and Marcus had once waited for the Apostles to appear in the windows of the great astronomical clock in Prague.

A fleeting glance at the undamaged clockface led her to quicken her step, as she crossed the road to the church hall. This had been the gift of a Regency Wemlock, allegedly after losing a bet with the rector that he could name all seven of the Deadly Sins (he had overlooked Pride). She felt a twinge of envy for a time when the rector could rely on his patron's munificence to fund building works. Her eye drifted to the row of almshouses, newly converted into three luxury homes, and the envy turned to shame. Taking a deep breath, she entered the hall. The two wardens were busily arranging the chairs in a circle: Alec Whittle, a retired auctioneer, in his all-weather sludge-grey cardigan, the loose leather patch on his left elbow a product of persistent scratching; and Petunia Wyatt, widow of the late area coroner and commandant to an army of stray cats. Marcus had nicknamed the pair Slough and Despond, unfortunately in the hearing of their son, Xan, who, at fourteen, used every parental indiscretion to his own advantage.

The hall swiftly filled with the elderly women, who were not only the backbone but the blood and sinew of the church. Eager to attract a younger, more mixed congregation, she took comfort from the thought of Rodger Ashdown, the ever-jovial plumber, who'd rebuffed her invitation to an Open Saturday, explaining, 'When the mortgage is paid and the kids are through school, then I'll have time to think about the Man Upstairs.' She doubted that Lewis Heathcote, a Nantwich wine merchant and the only man in the hall under forty, had ever applied for a mortgage, but that couldn't be the only reason he and Keung, his Cantonese lodger (the euphemism was their own), were among her most faithful congregants. She greeted him with the beaming smile that Xan accused her of saving for anyone gay, black, disabled or living in social housing. Determined to prove him wrong, she deflected its full force on to Lewis's neighbour, Daisy Quantock, who looked understandably startled.

If anyone were likely to oppose her proposal for the new lighting system, it was Daisy. Prone not only to speak her mind but to pronounce on the virtue of doing so, she had spearheaded the opposition to the paintings themselves thirty-two years ago, taking her case as far as the consistory court where, in another black mark against Clarissa, it had been dismissed by her father. Even so, she had remained a stalwart of St Peter's, as well as headmistress of its primary school, until, outraged by Father Vincent's introduction of the Roman Missal and sacramental confession, she led a small group of recusants to join the village Free Church. She had re-entered the Anglican fold on Clarissa's appointment, announcing her return with a graceless gibe that a woman rector could hardly be worse than a womanish one.

On her left (the chair between them conspicuously empty), sat Pamela Salmon, Clarissa's closest friend and ally, who'd succeeded Daisy at the school, her innovations incensing her predecessor ('Stars just for turning up!'), long before the current uproar over relationships teaching. She greeted the remaining members of the council and took a seat next to Wendy Plowright, the district nurse and lynchpin of the flower-arranging rota. She accepted a cup of tea from Shirley Redwood, the parish secretary, discreetly pouring the spillage back from the saucer, and a brownie from Hetty Blakemore, the doyenne of the homemade produce stall at the Autumn Fayre.

Clarissa opened proceedings with the Collect of the Day. Shirley read the minutes of the previous meeting, her muted tones accompanied by the whistle of Hetty's hearing aid. Alec reported on the progress of the Churches Together group and Petunia on the printing of the new welcome pack. Daisy, the recently elected safeguarding officer, explained that she was still awaiting instruction on whether PCC members themselves required DBS checks. Katy James, the refreshments organiser, expounded on the revised – 'one might say refreshed' – rota ('There again, one might not,' Wendy murmured), before thanking Lewis for the gift of a state-of-the-art coffee machine, which, she confessed, was 'a little complicated for some of us oldies, who can't tell our macchiatos from our flat whites'. Amid a ripple of sympathetic laughter, Lewis, who took his coffee very seriously, sat stony-faced, before offering to give the team a demonstration, where-upon Katy looked even more flustered.

Pamela, whose husband Brian was tower captain, reminded members that it was St Peter's turn to host the annual South Cheshire Six-Bell Striking Competition, to which all were invited. Clarissa then relayed a request from Dickon Yates's niece to install a memorial bench in the churchyard to her late uncle, which, after warm recollections of the much-missed Dickon's idiosyncrasies, was unanimously agreed.

'Now to the main business of the day: the lighting of the Wemlock panels!' She heard – or imagined she heard – the sound of positions becoming entrenched. 'Seward Wemlock's paintings are master-works: treasures that we're privileged to hold in trust. But we don't display them to best advantage.'

'Are we an art gallery or a place of worship?' Daisy asked, dusting down a musty argument. 'I only seek clarification.'

'You already know the answer.'

'Your answer.'

'The answer of bishops and priests through the ages. The beauty of the art is an aid to worship. Just as it was with the original wall paintings six hundred years ago.'

'Back then the peasants were illiterate. Happily, that's no longer the case. At least it wasn't when I had charge of the primary school. I'm aware that there are different priorities now.' Clarissa gave thanks for Pamela's restraint. 'Besides which, there are all the stories about Wemlock's private life. The various women at once . . . I mean one after another . . . at any one time.'

'Give her enough rope,' Wendy whispered audibly.

'I suspect that if you looked closely at any artist, very few would meet your exacting standards,' Lewis said.

'Not only artists,' Daisy replied pointedly. 'But most have the decency to keep their indecency to themselves. Lord Wemlock flaunted his. Models from London lolling about, wearing next to nothing. His wife – his common-law wife that is – and his brother's widow sharing a "love rota". It's no wonder that daughter of his went mad.'

'That's pure speculation,' Clarissa said.

'It's the truth. It's no secret that I had my differences with Father Vincent. But at least he saw the danger in Wemlock's Eden. Hence the curtain he put up to hide it from impressionable minds. You'd not been here five minutes when you tore it down. Now look what happens! Only last month, Hayley Seagrove and that lad from Maynard's farm were caught kissing in the transept.'

'I don't think we can lay that at Seward Wemlock's door,' Clarissa said mildly.

'Or at Clarissa's,' Pamela interposed, 'since the PCC endorsed her decision.'

'I wasn't a member then!' Daisy said, the tell-tale vein in her forehead throbbing. 'More's the pity!'

Clarissa would have laughed off the incident, were it not for the ramifications in the village and, indeed, in the rectory itself, where Xan denounced any attractive girl who failed to show an interest in him as a 'slag'. Although she could think of no more suitable setting for young lovers to meet than a church, she acknowledged that the majority of her congregation drew a sharp line between the sacred and profane. It was Marcus who, on their arrival in the parish, had insisted she remove the curtain, arguing that its very presence signified an outrage that didn't exist. What neither of them had known was that Andrew Leaves, the model for Adam, had subsequently married Daisy's daughter Susan. So, having made her peace with St Peter's, Daisy was affronted by her naked son-in-law every Sunday morning.

'I fear we're straying from the point here,' Hetty said. 'I'm sure that we all share your horror at Hayley's behaviour.'

'She wasn't there alone,' Pamela said, although it was apparent that Hetty took the boy's delinquency for granted.

'If the lights were brighter, there'd be fewer snares . . . dark spaces . . . shadows,' Katy said diffidently.

'As I understand, the proposal isn't to relight the entire church but simply to spotlight the paintings,' Alec said.

'In principle,' Clarissa said. 'But we must be open to all options. It may be that spotlighting the paintings makes the rest of the church look drab. Now's not the time for half-measures. Seward Wemlock's work is attracting ever more interest. As many of you know, it's to be the subject of a major retrospective at the Tate in 2021.'

'Curated by your husband,' Lewis said, with an encouraging smile.

'Indeed. It's bound to have a knock-on effect. And with the growing number of visitors heading here from their canal boats or stopping off on the Sandstone Trail, we must do everything we can to entice them into the church. This is a real chance to increase our income: not only postcards and guidebooks but tea towels and T-shirts, mugs, paperweights . . . I'm talking off the top of my head. Not to mention the queues for Katy and her team's delicious teas.'

'Oh dear,' Katy said, 'I'm not sure whether we can—'

'I'm not sure whether anyone can,' Petunia cut in. 'Where will we find the manpower . . . that is, people power,' she said, in deference to Clarissa, 'to supervise these hordes? Look how stretched we are on Open Saturdays! They're a lovely idea, Rector, I'm not saying otherwise. Let the rest of the village come and see what we're about . . . flag up all our various activities. But in practice, what happens? Warren Davies drops in for free tea and biscuits while he reads his paper. Travis Crook from your Doubters' Group turns up to make mischief. And three lots of parents from the Chapel Hill estate dump their children in kiddies' corner while they slip off into town to shop.'

'Kiddies' corner!' Daisy harrumphed.

'But with the extra money we generate, we can afford to pay attendants,' Clarissa said.

'Instead of volunteers?' Katy asked, with a pained expression.

'Absolutely not. They'll always be needed. But we're jumping ahead of ourselves. All we have to vote on for now is whether to employ the consultant. He or she will let us know what's feasible. I'm sure we'll have many, many more meetings before we reach a final decision.' She strove to keep the edge from her voice.

The motion was carried by a margin of eleven to three. Clarissa snapped shut her file in relief and closed the meeting with a prayer. Gathering her coat and bag, she asked Alec to lock up, while she hurried home to see what havoc her son had wreaked in her absence.

She felt a pang of guilt, since she knew how Xan hated being used as an excuse, but it did well to remind them that she had responsibilities elsewhere.

She headed for the door amid a flurry of goodbyes and returned to the rectory, which was deceptively quiet. Even alone, Xan preferred to cocoon himself in his bedroom than to occupy the rest of the house. He reminded her so much of Alexander, although there was no one she could tell: not Marcus or her mother, who would each have cause for concern, and certainly not Xan himself, who took being named after his dead uncle as evidence that his parents had never respected his individuality.

'I'm back!' she called, to the usual silence. She walked into the kitchen, gazing in resignation at the remnants of his recent meal. She pondered heating up the leftover chilli but opted instead for a glass of Sauvignon, taking a moment to relax before going upstairs to check on Xan.

For fourteen years, she had sought to reconcile the demands of work and family. She'd made it clear, first in Putney and now in Tapley, that she would answer to *Vicar*, *Reverend*, *Clarissa* or even *Hey you!* but never to *Mother*. The weight of associations made it more than just the feminine of Father, and there was only one person entitled to use it: Xan. The irony was that he rarely did. He regarded it as a sign of maturity to address his parents by their Christian names. She was Clarissa to her face and the Rev in report, Mum when he wanted something, and Mummy only when he was ill.

Whereas she had thrilled to a clerical childhood, with its privileged place in parish life, Xan resented it. It was doubly painful that, after years of battling her father over the legitimacy of her vocation, she should now be challenged by her son. 'You choose to wear a dog collar. What about mine? Treated like the rectory pet by every weirdo and wrinkly!'

Xan was equally resentful of her age. She'd been mortified when he first went to nursery and asked her why she was the only mother with grey hair. That Christmas he'd announced to a startled Santa that his best present would be younger parents. Years later, when they moved to Tapley, Pamela, not yet her confidante, asked if she would clarify his circumstances, since he'd told everyone at the school that he wasn't her son but her grandson, the illegitimate child of her teenage daughter.

Shocked, she assured her that she was indeed his mother. Later, when she confronted him, Xan was defiant.

'I'm ten and you're fifty-four. If you'd had a daughter at nineteen—'

'I've never had a daughter!' Clarissa replied, biting back *More's the pity.*

'I've only got your word for that.'

'Would you like to see your birth certificate?'

'So what? You could have forged it.'

Marcus laughed off the fiction. 'All kids tell stories to make themselves more interesting.'

'Really? I must have been as dull then as I am now. No wonder Xan wants to disown me.'

'I went through a stage of claiming to be adopted. We should be grateful that he's allowing us a role in his conception, if only at one remove.'

It was easier to charge her husband with making light of her concerns than her son with fuelling them. Clarissa realised that it was Marcus's way of coping with his semi-detachment from family life. Even so, it was particularly hurtful from one who'd shared the anguish of hoping, trying and, in her case, praying for a child. Would Xan declare so often that 'I never asked to be born' if he knew that his birth had undermined their marriage?

Whatever reasons either of them might cite for their gradual estrangement, she had no doubt that her struggle first to conceive, and then to carry a child to term, had been paramount. She even wondered whether her own unanswered prayers had led to Marcus's apostasy. She recalled his dismay during the St Cuthbert's pilgrimage to Bethlehem, when he'd scoffed at the legendary potency of the Milk Grotto, only to catch her sneaking back to light a candle. For all the emotional strain and clinical humiliation, he'd put his trust in IVF. Then, two years after the miracle of Xan's birth, she'd pleaded with him to try again. No matter that he himself had grown up as a happy, well-adjusted only child, she insisted on Xan's need for a sibling. No matter that both Marcus and the doctors warned her that, at forty-six, her chances of success were slim, she professed her faith in a higher power. And because he loved her – she must always remember that – Marcus had agreed to a further treatment cycle, which failed.

Even so, he never reproached her. He was tender and patient, avowing that no second baby could ever be as perfect as Xan. It wasn't until much later that she understood it was a strategy for withdrawal. With every thought focussed on her mewling or sickening or

16

teething or toddling son, she'd been blind to the fact that her strapping six-foot-two husband felt neglected. Over time, she noticed that he mentioned one of his colleagues more frequently than any other: Helen Leslie, the newly appointed assistant curator of photography, a twice-divorced forty-year-old, with two teenage sons. She was spirited, sharp and the author of a well-received monograph on Lee Miller. His admiration for Helen was all the more striking, given his disdain for her specialism. It was as if he'd been willing Clarissa to confront him and, when at last she did, he confessed to their affair.

Honesty, as she instructed her bridal couples, was the key to a lifelong partnership. Although she felt emptier than at any time since she'd lost her last embryo, she was grateful that he'd made no attempt to dissemble. That, together with his contrition, gave her hope that she might salvage her marriage. The three of them met, at her request, in a World's End café, carefully picked for equidistance and neutrality. Despite her mistrust of Marcus's puppyish guarantees, she genuinely liked Helen. She was forthright and droll, affectionately puncturing Marcus's pomposity, neither apologising for their liaison nor parading her sexual supremacy. Moreover, she made it clear from the start that she had no intention of asking Marcus to choose between them.

'Whatever the two of you decide, that's your business. Please don't make it mine. I've had two disastrous marriages; I've no desire for a third.'

The question for Clarissa was whether she wished to make a clean break or remain in an imperfect union. The answer, which struck her with unexpected force, was to remain. She wanted a husband but, more than that, she wanted this husband. For all his flippancy, his elitism, his increasing intolerance, and even his loss of faith, she loved him and couldn't envisage a life without him. Besides, however much she assured her congregation that sorrow and adversity were not scourges, she couldn't shake off the feeling that her preoccupation with Xan was to blame for Marcus's drifting away. Her duty to her parishioners was a further reason for preserving the status quo. When many had only just accepted a woman at the altar, it would be unconscionable to confront them with a divorcee.

Her greatest fear was that she was emulating her mother, settling for the husk of a marriage rather than daring to face the future alone. But with Marcus pledging that his love for her hadn't died, it would have been perverse to have rejected him out of pique or pride. True to form, he compared himself to a Cubist portrait, with eyes and mouth pointing in opposite directions. She could bear it, as long as they pointed in the same direction when he was with her.

'We're not Mormons,' she declared, when he proposed inviting Helen to dinner; there were limits to the goodwill she was prepared to extend to her rival. They met every few months at Tate functions where, if any of the other curators were apprised of the situation, they had the grace not to show it. Her hopes that the affair would burn itself out were frustrated, leaving her, Marcus, and presumably Helen, to adjust to the new pattern of their lives.

The pattern was formalised when she was instituted at St Peter's. Marcus spent his weekdays in London with Helen, whose sons had both left for university, and his weekends and study days in Cheshire. Xan, who grew up taking Marcus's regular absences for granted, while protesting every time that Clarissa left the house, argued fero-ciously that he should be allowed to stay in London, blaming her for cutting him off from his friends and dragging him 'up north', which he pronounced as though it turned his stomach. He was so intent on punishing her that, for several months, he refused every invitation to play days and parties, claiming that his classmates were 'muppets and retards', adopting a pose of misery that punished nobody more than himself.

A month before his tenth birthday, she tentatively suggested that they might celebrate it, fully expecting the usual invective, only to be taken aback when he agreed. Pressing his advantage, he refused to invite anyone to the rectory, demanding that she take his whole class to see the birds of prey at the Cheshire Falconry. The party was a turning point. Almost overnight he was reconciled to Tapley, exchanging his metropolitan contempt for the proud provincialism of his two new best friends, Matthew Salmon and David Leaves.

She was convinced that Xan knew nothing of Helen's existence and regarded his father's arduous weekly commute as confirmation of her own indifference to everyone but her parishioners and God. Marcus had long since informed her that Helen had no objections to their sleeping together. She bit her tongue before remarking on his mistress's generosity. But, having been granted the licence, he rarely exercised it. She'd come to terms with their lack of physical intimacy, dwelling instead on their emotional attachment. But, as he hit puberty, Xan appeared disturbed by their reserve.

'If you're worried about shocking the child, I'll go outside,' he'd said the previous month, on seeing the discreet peck that Marcus gave her on arrival. More recently, he'd sought to eliminate their need for separate rooms by sending them web links to anti-snoring tablets, clips and sprays.

Aching to see him now, she dismissed thoughts of food and went upstairs. Her knocks unanswered, she followed the injunction on his door to *Enter at Your Own Risk*. The immediate risk was asphyxiation from the fug, followed by ruptured ear drums, as he shrieked at a higher pitch than he would have wished: 'Can't you ever knock?'

'I did three times,' she replied as, in one sweep, he tore off his headphones and slammed shut his computer, making her wonder whether Marcus's suspicions that he'd found a way round the spyware were justified. 'How's tricks?'

'Great. Brilliant. Never better.'

'Did you have enough to eat?'

'Amazing news: the child has learnt to use the microwave!'

'Pity the child hasn't learnt to use the dishwasher,' she replied, stooping to pick up his plate from the floor.

'Was there something you wanted or did you just come up to torture me?'

'The latter. Have you done your homework?'

'Zzz!'

'Do you need any help?'

'What do you know about transverse waves?'

'Not much, I admit.'

'Well then?'

'You could enlighten me.'

He groaned and buried his head in the pillow.

'Come here and give your old mum a hug,' she added, wishing that she'd dispensed with the *old*.

'Ugh! Boundaries!' he replied, but she caught the ghost of a smile as she leant over and ruffled his hair. It was clear that, for all his protests, her cosseting comforted him. 'Where have you been?' he asked, 'does Dad know you're such a stay-out?'

'I told you, I had a PCC meeting.'

'Yeah, Pathetic Christian Cretins.'

She refused to be provoked, any more than by his large poster of the crucified Christ, above the legend: *Wanted for Crimes Against Humanity*. 'You're entitled to your opinion.'

'That's good to know.'

'But if you want me to take it seriously, I suggest you come to my Doubters' Group. Six thirty every second Tuesday.'

'Another group! Why does everything have to be a group with you?'

'You never want to discuss it on our own.'

'I don't want to discuss it at all! You say to respect other people's beliefs. Muslims and Jews and Hindus. Why not atheists?'

'There has to be a first cause, Xan. That's all I ask you to remember when you're studying transverse waves or whatever. I'm sure scientists will advance more and more ingenious theories for what happened before the Big Bang. But nothing comes from nothing. So, unless you're going to argue that the universe itself is God and willed itself into being, there must be a creator.'

'Have you finished?' Xan asked coldly, just as her phone rang.

'Saved by the bell!' Clarissa said.

'Don't answer it!'

'I thought you'd had enough of me.'

'It's not right that all the saddos are able to hassle you whenever they feel like. You should complain.'

'My boss has more important matters to attend to.'

'The bishop?'

'He's just my superior. I answer to a higher authority.'

'I give up!' He fell back on the bed, revealing a band of pale stomach, which she resisted the urge to tickle. Instead, she took out her phone and played the message.

'It's Mr Yarrow,' she relayed to Xan. 'He left his shopping bag in the organ loft when he was practising this afternoon. He's bothered about his frozen peas.'

'He should be bothered about his frozen brain. His pea-brain.'

'Shush!' she said, as she returned the call. 'It's all right; it's gone straight to voicemail . . . Reginald, hi! It's Clarissa. There's no problem. I'll pop down to the church and retrieve the bag. I'll put the peas in the freezer. You can collect them tomorrow. Blessings!' She turned to Xan. 'I'll be five minutes.'

'You can't go out now. It's dark. You'll trip.'

'I'll take a torch.'

'You could get mugged.'

'I'll be fine. Don't worry,' she said, touched by his truculent concern.

'I'm not worried. It's your funeral.'

With a smile that he studiously ignored, she went downstairs, threw on her coat and set out. Reaching the church, she was perturbed to find that the alarm was switched off. Only a handful of people knew the code, and she'd impressed on them all the need for vigilance. There'd been a spate of burglaries in churches across the diocese, which the police had advised them not to publicise for fear of copycats. How would they be able to replace the Victorian candlesticks and plate, let alone repair one of Seward's vandalised panels, if the insurance conditions hadn't been met?

She heaved open the door. All was dark, apart from a faint glow issuing from the ringing chamber, which vanished at her brisk 'Hello!' The silence was palpable, as if the effigies in the Wemlock chapel were holding their breath. She climbed the belfry's spiral staircase, conscious that, were any thief or miscreant to hurtle down the forty-two uneven steps, she'd be knocked flat, thereby bearing out Xan's warning. Breathless, she reached the chamber and turned on the light. The six bell ropes, with their brightly coloured sallies, hung in front of her. To one side, pressed against the wall, as though trying to merge with the memorial plaques to past tower captains, was Brian Salmon, and to the other, slumped on a bench, was David Leaves.

Neither spoke, giving Clarissa a moment to speculate on why they were alone in the dark. Was it part of David's bell-ringing training: depriving his other senses in order to sharpen his hearing? If so, why were Brian's head in his hands and his spectacles beside him on the bench? Why was David barefoot, with his shirt half-buttoned and the hem poking through his flies?

'I heard a noise. I'm sorry. I didn't mean to startle you.' Marcus was right: why should she always be the one to apologise? 'What are you doing?'

Appearances to the contrary, there had to be an innocent explanation.

At last Brian broke the silence. 'I was giving David some extra practice before the competition.'

'It's my fault,' David said, drawing away from the bench. 'You mustn't blame Brian. You mustn't. It's all me. I came on to him.'

Brian emitted a groan as rumbling as the tenor bell, but Clarissa refused to be diverted. 'You're fifteen. It's an assault.'

'That's not true! I wanted it. I begged for it. I love him.'

'Stop it!' Clarissa said. 'Put on your shoes, tidy your clothes, and go home to your parents.'

'I love him.'

'Do as she says,' Brian told him. 'Don't make things worse, please!'

David stepped into his shoes without untying the laces, in a manner so redolent of Xan that Clarissa wanted to scream.

'I know how it looks, Clarissa,' Brian said. 'And I've no right to ask. But I beg you not to tell Pamela. For her sake, not mine.'

'He's fifteen; it's an offence. A crime.' Try as she might, she couldn't banish the word *sin*.

'I'm practically an adult,' David said. 'More responsible than my dad. So my mum says.'

'This isn't what she meant!'

'If we promise never to see each other again—'

'No!' David shouted.

'If we promise never to see each other alone,' Brian repeated grimly. 'Can't you forget this ever happened? There's no need to mention it to anyone.'

'There's every need. There are rules.'

'A code of discipline?'

'And of decency.'

'We are decent!' David said.

'You're a child, David,' Clarissa said, her words confirmed by his snivels. 'Go now, both of you. I have to think.'

'Think of the lives that will be torn apart,' Brian said. 'Not mine, that's nothing.'

'That's not true!' David said.

'Pamela's and Matthew's and Margaret's, and David's parents'.'

'I don't give a shit about them!'

'Of course you do,' Brian replied. 'And David's life too. Think of that.'

'I won't have a life. I'll kill myself.'

'Don't talk nonsense!' Clarissa said, in unison with Brian, making her shudder. 'Just go now. Go home, both of you. You shouldn't be here. I need time to think.'

She watched as they quit the chamber. She didn't want them to leave together, but nor did she want either to remain behind. She glanced at the ropes, hanging taut and untouched, then switched off the light and walked warily down the stairs.

She attempted to weigh up her conflicting responsibilities, but the calculation weighed her down. She made for the door, only to remember the abandoned shopping bag. Climbing up to the organ loft, she felt a surge of bitterness towards Reginald, all the more acute for being unjust. If he'd been less absent-minded, she wouldn't be in this predicament . . . She stopped dead in her tracks. What sort of priest – what sort of person – would put her own peace of mind before ending a boy's abuse? In normal circumstances (the phrase mocked her), she'd pass the matter on to the parish safeguarding officer, but Daisy Quantock was David's grandmother. Desperate for guidance, she slipped into a pew and knelt to pray, but the voices in her head muffled her petitions. So she moved to the porch, reset the alarm and rang Marcus. But he didn't reply either.

Two

'What's up, bro?'

'Sup. You?'

'Stuff, y'know.'

'The Rev around?'

'S'pose.'

Clarissa listened to the terse exchange with mounting horror. As a rule, she was intrigued by snatches of conversation between Xan and his friends, the dropped syllables as indicative of the generational divide as dropped aitches were of class. But she'd spent a sleepless night, finally taking a pill two hours before the alarm, and woken, her head pounding and fuzzy, with no clearer idea of how to proceed. Now David, the very last person she wished to see, was in the hall talking to her son. She poured herself a third cup of coffee, aware that she'd regret it later.

'The D-man's here to see you.' Xan appeared at the kitchen door, showing no curiosity as to why his friend should choose to come ten minutes before they were due to catch the school bus. David stood behind him, his unease so patent that Xan's indifference seemed culpable.

'Can I have a word?'

'Not now, David. You have school.'

'Just a word. It's important.'

'Want me to wait?' Xan asked him.

'No need. Later!'

'Affirmative.' Xan raised his arm to give David the fist bump, which had recently replaced the hi-five among their set. 'Chill, Clarissa,' he called as he left, his irreverence lost on his friend who had more urgent concerns. As the door slammed, Clarissa turned to David, who looked younger than ever in his blazer and tie.

'About what you saw – what you thought you saw – last night,' he said, his voice steeped in anguish.

'We can't discuss it now. You'll miss the bus.'

'Who cares? I'm not going to school. I can't ever go back there again.'

'Nonsense!'

'You mean you're not going to say anything?'

'Sit down, David. You're making me nervous.' She gulped her coffee. 'Would you like something to drink? A glass of milk or orange juice?'

David perched with one buttock on a stool, as if anxious to appease her while asserting his independence. 'Brian's like a father to me.'

'Fathers don't have sex with their sons.' She realised that she had no idea what they'd done together and prayed that it was a quick fondle.

'Not in our fucked-up world. But in ancient Greece and Papua New Guinea it was common.'

'What?'

'Sex is merely a cultural construct.'

'Did Brian tell you that?'

'No! I googled it . . . Dad never touches me.'

'I should hope not. I didn't for one moment suppose—'

'No, I mean never – never at all. Not even on my arm or my shoulder. It's like I gross him out. Like I'm dog shit or something he can't bear to pick up. And it's not just sex – that's your dirty mind – it's talk. Brian talks to me about everything. He's so much cleverer.'

'He's so much older.'

'So's Dad and he doesn't know squat. Ask my mum! He's only been abroad twice in his whole life.'

'It's not a competition. We can't choose our parents. And if we could, it certainly wouldn't be in order to sleep with them. Brian may not be your father, but he is Matt's – your oldest, closest friend. Have you thought about him? How can you go to his house, seeing his mother and sister, after what you've done?'

'I don't. I won't. I hardly ever do now anyway, not with this row between Mum and Mrs Salmon about sex at the primary school.'

'Sex education . . . that is relationships education. I understand that you're hurting, David.'

'Only because of you.'

'Believe me, I want to do what's best for everyone. And you can come to talk to me any time. Just not right now. I have to go. I'm due to take the school assembly in half an hour.'

'You won't say anything to Mrs Salmon?'

'I'm still trying to decide.'

'They'll put me in care. Let them! I don't care. I'll be better off there than I am at home. Then all the paedos will rape me and it will be your fault. What if they send Brian to prison?'

'Let's not speculate.'

'Why not? It's true, isn't it? If they do, I'll kill myself.'

'You must promise me on whatever you hold most dear that that's just an empty threat.'

'You mean like on my mother's life? No way. But I'll swear on Brian's.'

'That won't be necessary,' Clarissa said. She was struck by the intensity of his feelings and, their furtive assignations notwithstanding, wondered if it were the same for Brian. She'd assumed that he'd simply tried his luck, resting his hand on the small of David's back – or lower – as he guided his grip on the sally, or rubbing against him as he tested the weight of the bells. But what if their liaison had been going on for longer and the ringing were a smokescreen? David had always been the best-looking of Xan's friends. At fifteen, he had the same fresh-faced glow that had made Seward Wemlock choose his father as the model for Adam. When had Brian first been attracted to him? This year? Last year? When he was twelve, eleven, ten?

'You must go. You can still catch the 8.50 bus into town and be in time for second period. If you miss it, the school will contact your parents, which will only make matters worse.'

'So what? I'm a criminal already, aren't I?'

'Of course not. You've done nothing wrong.' He seemed so lost and frightened that she longed to give him one of her trademark hugs but, thinking better of it, clasped his shoulder and looked him in the eye. 'You must understand that you're the victim in all of this.'

'And you understand nothing. None of you. You don't know what it's like in here.' He jabbed his forehead. 'And you won't. Not in a hundred million years.'

David turned on his heel. She followed him into the hall, where he bumped into the umbrella stand, yelped and stomped out. The day had begun badly and looked set to get worse. She was no nearer to reaching a decision about Brian and David, and loath to involve Daisy. In forty minutes, she would be standing in the school hall alongside Pamela, whose marriage, happiness and, indeed, entire future lay in her hands.

She gathered her bag and coat and left for the church hall. The dank air matched her mood and permeated her clothing. Entering the hall, she went straight to the cramped office, with its bank of filing cabinets, shelves of mildewed parish registers and the wormy sounding board from an ancient pulpit, which she shared with Shirley Redwood and Titus, her mephitic corgi. Dubious of Shirley's claim that Titus doted on her, Clarissa gave the slavering dog a perfunctory pat as she made for her desk.

Shirley was already hard at work and well into her daily packet of chocolate digestives. With Lent less than two weeks away, Clarissa dreaded the annual abstinence which, given her secretary's frayed nerves, would be a penance for them both. Now in what Marcus had caustically dubbed her *crimplene years*, the once pretty Shirley had let herself go. In a bid to boost her confidence, Clarissa had rigged an Autumn Fayre raffle to ensure that she won a makeover voucher from Aphrodite's of Nantwich. But Shirley had donated it to a neighbour, explaining that 'it would be wasted on me'.

With enviable efficiency, she was typing the minutes of yesterday's meeting. She'd just fielded a call from a young woman 'on the estate' (her squirm sufficient to identify it), who wanted to marry at St Peter's but was reluctant to attend a service. 'I could tell she was living in sin,' Shirley said, lowering her voice, although there was no one else in the building.

'Then I should publish the banns as soon as possible,' Clarissa replied.

'Of course,' Shirley said, her tone suggesting that Father Vincent, for whom she'd toiled devotedly for twenty-five years, would not have been so shallow. 'That tramp – I mean down-and-out . . . or is it vagrant? I get so muddled – is back.'

'Poor man! There must be something we can do for him.'

'I offered him a bus pass to Nantwich and vouchers for the food bank,' Shirley replied, with a snort. 'He said he wanted money not charity, and sloped off.'

Clarissa glanced at the clock, its inscription *Take time for God* a permanent reproach to one whose habitual thought was *God, is that the time?* She scanned her diary, relieved to find that the schedule was too tight for her to ring Daisy Quantock. With a knowing smile, she left Shirley to 'man' the fort and headed to the school.

With its black-and-white, timber-framed cottages, cobbled streets and deep gutters, it was possible for a visitor, especially one taking tea in Jayne's Country Kitchen, to imagine that little had changed in Tapley for centuries. But like so much else about the village, it was an illusion. As property prices soared, many homeowners sold up and moved to the Chapel Hill estate, leaving the High Street, once wide enough for the monthly cattle market, choked with the new owners' four-by-fours. The 300-year-old Wemlock Arms, said to have been frequented by Dick Turpin, was now a gastropub and boutique hotel, loved by the incomers and loathed by the locals, who transferred their custom to the Coach and Horses on the Burland road. The sleepy village shop had been bought by Mr and Mrs Chabra and turned into a seven-day-a-week convenience store. The Old Constabulary was now a museum devoted to the history of cheesemaking and watercress farming, trades that had formerly employed half the village. As she strode past, shouting a hasty 'Blessings!' at Tricia Harding, the museum's curator, Clarissa gave thanks that, despite their mutual suspicion and, at times, overt hostility, there was one thing that united Tapley's sundry residents. From the ages of five to eleven, their children all attended St Peter's school.

She entered the school gates, newly equipped with magnetic locks and security cameras, and hurried through the hotchpotch of buildings, past the Victorian schoolmaster's house turned administration block, and the two HORSA huts still in use as classrooms, to the 1970s assembly hall. Mouthing apologies for her lateness, she joined the staff on the platform. At a cue from Pamela, the two hundred pupils rose as one.

'Good morning children,' she said, struggling to soften her voice, which an ill-disposed critic in her BBC days, had described as 'pickled in privilege'.

'Good morning, Reverend Clarissa,' they chorused, stumbling as ever over the protracted name.

Ignoring the adults' bored faces, reminiscent of the *Today* programme presenters during her stint on 'Thought for the Day', she told them the story of Jesus's encounter with a rich young man, who wanted to follow Him but refused to give up his possessions, leaving Jesus to explain that it was easier for a camel to pass through the eye of a needle than for a rich man – or woman – to enter Heaven. In an effort to engage the children, she first took a needle from her bag and pretended to prick herself, triggering a gratifying wave of gasps, and then asked for suggestions of other animals too big to squeeze through the needle's eye, drawing an enthusiastic response from year four, who'd recently visited Chester Zoo. After the lions, elephants, giraffes and gorillas, a whey-faced boy with suspiciously close-cropped hair called out: 'Lice!'

'Yes, indeed. Well done!' she replied, flustered. 'Although to be precise, a louse is . . . lice are insects, not animals. So what does the story teach us? Hold on a moment!' she said to a boy, who bounced up and down, waving his hand: an alpha male in the making. 'Everyone will have a chance to speak.'

'I think George is asking to be excused,' Pamela interjected.

'Yes, Miss. I want a widdle,' he replied, to a gust of laughter and Clarissa's embarrassment.

'Of course. Go ahead,' she said, as George scurried out, clutching his groin. 'Now what have we learnt? Anything?'

With none of the children venturing a suggestion, Clarissa opined that 'in my view, the lesson isn't that we should all become paupers, but rather that we shouldn't place too much value on material things – that's any kind of thing, not only cloth. Now, let's all bow our heads in prayer.'

She thanked God for home and school, for family and friends, for lessons and games, for activity and rest. She asked Him to fill their hearts with happiness, their minds with inspiration and their hands with creativity. Then, after committing all the pupils at St Peter's to His loving care, she watched them file out of the hall, before following Pamela to her office (rebranded from Daisy's *study*). Her lips twitched in a weak smile when Pamela, moving to the Nespresso machine, made her usual joke about trading in Brian for George Clooney.

'*Napoli, Firenze, Indonesia, Capriccio* or *Fortissio Lungo*?' she asked, listing the various flavours.

'*Lungo* please. I need the hard stuff.'

'One of those days?'

'And it's barely begun.'

Clarissa switched on her phone and longed for a (minor) emergency. How could she sit here blithely chatting after what she'd witnessed last night? She'd been instituted as rector of St Peter's a few months after Pamela's appointment as headteacher of its school and had swiftly recognised a kindred spirit. To Pamela alone she'd confided the truth behind the cover story that she'd moved north to be closer to her ageing mother: namely, that she'd been trying to regularise her relationship with Marcus. She'd thought that putting some distance between them would help; instead, it had widened the gap. In return, she was the first person (not excluding Brian) to whom Pamela had shown her mastectomy scars, breezily claiming to have been so flat-chested that they made little difference. More recently, she'd given her a blow-by-blow account of her perimenopause: 'No

35

breasts but the heaviest periods in history'; the crippling fatigue; the non-stop peeing; and the dryness that made sex more uncomfortable than ever ('Thank God for Brian's restraint!').

Clarissa grabbed her cup and drained it in a single swallow.

'You did need it! Things are tough at this end too.' She pointed to the pile of post on her desk. 'When I remember how I used to lament the lost art of letter writing!'

'More hate mail?'

'And then some! You'd think I'd been forcing four-year-olds to put condoms on cucumbers.'

Pamela's distress was palpable. Last autumn, with the full support of the governors, she'd introduced relationships classes into the curriculum. It wasn't true, she'd said in her proposal, that all happy families were the same. Even in a sleepy village like Tapley, there was a world of difference. She'd cited Boy A, who'd used his mother's hysterectomy as an excuse for absence two years running. It was only when Pamela questioned her that she discovered she lived with another woman, who'd also had cervical cancer. They were scared that, if their relationship were exposed, their son would be picked on. A and others like him needed not just to learn about alternative families but to have their own validated. Yet her carefully selected storybooks had scandalised Susan Leaves, a teaching assistant, who didn't hold with boys wanting to be mermaids or a pair of male polar bears raising a cub.

Susan was Daisy Quantock's daughter and conclusive proof of the power of heredity. Clarissa knew her largely through Xan since, unlike her mother, she hadn't returned to St Peter's on Father

Vincent's retirement but continued to worship at the Free Church. Xan had repeated David's assertion that his mother didn't want to see his father 'bollock naked' every Sunday morning, at which Marcus, a stickler for accuracy where art was concerned, declared that, technically, it was buttock naked, since Seward had painted him in profile, taking care to conceal his genitals. Impatient with the boy talk, she'd chimed in that, ontologically, he wasn't naked at all, since the Prelapsarian Adam had known no such concept, prompting both husband and son to groan.

Clarissa who, as chair of the governors, had found herself at the heart of the dispute, acknowledged that Susan's objections, however misguided, were sincere. She held that the danger to young children from even the most coded allusion to sex was greater than that from ignorance. Nevertheless, Clarissa agreed with Pamela that the place for her to air her grievances was the staffroom, rather than the petition she'd circulated, first among the parents and then on social media, protesting against a 'vicious attempt to indoctrinate our innocent, divinely created children'.

'I don't know about you,' Pamela had said to Clarissa, when they were still able to joke about it, 'but I feel that Brian and I played a part in creating our two.'

The petition went viral: the word particularly apt given its toxicity. It attracted support from evangelical Christians and conservatives of all faiths. After articles in the local press and a three-minute report on *North West Tonight*, Susan's supporters planned to mount pickets at the school gates, a threat which, mercifully, had yet to materialise. Pamela demanded that she withdraw the petition and, when she

37

refused, was left with no choice but to dismiss her, whereupon Susan took her case to an employment tribunal. The date of the hearing had yet to be set. The village, meanwhile, split into rival camps: some acting on principle; others from boredom and malice. Clarissa feared that their positions would become even more entrenched should she (*should she*?) reveal what had taken place between Pamela's husband and Susan's son.

'How's Matthew?' she asked, stalling.

'Fine,' Pamela replied, surprised. 'Why? Has Xan said something?' Clarissa shook her head. 'Although you'd do better to ask his computer. It sees a lot more of him than I do.'

'Snap. Xan talks airily of a future where computers rule the world and humans do their bidding. I tell him that he's living in it now. So much for all my hours of agonising at college over freewill and determinism! He sits at his keyboard, thinking he's in control when algorithms define his every click.'

'Matthew's so ham-fisted! He can't even open a cereal packet without spilling it all over the table. Yet he texts like a concert pianist. Who to? Brian thinks we should give him his head.'

'Really?'

'But I can't. Perhaps it's a mother thing? That said, I'm less concerned about Margaret. At least she deigns to speak to us. Matthew knows that I've one cast-iron rule: no history, no phone! The moment he wipes a single message, I cancel his contract. He calls me Mrs Stassi. Claims that it's child abuse.'

'That's harsh.' Clarissa winced.

'You'll understand if I'm a touch oversensitive right now. I can't stop worrying. He thinks he's invincible. Yet you hear of even the most clued-up kids being targeted online.'

'My one wish is for Xan to be happy. Having a bishop for a father – to say nothing of a bishop's wife for a mother – wasn't a bed of roses, but all in all I had a happy childhood. I want as much for him. Marcus complains that I indulge him. Maybe it's having had him at forty-four?'

'You'd have been the same if you'd had him at fourteen. Ouch!' She gave a brittle laugh.

'He thinks I'm always judging him: that because of this' – she tapped her collar – 'I expect him to behave like a saint. It's so unfair; he's full of curiosity when Marcus takes us to galleries and explains how painters have treated all manner of biblical subjects. But Heaven help me if I try to explain what they represent!'

'Brian seems to have given up on . . . no, shied away from Matthew. He longed for him to join the ringing band, but it was never on the cards. I suppose it's the same as when Xan quit the choir. Too close to home.'

'Does Matthew still see much of David Leaves?' Clarissa asked casually.

'Of course. Why wouldn't he? True, it's been a little awkward since the business with Susan blew up. But why should our kids fight our battles?'

'No reason.'

'Though now that David's taken up ringing, I think Brian sees as much of him as Matthew.'

'Really?'

'He's giving him extra practice before the competition. He says he's a natural, never stops singing his praises. I suspect he does it to reproach Matthew. Not that it has any effect. Andrew was dead against David signing up. You know as well as I do – better – how he feels about St Peter's. But he relented when Brian explained that a training session was as good as an hour's workout. Climbing, stretching, pulling weights: the tenor bell weighs a ton – literally! It keeps Brian in trim. He insists that the Exercise – they call it *the Exercise* – separates the men from the boys.' Clarissa flinched. 'Is something wrong?'

'No. I've just seen the time. I'm due at Chapel Hill. I promised to call in on Lizzy Heaton.'

'Isn't she the woman who was mugged?'

'Yes, except that she wasn't. As the police pointed out, a mugger doesn't blacken your eye and break your ribs and then leave you with your purse and rings. The culprit was her partner, but she refused to press charges. Now her mother tells me that her brothers have seen him off. When I asked how, all I got was: "You don't want to know, Vicar!"'

'Good on them! The "Stand by Your Man" routine has to end.'

Clarissa feared that Pamela would rue her words. The question of Brian and David lay heavy on her: during the half-hour she spent with Lizzy; on her return home for lunch; and even as she prayed the Daily Office. Immediately she'd said the Grace, with an added entreaty that God might forgive her distraction, she set off for Leighton Hospital to visit Peter Mainwaring, whose wife Gillian was a regular at the Eight O'Clock. He'd declined markedly since her last visit, when he'd greeted her with a resolute: 'Touting for business, Rector? Sorry to disappoint you. I'm not ready to meet my maker yet.' Moving to the bed, she pressed the cold hand, resting on the barely ruffled counterpane, and watched the morphine dripping steadily into his withered wrist.

She said a short prayer over Peter, whose eyes flickered: a reflex which Gillian hailed as a recognition, and returned home to find Marcus busy in the kitchen. 'Hello, old stick!' he said, looking up from a half-dismembered chicken. At her ordination, he'd threatened her with divorce should she ever address him as 'My dear'. Yet he felt no qualms about his own dismissive – indeed, dehumanising – endearment.

Putting down the poultry shears, he moved to kiss her lightly on the cheek, waving his sticky hands to excuse the muted greeting. She felt a momentary disorientation, wondering whether, with so much on her mind, she'd mistaken the day. 'I wasn't expecting you till tomorrow.'

'Trouble at t'mill!' he said, in an overripe accent. 'I took advantage of a study day to escape. Plus, of course, I longed to see my beautiful wife and my son and heir.'

'Speaking of whom . . .'

'Or rather not speaking. I got the statutory grunt as he disappeared upstairs. Is all well?'

'As far as I know. I see little more of him than you do. The problem's not Xan but one of his friends.'

'Which one?'

'I'll tell you later. I need alcohol. Oh, you've opened the Saint-Émilion!'

'I told you: rough day.'

'Anything you'd care to share?'

'I'm not one of your parishioners,' he said testily.

'No, of course not,' she replied, wondering how she might have phrased it better.

'I had a massive run-in with our new curator, Herm.'

'Not another pronoun showdown?'

'Not at all. Why do you automatically assume it's my fault?' Clarissa didn't reply. 'Remember I told you how she'd called me out on my "gendered language": "man of letters", "cleaning ladies", even "golden girl", which anyone else would have taken as a compliment.'

'Isn't that a tad disingenuous?'

'It turns out I didn't treat her concerns seriously enough. So she made a list of phrases I'd used in recent meetings: "punch above our weight", "out for the count", "throw in the towel" . . . that sort of thing. She maintained I'd deliberately chosen them to exclude her. I suggested that someone who identified as non-binary should be as comfortable with metaphors drawn from boxing as from knitting. For which she made a formal complaint to HR, who've hauled me over the coals for mocking "their gender preference".'

'Herm doesn't have to be your best friend. Just try not to goad them!'

'How easily that "them" rolls off your tongue!'

'I'm far too much my mother's daughter for it ever to be easy. But I believe their self-respect outweighs my linguistic scruples.'

'Spoken like a true Anglican: that is a true twenty-first-century Anglican. Your lot virtually invented the language, thanks to Cranmer's prayer book. So what do you do after four hundred years of sterling service? Ditch it!'

'It felt more and more remote. We had to become accessible.'

'It's not like fitting ramps for wheelchairs! You've destroyed the mystery: the mystery embodied in words that sprang directly from the faith – the life-and-death faith – of the men who wrote them. Should God be accessible? Should art be accessible? Shouldn't we approach both in a spirit of awe: through the mystery that is the deepest expression of the divine? Cranmer . . . please let me finish,' he said, as she tried to respond. 'Cranmer and his colleagues were artists, with a poetic genius as great – if not greater – than Shakespeare's. I heard that poetry day in day out for eight years in the John's chapel. It's what drew me to the Church. But you've tossed it all away.'

'We still use the Prayer Book at the Eight O'Clock.'

'That's big of you! I should introduce you to Herm. You might find you've a lot in common. Her current mission is to coerce the Tate into making reparation for its role in the slave trade.'

'But I thought that it'd been investigated and cleared.' Clarissa took a sip of wine and wondered, guiltily, when she might shift the conversation from Marcus's issues to hers.

'Fully. The trade had been abolished years before Henry Tate, and Abram Lyle for that matter, were born. But that's not enough for Herm, since their fortunes derived from sugar plantations, which employed slave labour.'

'It's a valid point.'

'But it's not *the* point, not two centuries later. She's another one who's hot on accessibility. She's all for upgrading the photography collection. Photographs are popular, ergo they're good. But when you suggest the reason: that they present people with images that are easy to identify and easy to identify with; that they capture a moment (beautiful moments, powerful moments, meaningful moments, I grant), she sneers. I proposed that she spend time in the conservation department: examining the pentimenti; seeing how great artists have struggled to realise their vision; smelling the sweat beneath the paint. She looked at me with a mixture of condescension and pity, as if – I don't know – I'd told her to send a letter rather than a text. "I take it that your ideal artist is Seward Wemlock," she said. I forgot to mention that she's been against the retrospective since the day she arrived. "Not my ideal, no," I replied, "not with more than six centuries of Western art to choose from. But I regard him as one of the finest painters of the late twentieth century, and I've no doubt that the show will consolidate his reputation." Seward, of course, is anathema to her: not only a rich, white male but a peer of the realm, and a well-known philanderer. Which makes me equally culpable for championing him . . . You pride yourself on upholding the highest aesthetic standards, only to be told that you're flaunting your privilege.'

Clarissa's tussles with church leaders had taught her how hard it was for such men to acknowledge their privilege, but she refrained from saying so. 'Surely some of the others agreed with you? What about Perry and Otto?'

'Of course. But they're equally entitled, so they don't count.'

'And Helen?' she asked, careful as ever to keep her voice neutral.

'Fence-sitting. She loathes Herm's stridency but values some of *their* ideas, not least of course *their* endorsement of photography. I reminded her of Burke: all that's necessary for evil to flourish is for good men to do nothing.'

Clarissa grimaced.

'It may sound extreme, but for those of us who cherish art – who put our faith in it the way you do in God – the Herms of this world are on the side of evil.'

'No, that wasn't what shook me,' Clarissa replied, reflecting on her own predicament. She might not describe what she'd chanced on last night as *evil* (a word she preferred to avoid), but there were many in the parish who would.

'For Herm, feelings are paramount, in determining art as well as gender. This picture, this collage or, best of all, this performance piece, is good because it speaks directly to me, touches my inner core. Do you remember going to that lecture at the Courtauld by Niall Walgrave?'

'Vaguely.'

'He was a dwarf; you can't have forgotten. He judged a painting entirely on the prominence it afforded other "little people". This Velázquez is outstanding because we're in the foreground; this Rubens is tolerable because we fill half the canvas; this Van Dyck is inferior because we only fill a tenth . . . or whatever. We thought it ridiculous. At least I did. You thought it sad. But it's stayed with me because it was so bizarre. Nowadays, such subjectivity is the norm.'

'Your beloved Kierkegaard held that all truth was subjective.'

'That was just his point of view.' They laughed, and Marcus visibly relaxed. 'I'm sorry; I'm scarcely through the door – a day early – and I'm already dumping everything on to you. You must be relieved that it's only once a week,' he said glibly. 'I haven't asked about you. You mentioned one of Xan's friends. Not more teenagers French kissing in the church?'

'No, but you're not far wrong. I'll tell you the whole story later.' She was reluctant to embark on it while he was preoccupied with dinner and there was a danger of Xan walking in. Leaving Marcus to cook, she refilled her glass and went upstairs to draw a bath, an unwinding that felt less indulgent when he was at home.

Warmed both inside and out, she returned to find her husband and son sitting at table, the latter rolling his eyes as she said grace.

'Do you say grace when you're in London, Dad?'

'Don't stir things.'

'What about the gravy? Am I allowed to stir that?'

Seeing them together always cheered Clarissa. For all the hints of Alexander in his attitude, Xan was pure Marcus in his looks. And they were good looks. Although his face had filled out and his hair become strawy in texture as well as tint, Marcus was still a handsome man. Even in the darkest days of her infertility, he'd vehemently opposed adoption, arguing that, no matter how loving the parents, adopted children bore a lifelong burden of rejection. The truth, however, was that he'd wanted a child of his own blood. At the time she'd despaired, but now she was grateful since, as he stood on the verge of manhood, Xan not only gave her hope for the future but rekindled her past.

'How's everything at school?' Marcus asked him.

'Bor-ing!' Xan replied, yawning between syllables.

'So what would you rather talk about? You've given up playing football. You don't even watch it any more. You've no hobbies, at any rate none to speak of. What's happening in the land of Xan?'

'Nothing. You're right, I'm a black hole.'

'You can't live your whole life online,' Clarissa interjected, profiting by Marcus's presence.

'When you come down to London in May, the laptop's staying here,' Marcus said.

'You'll be at work!'

'Not every day. And you can explore the museums and galleries, catch up with old friends.'

'I've not seen them for five years!'

'I have good friends I've not seen for ten,' Clarissa said. 'That doesn't change things.'

'At your age nothing changes.'

'Except for children.'

Although she worried that Xan was too young and impressionable to roam around London alone and that Marcus's supervision would be lax, she was glad that they were spending the summer half-term together, not least given David Leaves' disclosure of his poor relationship with Andrew. Was it cod psychology to suggest that, had he had a more affectionate father, he wouldn't have looked for a substitute?

After bolting his food and grumbling that pineapple was 'not proper pudding', Xan scraped back his chair. 'Can the child leave the table?'

She longed to explain that repetition was the enemy of irony but was afraid that Marcus would quibble. 'Go on then.'

'Put your plate and cutlery in the machine,' Marcus added, as Xan made a dash for the door.

'I'll only get a rollicking. Clarissa always tells me I do it wrong.'

'I've shown you the right way so often,' she said, convinced that his bungling was deliberate. 'Don't worry; I'll do it.'

'Remember when we used to moan about families who sat in silence in front of the TV?' Marcus asked, as Xan headed upstairs. 'That now feels like the height of togetherness. Shall I help you clear?'

'Later. There's something I'd like to discuss with you first.'

'Uh oh! Is this an *uh oh* moment?'

'Yes, but not for us. Not directly.' She told him what she'd witnessed in the belfry.

He exhaled slowly. 'Well it makes a change from bats. X-rated ringing: who knew?'

'It's serious, Marcus. Brian was meant to be training him.'

'He certainly showed him the ropes.'

'I said *serious*! He's been tower captain for almost twenty years. I'd have trusted him with . . . anything.' She stopped herself naming Xan. 'He's my best friend's husband. How could he do it to her?'

'"A stiff prick has no conscience."'

A limp one was hardly a model of probity, but she let it pass. 'What am I to do?'

'Is that question genuine or rhetorical?'

'Genuine, of course.'

'Start with the basics. No one was hurt. And David did say that he was the instigator.'

'Can I believe him?'

'I wasn't there but, from what you've told me, yes. I suggest you do nothing. Erase it from your mind. Or, if that's impossible, draw a line under it.'

48

'What if the story leaks out?'

'How? There was no one else around.'

'I know. But these things have a way of surfacing.'

'So who are you concerned about? David or yourself?'

'That's not fair. David, naturally. Besides, any cover-up wouldn't just be laid at my door but the Church's. Can it weather another scandal?'

'They promised that they'd stop seeing each other?'

'Yes. Brian was terrified. With good reason.'

'And David *is* fifteen.'

'Barely.'

'Like all fifteen-year-olds, he'll have sex on the brain. You told me that Mrs Thing – '

'Thring.'

'Found that wad of soiled tissues under Xan's bed.'

'You said you'd spoken to him.'

'I did. I told him, next time, be sure to flush them down the loo. Don't give me that look! All those reports claiming that men think about sex every seven seconds: balls! But in their teens it's probably every three. David's finding his feet, along with other parts—'

'Thank you.'

'It's not as though he'll be scarred for life or turned gay – if such a thing were even possible. Think of all those Lotharios I knew at Christie's, who'd been at it like rabbits at school. I soon learnt that you never ask to bum a fag from an Old Etonian.'

'Can't you be serious for one minute?'

'I'm trying, without much success, to lighten the mood. Yes, what

Brian did is a gross betrayal of trust. And yes, he should have thought of Pamela and their kids and David and even the church. But you asked my advice; so, here it is: do nothing.'

'Would you feel the same way if it were Xan?'

'Of course not! Though I hope that I'd behave the same way. I've never felt the slightest attraction for a nymphet – of either gender! At least not for the last forty years. My sex life is strictly above board. But there but for the grace of . . . something or other, go I. You only have to read a few pages of Krafft-Ebing, or one of the other scientific treatises that in my youth I scoured for stimulation, to grasp the diversity of desire. We now view paedophiles as beyond the pale, but we haven't always. You don't need to go as far back as ancient Athens; just look at Victorian London and all those aristos having sex – quite legally – with twelve-year-old prostitutes. *Unripe fruit* anyone?'

'Thank God we live in a more enlightened age.'

'In some ways, but not all. We've made paedophilia the one unforgivable sin: Christ's blasphemy against the Holy Spirit. And it's as well to remember that Brian's not a paedophile.'

'I caught him in the act!'

'On the evidence, he's an ephebophile.'

'A what?'

'Attracted to adolescents: boys whose genitals are fully formed.'

'I'm not sure that Tapley will appreciate the distinction.'

'Which is another reason to keep it to yourself.'

'I have to look beyond the shock waves. These people are my parishioners; I've been charged with care of their souls.'

'You're on your own there, I'm afraid.'

'No, I'm not. I'm really not. I shall pray for guidance. Thank you for your thoughts; they've helped concentrate my mind.' She stood up unsteadily. 'I'm ready to drop.'

'Shall we listen to some Brahms?'

'You go ahead. I'll wash up.' He demurred. 'No, honestly. You cooked and I find it restful.'

'As you like.' He smiled and she stroked his arm, only for him to hand her a dirty plate.

Three

Clarissa missed sex. She was a 58-year-old priest who taught that marriage was a sacrament, but what she missed most in her own was the sex. Even with Pamela she referred to 'intimacy', but the reality was more visceral: it was the bodiliness, the fleshiness, the sheer humanity of the coupling; the unique *us*ness of the act which, notwithstanding the sweat and the mess and the involuntary noises, was an affirmation of her whole being. She wanted more than a marriage of true minds.

Her sense of loss was all the greater when Marcus was at home, his presence filling every room except the one where it was most needed. The rectory had six bedrooms and theirs were two doors apart yet, in her fancy, she heard him snoring, not the painful grunting she'd invoked to Xan to justify their separation, but a rhythmic snuffle. The rectory had only one bathroom, a vestige of its Victorian past that neither of her immediate predecessors, both bachelors, had sought to redress. She listened to him whistling as he headed for the shower, 'La donna è mobile' deepening her frustration as she waited her turn.

Losing patience, she marched to the bathroom and was about to pound on the door when she caught further snatches of Verdi, this time the 'Dies Irae', from beneath the splash of water. She stood, rapt as ever by the glorious singing. It was his voice that had first attracted her in Cambridge. Although she loathed the term, she'd been something of a groupie, attending choral evensong at St John's at least twice a week, preferring its contemplative liturgy to the more dramatic sound at King's. The music had transported her, but not so far as to blind her to the allure of the singers, in particular, the stocky tenor with the straw-coloured hair, amber eyes and high complexion, at whom she found herself gazing even during the Creed. She'd introduced herself after a service and, ignoring the gentle teasing of his friends, he'd invited her for a drink at the Baron of Beef. She learnt that this was his second spell in the choir, where he'd been a treble from the age of eight to fourteen. He was studying history of art and writing a dissertation on the religious imagery of William Blake, whose work had fascinated him ever since his schoolboy visits to the Fitzwilliam. Sensing a soulmate, she mentioned that her father was a bishop, a fact she rarely divulged, let alone on a first date. But as she soon found out, his interest in religion lay in the art that it inspired rather than the truths it revealed.

They rapidly became a couple, accepted as such by friends even before they admitted it to themselves. They shared meals, books and outings, memories and secrets, and, ultimately, bed: a momentous event for Clarissa, who'd forsworn sex before marriage, not to please her parents or fulfil a romantic ideal, but to honour God. They met each other's families, Clarissa timing his visit to Chester to coincide with Alexander's return from San Francisco, calculating correctly that her brother would absorb most of her mother's attention and father's disapproval. They mapped out their life together after Cambridge. While she tried to remain sanguine on seeing her male counterparts proceed to theological college, he was elated at gaining a place at the Royal Academy of Music. Then three months before graduation, he developed the vocal cord nodules that destroyed his singing career.

The disappointment would have crushed a lesser man. After his voice finally cracked in 'O come, let us sing unto the Lord' (an anthem she'd never since been able to abide), he was dropped from the choir. For a few dark weeks he refused to talk about it, and she feared for the future. Then on Ascension Day, she found a note in her pigeonhole, asking her to join him at noon in First Court, where his former colleagues were to sing from the top of the Chapel Tower.

Over lunch, he spoke of Mrs Hamilton-Brooke, a wealthy music lover who'd become his most devoted fan after hearing him in a Gents concert at the Wigmore Hall. On learning what had happened, she'd invited him to London for a 'dispassionate discussion' of his options (Clarissa suspected that the sixty-year-old widow's interest in Marcus was less dispassionate than he liked to pretend). A collector of paintings as well as singers, she urged him to try his hand at art dealing, promising to mobilise her friends on his behalf. She was as good as her word and, the autumn after coming down, he started on the front counter at Christie's.

Like all the setbacks in their early lives, it had drawn them closer together. The dashing of his hopes made him more sensitive to the thwarting of hers. He was vehement in support of her struggle for ordination: joining protests and raising banners, while always letting the women take the lead. Looking back, she suspected that his zeal sprang from a conviction that they were destined to fail. Was she wrong to date their estrangement to the IVF? Should she have seen the signs ten years before? Despite his professions of pride in her achievement, he made little attempt to adjust to her new role. He joked about presiding at vicarage tea parties, but when the archdeacon's wife invited him to join a candle-making group for clerical spouses, he was outraged. In the months after Princess Diana's fateful *Panorama* interview, he informed successive dinner parties that she was lucky to have had only three people in her marriage; she should try sharing her *spouse* with an entire congregation.

Smarting anew, she rapped on the door, demanding entry. Meanwhile, Xan emerged from his room, hair uncombed, tie askew and clean shirt already crumpled. He walked past, barely giving her a second glance, as if such commotions were commonplace.

'Morning darling,' she said, trying not to inhale his body spray. 'Are you going for breakfast?'

'Dur!'

He headed downstairs, and she turned back to the bathroom just as Marcus came out, his profuse apologies placating her until she was engulfed in a cloud of steam. Showering and dressing quickly, she made her way to the kitchen to find father and son at opposite ends of the table, the one absorbed in *The Times* and the other in his phone. Neither of them looked up or acknowledged her presence.

'Shouldn't you be off to the bus?' she asked Xan.

'I'm driving the boys,' Marcus said, turning the page. 'I've run out of razor blades. I had to use yours.'

'Gross!' Xan interjected.

'Mrs Chabra sells them at the shop,' she said.

'Only Gillette.'

'Are you taking Matt and David?' she asked, worried that he might let something slip.

'They're meeting us outside the pub.'

'So David went to school yesterday?' she asked Xan. 'When he came here, he looked peaky.'

'Peaky?' He laughed. 'No wonder, living with his dad! He's a fucking headcase.'

'Language!'

'Well he is. He makes the whole family – even his mum – do exercises, press-ups and shit, from the Canadian Airforce. Like he's preparing for a war. I tell you: don't ever play ping-pong with him. He goes mental if he loses.'

'Makes you appreciate your own dad, eh?' Marcus said.

'You're such a loser anyway.'

'Why did I ask? Come on, let's leave your mother in peace.' In a single move, Marcus put down the paper, gulped his remaining coffee and stood up. 'Will you still be here when I get back?'

'No, I have to go to Church House.'

'Any particular reason?'

'To see the diocesan safeguarding officer,' she said pointedly. While loath to admit it, even to herself, it was Marcus's attempt to downplay Brian's offence – however well argued, however well meant – that had convinced her she had to report it.

'Can't you two stop jabbering? We're going to be late,' Xan said, making for the door. 'Ciao, Clarissa!'

'Have a good day,' she replied, longing more than ever for a *Mum*.

With a thin smile, Marcus accompanied Xan out. After a per-functory breakfast, Clarissa moved to the chapel that Father Vincent had fashioned from the old laundry room. In place of his icons of the Virgin, she'd hung a portrait of *Jesus Christ the Liberator*, a hand-some black man robed in orange and white and wearing beads, which her father had been given on an official visit to Burundi. After his death, her mother had offered her the painting, which had earned her a measure of notoriety when it was displayed in her Putney study. These days, there was no one to see it but her cleaner, Maureen Thring, who gave it a wide berth, since it reminded her of Lucas, the Ghanaian engineering student who'd fathered her third child.

She prayed the Daily Office, with a special plea that God might incline the safeguarding officer to leniency. Comforted, she headed into work, where she found Shirley and Titus. 'Good morning . . . both of you,' she said, less disposed than usual to pander to her secretary's whims. She pulled up the rolodex and searched for Lisa Maxwell's number.

'Aren't you due at Wemlock Hall?' Shirley asked, with a sidelong glance at her digestives.

'I have to talk to Church House. I may need to reschedule.' Although reluctant to inconvenience them, she knew that they were one congregation that wouldn't notice the change. Aware of Shirley's curiosity – and doubtful of her discretion – she made a show of examining her phone. 'The signal's weak in here this morning. I'll pop outside.'

'Try this!' Shirley said, pushing the office phone towards her.

'They may keep me on hold for a while. I don't want to tie up the line.'

Followed by Shirley's reproachful stare, she stepped into the chilly hall and rang Lisa Maxwell, the diocesan safeguarding officer, only to be told that she was in a meeting with social services and wouldn't be available until noon. With an uneasy combination of foreboding and relief, she made an appointment for twelve thirty, returned to the office and informed Shirley that she would go to the Hall, as planned, and drive from there to Warrington. 'Is there anything in the diary for this afternoon?'

'Only the gerbil burial, straight after school,' Shirley said, with a sniff.

'Postpone it to five o'clock, would you? I'm sure to be back by then.'

She collected her car from the rectory and drove the two miles to Wemlock Hall. She announced herself at the gates, which slid open with a precision at odds with the crumbling piers, and proceeded cautiously up the rutted drive, the unchanging vista of poplars, paddock and copse a bittersweet reminder of her visits to Seward thirty years earlier.

Neither Seward, who had never expected to inherit the estate, nor Dora, whom he'd finally married a few months before his death, had shown much love for it. The Hall had been sold and turned into a home for psychiatric geriatric patients or, less harshly, the elderly and confused. Ozren Kovačić, who ran it with his wife Mirna, was waiting for her in the vestibule, shuffling his toupee like a cap. She followed him into the day room, previously the Wemlock dining room, the scent of mildew and beeswax replaced by that of cough syrup and sardines. Ten women and two men were dotted around: some slumped in their waterproof armchairs; others muttering, humming or rubbing their hands; one twisting the neck of her blouse as though trying to undo the invisible buttons; another registering their entrance with a penetrating cackle, before banging her head on the table.

'Just another day in paradise,' said the manager, who prided himself on his mastery of English idioms. At his nod, Blessing, one of the two nurses chatting together by the window, switched off the television, triggering a collective groan, although nobody appeared to have been watching it.

'It's the Reverend, come to take the service,' the manager said.

'Good morning, Reverend,' the second nurse said in a singsong voice, like Pamela prompting the children to respond at Assembly.

'Good morning to you,' she replied, flashing him a bright smile and struggling to remember his name.

'Benjamin's our newest recruit. He started on Monday,' the manager said, much to her relief.

'I hope they're not working you too hard,' she said lamely.

'Oh yes, very hard. But it is God's work.'

'Of course,' she replied, feeling squashed. 'Now I must attend to God's work too.' She opened her home communion set, prepared the vessels and put on her stole, while Benjamin and Blessing chivvied their charges.

'We must all look our best for Jesus,' Blessing told one lady, as she hauled her upright in her chair.

'Drop that!' Benjamin shouted at a gibbering man, who was clutching his neighbour's hand. Clarissa quaked, as he stood and saluted.

She stifled a wave of despair as she faced the torpid congregation. Apart from the odd mumbled *Amen*, a word that seemed to be more deeply lodged in their consciousness than *God*, the only engagement with the liturgy came from Benjamin and Blessing, the latter interjecting sporadic, disconcerting *Hallelujahs*. She began the distribution, keeping a wary eye on two of the communicants: one who'd bitten her thumb so badly when she placed the wafer on her tongue that the service had had to be halted while it was swabbed and bandaged; the other who'd spat out the wine with an imperious 'Too sweet.' But as they received the sacrament, with nothing more untoward than a licking of lips and a clicking of dentures, she almost regretted their compliance. It was hard to dispel the suspicion that she was literally thrusting God down their throats.

Led by the manager, she visited the four residents confined to their rooms. They climbed the central staircase, once lined with family portraits, and walked down the second-floor corridor, past hunting prints and photographs of servants, which hadn't merited the auctioneer's hammer. These mementos of the Hall's dead sat awkwardly alongside those of its living: the pictures; postcards; medals; certificates and other testaments to faded identities, exhibited in wooden cases on the bedroom doors.

Choked by the foetid odour, Clarissa entered the first room, greeted the impassive occupant, clasped an insensate hand and lifted the intincted Host to lips, which were clenched shut. In vain, she coaxed her to open them. 'It's no use,' Ozren said, 'she thinks it's a pill.'

Consuming the Host herself, she departed with a muted 'Blessings!'
She moved on to a former Salvation Army Major, now a frightened
old woman who, having grown up with stories of grandparents sent
to the workhouse, was convinced that she too had been consigned
to one. She was whimpering when Clarissa arrived and whimpering when she left, the sacrament a momentary distraction from her
distress. Next came Lucy Dutton, immortalised in Seward's spandrel; although the apple-cheeked artisan in a white cap and starched
apron, holding a wheel of Cheshire cheese, bore scant resemblance to
this whiskery husk, babbling to herself in a corner, having been banished from the day room for throwing a vase at the TV newscaster,
whom she had accused of impregnating her.

Clarissa's final call was on Andrew Leaves' mother, Lily, her
identity not merely faded but warped. She, who'd been one of Father
Vincent's most ardent adherents, so intent on maintaining her son's
purity that washing his mouth out with soap had been no idle threat,
was now a fount of obscenity, as helpless as a baby to control the filth
that spewed out of her. Having charged all the male staff with rape,
including Ozren, who eyed her charily, she herself had molested the
two male residents, bewildering one and traumatising the other. As
Clarissa gave her the consecrated wafer, she grabbed her hand and
clamped it on her breast. 'Stroke it, will you? Go on then; do it if you
want!' She cackled. 'Priests, you're the worst of all.'

On leaving the home, Clarissa felt such a strong urge to speak to
her mother that she rang her from the car.

'Who is this?'

'Me, Mother.'

'I knew it the moment I heard the traffic. Other daughters ring their mothers when they're sitting down quietly.'

'I am sitting down quietly.'

'In a car! Isn't it against the law?'

'Not if I keep my hands free.'

'It should be. How can you concentrate?'

'On the road, Mother, or on you?'

'Both.'

As usual after visiting the Hall, Clarissa felt doubly grateful for her 84-year-old mother's health and lucidity. Few phrases filled her with more terror than *granny annexe* but, sanctioned by Marcus who, she reckoned, secretly enjoyed hearing her mother find fault with her, she'd invited her to move in with them in Putney. Julia had flatly refused, determined to stay in the house in Handbridge, which she and St John had bought on his retirement. As the widow of a bishop, she took an active interest in cathedral affairs and worshipped there most weeks. Moreover, she'd formed a close attachment to a neighbour, Richard Birkensall.

Initially suspicious of anyone – never mind a fifty-year-old architect – who consorted with her mother by choice, Clarissa now regarded him as a godsend. He'd nurtured Julia's enthusiasms, the latest of which was gardening. After rhapsodising over her display of early flowering camellias, 'a carnival of pink and crimson', she declared that 'Richard taught me this ancient Chinese proverb. "If you want to be happy for an hour, roast a pig" – that may be easier in China – "if you want to be happy for a year, marry; if you want to be happy for a lifetime, plant a garden."'

Clarissa couldn't decide whether she'd quoted it as an example of Richard's wit and wisdom, a belated admission of the problems in her own marriage, or a veiled comment on those in her daughter's, about which she knew far more than was desirable.

Arriving at Church House, she was sent straight in to see Lisa Maxwell. She'd met her only once, on the safeguarding refresher course the previous year, when she'd been impressed by her commitment, integrity and lack of personal vanity, but above all by her confidence, as a thirty-year-old former care worker, in handling the facetiousness and, at times, barely concealed contempt of the senior male clerics, who resented having to take part. After a crisp greeting, she returned to her desk, beneath a saccharine portrait of Jesus holding a tow-headed girl on his knee. Clarissa was struck by the irreverent thought that, with no witness other than the divine dove, the Lord was in breach of Lisa's own guidelines.

'I presume this is about the headteacher . . . Mrs Salmon,' Lisa said, dispensing with the niceties.

'I beg your pardon?'

'Your request for an urgent meeting. We've received a complaint that she's been hugging children as young as four.'

'Are you serious?' Clarissa asked. 'What sort of world is it when a teacher can't comfort a crying child without risk of censure?'

'I'm merely reporting the complaint, which we're required to investigate. Wasn't it you, at last year's training day, who argued forcefully that women were no more naturally virtuous than men?'

'That sounds like me,' Clarissa replied, recognising her call for gender parity at all costs. She realised that, whatever the outcome of her meeting with Lisa, it would affect not only Pamela's marriage but her position at a school mired in controversy. In sober tones, she recounted what she'd seen on Wednesday evening. To her surprise, Lisa's immediate concern wasn't the abuse itself but why she'd waited a day to report it.

'Daisy Quantock, our parish safeguarding officer, is the grand-mother of David, the boy in question. I was afraid that it would cloud her judgement.'

'Have you discussed it with anyone else?'

'Only my husband.' She wanted to add 'and the Almighty' but feared that His name would carry little weight in a diocesan review.

'We must notify the police at once. I'll ask the communications team to come up with some whys and wherefores, in case anyone gets wind of the delay. We can't be seen to be dragging our heels. Not after the Archdeacon of Congleton!'

'David claims to be in love with Brian. He swears that he made the first move.'

'That's classic victim talk. The tower captain will have groomed him.'

Clarissa yearned for the days when *grooming* was reserved for ponies.

'Still, I wonder if there's something to be said for dealing with them privately: trusting in their contrition.'

'That would be collusion! It's bad enough that you've left it till now. Right! Are you ready? Let's go.'

Springing into action, Lisa led her out to her car, its *Raise a Hallelujah* sticker raising Clarissa's hackles.

'Fill me in on the tower captain! How long has he been ringing? Was he DBS-checked? How many other children has he trained?' Lisa plied her with questions throughout the fifteen-minute drive to Arpley Street. Drawing up outside the police station, she declared that they would have to identify every minor with whom Brian had come into contact.

'Is that really necessary? Tapley's a tight-knit village.' She thought with horror of having to explain the inquiry to Xan. 'Must we chop off a leg to treat a sceptic toe?'

'But if the toe's left to fester, it will infect the entire body.'

Lisa ushered her into the station, her easy familiarity with both officers and procedures a mark of her many visits. They were escorted to an interview room, where Lisa outlined the crime, merely calling on Clarissa to corroborate certain details. The constable explained that a report would be sent to Nantwich, for detectives to follow up. When Clarissa asked how long that would be, his only answer was 'as long as it takes'.

Lisa drove her back to Church House, dropping her at her car with instructions not to talk about the case to anyone and to let her know directly of all developments. 'A twenty-four-hour flu!' she shouted triumphantly as she pulled away.

'What?'

'That's how we'll explain the delay if anyone asks.'

Drained and demoralised, Clarissa drove back to Tapley. Never had doing the right thing felt so wrong. She'd stuck to the rules as strictly as a confessor who, told by a penitent that the Chalice had been poisoned, proceeded to administer it, rather than break the

65

sacramental seal. Would her exposure of Brian have a similar effect – less lethal but still noxious – on her own congregation?

A text from Jenny Watkins, festooned with emojis, reminded her that she was due at Magpie Lane. Jenny, who ran the Chester East mobile library, and her husband, Dan, the self-styled 'big cheese of Leyland Dairies', were regulars at St Peter's, while their children, Emma and Frank, attended the Sunday Group. Cuddles, their pet gerbil, had died at the weekend and, for all her parents' promises that he was 'with Granny in Heaven', Emma was desolate; far more so, according to Jenny, than at the death of Dan's mother. They planned to bury him in the garden, and Jenny had asked Clarissa to say a prayer. Clarissa, for whom love was love, unbounded and unreserved, was happy to oblige.

Her readiness to perform such ceremonies had reached the ears of the archdeacon, who viewed it as female mawkishness, akin to Christina Rossetti elegising her cat. After a rambling discourse on animal souls, he agreed to turn a blind eye, provided that she confined the practice to mammals, birds and goldfish. There must be no amphibians, invertebrates or reptiles, least of all snakes.

Doctrinal debate on the afterlife of animals might engross the archdeacon, but it would be little comfort to a grieving ten-year-old and, as she entered the house, Clarissa didn't hesitate to assure Emma that Cuddles was in Heaven, looking down at them. With daylight fading, Dan led the way into the garden, gathering the company under a windswept sycamore. Clarissa, carrying the shoebox coffin, chided herself for wondering why, if Jenny could afford Ferragamo, her annual giving was so low. After handing the box to Dan, who placed it solemnly in the freshly dug hole, she thanked God for 'bringing us Cuddles, who was with us in times of joy and sorrow, who delighted us with his tricks, who soothed us with his gentle spirit—'

'He bit my finger!' Frank protested, to a concerted 'Shush!' from his parents.

She offered the blessing and then, with a glance at Jenny, who shrugged apologetically, picked up a pink beach spade and tossed soil into the grave. They went back indoors, where Jenny produced two plates of sandwiches, telling a sobbing Emma that 'it's just like Granny's funeral'. Dan fetched a bottle of whisky, deflecting Jenny's frown with 'it's just like Granny's funeral'.

Clarissa departed, after giving Emma a hug, licensed by her parents' presence. She longed to reflect on the day's events but, returning home, she found Marcus waiting for her in the hall.

'I heard your car in the drive,' he said. 'You took your time.'

'I've been burying a gerbil.'

'How did it go?'

'The burial?'

'No,' he said with a sigh, as though she were being wilfully obtuse. 'The interview with the safeguarding woman.'

'I told her what I knew and gave a statement to the police, who are now investigating. I'm shattered. Is there a reason we're standing out here?'

'Not really. Go and sit down. I'll open a bottle.'

'Just a small glass for me. I have the Bible study group.' She moved into the sitting room and flopped down on the sofa, tucking her legs beneath her. The prospect of a lengthy discussion on the Psalms with several of her most opinionated parishioners, however grim, would at least occupy her mind while she waited for the police to act. This must be how it felt for soldiers who received intelligence of an imminent attack . . . worse (she thought of the unsuspecting Pamela), who couldn't send word to their comrades in the front line. There, the analogy broke down, since the attack was one she'd precipitated herself by disclosing their position to the enemy.

Marcus brought in the wine and handed her a glass, which was fuller than she'd specified.

'Cheers!' he said, and she echoed the toast, rubbing her eyes and pinching the bridge of her nose. 'You look worn out.'

'This should do the trick. But I must go easy. I've yet to check on this evening's psalm, but I doubt it's 104.'

'You've lost me.'

'In which David (or A. N. Other) praises God for *wine that maketh glad the heart of man.*'

'I've something to say that won't gladden your heart. Far from it.' Marcus moved to the door. 'Xan,' he shouted, 'come down here!'

'Something to say to him or about him?' Clarissa asked, unsure which would be worse.

'About . . . and with. He's in trouble at school. Serious trouble for – there's no polite way to put it – slut-shaming.'

'Do you mean David?'

'What?'

'Have they found out about him and Brian?'

'No! At least not that I know of. Why do you ask?' He stepped into the hall. 'Xan, get down here now! Don't make me come up!'

'Because it's on my mind.'

'Even in these gender-inclusive days, I don't think *slut* is used about boys. Besides, David's not the only one at risk. Xan!' he roared, just as their son entered the room, making a play of wiping spittle off his face.

'I'm not deaf. Oh, it's the Rev.' He spread out his arms. 'Crucify me now!'

'That's not funny,' Marcus said.

'Or appropriate,' Clarissa added. 'I don't know what's got into you lately.'

'That's because you never listen to me.'

'How can I when you refuse to talk?' She stood up and moved towards him, only to be left stranded as he backed against the fireplace. 'What happened at school? Your father told me you're in trouble.'

'Ask him. He knows the whole story. He was called in by the head.'

'I'd rather hear it from you.'

'Why? So you can torment me?'

'Like you tormented some poor girl?'

'Then you do know?'

'Just tell your mother what happened,' Marcus interjected.

'Matt and I spray-painted *Slag* on this girl's locker, OK?' Xan said, his defiant tone belied by his defensive stance. 'I understand it was stupid and wrong and sexist, and I'm sorry, OK?'

'Which girl?'

'What difference does it make? You don't know her; you don't know everyone. Ruth Taylor. She's a Seventh Day Adventist. They're even screwier than normal Christians. Her parents don't let her wear deodorant. Mandy Skeritt said that, when she had her period, she wouldn't use a tampon, because it'd be like losing her virginity. Gross!'

'That's medieval!' Marcus said.

'Even if her mother won't discuss it with her, haven't you covered menstruation in RSE classes?' Clarissa asked.

'See, you never listen! I've told you before; they're pants. Mr Brown putting a condom on his fist to show how it stretches. Then, when it rips, telling us that the withdrawal method has always worked for him. Except twice. Ha ha! Since everyone knows he has two kids.'

'We seem to be straying from the point,' Clarissa said.

'But it is the point!' Xan replied, his anguished face melting her anger. 'Her parents won't let her take the classes. She's the only one out of the whole year. David's mum would be proud of them. But it's sick. They should be done for child abuse.'

'What?' Clarissa felt her heart jump.

'Course it is. Don't they realise what school's like: how the other girls take the rip . . . call her a square bush? You blame boys for everything, but it was the girls who got her to get her tits out to prove that she wasn't a prude. It was one of them who filmed and whatsapped it.'

'To you?' Marcus asked.

'To everyone.'

'Did you share it?' Clarissa asked sternly.

'Only to Steve Brooks. He's at Nantwich High, so he doesn't know her.'

'And that doesn't count?'

'OK, OK. Get off my case, can't you? If I share a picture of a corpse, does it make me a murderer?'

'No, but sharing a picture of a naked fourteen-year-old is a crime.'

'Please don't go all churchy on me!'

'I'm not. I'm going all policey . . . all courtsy . . . all criminal-record-for-the-rest-of-your-lifey.'

'I've said I'm sorry; what more do you want? Matt and I have detention every afternoon for two weeks. Just because we were caught spraying the locker! What about the rest of them who've got off scot-free? Any other parents would be down at the school, kicking up a stink about the injustice.'

'Is this your way of saying sorry?' Marcus asked. 'You have no idea of the seriousness of what you've done.'

'You can talk,' Xan said, reddening under his parents' gaze. 'You look at naked pictures all day long.'

'Don't be absurd! It's hardly comparable.'

'Why? Because some pervy painter has spent months leching over a model?'

'And I don't write *Slag* or any other juvenile insult underneath them,' Marcus said, parrying the question.

'Yes, I think we can all agree that the child is a great disappointment,' Xan said.

'We most certainly cannot,' Clarissa said, torn between remonstrance and compassion.

'Lucky I'm staying at Matt's tonight, so you won't have to put up with me under your roof.'

'What?' Clarissa said, exchanging a startled look with Marcus.

'It's Friday. Our sleepover.'

'Is it just you?' Clarissa asked, her stomach churning. 'Or is David going too?'

'No. He's so gay.'

'What?'

'He's been acting weird for weeks.'

'It's out of the question. There'll be no more sleepovers from now on.'

'You can't do that! We've already been punished at school.'

'It's not a punishment.'

'Then what is it? What's happened? Tell me!'

'Trust me, you'll find out soon enough. Dad'll make your dinner tonight. I have the Bible study group.'

'Yeah. Of course you have.'

As Xan stood, shoulders hunched, hands clenched, eyes lowered, Clarissa felt a surge of tenderness towards him. He was a fourteen-year-old boy, whose hormones were acting on him like the itching powder which, in the more innocent – if no less callous – days of her youth, she and her friends had sprinkled in their enemies' knickers. His faults were the waywardness of adolescence, and she feared that learning about Brian and David wouldn't help.

'Why did you bother to have me if you hate me so much?' he said, leaving the room.

Marcus raised the wine bottle speculatively; she nodded and passed him her glass. 'Should we be worried?' she asked, returning to the sofa.

'Isn't that what giving a hostage to fortune means?'

'I just wish I could offer him what he needs.'

'What he needs is a girlfriend. To requite his feelings. To stop him resenting the 99.99 per cent of the sex who aren't and never will be attracted to him. And most important of all, to make him feel good about himself.'

'You seem to know a lot about it.'

'It may come as a surprise, but I was fourteen myself once. Though perhaps I should say fifteen or sixteen, considering I was such a late developer. At fourteen, I was having brattish conversations about the respective merits of Byrd and Tallis. My greatest fear was that my voice would break and I'd be chucked out of the choir. One of the baritones told us that wanking would bring it on sooner. So wet dreams were a double nightmare. When that same creep lent us a Victorian manual of anti-masturbation devices—'

'There really were such things?'

'Complete with graphic illustrations! Sheaths attached to bells that rang to alert your parents at the first hint of arousal. Spiked rings like cigar-cutters that bit into an erection. But while my fellow choristers gaped in horror at the instruments of torture, I wanted one if it would keep my voice pure.'

'Poor you! I had no idea.' She felt her tenderness extend to a second fourteen-year-old, one more like their son than she'd supposed. 'So what's the solution for Xan? Praying that he makes it through adolescence as unsullied as possible?'

'You have more faith in the power of prayer than I do.'

Clarissa stood and walked to the door, pausing behind his chair to kiss the crown of his head. 'I need to freshen up before I go out.'

She went upstairs, hovering outside Xan's door, her hand poised to knock, only to move away, blaming her failure of nerve on pressure of time. Marcus's recollections of his teenage years had prompted her own: of a world so remote that it might have been sepia-tinted. She'd attended an all-girls' school, where the mistresses warned their pupils to steer clear of boys, as if they were venomous toads or snakes, ever ready to spit their poison. Until she'd joined the Christian Youth Group at the age of fifteen, the only boys she'd encountered were Alexander's friends, who barely acknowledged her existence. At the youth group, the boys – and girls, for that matter – were as serious as the texts they were discussing. Indeed, the only appreciable difference between the sexes was that it was the girls who poured the orange squash and passed round the biscuits.

After a quick wash and a dab of toilet water (a phrase that had rendered the five-year-old Xan prostrate with mirth), she went down to the study and read through the psalm, before returning to the sitting room, to find Marcus much as she'd left him. 'I hope that the parish appreciates what a glamorous rector it has,' he said, watching her rifle through her bag.

'Why, thank you, kind sir,' she replied, although a glance at the now empty bottle blunted the compliment. 'It's amazing what a pair of ritzy earrings will do.' She gestured to the silver filigree butterflies. 'Lord knows how I'm going to face Pamela!'

'Are you sure she'll be there?'

'Of course. She's leading the meditation.'

'I can't believe that she doesn't suspect something. It doesn't say much for their sex life.'

Clarissa bit her lip. 'As I understand, it's been fairly non-existent since her operation.'

'You'd think he'd find the lack of breasts a turn-on.' She looked at him. 'Sorry, that was tasteless. Besides, no one can ever know what really goes on between husband and wife.'

'True! Half the parish envies us. They think that our routine separation adds spice: every weekend a second honeymoon.'

'Let them think what they like! What does it matter?'

'I feel such a hypocrite, pretending that we have the perfect marriage.'

'We have the perfect *arrangement*. Remember, this is what you wanted.'

'I know,' she said, longing to point out that wants changed over time. Helen may have spared him the need to choose, but she'd made no such pledge. Why hadn't she been more militant in her own cause, rather than trusting to marriage vows and fatherhood, loyalty and habit, to say nothing of love, to inform his choice? Not only had she enabled him to have his cake and eat it, but she'd mixed the batter, piped the icing and brushed up the crumbs. 'I have to go. The fridge is full. I'll leave you to see to the prodigal.'

'That's fine. So which psalm is it tonight?'

'Sixty-two. *Truly my soul waiteth upon God, from Him cometh my salvation.*'

He hummed a few bars. 'The Purcell setting,' he said, as she stared at him blankly.

Four

There was far too much *sin* at the Eight O'Clock. As she repeatedly exhorted the smattering of worshippers to bewail their sinfulness and repent their sins, while assuring them that Christ 'humbled Himself even to death upon the Cross for us miserable sinners', Clarissa despaired of the Prayer Book's emphasis on human failings. Was it heretical to suggest that God's mercy was so boundless that the Eucharist should focus not on our wickedness but on His love? As she broke the bread and raised the cup, she longed to assure them that, by taking human form, Christ had sanctified the flesh, not stigmatised it. Then a rash glance at the ringing chamber gave her pause.

The service over, she returned to the rectory, with a mere half hour in which to have breakfast, put the joint in the oven and tidy the sitting room, as well as ensuring that Marcus left in good time to collect her mother and Xan was up and dressed. Her 'Rise and shine!' going unanswered, she poured Xan a glass of orange juice and took it upstairs. After a loud knock, she strode into his bedroom, throwing open both the curtains and the window. He squinted at her with tousled resentment, as she urged him to make haste, with a reminder that his routine exemption from Sunday worship hinged on attendance during his grandmother's visits. Impervious to his protests, she hurried downstairs and back to church.

After checking on the sidespersons, she made her way to the vestry, welcoming the choir as they dribbled in. She felt a tremor of unease as young Jeremy Bridge pulled off his hoodie, exposing his bare midriff to Pete Darwin and Roger Simmonds, the two basses. She wondered whether, like so much else, the robing facilities would now have to change. As if to highlight her fears, the bells began to peal.

She had assumed that they would be silent. Was Brian braving it out? He hadn't contacted her since Wednesday. Did he think that, by refusing to acknowledge the problem, it would go away? Or else that her closeness to Pamela would induce her to break the rules rather than cause her friend pain? Then again, was Brian even in the chamber or had he called in sick and asked one of his colleagues to deputise?

As the opening bars of 'Come down, O Love divine' resounded through the church, young Tilda Jenkins, lately promoted from acolyte to thurifer, her rainbow-streaked sneakers poking out from beneath her cassock, led the introit procession. Passing along the nave, Clarissa was alerted to a familiar trill on 'O let it freely burn'. She looked round to see her mother in a plum tweed coat, standing between Marcus and Xan and immediately behind Pamela, Brian and their daughter Margaret. Julia kept her gaze trained on the hymnal, but Xan fixed her with a ferocious glare, no doubt intensified by Matthew's absence. She reached the sanctuary just as Reginald pulled out all the stops for the final verse, moved to the altar and turned to welcome the congregation.

The service proceeded seamlessly, although Clarissa always felt on edge in her mother's presence. As she mounted the pulpit, she was eight years old again, waiting in the wings at her ballet showcase. Taking her text from the morning's reading – *Consider the lilies of the field, how they grow; they toil not, neither do they spin* – she referred to its apparent contradiction with other of Jesus's teachings, such as the Parable of the Talents, and announced that her sermon would address the notion of *gospel truth*, which had come under fire at a recent Doubters' Group meeting.

She was momentarily thrown when her greeting to two of those doubters prompted an audible stir, and a menacing stare from Daisy Quantock, who scoured the pews as if the ferreting out of unbelievers were part of her safeguarding role. Pressing on, she noted how 'even with the many records now available, our memories of events differ widely. That's certainly the case within my own family, as my husband, mother and son, here today, can vouch.' Several people, grateful for the distraction, turned to the trio, who responded by respectively grinning broadly, nodding graciously and squirming in his seat.

Pausing to regain their attention, she declared that 'far from dwelling on the disparities in the Gospel narratives, I'd be sceptical if the Four Evangelists, writing forty years and more after Jesus's death, relying on their own and their informants' fallible memories, had spoken with one voice. Any disparities are a problem only for those who regard the Bible as the unequivocal word of God: those with no understanding of how books, including holy books, are written, codified, edited, translated and revised. Much as I deplore the creationist argument that God planted fossils to test our faith, I firmly believe that the inconsistencies in the Bible serve a purpose: to show that there can be no authoritative interpretation of the Scriptures and that we must each of us exercise our God-given judgement as we read them.'

She quit the pulpit and prepared for the Eucharist. She was grateful that, despite dismissing it as 'like being given a sweet after visiting the dentist', Xan lined up with Marcus, directly behind Brian, one of the few who might have benefited from the strictures of the Eight O'Clock. As ever, Julia kept to her seat since, while she may have been *in love and charity with her neighbours*, she remained in contention with the priest.

At the end of the service, Clarissa took up position in the porch. She smiled faintly when Xan, who'd long since ascertained that his obligation didn't extend to 'hobnobbing with the God-botherers', rushed out, shook her hand and thanked her 'for a lovely liturgy, Reverend'. He was followed by Neil Francis who, eager to parade his erudition, expounded on the lilies of the field, creating a bottleneck on the steps. Several people slipped past with mouthed thanks, expressive glances at children and watches, and, in Tricia Harding's case, a cryptic gesture that might either have been a request to ring her or an invitation for a drink. Curtailing Neil's discourse on Galilean wildflowers, she pounced on Benjamin, the new care assistant at Wemlock Hall, whose regular attendance would double the BAME representation at the church. Having secured his promise to come to tea on his next afternoon off, she returned inside, where Katy James and Hetty Blakemore were serving the coffee and biscuits, which, for some of her parishioners, were as meaningful a communion as the bread and wine.

In one group, Marcus was pointing out details of the Eden painting to the Misses Charlton who, deprived of a male rector to fawn over, had seized on the next best thing; in another, her mother in best fete-opening mode was holding forth to Shirley and Mrs Redwood, Lewis and Keung. As she headed towards them, she was waylaid by Pamela, accompanied by a flushed, uneasy-looking Brian.

'Have you got a moment?' Pamela asked.

'I really must rescue Lewis and Keung from my mother.'

'How about later? Or else call me this afternoon. I left you a voice-mail. We do have to talk about all this sex stuff.'

'What?' Clarissa's yelp triggered several turned heads and a terrified glance from Brian.

'Matthew and Xan spray-painting that poor girl's locker.'

'Yes, of course.'

'Brian was outraged, weren't you?' He nodded wretchedly. 'I was quite taken aback. It's usually me who's left to lay down the law.'

'I don't believe in double standards,' Brian said, in a strangulated voice. 'Jack the Lad, Jill the Slag.'

'Highly commendable,' Clarissa said, as coldly as was possible in front of his wife.

'He let rip. I was afraid he'd reduce Matthew to tears. I know you're just as angry: banning sleepovers and so forth. I agree one hundred percent that they should be punished. But "for ever"? Really?'

'I promise we'll discuss it soon. Now I must . . .'

Without further explanation, she made her escape, painfully aware of having offended her friend.

'Whatever's the matter, darling?' her mother asked.

'It's nothing. Don't worry.'

'In which case, there's no excuse for that frown. I used to tell her as a child,' she said, playing to the crowd, '"if the wind changes, your face will stick."'

'Did you? I'm sure you did.'

'Excellent sermon, Clarissa. Thank you,' Lewis said. 'Real food for thought.'

'Yes, indeedy,' Mrs Redwood said. 'I always tell Shirley – don't I, girl? – the Rector's sermons are so meaty we can save on the Sunday roast.' She laughed, revealing alarmingly white false teeth.

'Not now, Mother!' Shirley said.

'Not that you'll have an appetite after all those biscuits. Three she's had already. "Leave some for other people," I told her. Not that I'm counting.'

'I'm sure there are enough to go round,' Julia said placatingly.

'But she's pre-diabetic. Which is diabetic in two years' time, you mark my words. Who's going to look after me if she has her leg off? I've only 10 per cent kidney function.'

'Remarkable!' Julia replied.

'Talking of the Sunday roast, we must be on our way, Mother. I'm needed in the kitchen.'

'Preaching one moment, cooking the next: she's a marvel, my daughter,' Julia said, her face falling when her listeners concurred.

Clarissa excused herself, made her way to the sacristy and disrobed. Returning to the nave, she said her goodbyes, apologised for not helping Hetty and Katy with the washing-up and leaving Alec to lock up once again. Although she invoked her mother's visit, her main concern was to avoid confronting Pamela or Brian. But no sooner had she collected Marcus and Julia than Brian scuttled towards them.

'Clarissa, may I have a word in private?'

'Sorry, Brian,' Marcus interposed. 'I'm going to claim a husband's prerogative and whisk her away.'

Marcus ushered the two women into the porch. Julia turned to him as she descended the steps. 'I'm surprised that you were so short with a parishioner. St John would never have countenanced it.' She gave a hollow laugh. 'My mistake. It's easy to forget that you're not the rector. Times have changed.'

'If you're growing forgetful, Mother, you should speak to your doctor,' Clarissa said. 'He may have some pills that will help.'

Marcus gave her an admonitory look as he opened the lychgate.

'Don't try to be clever, Clarissa,' Julia said. 'You know very well what I mean. It's lucky you have such a forbearing congregation. I always enjoy talking to that wine merchant. He reminds me of Richard. Such a charmer! And so kind of him to give a home to the Chinese boy!' Clarissa, inured to her mother's guile, exchanged glances with Marcus. 'Do you remember, when you saved all your pocket money to sponsor that little Indian girl?'

'It's hardly the same. She was a destitute orphan. Keung is a postgraduate business student. What's more, he's Lewis's boyfriend, not his protégé.'

'Must you cheapen everything?'

They arrived home where, dismissing Marcus's offer of help, Clarissa made straight for the kitchen and left him to entertain her mother. 'You owe me big time!' he said, as he fetched ice for the gin and tonic, which, under Richard Birkensall's tutelage, she'd substituted for her pre-prandial sherry. Fearing that the strain of the past few days would cause her to snap (and snap at her mother), Clarissa spun out her preparations, before joining the others in the sitting room.

'Are we nearly there?' Marcus asked, as she entered.

'Give it half an hour. I've just taken the lamb out of the oven.'

'Your mother was complimenting you on maintaining such an active congregation,' Marcus said.

'Really?' Clarissa asked in amazement.

'What was it you said?' Marcus turned to Julia, who gave him no help. '"It's no mean achievement when churchgoing is seen as just another Sunday hobby, on a par with yoga or hang-gliding."'

'In Tapley?' Xan interjected, through a mouth full of peanuts. 'I wish!'

'Then again, St John always expected higher attendances in a country parish than in town,' Julia said. 'Fewer distractions. Not that there weren't distractions enough this morning.' Clarissa sighed. 'All those children running about. Although I grant that it's harder for a woman to keep discipline.'

'We aim to be a child-friendly service.'

'Not for this child!' Xan said. 'I'm hungry,' he screeched, as Marcus snatched the peanut bowl away from him.

'Your father would never have stood for it,' Julia said to Clarissa.

'Alexander used to claim that Father rebuked babies for crying during christenings.'

'That's a wicked thing to say when your brother's not here to defend himself.'

It was her father who should have been defending himself, Clarissa thought, but she let it pass.

'I'd always understood that country people set great store by tradition,' Julia said.

'Some, yes. There are no hard-and-fast rules.'

'So they approve of the new-fangled liturgy? *We have sinned against God and our neighbours.* It sounds as if we've stolen their lawnmowers. What's wrong with *God and our fellow men*?'

'Have you looked in the mirror lately?'

'It's standard usage!'

'Must we go through this each time you come?'

'It upsets me each time I come.'

'I'm truly sorry. But I refuse to be lectured on language by someone who sent me to an all-girls school, whose speech day anthem was "Let us now praise famous men".'

'I never knew that,' Marcus said. 'Was it the Vaughan Williams or the Finzi setting?'

'Ur, Dad!' Xan said.

'You're missing the point, Marcus,' Clarissa said.

'No, no one's permitted to make a point but you,' Julia said.

'Excuse me! For the first dozen years after I was priested, you wouldn't even attend a service I conducted. You still won't take communion from me.'

'It would be trampling on your father's memory.'

'You're not the only one who remembers him. He had many admirable qualities, but he was no saint. He was selfish and domineering and pompous. He kept you under his thumb.'

'If I'd talked to my mother the way you talk to me . . .' Julia dabbed her eyes. Whether her tears were spontaneous or studied, the effect was the same, notably on Xan, who sat beside her and stroked her arm.

'Thank you darling,' Julia said, between sobs. 'At least somebody in this family cares.'

'You're such a bully,' Xan said to Clarissa. 'And a hypocrite. You criticise Granny's marriage, when everyone knows you're covering up Dad's affair.'

'What?' Clarissa said.

'Have you been snooping through my phone?' Marcus asked.

'No!' Xan replied indignantly. 'You're the one who does that. I believe in the right to privacy.'

'Then how come you know?'

'Granny told me.'

'Mother!'

'I didn't want Xan to blame Marcus.' She looked at Marcus. 'I didn't want him to blame you. I've seen what happens when a son turns against his father.'

'You told your mother?' Marcus asked Clarissa.

'In a moment of weakness, years ago at St Cuthbert's. I was angry and hurt. I needed to sound off to someone. I should have known.'

'You've no right to attack Granny. At least she's honest. While you two are liars and frauds.'

'Thank you, darling,' Julia said. 'But, remember, we're taught to honour our parents. Even though they may not always deserve it.'

'Tell me about it!'

'What was that joke about grandparents and grandchildren

85

getting on so well because they share a common enemy?' Marcus asked Clarissa.

'It wasn't a joke.'

'I didn't want Xan to blame you either, Clarissa,' Julia said. 'Leaving London . . . breaking up the family home.'

'You know how I've never allowed parishioners to call me Mother?' Clarissa said to Marcus. 'I thought it was to keep it special for Xan. I'm no longer so sure.'

'Let's have some lunch,' Marcus said. 'We'll all feel better. We can start on the melon while we give the lamb time to rest.'

Leaning heavily on Xan, Julia stood up and headed for the dining room, when the doorbell stopped them in their tracks.

'No! Don't people realise it's lunchtime?' Xan asked. 'They do it on purpose.'

'You go through,' Clarissa said. 'Don't wait for me. I'll get rid of them.'

The moment she opened the door, she knew that she'd spoken too soon. Pamela stood before her, wild-eyed, grey-faced, her lips moving wordlessly.

'Come in,' Clarissa said, forcing a smile, while her stomach felt both gapingly empty and full of rocks.

'Brian's been arrested.'

'Come in,' Clarissa repeated, as Pamela remained transfixed.

'It's Sunday. We'd only just got home from church. His parents had arrived for lunch. Couldn't they have left it till tomorrow? It's Sunday!'

'You're in shock.' Clarissa took hold of her arm and recoiled from its brittleness.

Pamela drew back. 'You haven't asked why. *Sexual activity with a child.* That's what they said. *With a child!* I'm going to be sick.'

'Quick! Through here.' She pulled her through the doorway and into the cloakroom, which was close, but not close enough to prevent her vomiting outside the bowl.

'I'm so sorry. Where are your cloths? I'll clear it up.'

'Leave it. It's nothing. It can wait.'

'I want a cloth, Clarissa.'

'You just need to wipe your mouth. Here.' She turned on the tap and drew a resistant Pamela to the basin. When she stood immobile, Clarissa cupped some water in her hands, splashed it on her face and dabbed it with a towel. 'Let's go through to my study. Would you like some brandy?'

'You're offering me a drink?'

'For the shock.'

Pamela gazed vacantly at the vomit. 'Yes, of course.' Clarissa steered her through the hall, calling for Marcus along the way.

'You have company?'

'Only my mother.'

'I've interrupted your lunch. I'm so sorry. I'll come back later.'

'Are you serious?' Clarissa said. As Marcus appeared at the kitchen door, she asked him to bring a glass of brandy. With a tactful nod, he returned to the sitting room, while she led Pamela into the study, settling her in the comfortingly cracked Chesterfield, before drawing up her own chair closer than the norm.

'*Sexual activity with a child.* Did I tell you that?'

'Yes. You don't need to repeat it. Unless, of course, it helps.'

87

'They used that expression they do on TV. "You don't have to say anything but it may harm your defence . . ." You know the one. It made it seem both more and less real at the same time.'

'Have they taken him to the station?'

'I presume so. Yes. Where else would they have taken him? He didn't deny it. You'd think he'd have told them it was all a mistake. Salmon's a common enough name. But instead, he asked me to call a solicitor. Why would he want a solicitor if he's innocent?'

'He'll need legal representation,' Clarissa said, wondering when to admit to her own involvement.

Marcus brought in a bottle of brandy and two glasses. 'Just in case,' he said, as he put them down next to Clarissa.

Pamela looked up at him. 'Hello Marcus.'

'Hello.'

'At least when you cheat, it's with a middle-aged woman. *Sexual activity with a child!*'

'Thank you,' Clarissa said, as Marcus lingered awkwardly. 'If we need anything else, I'll call.' He walked to the door. 'Just a sec!' She turned to Pamela. 'Did you ring the solicitor?'

'What solicitor? We've never had one, except for our wills.'

Clarissa moved to her desk and took out an address book, which she handed to Marcus. 'Will you ring Dale Robertson and ask him to go to Nantwich police station? Explain as much as you can.'

'Of course.'

'The number's under S,' she added, as Marcus went out.

'Robertson. Isn't he the one representing the school at Susan's tribunal?'

'He's the best.'

'*Sexual activity with a child.* Oh God! Susan will have a field day. I defile children's minds, while Brian defiles their bodies.' Clarissa wished that that were the only connection to Susan. 'The police must be thinking of it already. After they drove Brian away, two officers ransacked the house. They seized all our computers: mine and the kids' too – the kids! – our DVDs, old VHS tapes, even the model of Priapus, which Brian's cousin Derek brought back from Turkey. We used it for hanging keys. Why didn't I throw it away?'

'You'll get it back.'

'I don't want it back!'

'I meant everything they removed.'

'Do they imagine we're running a family vice ring? The kids need their computers for school.'

'We'll find them replacements. Don't worry. Drink this.' She poured two glasses of brandy, handed one to Pamela and took a sip from her own.

'No, I must go home,' Pamela said, setting aside the glass. 'I should never have left them. Brian went without a word to any of us. Margaret was screaming; Matthew hugged her. He hasn't done that in years. Len, Brian's father, had a heart bypass last summer. He looked worse than he did after the op. The police sealed everything in plastic bags. They made me sign for them, as if they were collecting the stuff for repair. Matthew just stood and watched. He spends his life on that computer. He rants and raves when I tell him to switch it off. He just stood there and watched them take it away.'

'Have some brandy. You'll feel better. Then we'll go back together.'

'*Sexual activity with a child*. What child? What age? What age is a child? We've stayed at family hotels. I've never seen him so much as glance . . . He's led your Holiday Fun Club. You wouldn't have asked him if you'd had the least suspicion . . . if the thought had ever occurred to you. You'll speak up for him, won't you? You'll be a character witness in court. Court!'

'Pamela, listen to me.'

Pamela looked at her. 'You've got your church face on: your God-will-see-us-through-it face. I want the other face: your best-friend face; your this-is-all-a-dreadful-mistake-and-Brian-is-innocent-face.'

'Believe me, I wish that he were.'

'How do you know?' Pamela stood up slowly. 'Do the police notify clergy when they arrest one of their parishioners?'

'Nothing like that. I know the boy in question.'

'Boy? So it was a boy. I'd thought . . . *Sexual activity with a child*. I suppose it was fifty-fifty. "Congratulations, Pamela, you have a beautiful baby boy!"'

'Please sit down.'

'Don't fucking well tell me to sit down! What boy?'

'David Leaves,' Clarissa replied, confidentiality no longer an issue.

'Susan's David?'

'Yes.'

'That bitch!' She let out a bitter laugh. 'Are there no depths she won't stoop to to get back at me? Isn't it obvious? She's pressurised David into accusing Brian.'

'No. I was the one who reported them.'

'You?'

'I caught them together in the ringing chamber.'

'They were practising for the competition.'

'Not only that.'

'What did you see? Tell me, I want every last detail . . . No, no, I don't. Tell me!'

'They broke apart the moment I walked in.'

'Then you saw nothing! Brian was helping David with one of the bells. They're so heavy. They heard you coming and took you for a thief.'

'David's flies were undone.'

'Teenagers are messy dressers. Look at Matthew! Look at Xan!'

'But not David. Never a hair out of place. Besides, they didn't deny it.'

'So you went to the police?'

'No, the church authorities.'

Pamela picked up the glass of brandy and downed it in one. She moved to the window. 'Am I so repulsive?' she asked impassively.

'You know that it's not about you.'

'I know that's what people say. "It's nothing to do with the wife." But that's just words. I disgust him so much that he risked everything – family, home, marriage – for a fifteen-year-old boy. And one with chronic bad breath.'

'There are no rules to sexual attraction. Remember Terence: "Nothing human is alien to me"?'

'This is my life, not *University Challenge*!'

'I'm sorry.'

'How long have you known?' Pamela asked, returning to the body of the room.

'Only a few days.'

'Couldn't you have warned me? If not for my sake, then for the children's. You're supposed to be my friend.'

'I wanted to,' Clarissa said, wincing. 'I held off saying anything for as long as I could. I prayed for guidance.'

'What: "Take this cup away from me"?'

'You must see that I had no choice.'

'But you did.' Pamela knitted her brows. 'You chose the Church.'

'Believe me, if there's anything I can do . . .'

'You've done it already. Now you'll have to testify against him at the trial. It will be your evidence that convicts him.'

'I'll say everything I can in mitigation.'

'Why? Because of our friendship? Because only God can judge? Don't bother! Let them lock him up for the rest of his life and throw away the key.'

'That's the pain speaking.'

'Is it? Then it knows the right thing to say. What he's done is evil. You may dislike the word but, right now, I'm not that concerned about your sensibilities. He's destroyed his family. He's destroyed his parents (how we used to laugh at the way they doted on him!). And who knows how deeply he's damaged that boy? One of his son's best friends. They grew up together . . . No! You don't think—'

'No, I don't.'

'You don't know what I was going to say.'

'I do, and it's *no*. Brian loves Matthew. He loves both his children. He'd never do anything to hurt them.'

'Too late! I've never trusted David. That may be a cruel thing to

92

say about a child, but it's a fact. He spent half his life at our house, long before you and Xan moved here. We'd find him playing with the train set or watching TV, even when Matthew wasn't around. We felt sorry for him, saddled with that father. But all the time he was preying on us, trying to get his feet under the table . . . no, between the sheets.'

'You know that's not true.'

'Now it all makes sense. People will say that David's the victim. But it's Brian. David manipulated him from the word go.'

'How? Matthew and David have known each other since primary school. Are you suggesting that he's targeted Brian since Reception? He came to see me. His one concern was to exculpate Brian. He claims he's in love with him.'

'I think I'm going to be sick again.'

'Here.' Clarissa grabbed the wastepaper basket and handed it to Pamela, who retched loudly before sitting down with the empty basket on her knee.

'David's fifteen. Brian and I have been married for twenty-two years. What does he know about—'

She broke off abruptly as Xan rushed into the room. 'This is brutal! Matt just texted.' He made for Clarissa, phone in hand, before catching sight of Pamela in the high back chair. 'Oh shit!'

'What has Matthew texted?' Pamela asked.

Marcus followed Xan into the room. 'I told you not to disturb your mother.'

'Nothing. Just a joke.'

'What joke?' Pamela continued implacably.

'Something about his dad being arrested,' Xan mumbled, staring at the floor.

'Show me.'

'Go back to Granny, darling. I'm sorry to have taken so long, but something's cropped up.'

Needing no second invitation, Xan headed to the door.

'Show me please,' Pamela repeated. 'I could do with a laugh.'

With an imploring look at Clarissa, who nodded bleakly, Xan passed his phone to Pamela. She studied it and handed it back.

'Thank you. Although for your information – in case you intend to spread the news – the word is spelt with an A. P A E D O.'

'No one will be spreading the news, Pamela,' Marcus said. 'Come on, Xan.'

'Honest, I won't,' Xan said. 'And I don't believe it. No way.'

Marcus put his arm round Xan's shoulder and led him from the room.

'Why would Matthew do that?' Pamela asked.

'Because he's angry? Trying to hit back? To ease the pain? To dissociate himself from his father? Your guess is as good as mine.'

'Did Brian think for a moment what this would mean for his son. Just imagine all the questions he must be asking himself? "Does he feel the same way about me? Will I be like that when I'm older? Is there anyone left I can trust?" And that's just for starters. I've moaned to you so often about not knowing what goes on inside Matthew's head. I do now.'

'Maybe this will bring the two of you closer.'

'There's very little I can be certain of any more, but one thing

I do know is that, whatever the rights and wrongs of it, he'll blame me. I must go home. Find out what else the kids have been saying. I shouldn't have left them with their grandparents. But I had to get out of the house.'

'I'll come back with you.'

'Thanks, but no. I have to do this on my own.'

'That's not true.'

'I'm afraid it is. But what is it I have to do? Do I wait for him to return from the station and ask how it went, as if it were a day at the office? Will he be returning tonight at all or will they keep him in the cells until morning, when the magistrates set bail . . . that's if they do.'

'One way I can help is by liaising with Dale Robertson. I'm sure he'll be at the station by now.' A flicker of doubt entered her mind at the thought of his weekend round of golf. 'I'll find out how things stand.'

'Tell him that I don't want Brian home. I'll pack a bag with his toothbrush and underwear and shirts and shaver and anything else he needs. I don't want him to feel dirty . . . oh! But I don't want him back. Not now, not ever.' She walked to the door. 'You don't know how lucky you are that your husband is a mere adulterer.'

As she followed her out, Clarissa saw that the brandy had taken effect. Worried that to insist on accompanying her would distress her further, she closed the door on the tottery figure and made her way to the kitchen.

'What are you doing?' she asked her mother, who stood at the sink scouring pans.

'What does it look like?'

'There's no need.'

'Nonsense. We can't leave you to do everything. Truth to tell, these pans could do with a good scrub. It looks as if they haven't had one in years.' Clarissa smiled wanly; at least some things hadn't changed. 'I've kept your lunch warm.'

'Thank you, but I'm not hungry.'

'That's neither here nor there. You can't solve the world's problems on an empty stomach. Do as you're told for once.'

Relieved to relinquish control, Clarissa sat down at the kitchen table, while Julia took a plate from the oven and set it in front of her. She ate slowly, unsure whether the food were flavourless or she'd lost all sense of taste.

'I know that Pamela's been a good friend to you, but people expect too much.'

'Did Marcus tell you what's happened?'

'That her husband's been having an affair? Yes. It's always the quiet ones.'

Clarissa wondered whether that were true. In what respects could Marcus be accounted quiet? 'Where is Marcus?' she asked, abruptly aware of his absence.

'In the garden, playing football with Xan.'

'Really?' She turned to the window, to see the two of them on the lawn.

'Xan was upset for his friend. He's more sensitive than you give him credit for.' Clarissa swallowed half a potato rather than protest. 'Marcus suggested that they had a game and he jumped at it.'

'I'm astounded.'

She cleared her plate but refused pudding. 'Please don't be offended, but I have to go out.'

'Now? Your father's Sunday afternoons were sacrosanct.'

'I'm sorry.' However much she might wish to put it off, she knew that she had to pay a call on the Leaves, the second family her testimony would tear apart. 'I hope it won't take too long. Will you be all right on your own or should I ask Marcus to keep you company?' She gazed outside, loath to break up the game.

'I may be old, but I'm perfectly capable of occupying myself for an hour.'

Touched by her mother's tenacity, Clarissa planted a kiss on the nape of her neck and set out. She drove the half-mile to Meadow Lane, a grim misnomer for the twin rows of pebble-dashed houses, built on the outskirts of the village which, in the early 1930s, had yet to preserve its heritage. Unlike their neighbours, who'd adorned their facades with porticos and panels, artificial bay trees, a St George's flag and coloured lights, the Leaves had kept theirs in an authentic state of anonymity. Clarissa rang the bell and peered through the frosted glass. The door opened and the strips of blue and green coalesced into Susan, her well-scrubbed face looking more raw than ever.

'We were expecting you.'

'Then you know,' Clarissa said, seeing no need to elaborate.

'The police came this morning. They said it was you who found them.'

'Our organist had forgotten his shopping.'

'What were they . . . No, don't answer! I don't want to know. I'll know soon enough. The police asked David to make a statement. He refused. He swore blind that nothing happened. But it did, didn't it? I knew the moment I heard. Andrew says he'll take him to the station tomorrow, if he has to drag him by the hair.'

Clarissa shivered.

'Not that he would. It's just talk.'

'Who is it?' Andrew called.

'The rector.'

'Bring her in.'

Clarissa followed Susan into the sitting room. Andrew was standing in front of a heavy, mushroom-tiled fireplace, next to a set of shelves housing Susan's collection of pincushions. Daisy Quantock and her granddaughter, Rosemary, were sitting at opposite ends of a chintz sofa. David was slumped on the floor, his back against the window seat, half-hidden by a full-length curtain.

'We were expecting you,' Andrew said.

'You,' Daisy echoed.

'I came to see if there were anything I could do.' She hovered, waiting for an invitation to sit down.

'Haven't you done enough?' David shrieked. 'Liar, liar! You're a liar. This is all your fault. We didn't do anything wrong!'

'Quiet! Stop snivelling!' Andrew shouted. Clarissa feared that he'd tell him to take his punishment like a man. Any lingering qualms about her decision to speak out were banished by the sight of David, defenceless, wiping his eyes and nose on the back of the curtain.

'You reported them,' Andrew said, 'but you didn't see fit to say anything to us, the boy's parents.'

'I followed the protocol.'

'I am the protocol!' Daisy said.

'In ordinary circumstances, yes. But I was afraid that there'd be a conflict of interests . . . a lack of objectivity. I know that there would have, had it been me.'

'But it wasn't, was it?' Andrew said. 'The kiddie-fiddler didn't pick on your son, only mine. I'll punch his lights out.'

'Andrew please, this isn't helping,' Susan said.

'It's helping me.' He clenched his fists as menacingly as if LOVE and HATE were tattooed on the knuckles.

'May I?' Clarissa addressed Susan, indicating an empty armchair.

'Yes, of course. What am I thinking?'

'We all know what you're thinking,' Andrew said. 'Just what was it that pervert did to David?'

Rosemary began to cry. Susan moved to the sofa, squeezing between her mother and daughter: three generations united in gloom. Clarissa, meanwhile, took her seat, trying to ignore the antimacassar scrunched under her shoulders.

'Bell ringing!' Andrew exclaimed. 'I was against it from the start. What sort of hobby is that for a fifteen-year-old lad? But Salmon gave me all the guff about upper body strength. Upper body! Look at him! Nothing but skin and bone. He hasn't got a body at all.'

'You may not think so,' David said defiantly. 'Other people do.'

'I swear I'll swing for him.'

'Not in front of the rector!' Susan said.

'If you lay a finger on Brian, I'll kill myself.'

'Did you hear that?' Andrew asked Clarissa, who'd heard it three days before.

'I came to tell you that he's been arrested.'

'Thank God!' Susan said.

'They should put him away for life,' Daisy said.

'He didn't do anything!'

'They may not send him to prison,' Clarissa said, eager to reassure David, who was twisting the curtain distractedly.

'You can bet on it,' Andrew said. 'For him it'll be all community service and counselling. Tell him from me that he'd better not show his face again in Tapley. Or else he won't have any face left to show.'

'I'll kill myself!'

'For Christ's sake, this isn't a game!' Andrew said, rounding on his son.

'Andrew please . . . Rosemary!' Susan said. 'If nothing happened between you, David, why are you so worried about him?'

'He was kind to me. He took me seriously. He never called me a waste of space.'

'Nor did anyone else.'

'You liar! How can you say that? You've heard him.'

'The man is your best friend's father. Did you never think about Matthew?'

'Matt doesn't appreciate him. He makes fun of him. He's no idea how lucky he is. If he was my dad—'

'You'd what?' Andrew asked.

'I love him!'

'Don't say that!' Daisy chimed in. 'Don't you ever dare say that again.'

Rosemary's sobs grew louder. 'Go upstairs dear,' Susan told her, but she made no attempt to move.

'You're all such hypocrites,' David said, refusing to let the matter rest. 'And you're the worst.' He stared at Clarissa, who blenched on hearing the accusation twice in one day. 'Christians spout off about love, but you punish it.'

'What your grandfather and I had was love,' Daisy said. 'What your mother and father have is love.' Clarissa detected a slight hesitation. 'What that man did to you was a sick perversion.'

'He did nothing. Just . . . Not that I didn't want him to. I begged him to fuck me.' His parents' and grandmother's faces contorted in disgust; Rosemary hugged her chest and laid her head on her knees. 'But he was afraid of hurting me, even though I said I didn't care.'

'First thing tomorrow we're going to the doctor's,' Susan said. 'You're having a thorough examination.'

'Good. I'll show him my bruises, but they're not from Brian.'

Susan stood up and moved to David, crouching clumsily beside him. 'You're the victim here. Nobody blames you.'

'He does!' David pointed at his father.

'He's revelling in all the attention,' Andrew said.

'He doesn't know his own mind,' Daisy said.

'It's my mind . . . my body.'

'I don't think this is helping,' Clarissa said. To her surprise, she missed the routine offer of tea, which might have eased the tension.

'You're a fine one to talk!' Daisy said. 'Why else didn't you inform his parents, if not to protect your friend, the so-called headteacher? She'll be taken down a peg or two.'

'There's no connection, Mother,' Susan said.

'Isn't there? You lost your job because she brought in relationships teaching. She needs to sort out her own relationship.'

'How is Pamela?' Susan asked, reminding Clarissa that, until recently, they'd been colleagues.

'Distraught. Incredulous. Angry. Much as you'd expect.'

'And the children?'

'Never mind her children,' Andrew said, 'think about your own!'

Clarissa looked at David and Rosemary, both of them seeking to disappear: the one behind the curtain and the other into her own lap.

'This is exactly why I told you he should have nothing to do with that church,' Andrew added. 'They can change the rector. They can change the services. But they can't change the fact that it's a Wemlock church. And all those Wemlocks were evil.'

'If you search hard enough,' Clarissa said, 'you'll find that every family has skeletons in its closet.'

'Yes, and the skeletons in theirs are my ancestors: the Leaves they worked to death on their land . . . in their mines. My father was killed when a shaft collapsed at Bickerton, and they never even sent a wreath.' Seeing Susan and Daisy exchange glances, Clarissa wondered whether Andrew were keeping up the pretence for the children or if he'd told himself the story so often that he believed it. 'But what does that matter when they paid for the upkeep of St Peter's? They even have their own chapel. And the painter, your friend Seward: he was the worst of the lot. I warned you about him when you first came up here, bright-eyed and bushy-tailed. Call yourself a reporter! Even then, all you cared about was the good name of the Church.'

'That's not—'

'You were a reporter?' David asked, letting go of the curtain, which twirled free.

'She worked for the BBC,' Daisy said. 'She made a programme about Lord Wemlock's paintings.'

'I did investigate,' Clarissa said, perturbed by the renewal of the charge, 'but there was no evidence.'

'His other daughter went loopy and attacked him. What more evidence do you need?'

'Evidence of what?' Susan asked. 'You're talking in riddles.'

Susan's bafflement, coupled with that of her mother and children, convinced Clarissa that Andrew had never repeated his claims. At the very least, Tapley had been spared Daisy's tirade against 'incest in Eden'.

'I'm saying nothing. I did once, and look where it got me! She knows what I mean,' Andrew replied, turning to Clarissa.

His choked voice cracked open the shell, which had been formed by years of disillusion. She saw him again as he had been at fifteen, the same age as David was now: sturdier, more pugnacious, but with a head equally full of secrets. The biggest, which he'd shyly confided to her after she'd sworn that it wouldn't be broadcast, was his dream of becoming an artist. He'd shown her his portfolio: sheaves of woodland sketches; several of rabbits, foxes and birds, but most of bugs and beetles, roots and ferns, drawn with a passion and precision that dazzled her. She recalled the tears, which he'd struggled to stifle, on meeting someone who believed in him, and longed for him to reconnect with that vulnerable adolescent the next time he belittled his son. He'd been so keen to watch a famous painter at work that he'd overcome his inhibitions to pose naked. But somewhere between sitting for Seward and quitting school, he'd renounced his artistic ambitions.

It was clear that his change of heart had been linked to the allegations he'd levelled against Seward. They were so preposterous that, after the initial thunderbolt, Clarissa had been able to put them from her mind for thirty years. Dredging them up, she recalled that Andrew had had a flirtation with Seward's elder daughter, Laurel, who, in his account, had ended it because she preferred to sleep with her father. Notwithstanding Laurel's desire to shock, Clarissa refused to credit that she would blurt out something so private – so shameful – let alone to a jilted boyfriend. She attached more weight to Father Vincent's view that Andrew, a practised fantasist, had concocted the story to deflect his own guilt at the souring of the affair. Nevertheless, he'd been so disturbed that he'd given up posing, despite having described it on tape as the most exciting thing that had ever happened to him.

Had she dismissed the allegations too easily? Even today, when so many pillars of the Church had crumbled, it was inconceivable that Seward, blessed not only with a God-given talent but a devout faith, would have been capable of such depravity. On the other hand, there was no doubt that Andrew's suspicions of him had cast a shadow over his entire life. More than thirty years on, it was impossible to ascertain the truth. But the slightest chance that she had failed the father made her doubly determined to support the son.

'I was against those paintings from day one,' Daisy said, as if reading her mind. 'I told Lily that she was a fool for allowing Andrew to get involved. And though it gives me no pleasure to say so, she's paying for it now. A woman who never let a coarse word pass her lips using language that would make the angels blush.'

'That's got nothing to do with David,' Susan said.

'I beg to differ. How can you expect the boy to behave decently when the first thing he sees as he enters the church is a life-size picture of his naked father?'

'If it were up to me, he wouldn't enter it at all,' Andrew said.

Daisy turned to Clarissa. 'And now you plan to shine more light on it. I've said it before and I'll say it again: a church is no place for flesh.'

Clarissa wondered what she made of the millions of crucifixes on altars across the globe: the twisted figure clad in nothing but a loincloth. Or was it just sensuous flesh to which she objected, Christ's nakedness being justified by His suffering?

'I realise that this is a very painful time for you all,' she said. 'I have no easy answers. Rest assured that I'm here to help in any way I can.'

'What more could we want?' Andrew asked.

'Enough now,' Susan said. 'Reverend, what will you think of me? You must be parched. Can I get you a cup of tea?'

Five

Clarissa ran down the High Street, hotly pursued by a bull. As she passed the Wemlock Arms, its bellow turned into a bell. Seizing the chance to escape, she sat up in bed, only for her conscious mind to plunge her into deeper confusion. The clangour that tore through her sleep was the tenor bell, its muffled toll redolent of Remembrance Sunday. The chimes quickened, as if somebody were raising the alarm. Her first thought was *Fire*, but dashing to the window, she saw no thread of red in the blanket of darkness. After checking on Xan, who lay blissfully undisturbed, she headed downstairs, where she grabbed her keys, threw a coat and scarf over her nightdress, sank her cold feet into a pair of wellingtons, and set out.

The peal had ceased and the air was so still that she heard her own ragged breath. With no glimmer of moonlight in the leaden sky, instinct guided her to the lychgate. As she hurried down the path, a pounding, panting ball of fur hurled itself at her from behind a grave. After a momentary dread, she recognised Alec Whittle's Ajax, who led her to his master, standing beside the porch with Hetty Blakemore and Alan Millington. Alec, out walking the dog, had been the first to arrive on the scene, swiftly followed by Hetty, a chronic insomniac, and Millington, a retired army major who lived across the road in the former almshouses, although his only contact with the church was to issue regular complaints about the cars blocking his view.

Alec, bemoaning numb fingers, fumbled with the lock which, with the alarm switched off, must have been secured from the inside. Hetty, still exercised by Hayley Seagrove and her boyfriend's 'sacrilege', speculated that a group of teenagers had broken in and, 'drugged on cracked cocaine and cannabis', sounded the bell. Millington claimed, with unseemly relish, to have read of subsidence setting off spectral peals. Clarissa suspected that the explanation was at once more mundane and more sinister. Brian had not been back to the village since his arrest. According to Pamela, he was living in a bail hostel in Crewe and had rebuffed all her attempts to visit him. Clarissa had refused to add to her woes by requesting the return of the church keys, but, as Alec unlocked the door to reveal a ghostly light emanating from the ringing chamber, she feared that her solicitude had been misplaced.

Her chest constricted as she lumbered up the worn, winding tower steps, cursing her choice of footwear. Behind her came sighs of effort from Alec and impatience from Millington. Hetty, due for a replacement hip, remained at the bottom with Ajax. Clarissa reached the ringing chamber, where a glance through the open door confirmed her fears. Brian was dangling from a bell rope, the slack coiled around his neck. Moving hesitantly towards him, she saw that his face was grey, his eyes red and his mouth speckled with foam. His shirt had either fallen open or else been torn by hands, which were now clenched, revealing a patch of pallid skin. He had wet – and, to judge by the smell, fouled – himself. An upended chair lay beneath him.

Clarissa stood transfixed, while Alec checked the pulse. 'Dead,' he said shortly. She sank to her knees, trusting that God would listen to her heart, since her mind was a void. As sentience returned, she found words to pray for Brian and all who loved him, and for the parish and all who would be wounded by this further desecration of the church.

She stood up, shaken by the knowledge that the last time she'd entered the chamber, Brian had been alive. Now, he hung like a carcass in the Wemlock Hall game larder. The last time she'd entered, he'd been with David. Now, he'd come back alone. He'd tied the rope and climbed on to the chair alone. So why did she feel as though she were the one who'd kicked it away?

Millington flipped open his phone and prepared to ring the police.

'Is there a signal in here?' he asked.

'Yes,' she replied, tempted to remind him of his protest against the 'unsightly' antenna on the spire.

Leaving the men to wait for the officers, she dragged herself down the steps, anxious to speak to Pamela before the patrol car arrived and the village rumour mill started grinding. One of its chief operatives was in the porch, vigorously stroking Ajax. Clarissa gave her a rushed report, swearing her to secrecy until the family had been informed.

'What an ass!' Hetty said. 'What an utterable ass!'

The blush of dawn on the tumbledown gravestones heightened

Clarissa's sense of mortality. She returned to the rectory to shower, dress and write a note for Xan, explaining that she'd been called out in an emergency. She set off, striding through streets deserted apart from a Leyland Dairies delivery van and Mr Chabra opening the shop. Reaching the Salmons' house, she pulled the cord on the bronze bell and was struck afresh by the image of the strangled Brian. Pamela, face haggard, hair matted and wearing a man's camel dressing gown, answered the door.

'Clarissa, what on earth! It's ten to seven.'

'May I come in?'

'What's wrong? Tell me! It's Brian, isn't it?'

'Shall we go through to the sitting room?'

Pamela stepped aside without answering and Clarissa entered the hall, treading on an envelope, which she reflexively bent to retrieve. There was a single name written in a steady hand, and she duly surrendered it. 'It's from Brian,' Pamela said, in a voice drained of emotion. 'He's dead, isn't he?'

'Yes,' she replied, her hospice training coming to her aid, as she took her friend's limp arm and led her to the sofa.

'When?'

'During the night . . . the early hours. I'm so sorry.'

'Two weeks ago, everyone would have grieved with me. I'd have been suffocated by sympathy. But now? I can already hear them . . . or maybe I can't. Maybe they'll have the kindness to whisper. But I'll see it etched on their faces. "It's the best solution . . . a clean break . . . deep down, she must feel thankful." But I loved him. Whatever he did: whatever he was: I loved him! I can't help it. Is that wrong?'

'Of course not. He loved you too,' she replied, convinced that, however misguidedly, Brian had been trying to spare her from suffering.

'Maybe once. Why did the hostel ring you? When I went there, they wouldn't let me through the door. Did he shut me out completely? Did he name you as next of kin?'

'He's written to you. See!' She pointed to the crumpled envelope in Pamela's hand. 'He'd never shut you out.' Pamela looked slowly down at the letter. 'Would you like me to read it?'

'No!' She clasped it to her breast. 'It's mine. He wrote it to me! He must have slipped it under the door during the night. But how? The hostel has a strict curfew. Not all the men are on bail. Some have been in prison for violent crimes. Is that what happened? Did one of them discover that he was a . . . a . . . I can't say the word.'

'No, not at all.'

'Then how? Why? What do you know?'

'Can I get you anything? A cup of tea?' she asked, playing for time.

'Tea, tea! Don't I pee enough as it is? Will tea bring him back? Tea!'

'The hostel didn't call me. I found him . . . heard him. I was woken by the ringing.'

'The doorbell?'

'The church bell. I'm so sorry, Pamela. He hanged himself in the belfry.'

'Oh God!' She clutched her throat, either to stop herself choking or to share the pain. Gently but firmly, Clarissa prised her hand away.

'Why there?'

'It was somewhere he knew well, somewhere he felt safe.'

'Somewhere he'd been with David.'

'Somewhere that was precious to him long before David was born. He loved those bells. He knew that the tenor bell would take his weight: that he would just have to remove the slider.'

The more she sought to reassure Pamela, the more she unsettled herself. She'd assumed that he'd wished to atone in the place where he'd offended. But what if it were the reverse: a gesture not of repentance but of revenge? He'd known that his death knell would reach the rectory. If suicide were as much an act of aggression as of despair, had it been directed at her?

'How long does it take to hang?'

'Not long. Minutes . . . if that.'

'Did he look peaceful?'

'He looked still.'

'Where is he now?'

'As far as I know, where we found him.'

'You left him up there?'

'Alec Whittle is with him, and Major Millington from the almshouses. They're waiting for the police.'

'Was there no one else? He couldn't stand Alec. He called him Mr Pecksniff.'

'What?'

'From Dickens. That's something you didn't know about him. He was a voracious reader. He wasn't just . . .'

She began to cry, enabling Clarissa to comfort her without the entanglement of words. As the sobs became sniffs, Pamela pulled out of her embrace. 'It's my fault. This would never have happened if I'd taken him back.'

'You had no choice.'

'You of all people should preach forgiveness.'

'His bail conditions specified that he must stay away from children. Including his own.'

'The children. Oh God! How . . . what am I to tell them?' She turned to the door, as if they might be eavesdropping.

'Would you like me . . .?'

'No, I'm their mother. It's my job.' She turned back and, as if noticing the letter for the first time, tore it open. Rubbing her eyes, she read it or as much of it as she could see through her tears. 'The children,' she repeated, before staggering upstairs.

Alone and ashamed of her throbbing headache, Clarissa glanced at the letter, which Pamela had left behind. Peering down, she skimmed the short paragraph, as though by not touching it, she would rebut the charge of prying. Given the neatness of the script, there was little chance of a coroner's verdict that the balance of Brian's mind had been disturbed. He assured Pamela of his love for her and the children and apologised for the hurt and disgrace that he'd brought on them. Was she wrong to detect a touch of self-pity in his insistence that they would be better off without him and even of irony in his subsequent instruction that his life insurance policy was in the drawer under his bed? She was both moved and angered as, deftly avoiding the issue of age, he declared that he'd 'never felt any previous attraction to my own sex' and explained that 'something unknown, unexpected and utterly irresistible was opened up in me by David'. Acknowledging that he had no right to ask, he appealed to his wife not to blame David and to protect his identity, so that 'in time, he, like the rest of you, might think of me with a vestige of affection'.

'Unknown, unexpected and utterly irresistible': that was as fair a description as any of sexual desire. It was no wonder that St Augustine, himself no stranger to such desire, had made it the root of Original Sin. A firm believer in Original Virtue, she abhorred the Augustinian doctrine, but, with a lifetime's experience, reinforced by Brian's letter, she couldn't altogether dismiss it. Yet if she were to borrow – indeed, to redeem – the traditional imagery, the source of human suffering would not be the serpent that tempted Eve to pluck the fruit, but rather the worm in the fruit itself. In the temporal world, everything was subject to decay.

Startled by her ringing phone, she rummaged agitatedly in her bag, relaxing when she saw that the call was from Xan. Having woken to discover her note, he wanted to know more about the emergency. Fearing that he'd hear from someone else, she explained as simply as she could that Brian had killed himself. To her relief, he didn't press for details.

'Shit! Shall I come over? Shit, what do I say to Matt?'

'Not now. His mother's only just telling him.' She listened for voices, but the house was eerily quiet. 'I'll find out whether he'd like you to visit him after school.'

'Do I still have to go?' he asked, sounding so wretched that she allowed him to take the day off. She promised to be home as soon as possible, ending the call just as Pamela returned downstairs.

'In the kitchen!' she shouted. 'I'm making Margaret a smoothie.'

Clarissa moved to join her. 'You've told them?' she asked, bemused by the protracted silence.

'She likes it frothy,' Pamela said, tearing the skin off two bananas and tossing them into the blender, along with sugar, almonds and half a pint of milk.

'Is there anything I can do?'

'How about turning back the clock? No. Margaret howled when I told her. I put my arms round her, but she pushed me away, clinging to Hiccup, that's the elephant Brian won for her at Knutsford fair, when she was four or five. Do you think that she made the connection?' Her lower lip trembled, but she bit it hard.

'And Matthew? Sorry, did you say something?' Clarissa asked, as Pamela switched on the blender.

'She likes it frothy,' she replied, giving the drink another whisk.

'What about Matthew?'

'He won't eat bananas.'

'No, when you told him.'

'I'd barely begun to speak when he flung a pillow over his head. I pulled it away and he clamped his hands over his ears. I prised them off and, the next thing I knew, we were fighting. Just like when he had his ears syringed as a child. They were full of wax, like his father's.' She whimpered but, when Clarissa took a step towards her, she shook her head furiously. 'No. I have to take this to Margaret. Then I must get dressed. The police will be here and want me to identify the body. That's how it's done, isn't it?'

'I think so, yes. But only when you feel up to it.' She pictured the pendent corpse and trusted that the mortuary staff would have wiped his spittle-flecked mouth and shut his bloodshot eyes. 'Although I'm sure that somebody else . . . I can go if you'd prefer.'

'No, I want to see him. I need to see him one last time.'

Pamela carried the drink upstairs. Feeling hungry, Clarissa opened a packet of fig rolls and made herself some coffee. The biscuits put her in mind of Shirley, whom she started to text, struggling to find words that would alert rather than alarm her, when Matthew appeared, wearing his school uniform.

'Matthew, I'm so—'

'I'm starving.'

'Yes, of course. I'll—'

'I'm famished.'

'I'll make you some breakfast. What would you like?'

'Bacon, eggs, sausages, tomatoes, beans.'

'I'll do the best I can.' She moved to the fridge, pausing as she passed him. Seeing him flinch, she decided against a hug. 'I'm so sorry,' she said, as she put the frying pan on the hob.

'Why? He didn't care about us, so why should we care about him?'

'He cared about you deeply.'

'Is that what they teach you to say at vicar school?'

'They teach us to tell the truth,' she replied, with more conviction than she felt.

'Then how come he took the coward's way out, leaving us to clear up the mess?'

'Who knows what he was thinking? No one that desperate can

have been thinking straight. The one thing I'm sure of is that he thought he was making things easier . . . cleaner . . . tidier for you all. He wanted to spare you the burden of a trial.'

'What burden? We weren't on trial. We didn't even have to go to court. He did it for himself; he knew how nonces are treated in prison.'

'That's a sad way of looking at it.'

'You said you'd tell the truth. Well I'm glad he's dead. Do you hear me? Glad!'

He burst into tears and pounded his temples. Leaving the bacon and sausages to sizzle, Clarissa lifted him up, feeling his resistance crumble as he buried his face in her chest.

'Your father did love you, I promise you that. Whatever he did to hurt you wasn't deliberate.'

'I can smell burning,' Matthew mumbled through his sobs.

'Just a moment!' She hurried to the stove and switched off the gas. 'I hope you like your bacon crisp.' She cut a tomato and added it to the plate, which she took to the table. 'Too late for the eggs, I'm afraid. How many slices of toast would you like?'

'Four,' he replied brashly.

'Right you are. Eat up and then maybe you should change into something more comfortable.'

'I'm going to school.'

'I don't think that's a good idea; you're still in shock.'

'No. I was in shock two weeks ago when he was arrested. I'm perfectly fine now.'

'Then you should stay to support your mother.'

'That's why I can't miss any lessons. I must get my grades. There'll be no help from my dad – Brian. It's all down to me. I've texted Xan and David that he's dead and to meet me at the bus stop.'

'You've texted David?'

'And Xan.'

'I'm sorry, but I must dash. I told Xan he could take the day off school and come round to see you later. I need to warn him of the change of plan. Don't worry about the bus; I'll drive you. Tell your mother I'll be back.'

Leaving Matthew perplexed, she went out. Her one thought was to ring Susan and prevent David from replying rashly – incriminatingly – to the text. Not having the number in her phone, she braced herself and rang Daisy.

'I can't say I'm surprised,' she said, on hearing the news. 'He always was a quitter.'

'I'm in rather a rush,' Clarissa replied, raising her voice to include Tricia Harding heading towards her as she left the shop.

'At least he's done the right thing by David. The scales will finally fall from his eyes.'

'That's why I have to speak to Susan,' Clarissa said fiercely. 'It's urgent.'

Furnished with the number, she rang Susan, who answered at once, apologising for the background noise. She described how David had received Matthew's text during their morning workout. Andrew's fury at the interruption had intensified when David collapsed in the middle of a squat. While she tried to comfort him, Andrew had taunted him that suicide was for sissies. David ran upstairs, screaming that he was ill, but Andrew had followed, pulling off his singlet and forcing him into his uniform, asserting that, if Matthew, whose father had died, was going to school, then so was he.

After repeating her offer to drive the boys, Clarissa urged her to impress on David the need to conceal his relationship with Brian, both to protect himself and to respect Matthew's loss. She returned home to find Xan, dressed for school, sitting at the kitchen table, staring at a bowl brimful of cereal. For once, he neither groaned nor squirmed when she stood behind him, one hand on his shoulder and the other stroking his over-gelled hair.

'How did he do it?'

'He hanged himself from one of the church bells.'

'Swinging to and fro till his skull cracked?'

'No!' she replied, recoiling from the ghoulish image. 'Strangled by the bell rope.'

'Have you ever thought of killing yourself?' he asked haltingly.

'No, never. I promise.'

'Because of God?'

'In part,' she replied. 'Even when I've been at my most miserable ... despairing, I've known that my feelings weren't the best measure of God's plans. Besides, never for one moment could I conceive of ending my life when I have you.'

'Brian had Matt and Margaret.'

'I'm not Brian. I give you fair warning that I shall be around for a good while yet. Now eat up! You have two minutes to get ready and into the car.'

Seizing on the rare dispensation, he wolfed down the cereal and headed outside, barely complaining when, keen to create a buffer between David and Matthew, she insisted that he sit in the back. They first picked up Matthew, who slid in lankily next to Xan, to be greeted by a laconic: 'Sorry, bro. It's brutal.'

'Sweet choice of words!'

'Would you like some music?' Clarissa asked.

'Whatever,' Xan said, so grateful for the distraction that he tolerated Radio Three. A few moments later, they turned into Meadow Lane, where David, his puffy eyes and dishevelled hair at odds with his spotless uniform, stood waiting.

'Sorry to hear about your dad,' he mumbled, as he stepped into the car.

'He did what he did. It's done.'

'Have you been crying?' Xan leant forward and grabbed David's arm.

'Leave off!'

'Xan, sit back!' she said. 'Do you want us to have an accident?'

'It's allergies,' David said.

'To what?'

Clarissa turned up the radio, her stomach settling as the stately melody filled the car. She tentatively identified it as Dvořák, only for the presenter to announce that it was Grieg's 'Funeral March in Memory of Rikard Nordraak'.

'Will Matt's dad have a funeral in church?' Xan asked.

'That's not a discussion for now. It depends on his family.' She glanced at the rear-view mirror, but Matthew's face was blank.

'What about *Hamlet*, when Ophelia's only buried in holy ground by special command of the king?'

'Xan, this isn't helpful.' She was reluctant to turn up the volume in case the entire programme was devoted to funeral marches and requiems.

'I couldn't give a toss where he's buried,' Matt said. 'I shan't be going.'

'He's your father!' David said.

'So? Your dad may be a gobshite, but at least he's not a paedo.'

Sensing David's distress, Clarissa patted his thigh.

'Keep your hands on the wheel!' Xan shouted, with what she prayed was jealousy, rather than suspicion.

'No one's told me . . . how did Brian – your dad – die?' David asked, with a telltale catch in his voice.

'Not now, David,' Clarissa said. 'I'm sure that Matthew doesn't want to talk about it.'

'Why not? Everyone else will. He hanged himself – what a dork! He hanged himself from one of his precious bells. In the tower where you trained. You're lucky he never tried it on with you.'

'Who says he didn't?' Xan interjected. 'We don't know that. Why not ask him?'

'Don't be ridiculous!' Clarissa said. 'You should think before you speak.'

'I am thinking. He looks all cut up.'

'So were you when you heard the news.'

'But I didn't cry.'

'Some of us have feelings,' David said.

'Yes, let it go,' Matthew said. 'It's the D-man. He wouldn't . . . Dad wouldn't . . . You didn't . . .'

'I did. He did. I loved him.'

Matthew rammed his head against the seat, jolting David forward.

'You dickhead!' Xan shouted at David.

'I loved him and he loved me.'

'That's enough, all of you! I'm going to stop the car.'

'You can't,' Xan said. 'We'll be late for assembly.'

'Some things are more important. We need to talk.' She pulled in to the kerbside, triggering a blast of horns. 'Listen to me please,' she said, twisting round, the seatbelt the least of her constraints. 'Brian loved you, Matthew, and he cared deeply for you, David.' Xan snorted. 'But the feelings weren't the same. He was very confused. That confusion is what killed him.'

'No, he killed him,' Matthew said, punching the back of David's seat.

'No, she did,' David said, pointing to Clarissa. In a flash, he opened the door, narrowly missing a buggy, leapt out and bolted down the street.

'David!' Clarissa shouted through the open door.

'Leave it!' Xan said.

Losing sight of him, she pulled the door closed.

'Why did he say you killed my dad?' Matthew asked.

'He wasn't speaking literally.'

'Then not-literally?'

'I caught your father and David together in the ringing chamber.'

'You mean together, like *together*?'

121

'Let's not rake it up now.'

'And you said nothing?' Xan interjected.

'Not to you, obviously.'

'What about Mum?' Matthew asked.

'It's complicated. The Church has rules. I'm worried about David.' She scoured the pavement in case, by some miracle, he'd reconsidered and returned.

'Why?' Xan said.

'Do you still want to go to school or would you rather go home?' she asked Matthew. 'We can talk about this with your mother.'

'School. Like Xan said, the first period's *Hamlet*.'

Clarissa started the car and drove the half-mile to the school in a welcome, if oppressive, silence. She parked, and the boys clambered out without a word. She watched them disappear into the crowd, before getting out herself and walking into the lobby. En route to the principal's office, she ran into Mrs Harrold, the boys' year teacher. Taking her aside, she told her first of Brian's death and Matthew's wish to carry on as normal, and then of David's flight, which she attributed solely to distress at having to withdraw from the Six-Bell Striking Competition. Happy to have avoided the principal, a fervent evangelical, she asked Mrs Harrold to contact David's parents, while she went in search of him.

Back in the car, she rang to warn Shirley that she would be delayed. 'The church is closed,' the secretary replied, bubbling with excitement. 'The police have declared it a crime scene. They've stuck black-and-yellow tape all over the porch. Like liquorice-flavoured rock.'

Clarissa crawled around the neighbourhood, to a cacophony of hooting. After forty minutes, she lost heart and headed to the police station, informing the desk sergeant that she'd come to give a statement about Brian's suicide. After a brief interview with the coolly efficient investigating officer, she returned to Tapley, parked outside the church and inspected the porch, with its cat's cradle of tape, two ends of which were flapping in the breeze. Wary of being waylaid, she hastened to the office, where Shirley, aching from Lenten abstinence, was avid for news.

'So dreadful!' she said piously. 'Poor Mrs Salmon! And to think he was wearing her bra and pants.'

'What?' Clarissa asked. 'Who on earth told you that?'

'Jayne in the café. I just popped out for a five-minute break. The phone hasn't stopped all morning.'

Which she was paid to answer, Clarissa thought with a rush of irritation. 'Unlike Jayne, I was there,' she said. 'He was wearing his own shirt and trousers. He wasn't a transvestite.'

'He was something still worse, wasn't he?' Shirley said, refusing to back down. 'Little boys.'

'Did Jayne tell you that too?' Clarissa asked coldly.

Shirley's lips quivered. 'Of course not. I don't listen to gossip. There was a reporter here from the *Nantwich News* . . . well-turned-out but a terrible skin. She said he'd been up in court last week.'

'He's dead. Isn't that enough?'

'But little boys—'

'One boy. And not so little. He was fifteen years old. I'd be grateful if you'd make that clear to anyone else who doesn't listen to gossip.'

123

The news travelled fast and, over the next hour, she received calls from two mothers and one father, worried about Brian's unsupervised access to their sons during last summer's Holiday Fun Club. No matter that he'd given up his time to run several group activities (she emphasised *group*) for teenagers, who would otherwise have idled about the village, he was a pervert from whom no boy was safe! Even his sheltering them in the Thatch Inn during a freak storm was interpreted by one mother as an attempt to inebriate her son. 'Would you rather he'd caught pneumonia,' she snapped, slamming down the phone. As Shirley gasped and Titus growled, she regretted her bluntness. It was understandable that parents were anxious. Nevertheless, was Brian to have a one-word epitaph?

Leaving an aggrieved Shirley to take messages, she walked to the rectory and prayed the Daily Office before the image of Christ who, as liberator of the world, had more pressing concerns than illicit sex in an English village. After a quick lunch, she set off for the Chapel Hill estate, stopping at the Chabras' to buy the bread, milk and vegetables that she took, along with the weekly Eucharist, to Marion Fairweather. The acrid smell of incontinence pads pervaded the airless flat, as she gave her the sacrament. Ignoring the five-pound note in its usual place by the kettle, she made the mandatory cups of tea and left with a promise to feed the cat if Marion were sent to hospital with this week's undiagnosed ailment.

Switching on her phone as she returned to the car, she found a text from Susan to say that David had been picked up in Brookfield Park and the police were bringing him home. Relieved, she decided to call on Pamela, whose mask of composure slipped the moment she recognised her visitor. In a voice edged with anguish, she whispered that Len and Josie were there. Clasping Clarissa's wrist, as though afraid that she might escape, she ushered her into the sitting room, where she shook the bereaved parents' hands (Josie's making barely an impression) and offered her condolences.

'Josie has been telling us about Lorraine, Brian's fiancée before he met me. Lovely girl!' Pamela said, emboldened by Clarissa's presence.

'It all came flooding back.' Josie turned to Len. 'He was always a ladies' man, wasn't he?'

'There were lasses, yes.'

'Now he'll never have the chance to clear his name.' She sniffed back her tears.

Pamela moved to the door, beckoning Clarissa, who followed with an apologetic smile at Len and Josie.

'I presume Matthew got to school all right?' Pamela asked, as they moved into the kitchen.

'Fine,' Clarissa replied, gulping. 'He should be home any moment.'

'It's their last day of detention.'

'I'd forgotten. Surely they'll let him off it?'

'He didn't want special treatment. He can't have it both ways.'

'I suppose not.'

'Though his father managed,' Pamela added, with a laugh that turned into a snarl.

'Where's Margaret?' Clarissa asked quietly.

'In the bathroom. She's taken two baths today already, to my certain knowledge. Maybe a third while I was at the mortuary.'

'You identified the body?'

'The attendants had the decency to cover his neck.'

'Then the worst is over.'

'Is it? The policewoman said that they'll hold a post-mortem tomorrow. Since there's no suspicion of foul play, she expects the coroner's office to release his body soon afterwards. My next job is to plan the funeral.'

'You don't have to make any decisions yet.'

'I know that the sensible thing would be to opt for the crem. Immediate family only. Hell, I'd best get back to them! They look as lost as on their first trip abroad . . . But it should be in the church. Those bells meant everything to him. It may be asking for trouble, but I couldn't bear anything hole-and-corner.'

'It can be as grand as you like. And not just because it's you. It's enshrined in law. We all have a right to a funeral in our parish church.'

Her hope that the right would be respected was swiftly dashed. While neither of the wardens protested to her face, Petunia wasted no time in complaining to the archdeacon, who rang her that same afternoon, his manner the customary mixture of condescension and coercion. After the statutory two minutes of small talk, his tone hardened.

'I've received representations about the inexpedience of conducting Mr Salmon's funeral at St Peter's.'

'May I ask who from?'

'They were made in confidence. Let's just say that the person in question has a florid demeanour.' As he chuckled to himself, she refused to give him the satisfaction of acknowledging the pun. 'I'm well aware that the dead must be buried. However great the late Mr Salmon's sins, he was no Jezebel, whose carcass *shall be as dung upon the face of the field in the portion of Jezreel*. But under the circumstances, isn't it foolhardy, to say the least, to hold the service in your own church? And I'm not just thinking of you. Given the imminent employment tribunal, can Mrs Salmon afford the hullabaloo? Wouldn't it be wise to go somewhere nearby, say St Timothy's?'

'You forget that St Timothy's is a dissenting parish. They wouldn't allow me to officiate. Besides, Brian Salmon was tower captain here for two decades. He made a significant contribution to church life. That deserves to be celebrated.'

'Well, I have no power to compel you,' he replied, with a sigh. 'I pray your parishioners see it the same way.'

The first test of their opinion occurred the following Sunday, when she included Brian in the prayers for the souls of the faithful departed. Although shielded on either side by the well-liked Hannah Richards and Dickon Yates, his name provoked a distinct intake of breath. Worse was to come when she read the notices, announcing 'the funeral of the former tower captain, Brian Salmon, at three o'clock next Thursday, to which all are welcome'.

'He's not welcome!' cried a voice from the back of the nave, which she identified as that of Logan Drinkel, one of the parents who'd been exercised by Brian's presence in the Holiday Fun Club.

'Hear hear!' shouted Angela Wilcox, whose son, James, was the choir's leading treble. 'Have you no morals?' she asked Clarissa, who stood aghast. Years of dreading an objection to the banns had failed to prepare her for this. Angela rose and strode into the nave. 'Come on, James, we're leaving.' He sank into his seat. 'I said: "Come on!"'

With cheeks as red as his cassock, James sidled from his stall and slunk down the side-aisle, where his mother propelled him to the door. Clarissa turned to the shocked congregation, among them Pamela sitting, shamefaced, alongside her parents-in-law. She was eager to offer her what comfort she could, so when Reginald Yarrow peered down from the organ loft, waiting for the cue for the final hymn, she shook her head and gathered her thoughts. As the agent of Brian's lost reputation, it was fitting that she should be the one to salvage it.

'Our faith should never become cosy. It must rise to the challenges and complexities of life. There has been much fanciful – some might say, hysterical – speculation about the nature of Brian's offence. He was not a seasoned paedophile. Technically, he wasn't a paedophile at all, but rather an ephebophile – don't worry if you don't know the word; I didn't myself until a few days ago. It means somebody who's attracted to adolescents. And from everything we know, in Brian's case there was only the one. Moreover, the boy – the adolescent – in question has confirmed that he was neither manipulated nor constrained. On the contrary, he was the initiator. None of this justifies Brian's behaviour, but it does mitigate it. So I trust that you'll understand – and, indeed, endorse – my decision to hold his funeral here in church.'

Fearing another outburst, she quickly gave the blessing. She nodded to Reginald, who blasted the opening chords of 'O Jesus, I have promised'. The congregation rose to sing, and she followed the depleted choir down the nave and into the vestry. Leaving them to chew over the furore, she made her way to the porch.

'I hope you don't think that I traduced David,' she said to Daisy Quantock, who was hurrying past.

'He's done a good enough job of that himself.'

'How is he?'

'Bruised.'

'Yes, Xan told me about the scuffle at school.'

'How interesting that you should latch on to that!' she said acidly. 'I was referring to his soul.'

She walked away, leaving Clarissa chastened. 'I'm so sorry that you were subjected to that,' she said to Pamela, who hung back until the crowd had dispersed.

'It's my own fault. What was I thinking of: rubbing people's noses in it?'

'You've done what you thought best for yourself, and for Brian.'

'I wish I had a shred of your conviction.'

'Thank you . . . thank you for speaking up for him,' Len said, taking her right hand in both of his and shaking it vigorously.

'I only did what was right,' she said, gently freeing herself as she turned to Josie, hiding in her husband's shadow. 'How are you bearing up?'

'I just want the week to be over.'

'It will be a lovely service, I promise.'

One thing that she couldn't promise was the choir. While more discreet than Angela, the parents of the remaining five trebles, girls as well as boys, made plain their disapproval by refusing to let their children miss an afternoon's schooling, a particularly feeble excuse given that they all went to St Peter's. Meanwhile, the adult choristers found themselves unable to take the time off work. Even the long-retired Roger Simmonds had an urgent hospital appointment. Reginald, however, agreed to play the organ and, crucially, there would be a funeral toll. Heedless of the spondylitis that had occasioned his resignation as tower captain twenty years earlier, Len Salmon declared that, if no one else were willing to do it, he would ring the tenor bell himself. But Annabel Thynne, whose stature belied her strength, stepped forward, wishing, she said tearfully, to honour Brian's thirty-two years in the band and their twenty-year friendship.

Marcus was arriving from London on Wednesday evening, and several of Brian's relatives were due to attend, but Pamela had little idea of how many mourners to expect. Despite a steady stream of casseroles and cakes, few of her neighbours had ventured into the house, the usual strain of condolence visits accentuated by both the manner of Brian's death and the seething, silent presence of Matthew, who emerged from his room only to cause the guests embarrassment and his mother pain.

He was at home for a week, having been suspended from school for smashing David's head against a locker.

'It sucks! They punished Matt, when it should have been David,' Xan told Clarissa.

'It was an unprovoked attack.'

'Course it was provoked. He was shagging Matt's dad.'

'David's hurting too. You should show him some compassion.'

'Why, because I'm your son?'

'No, because he's your friend.'

'No way am I friends with that bender!'

'It isn't headlice. You won't catch it.'

'You're as bad as the girls at school. They've dissed him up to now. But as soon as they find out he's gay, they're all over him.'

'Maybe they don't feel threatened by him.'

'They can't take real blokes. Same as you. It's why you don't care about Dad and his tart in London.'

'She's not a—'

'Instead, you're hooked on Jesus. Gentle Jesus meek and mild! What sort of bloke lets Judas kiss him . . . gets himself whipped and stuff. It's messed up!'

Xan's accusations stung. After a lifetime in clerical circles, she was well aware of those whose reverence for both the body of the dead Christ and the priests who represented Him carried an erotic charge. In its drive to regulate sexuality, the Church had channelled it into some dark and dubious places. The early Christians had been less inhibited. It was Seward Wemlock who'd introduced her to the sects that used sex in their rites, their names unsurprisingly absent from the theology tripos. Although she baulked at their excesses, which Seward had detailed in a patent attempt to shock her, they offered a welcome corrective to the Church's subsequent denial of the flesh. As ever, there was a happy medium and, as she stood in St Peter's on the eve of Brian's funeral, she marvelled yet again at how Seward had found it: imbuing all his figures, earthly and celestial, with both a corporeal dignity and a spiritual glow.

Lost in thought, she was roused by the slow scrape of the door, as if someone were trying to slip in unobserved. Turning towards it, she made out a tall, thin man in a beret and soutane, silhouetted like the motif on a liqueur label. Doffing the beret, he looked around intently, before advancing and genuflecting to the reserved sacrament.

Her gasp made him jump. 'Rectoress,' Father Vincent said, 'I didn't see you.'

Her amazement that he should venerate the sacrament, consecrated by her, in a church he believed that she'd polluted, outweighed the barb. 'I'm speechless,' she said, wondering whether the obeisance was instinctive. 'This must be the first time you've set foot in here since I arrived.'

'Say rather since I departed.'

They walked towards each other like prize fighters before a bout. At seventy-five, Father Vincent remained an imposing figure, with a full head of fine silver hair above the high brow, deep-set eyes and pale, gaunt features, which had led the ladies of the parish to extol his ascetism, even as the children nicknamed him 'the Skull'.

'What brings you to Tapley?'

'Fidelity. Concern for my former flock. Although I usually prefer them to visit me in Chester. I wouldn't wish to tread on your elegant toes.'

'Very thoughtful of you,' Clarissa replied, shuffling her sneakers.

'But the events of the past two weeks have caused great distress. I've received supplications from several quarters.' He put his finger to his lips, as though she were about to ask for names. 'So I answered the call. Once here, I was seized by an overwhelming urge to look inside.'

He glanced round. 'I'd forgotten . . . no, I'd refused to remember how beautiful it is.'

'There's been nothing to stop you visiting.'

'Hasn't there?' He fixed his eyes on the altar. 'You won't expect me to approve of the reordering.'

'I wanted the altar to be at the heart of the church, not a priests-only party from which everyone else is excluded.'

'My spies – I speak figuratively, of course – reported that you didn't get your way without a struggle.'

'You'd trained them well. Many people thought that the change was presumptuous. They felt unworthy of having Christ in their midst.'

'With good reason.' He turned towards Eden. 'There's one change I do applaud.' She looked at him in surprise. 'The removal of the curtain! I allowed myself to be pressured into putting it up. Although in my own defence, it was the simplest way to defuse the controversy. You must remember; you were involved in it.'

'As a commentator.'

'Quite. I still have my tape of the programme. You were a first-rate broadcaster. You missed your calling.'

'Some would say I'd found it.'

'No doubt.' He surveyed the church. 'Such miraculous paintings! They're the reason I stayed in the post for so long. Seeing them day after day for thirty years has been the supreme privilege of my life.'

Clarissa followed his gaze. It made no sense that a man so zealous to condemn human frailty should cherish paintings which, in her view, did the exact opposite.

'This is Wemlock's masterpiece,' he said, turning back to Eden.

'Youth in all its innocence and beauty, before nature and desire defile it.'

The contradiction started to make sense.

'My husband is currently curating the first full-scale retrospective of Seward's work. Do you remember Marcus?'

'Of course. One of the coming men at Christie's.'

'He moved to the Tate a few months before I was accepted for training. The exhibition is bound to generate interest in our paintings. We're planning how best to exploit it.'

'I'm sure you are,' he said, with a cryptic smile. 'Such a shame that Laurel isn't here to advise.'

'She hasn't been seen in Tapley for years. Marcus wrote to her but has yet to hear back. I shall invite her to any celebrations.'

'You can save yourself the trouble. She died last autumn.'

'Really? I had no idea.'

'She swallowed bleach.'

'How appalling! I'm so sorry. Bleach? Are you sure you don't mean Sorrel? She was the one who was committed.'

'I do know which is which!' he said gruffly. 'Laurel . . . it was definitely Laurel. One of her daughters discovered her body.'

'It gets worse.' The conjunction of the suicides disturbed her. 'She must have been what age?'

'Fifty. The same as him.' He stared at the adolescent Adam.

'And as Brian. I wonder whether Andrew knows about Laurel.'

'He won't care. He closed that chapter before the paint was dry on the canvas. He never entered the church again, at least not while I was rector.'

'Nor since.'

'He blamed me for persuading him to pose. Such ingratitude! He should give thanks every day of his life: to have been blessed with an immortality denied to all but a select few.'

'Surely the blessing of eternity is enough?'

'How principled of you!'

'Have you been to the Hall to visit his mother?' she asked quickly. 'I know that you and Lily were close.'

'Never again! It's more than flesh and blood can stand. I don't reproach her for losing her mind, just for what's left inside it. I could never abide to hear filth, least of all from a woman.'

'Count yourself lucky you weren't within earshot of my delivery room!' She stifled a smile at his shudder.

'I've detained you long enough. Doubtless the whole of Tapley is lining up for your ministrations.' With a curt nod, he strode out, leaving Clarissa feeling as though she'd been brushed by a venomous butterfly. She returned to the office, where she received calls from both the Nantwich police and the archdeacon, warning of demonstrations planned for the funeral. A Facebook group, Concerned Christian Mothers, invited all those opposed to the Church's 'support for paedophiles' to gather outside St Peter's on Friday. Appalled, Clarissa trusted that, as with the threatened picket at the school, no one would turn up. The inspector, less sanguine, undertook to dispatch two of his officers, while the archdeacon promised to pray for her.

Pamela agreed that, as a precaution, the coffin should be placed in the chancel before the service. Len and Josie proposed to keep vigil and, at one o'clock, Clarissa sent Shirley to them with coffee and sandwiches, which they declined. An hour later, Marcus, stationed in the porch, reported that a dozen protestors had assembled at the lychgate, overseen by two policemen, who looked little older than Xan. Clarissa set off for the church, accompanied by Shirley, who cheerily remarked that 'Mother is fuming at having to miss all the drama.' Grateful for once that her gender granted her a measure of anonymity, she swept past the protestors, sickened by their placards, which ranged from the succinct *Jesus Wept* to the scurrilous *Church Loves Perves*. One elderly woman had so misjudged the lettering of *God Hates a Child Abuser* that, even close up, it appeared to read *God Hates a Child*.

It was a relief to find that, forty minutes before the ceremony, the mourners already outnumbered the protestors. She thanked Alec and Wendy, the acting sidespersons, assuring them that their duties would be limited to welcoming visitors, handing out orders of service and taking the retiring collection for *The Ringing World*. Alec, more apprehensive than Wendy, pointed to Major Millington in a nearby pew, who'd offered to help in the event of trouble. Insisting that the police had everything under control, she made her way through the church, where she spotted a pair of strangers examining the spandrels. Something in their trim beards, shiny suits and guarded manner put her in mind of evangelical pastors, and she feared that, alongside the public protest at the gate, they intended to disrupt the service itself. She greeted them charily, only to learn that they were surveyors, come to pay their respects to their late colleague.

'It doesn't add up,' one said. 'With us, he was a regular guy, always talking about his wife and kids. It doesn't add up.'

The bell began to toll. Clarissa pictured Annabel alone in the ringing chamber, her loyalty to her former captain numbing the ache in her arms. With more mourners arriving, she headed into the sacristy to vest, returning as the knell drew to a close and Reginald Yarrow played the stately opening chords of Elgar's 'Nimrod'. She welcomed the congregation, delighted to see rows, which she'd feared would be empty, dotted with mourners: some, her parishioners; others, Brian's family and friends. Pamela occupied the front pew, between her children: Margaret, staring incredulously at the coffin; Matthew, scowling into space. Behind them sat Len and Josie, clutching each other's clenched hands. Further back were an unexpected trio: David Leaves, his bruised jaw still livid, beside his parents. She wondered what had prompted Andrew to break his vow and cross the threshold. Was it the satisfaction of seeing his enemy consigned to the grave, or had he taken pity on his son?

The organ's dying fall cut short her conjecture. She opened the service with the bidding prayer. After two hymns, one of which – 'The Sacred Bells of England' – was unfamiliar to her, and the poem 'If I Be the First of Us to Die', read with surprising gravity by Brian's cousin, Derek, whom she'd previously encountered drunk at parties, Clarissa mounted the pulpit to deliver the eulogy.

'We're gathered together to celebrate the life and mourn the death of Brian Salmon. Brian was many things: a devoted husband, father and son; a chartered surveyor, who built his firm into the foremost in the area. Here at St Peter's, we recall his enthusiastic engagement with a range of activities, and there are many Tapley children whose summers were enriched by his leadership of the Holiday Fun Club.

Above all, we recall his twenty years as tower captain, which lent so much to our worship.

·'We can't ignore the painful events that preceded – and pre-cipitated – his demise: events that have led a baying mob to muster outside, ostensibly in the name of Christ, but without one jot of the compassion that is the essence of His being. I ask you, how would Christ, who reached out to the leper, treat those reviled as moral lepers today? Would Christ, who assumed our flesh and knew the power of temptation, reject those whose flesh has proved too weak to resist it? Would Christ, who taught us to *Judge not, that you be not judged*, set out a list of exemptions? Would Christ, who told Peter to forgive his brother seventy times seven, say: "But the 491st time . . . the 491st sin" – I trust that my maths is sound – "is one too many"? No! His mercy, like His grace, is absolute. So let us remember His instruction to an earlier mob, one that denounced the woman caught in adultery: *He who is without sin among you, let him throw a stone at her first.*'

No sooner had the words left her mouth than a stone shot through the air and cracked the coffin. A stunned silence was followed by an uproar. Clarissa looked round for the culprit, but the congregation were all seated and Alec and Wendy were guarding the door. There was no way that any of them could have thrown it. Awestruck, she gazed heavenwards, feeling a rush of heat to her head and nausea in the pit of her stomach. The last thing she saw as she sank to the ground was the dissolution of Eden.

TWO

1987

One

I walk through the colonnaded portico and into the body of the church. A cascade of coloratura sweeps over the low hum of chatter on the dais, where the singers have been rehearsing. I recognise seven of them, but the eighth is a new recruit, at first sight a recent graduate. As I wave to him, I feel a pang at the thought of Marcus. Had he taken up his place at the RAM, he too would be embarking on his professional career. I might have secured him an audition, although I suspect that he'd have owned the obligation less graciously than the one to Mrs Hamilton-Brooke. I'm still reeling from his announcement – admittedly, at a bibulous dinner party – that 'I have Christie's; Clarissa has Christ', as if the assonance established an equivalence.

I sense the singers smile as I step casually on to the dais and lift the altar cloth. Although the church will have been thoroughly searched, I can't forget the stories of both a Christ and a Churchill interrupting the live broadcasts when the department was evacuated to Bedford during the Blitz. At least their language adhered to BBC guidelines, which is more than can be said for that of the tramp, who bedded down overnight beneath this very altar, only to leap out in the middle of a hymn and curse the singers for waking him. A quartet of tenors and basses bundled him into the street. As not only the young-est but the only female producer in the department, I have to guard against naivety, but I trust that, at the end of the transmission, they gave him some money for food.

My flick of imaginary dust from the cloth fools no one, and I exchange a few words with the singers, who are heatedly discussing Edwina Currie's remark yesterday that 'Good Christians won't get AIDS'. I'd like to address it on air, but Jan, my super-efficient PA, has timed the script to the second. Not even 'The blessing of God Almighty, Father, Son and Holy Ghost' is allowed to run into the pips. With the hymns and reading chosen by the editor, Canon Buckley, and the prayers set out in *New Every Morning*, the producer-presenter enjoys little latitude. But while several of my colleagues regard their slot on the *Daily Service* rota as a necessary evil, I count it a privilege to work on a programme that has ministered to 'the sick and the suf-fering and the lonely' for more than sixty years.

Jan gestures to her stopwatch and I move to the desk, where I put on headphones and catch the last two minutes of *A Poet Speaks* (although, having missed his name, all I can say is that he speaks with a thick Scottish brogue). The red light flashes and I welcome listeners, careful to modulate my voice after some hurtful criticism. The service proceeds without incident, after which I shout my thanks down the cream-and-gilt nave to the organist; introduce myself to the new bass; and join the trio of women around a pregnant alto, taking my turn to feel the baby kick. While I wholeheartedly agree with Marcus that now is the time to focus on our careers (not to mention, finalise our wedding plans!), I can't help but feel broody.

I leave All Souls and return to Broadcasting House, glancing up at Prospero and Ariel, the figures making more sense after Marcus's disclosure that Gill carved a near-identical version, entitled *Abraham and Isaac*. I take the lift to the second floor, stopping to greet Joyce, the redoubtable mistress of the tea urn. As I enquire after her husband ('Trouble!') and her children ('All the better for you asking'), I have an uneasy suspicion that I'm turning into my mother. Clasping the regulation rock cake ('Men like a girl with meat on her bones'), I head off, past the door marked *Chief Assistant to the Assistant Chief*, which after two and a half years still tickles me, and enter the department. With his door ajar, I catch Canon Buckley's eye. 'Intriguing pronunciation,' he says cryptically and picks up his phone.

There are twelve producers in the department and the Canon is one of two not yet reconciled to my appointment. The other is Archie Ledbury, erstwhile provost of Chelmsford cathedral, a legend throughout the entire Corporation for having once travelled from Brook Green to Broadcasting House in his dressing gown and slippers, so dumbfounding the ticket collectors that they let him pass unchallenged. Both men cloak their disdain in elaborate displays of gallantry. Archie stands up whenever I enter a room and offers to carry the flimsiest file, yet should I make a suggestion at a meeting, he interposes a 'Charming, my dear! Now shall we put it to the men?'

The general assumption that, as much as I condemn the boys' club atmosphere, I owe my job to the old boys' network couldn't be more wrong. It's not my father I have to thank but – now it's my turn to be grudging – Mrs Hamilton-Brooke. The path to priesthood barred, I left Cambridge with no other aim than to avoid teaching. I took a temporary job in the Charing Cross library which, after nine months, was at risk of becoming permanent. Try as I might to share Marcus's excitement in life at Christie's, my dissatisfaction was driving us apart. At one of the many tête-à-têtes to which I wasn't privy, he confided his fears in Mrs Hamilton-Brooke's ample, maternal and, I trust, metaphorical bosom. She suggested that I consider religious broadcasting, where Vyvyan Blackwood, her cousin's brother-in-law or brother-in-law's cousin, was on secondment. Strings were pulled, and the head of department, Bruce Winward, invited me to lunch in the BBC canteen. I was so distracted by the sight of the Beverley Sisters, queuing for salads in matching pink chiffon, that it wasn't until the meal ended that I realised I'd been offered a job.

For all the rewards of broadcasting, I can't pretend that it's what I was put on this earth to do. There's no mistaking the groundswell of support in both the Church itself and society at large for female ministry, and Archbishop Runcie will ordain the first women deacons in Canterbury on 27 February. But I'm convinced that, after granting us this sop, the clerical hierarchy will close ranks against our priesthood. Of the many debts of gratitude I owe my colleagues, perhaps the greatest is for the example they've set by giving up livings, chaplaincies and prebendary stalls in order to work here. As Julian Wotton, former rector of St Magnus the Martyr and now the department's liturgy expert, explained: 'I've opted to exercise my vocation across the airwaves, rather than in the parish.' I thanked him because I knew that he meant it kindly, but the difference between us is that he had the choice.

144

For as long as I can remember, I've felt called to the priesthood. Even before I had words to articulate the fervour inside me, I yearned to be part of the mystery that Father celebrated at the altar (a mystery far more impressive than the magic tricks at my friends' birthday parties), which had the power to heal the sick, to comfort the sorrowful, and to sustain the dying. As a child, I wanted nothing more than to sit in Father's study while he wrote his sermons, or to sneak into the sacristy to watch him vest. Sometimes, he upheld the pretence that, if he ignored me, I was invisible; sometimes, he permitted me to stay, as long as I kept stock-still, feigning outrage at the inevitable rustle; sometimes, the outrage was real, at which point he would summon Mother to remove '*your* daughter', a doubly brutal rebuff.

I was deemed to be a daddy's girl which, for reasons I could never fathom, was more acceptable than Alexander's being a mummy's boy. But it was one thing to wish to be near him, quite another to wish to be like him, as I found when I crept into the sacristy, not to watch him vest but to try on his robes. Swamped by his cassock and surplice, part priest and part princess, I waddled down the nave to the altar, where I consecrated imaginary elements as if making tea for my dolls. A furious roar apprised me of his arrival, followed by the thud of footsteps as he ran up and tugged off the robes. With his claim that the angels would weep for me ringing in my ears, I believed that I was the wickedest girl alive, loathsome to both God and my father, whose sentiments, as ever, were the same.

My moment of truth came when Father was appointed Principal of Westcott House in Cambridge. Surrounded by male ordinands, I could no longer disregard the obstacles to my vocation. I threw myself into new activities: first ballet, winning prizes for politeness and posture, rather than skill; then fencing, taking a silver medal in the Eastern Region Under Twelves Girls' Foil. But I gave up both when we moved to Chester and Father confirmed me in the cathedral. My faith felt more urgent than ever and I longed to dedicate myself to God. With no other avenue open to me, I dreamt of becoming a religious. I was teased in class for picking *The Nun's Story* as my favourite novel. I identified passionately with Sister Luke, even though I swore that, were I to take vows, I would never seek laicisation, no matter how righteous the cause. Then at seventeen, I went on a week's retreat at St Hilda's Priory. In that place of intense prayer and sequestered spirituality, I discovered that my calling wasn't to the monastic life.

Far younger than Sister Luke (but then I wasn't the heroine of a three-hundred-page novel), I realised that my place was to be out in the world, and I applied to read theology at Newnham. Father urged me to choose something more practical, although I suspect that his main concern was that it might become practical. For once, Mother dared to defy him, happy to picture my career path as teaching RE, before marrying the school chaplain or one of the eligible young curates in the diocese. When the Senior Tutor asked me at my interview why I'd chosen theology, I replied: 'Because I'm going to be a priest!' – not *I want to be* but *I will be*. It was the first time that I'd spoken the words out loud since I was a girl of six, winning plaudits for filial devotion. Glancing across at Miss Hodges, the Director of Studies, whose tweedy figure I would come to know so well, I saw tears in her eyes. My audacity must have impressed them, since they offered me an unconditional place.

Thanks to Mrs Hamilton-Brooke, I'm neither instructing schoolchildren on Noah's Flood and St Paul's missionary journeys, nor pointing readers to the latest Catherine Cookson. Instead, I'm on the line to Lambeth Palace, asking whether, in the light of Mrs Currie's remark, the Archbishop would care to reflect on what constitutes a good Christian. So determined are our masters to ensure the programme's objectivity that Julian is recording a fifteen-minute segment for *Sunday* on women deacons, which has my name written all over it. Meanwhile I'm putting together a piece on the Church's response to AIDS, an issue of direct import to at least two of my colleagues. Although whether they'd be willing to acknowledge it is another matter.

Jan takes her lunch break and, with the office to myself, I ring Alexander. Bruce has urged me to maximise my expenses, 'which make the rest of us look bad', but, while I can't in all conscience put in bogus claims, I have no qualms about making regular calls to Cuba on the BBC's phone bill. 'Go figure!' as my Newnham friend, Belinda, would say.

Denouncing England as strait-laced, class-ridden and moribund, Alexander escaped abroad on leaving SOAS. After travelling in Thailand, Vietnam and Malaya, he settled in San Francisco, working in an organic greengrocer's, which would have appalled our parents even more, had they known that it was a hive of political activism. Through one of his *comrades* (a word that always sounds rehearsed), he secured a job at Radio Havana Cuba and moved there four years ago.

The station is Castro's version of the World Service, the difference, according to my brother, being that it makes no secret of its ideological stance. Armed with the Spanish he learnt from Bayardo, his San Franciscan boyfriend, he translates news reports into English and broadcasts them every morning. He's classed as a *foreign technical worker* (which is ironic given that he's the least technical person I know), with a salary and an apartment way beyond the means of the average Cuban. He's so desperate not to be thought an exploitative Westerner that he's generous to a fault. At the party he threw during my visit, I watched in disbelief as the guests openly pocketed the glasses. When I alerted him to it, he admonished me, explaining that theirs was the greater need, and reminded me that Jesus, whose radicalism he applauds even as he rejects His creed, enjoined the rich young man to give all that he possessed to the poor.

I was touched and humbled. Nevertheless, no Cuban subsisting on two dollars a week could afford to be so starry-eyed about the struggle. It isn't that Castro can do no wrong in Alexander's eyes, rather that any wrong he does is forced upon him by the capitalist West. So when we took a taxi driven by a moonlighting teacher, he maintained, after a long exchange in Spanish, that the man found it a welcome break from the classroom. Likewise, when we stumbled across a group of rough sleepers on the pot-holed streets of Old Havana, he insisted that they'd spurned the state's lavish housing subsidies and lived there by choice. His boyfriend Cesar, who accompanied us, whispered: 'This is why we loves him.' At first, I presumed that he'd muddled the pronoun as well as the verb, but when Alexander stopped at every corner to salute friends and strangers alike, I was no longer so sure.

Cesar, who appointed himself my guide during the visit ('since we are both of us knowing Alejandro is not depending') is a total charmer. Heart-stirringly handsome, tall and muscular, with olive skin, green eyes and lustrous black hair, he's a maintenance engineer at the radio station, but when he first moved to Havana, he worked as a prostitute, an experience that has left him remarkably unscarred. 'I give my fucks to both of the men and the women,' he said brightly, 'but I like most to give my fucks to the women, because I give my kisses to the men.' He illustrated it by drawing Alexander into a close embrace, at which I knew better than to blush.

Even Alexander can't gloss over the deficiencies of the Cuban telephone system, and I dial five times before we're connected. Finally, I hear my brother's voice, albeit as distant and crackly as on a Victorian wax cylinder. Given the state of the line, I've learnt to read nothing into his tone, but today the heaviness is palpable.

'No worries, little sis,' he says, in response to my question, 'I spent most of Tuesday in a police cell.'

'What?' I shriek, looking up to check that the door is closed.

'Just a misunderstanding. A couple of months ago, I filed a complaint against a police officer who's been harassing one of Cesar's friends, a flamboyant *maricón* – his term not mine. He's been biding his time and, yesterday, he arrested me for violating the residency laws. All nonsense of course, and I was released after a few hours.'

'Did you contact the embassy?'

'I don't want to disillusion you, but the days of *Civis Britannicus Sum* are over, at any rate in Cuba. Besides, I've long been a thorn in their flesh, and they'd be happy to see me rot in jail. No, I rang the

149

head of the station, who put in a call to the ministry and had me out of there pronto.'

'What's to stop the officer from trying it again?'

'Nothing, but he'll have to wait a while. I'm owed two months' leave and I'm planning to fly back to England at the end of March. As we speak, Cesar's applying for a *carta blanca*: that's an exit and, more to the purpose, a re-entry visa.'

The news elates me, and I assure him that Marcus will be as pleased as I am to have them to stay. I make a mental note to upgrade the futon and, dismissing his *warn*, promise to *tell* our parents.

After a frustrating 'no comment' on the Currie case from Lambeth, I leave the office early, trusting that my resolute stride indicates that I'm heading off on an assignment, rather than back to Bayswater to 'doll yourself up', in Marcus's arch phrase. I'm due at Christie's at six, for a reception prior to the auction of Modern British Art, which is only the second that Marcus has catalogued.

He's been on edge for weeks. Christie's has brought out all his insecurities. After getting to know his fellow cataloguers, he reported that he was the only one whose parents lived in a house with a number, as glumly as if they'd had an outside loo. I pointed out that his father was a solicitor and his mother a GP, but that's cold comfort when half of his colleagues are the younger sons of peers, whose tastes were formed in their families' picture galleries. Marcus, who takes his work very seriously, dismisses them as dilettantes, whose prime concerns are to quaff champagne and meet the right sort of girl. I doubt that I pass muster, although, as a bishop's daughter I have a certain cachet, especially if our fathers rub shoulders in the Lords.

I treat myself to a cab and join the sluggish traffic to King Street, where Marcus, looking drawn, waits for me in the lobby. Planting a sweaty kiss on my cheek and without a word about my new Katherine Hamnett dress, he grabs my arm and steers me up the stairs.

'Is everything all right?' I ask.

'What do you think?' he says tersely. 'One of the porters dropped a hammer on the Sickert he was hanging. There's a massive gash in the canvas. Jeff Norton – he's the in-house restorer – is hard at work on it. But all he can do in the time he's got is patch it up, use some invisible adhesive, and pray.'

'That's worked in the past, hasn't it?' I've been horrified by Marcus's accounts of the porters' carelessness in the warehouse, leading to punctured canvases, split panels, and precious mouldings shattered beyond repair.

'Just about. Bloody Neanderthals! There was a Munnings right next to it. It's practically valueless. Why couldn't he have smashed that?'

We walk into the first of the Great Rooms, where a jewel-encrusted wave beckons us to Mrs Hamilton-Brooke. Marcus kisses her on both cheeks, while I admire her porcelain complexion, sheath of jet-black hair and neon orange minidress, designed for someone a good thirty years younger but which she has both the confidence and the legs to carry off.

'Hasn't our boy done well?' she asks, taking me by surprise as she loops an arm through mine. 'I'm hearing great things about him. It won't be long now before he's summoned upstairs.'

'It's no more than he deserves,' I reply, wishing that I could share my pride in him with someone – anyone – else.

'Promise you won't tell him, but I have a friend who may be persuaded to part with a collection of Leightons. Twenty years ago, they were worth less than their frames. She wanted to get rid of them, but I told her: "Give it time and they'll come back into vogue." Was I right or was I right?'

'As always, Lettice,' Marcus interjects, using the name that, in spite of repeated requests, I have yet to adopt.

'You weren't supposed to hear that,' she says playfully, extricating herself from me and smacking his hand, all without spilling a drop of champagne. 'I've told her that now's the time to sell. And as it happens, I know the perfect young man to handle everything.'

'That would be brilliant,' Marcus says, as one of the directors advances towards us.

'Now, Marcus,' he says, glancing at me indifferently, 'you mustn't monopolise our most distinguished guest.'

'Flatterer!' Mrs Hamilton-Brooke replies, although her smile suggests the opposite.

'Don't say a word!' Marcus instructs me, as the director whisks her away.

I mime zipping my lips.

'A collection of Leightons! That would be a feather in the proverbial. Johnny Lennox just came back from Lausanne, with the promise of a couple of Boudins from one of his father's racing cronies. How can I compete with that? But a collection of Leightons . . . good old Lettice!'

'Take care that she doesn't get stuck between your teeth.'

Eager to brag to his colleagues, he conducts me into the

neighbouring room, where Tristram Beevor, Harold Yarmouth and Yorick Frobisher are standing beside a surrealist landscape, together with Tristram's girlfriend, Rosemary, and an unfamiliar couple. Marcus introduces me to Piers Duguid, who recently started on the front counter, and his sister, Lucy, whose glittery eyeshadow fails to conceal her boredom. Tristram and Harold pay me the compliments that Marcus neglected. 'You're out of your league, old chap,' Tristram says, prompting Marcus to redden, although whether at his good fortune or his oversight is unclear.

'How are you enjoying life with these reprobates?' I ask Piers.

'Reprobates? I don't know about that,' he replies, with a shy laugh.

'Poor Piers has had a simply agonising day,' Yorick says. 'Some old sea dog—'

'Actually, he was the last admiral of the fleet.'

'As I said, some old sea dog brought in a picture that the chairman had declared to be a masterpiece over lunch. It was patently painted on a photograph.'

'Must have been some lunch,' Harold says.

'I could tell at a glance,' Piers says. 'I didn't know what to do, so I promised to show it to somebody senior.'

'Quite right,' Marcus says. 'We've all been there. During my stint on the counter, I had to remind myself daily of the sign in a Turkish hotel: *Please leave your values at the desk.*'

An Albino waiter, with pronounced razor burn, proffers a tray of champagne.

'Don't mind if I do,' Yorick says, with mock gentility and a pointed leer.

I take a glass, drowning the memory of BBC plonk. 'None for you?' I ask Lucy.

'Not advised,' she drawls. 'I had an abortion on Monday, and alcohol increases the risk of bleeding.'

'I didn't know that,' I say, more sharply than I intend.

'Bully for you!' she replies.

'Rosie knows, don't you, dearest?' Tristram says, in what I trust is an attempt to put Lucy at her ease, but I fear is meant to put Rosemary down. 'She's had a couple. Not yet the time for a son and heir.' She grins vacuously and guzzles her champagne. 'Oops, I forgot!' He turns to me with a smirk. 'Does it offend your sacred principles?'

'Quite the reverse. Forcing someone to become a mother is as abhorrent to me as rape.'

'Must you?' Yorick asks, with an operatic cringe. 'It may not be my area of expertise, but I thought alcohol was supposed to help with abortions. Or is that only gin?'

'Cave!' Marcus says. All four cataloguers turn to the wall, as an immaculately dressed, silver-haired man, with a peacock feather buttonhole, approaches. Piers, nervously, turns back too soon, but the man walks past.

'Explain!' I tell Marcus.

'Victor Davenport-Adams, the chairman's brother-in-law. He has an Augustus John in the sale. Two experts have confirmed that it's a copy, but because he's family, the chairman insisted we keep it in.'

'Won't someone detect it?'

'We already have. As copies go, it's decent enough. Painted not long after the original. With what John fetches today, no forger would bother.'

'What does it matter, as long as it's good? Surely a picture has a value independent of the artist?'

'That depends how you define value,' Harold says.

'Who was it produced a programme on authenticating the Nag Hammadi scrolls?' Marcus asks.

'That's utterly different. A world religion is based on the canonical gospels. If those of Thomas, Philip and Mary Magdalene are found to be equally authoritative but to have been suppressed because they didn't fit the agenda of the early Church, then it has earth-shaking implications. The new portrait of Christ that emerges presents a huge challenge, not least to orthodox morality.'

'The market is our morality,' Harold says.

'That's just about the most disgusting thing I've ever heard!'

The shocked silence shows that I have crossed the line.

'I could listen to her talk all day. She's wasted on you, old chap,' Tristram tells Marcus. Though loath to be discussed in the third person, I'm grateful for his intervention. 'If you ever fancy a change of pace and two thousand acres of prime Herefordshire . . .'

'They're taken,' Rosemary interjects, with a glacial smile.

'Thanks for the offer, but I'm happy with my few hundred feet of prime Bayswater.'

The waiter returns, with a bottle of champagne. 'Can I fill anyone up?'

'Any time,' Yorick says.

'Oh, what the Hell!' Lucy says. 'Somebody grab me a glass.'

Two

Marcus takes the wheel as if by right. No matter that I passed my test first time, whereas he failed his twice. 'Practice makes perfect,' he said, on the only occasion I mentioned it.

'You do know that seventy-five per cent of road deaths are caused by men?' I reply.

'So? What's the betting that seventy-five per cent of drivers are men and at least seventy-five per cent on long distances? Mile by mile, that makes us safer . . . Idiot!' he shouts, as a Renault Turbo overtakes us on the inside. 'You of all people should know not to treat statistics as gospel,' he adds, flashing me the smile that makes me forgive him almost everything.

I shouldn't complain. While not exactly a New Man, he professes to be a feminist and to do his fair share of household chores (which is true, provided that *fair* doesn't mean *equal*). Kate Williams, my newly married friend on *Woman's Hour*, maintained that she 'would have been happy promising to love, cherish and obey had it not translated as cook, clean and empty the dishwasher'. At least Marcus irons his own shirts, which my mother takes as a welcome sign that we aren't having sex. The thought moves me to lean over and kiss him.

'What did I do to deserve that?' he asks, keeping his eyes fixed on the road.

'Giving up your weekend to come to Chester. Watching my father lay down the law and my mother kowtow to it.'

'What about watching their daughter challenge it? I wouldn't give up my ringside seat for the world.'

'I'm glad that one of us will be entertained.'

'Something happens to you on the way up the M1. The calm and collected Clarissa I know and love becomes a seething mass of contradictions, desperate for your father's approval while doing your utmost to antagonise him.'

'Thank you, Doctor Freud,' I reply, alarmed by how well he knows me.

'I'd say that the transformation takes place somewhere around Newport Pagnell. Beware, just a couple of junctions to go!'

'I take back the kiss.'

'You can't. It's stuck.'

The traffic is heavy, and it's past eleven when we turn into Abbey Street. Mother will be fretting and Father will have assured her that it's all in God's hands, which is episcopal parlance for 'Don't bother me with trifles.' I jump out to open the gate and Mother appears in the porch before we finish parking. The sight of her beaming face makes me feel ashamed, and I kiss her more effusively than she anticipates. Ruffled, she turns to Marcus whom, now that we're officially engaged, she greets with a peck on the cheek.

'Your father will see you at breakfast. He's exhausted, so I insisted he go to bed.'

'That's fine. We'll do the same. Cars were nose to tail on the motorway.' I slip off my Barbour and hang it on a peg.

'What's that?' Mother points to my jersey.

'What's what?' I look down to see the *Ordain Women Now* badge, which I wear as instinctively as the cross around my neck. 'Surely you can see, Mother?' I say, gall rising.

'Do you want to upset your father? Won't you tell her to take it off, Marcus?'

'It's more than my life's worth.'

'You bet!' I give him a warning look.

'But I might remind her of what she said about respecting other people's beliefs, when she put on a headscarf in the Blue Mosque.'

'Ha ha,' I reply sardonically, unpinning the badge.

'Thank you,' Mother says, as much to Marcus as to me. 'The first ordinations aren't until April, but you can't imagine the nuisance the women are already causing. Your father sent out a pastoral letter, requesting that they use the title Deacon Angela or Claire or whatever, and avoid The Reverend—'

'To which they're entitled.'

'That's as may be, but you'd have thought he were suggesting burning witches.'

'The impulse behind it is the same: male fear of losing power.'

'What you refuse to admit is that women do have power. We just exercise it differently.'

'I don't want pillow power or a word-in-your-ear power but altar power, pulpit power, shout-it-from-the-steeple-top power.'

Seething with frustration, I'm almost ready to put the badge back on.

'Mrs Thatcher has a lot to answer for,' Mother says sadly.

I lead Marcus upstairs, where we turn in opposite directions like children at a Victorian board school. As far as my parents are concerned, we share a flat for the same financial reasons that several single priests in the diocese take in 'lodgers'. *What the eye doesn't see* might as well be embroidered on a sampler in the hall. Under their own roof, propriety is stringently preserved. As usual, Marcus has been given 'the African room', my mother's grandiloquent term for its collection of tribal masks from Boga, the Congolese diocese with which Chester is linked; the carved hippopotamus head my uncle brought back from Namibia; and the portrait of a black Christ, presented to Father in Burundi, which he banished from his study after Alexander dubbed it *Jesus Guevara*. I head to my old bedroom, which even smells of childhood. The assorted books and records, photographs and memory boxes, Holy Land posters and prayer cards, comfort and embarrass me in equal measure.

I sleep fitfully. Despite my complaints that he hogs the bed, I miss Marcus's warm weight beside me. I knock on his door at eight and am rewarded with a minty kiss. His excitement is tangible, and we're set to break one of the strictest house rules, when my mother sounds the gong.

Curbing our laughter, we go down to the breakfast room to find Father in shirtsleeves, belly billowing over his belt, engrossed in *The Times*. He opens his arms in welcome, only to pick up his cup before I reach him. I kiss his bald spot and tidy the tufts of hair above his ears. He flicks me away with a sigh.

'Marcus, my boy, pull up a pew! Not literally,' he adds, with a chuckle. 'Heartfelt apologies for not receiving you last night. I'd spent the evening in Little Hanby, celebrating one hundred years of St Chad's: preaching the sermon, blessing the new kneelers, cutting the cake and ploughing through a plateful of coronation chicken. Would you believe that it was my third centennial of the week, on top of the fiftieth anniversary of *Dogs for the Disabled*? And what do you suppose they fed me at each one? You've guessed it. Coronation chicken! Do they consider it the height of haute cuisine? Would I be insulted if they served roast beef or even sausage rolls? Sometimes I'd like to throttle Constance Spry.'

'I thought she was a flower arranger,' Marcus says.

'And a cook. Take care! You won't win points with my daughter if you deny the gentler sex their achievements.'

I refuse to be drawn, as Mother brings in a dish of kippers. Marcus's fulsome thanks confirms her conviction that I fail to feed him.

'You must be thrilled about Alexander's homecoming,' I say.

'We're counting the days,' Mother says. 'It will be a joy to see him again.'

'That depends what he wants,' Father says.

'To see us all, of course,' I reply, although our most recent conversation gave me cause for concern: nothing specific, just a suspicion that he was keeping something from me.

'I know my son. Did I tell you what he sent me for my birthday? A book by some Marxist theologian entitled *Class Struggle in the Gospels*!'

Marcus splutters his coffee.

'I wish you'd accept his invitation to visit,' I say. 'It would open your eyes.'

'Yes, and the press would have a field day.'

'Then at least allow Mother to go. Alexander would look after her.'

'Oh really?' He harrumphs. 'Besides, she can't bear the heat. It would be Jerusalem all over again . . . Still, I suppose we should give thanks that he's settled. No longer the world's oldest shop boy.'

'Isn't it odd,' Mother says pensively, 'how both you children have ended up working for the radio?'

'Yes, they've both found their calling,' Father replies, at which Marcus gives me a stealthy kick.

'If you don't object, we thought we'd drive to Port Sunlight,' I say. 'Marcus wants to go back to the gallery. Of course, we'd love you to join us.'

'Hasn't your mother told you?' Father says, frowning. 'We've been invited to lunch by Seward Wemlock.'

'*The* Seward Wemlock?' Marcus asks incredulously.

'Are there others?'

'But that's amazing! Everyone? Me too?'

'Yes, of course. Unless you'd rather not.'

'Are you . . . I can't think of anything I'd like more.'

Marcus's elation feeds mine. As a girl, I remember how the Wemlock name would be spoken in hushed tones in cathedral circles, and his picture appear regularly in gossip columns, once with the caption: *The aristocratic artist's legendary appetite for women*, which made him sound like a cross between a fairy-tale ogre and Lord Byron. So I was doubly impressed when I first saw his work in Marcus's room at St John's. It was a portrait of Christ and Mary

Magdalene, modelled on the sixties photograph of John Lennon and Yoko Ono in bed for peace. With rich symbolism, the coverlet was formed of hundreds of scarlet-tipped white roses and, in place of the Amsterdam skyline, they were set against what Marcus described as one of Wemlock's trademark azure backgrounds. Two cherubs held scrolls inscribed with *Peace* in Hebrew and Latin. It had caused outrage when it was originally exhibited, with Wemlock's father denouncing it as 'a betrayal' (of what: his family . . . the Church . . . Christ Himself?), but I was enchanted. The figures combined a child-like innocence and a wounded gravity, and the whole composition conveyed a stillness, which was deeply spiritual.

Exhilarated, Marcus recounts his introduction to the artist's work. 'It was at a show at the Hayward, curated by Kitaj. There were paintings by Bacon, Freud and Hockney, as well as Kitaj himself but, for me, the standouts were the two Wemlocks. The first was the back view of a girl emerging from a pond; she might have been a water nymph or simply a schoolgirl taking a dip, sunlight streaming through the trees and dappling her flesh. It exuded sensuality, but it was the chasteness not just of the girl's posture but of the artist's gaze, which were so moving to a rather grubby teenager. I was sixteen,' he adds apologetically to Mother.

'And the second?' I ask, observing her confusion.

'That was a diptych. On one panel, Abraham releasing Isaac from the ropes with which he'd bound him for sacrifice; on the other, Jephthah fulfilling his vow to God by slaughtering his daughter. As if the juxtaposition weren't disturbing enough, inscribed on the frame above them was the phrase – from Proverbs, I think,' he says, with a nod to my father, '*The eyes of the Lord are everywhere.* Since then, I've seized any opportunity I can to see his work. It's not easy when he shows so rarely (though I took Clarissa to the Antwerp exhibition a couple of years back). No living artist – certainly none that I know – comes close to his luminosity. He's as consummate a draughtsman as a colourist, distilling landscape into a kind of spiritual geometry. I'm babbling. You must stop me babbling,' he says to me. 'If I start to babble, put your hand over my mouth.'

'I promise.'

'If I'd known you felt this strongly, I'd have introduced you sooner,' Father says. 'Wemlock Hall is little more than half an hour's drive away. Outside a village called Tapley: quaint and unspoilt, if something of a backwater. Vincent Slater, my former chaplain, is the rector.'

'I knew that Seward had returned to Cheshire. Word has it he's become a recluse.'

'The two aren't synonymous.'

'I didn't mean . . .'

'Don't worry, my boy, I was joking.' As ever with Father, it's hard to tell. 'Hereward, his elder brother, died a few years ago in a motor accident.'

'Round here?' I ask.

'No, in France. In a Formula – whatever – race. He had no children. Seward inherited the title. He lives at Wemlock with his mistress and two daughters.'

'Not *mistress*, dear,' Mother says. 'Call her his *common-law wife.* It's kinder.'

'You can call her what you like. I don't mince my words.'

'You'd never know it to look at her,' Mother says. 'She's perfectly respectable, though not all that forthcoming. Well, you'll see.'

'Valerie, Hereward's widow, lives with them.'

'They didn't think it fair for her to lose her garden,' Mother adds quickly, as though to remove any hint of immodesty which, until then, hadn't occurred to me. 'She transformed it. She's out there in all weathers, pulling up something or planting something else. You'd have thought she'd have enough to do indoors!'

'This isn't a purely social visit.' Father cuts through Mother's chatter. 'A few months ago, I had a brainwave. As you know, artists live by their own code.'

It's on the tip of my tongue to ask why, when I see Marcus nod approvingly.

'Whatever his peccadillos – and we need say no more than that – Seward Wemlock is a deeply religious man. I've asked him to paint a series of panels for St Peter's, Tapley's parish church, and he's agreed.'

'A series?' Marcus says. 'Extraordinary. What a coup!'

'This diocese once boasted some of the finest painted churches in the country. I've wanted to revive the tradition for some time.'

With only five years until his retirement, I suspect that he also wants to secure his legacy.

'Of course, there's no reason that a church artist should be a Christian. You'll point to Duncan Grant and Vanessa Bell in Berwick.'

He looks at Marcus who, despising the Bloomsbury Group, stays silent.

'But when the artist is a believer – I'm thinking of Sutherland,

164

Piper, Eric Gill and, of course, Stanley Spencer – the work isn't only more inspired but more inspiring. Which is when it struck me. The most celebrated religious painter – the man who's been hailed as Spencer's heir – is living on our doorstep. He's even patron of his parish church.'

'Does that give him carte blanche?' Marcus asks.

'Not at all. The church will still have to apply for a faculty, but that's just a rubber stamp. St Peter's is no architectural jewel . . . quite the reverse. Accretions left, right and centre. Far from destroying its integrity, the panels will give it the unity it lacks.'

'It's a beautiful idea, St John,' Mother says. 'And I'm sure dear Vincent will support it.'

'That goes without saying. If the project's a success, who knows where it may lead? Our current spiritual malaise springs – at least in part – from the poverty of the culture. Art was once the instrument of the Church but, in today's world, it's seen as its antithesis . . . even its scourge: art, all freedom, taboo-breaking and the shock of the new; the Church, all repression, conformism and tradition. But why, when their fundamental aims are the same: to deepen our understanding; to enrich our humanity; and, most importantly, to feed our souls?'

'Amen to that!' Marcus says. 'Sometimes at John's, when I was singing a Bach chorale or a Tallis motet, I'd feel not just uplifted but transfigured.' He turns to me. 'As I told you then, it felt like being touched by God. I've tried so hard to recover that feeling but, since I gave up singing, I can't.'

'You could try prayer,' I say gently.

'Words alone – at least my words – aren't enough.'

'That's precisely my point,' Father says. 'Art is a gateway to God. Look at the Eastern Church, where icons aren't just sacred images but sacred objects, worthy of veneration.'

'Isn't there a risk that people will revere the images rather than what they represent?' I ask.

'Not in rural Cheshire!' Father replies. 'All my life I've grappled with the concept of the Trinity. You'll recall the introduction to my book, where I question whether I'll ever be able to present it more neatly than in the conjuring trick I used to perform for children: the one where I pulled a handkerchief from a hat, replaced it, and pulled it back out, first, as three attached handkerchiefs, then, as three separate ones and, finally, as a single handkerchief again, in an attempt to show both the individuality and interconnection of the Three in One.'

'That was you?' I ask. 'How strange! In my memory, it was a magician at a friend's birthday party.'

'I admit that the question was somewhat disingenuous, since, after discussing all the great Trinitarian theologians from Nyssa and Augustine to Abelard and Aquinas, I set out my own stall.' He breaks off to address Marcus. 'If you haven't yet read *Visible, Invisible and Indivisible*, remind me to give you a copy. It's been through so many editions, I have plenty to spare.'

'That would be wonderful,' Marcus replies, prompting me to return the kick.

'I'd say that my approach was closest to Abelard's. He envisaged the Father as Power, the Son as Wisdom and the Holy Spirit as Benignity. My own personifications, as expounded in the book, are the Father as Creativity, the Son as Love and the Holy Spirit as Moral Responsibility. To my mind, they're not just the three primary aspects of God but the three that we, as beings made in His image, must strive to emulate. Creativity is a way not only to engage with God but to manifest Him.'

For years, I've esteemed Father's scholarship more than his parenting. Yet I fear that he attaches too high a value to art. In a temporal world, it's natural to give fathers precedence over sons, but in eternity there are no such distinctions. Creativity is nothing without love, as anyone who has seen the paintings of the Reverend Thomas Philpotts can attest. For all their technical skill and visceral force, every brushstroke is imbued with hatred. While there's no danger of that with Seward Wemlock, his chequered romantic history makes me wonder about the third element in Father's scheme: moral responsibility.

At noon, I squeeze beside Marcus in the back seat of Father's *chariot of fire*: more prosaically, his ancient Rover. The journey is marked, like scores of its predecessors, by my parents' bickering: first, about the quickest route out of the city; then, about the 'new-fangled' (Father), 'two-year-old' (Mother), one-way system; finally, about the speed limit on the A41.

'No one can accuse me of driving too fast!'

'No dear, you're driving too slowly, which is why there's all this beeping.'

Marcus's hand sweats into mine as we reach the elegant gate piers of the Wemlock estate. We judder over the cattle grid and trundle down the long tree-lined avenue to the house, which, with its four-columned portico and Palladian windows, crowned by fantastical Gothic turrets and pinnacles, has a higgledy-piggledy charm. A maid with a built-up shoe greets us and leads us into the great hall. It's a cavernous room with a hammerbeam roof, an ornate staircase with heraldic beasts on the balustrades, four dun-coloured tapestries of hunting scenes on the whitewashed walls, and a large empty fireplace, in front of which we intuitively gather.

Seward Wemlock enters, blowing on his hands. At little more than five foot six, he's smaller than I expect, with a pugilist's compact physique. His eyes, which protrude slightly, are a piercing blue, his lips thick, and his dimpled cheeks and strong jaw unshaven. Most striking for a man in his late fifties is the full head of reddish-gold hair, to which his photographs fail to do justice.

'My Lord Bishop,' he says, shaking Father's hand.

'My Lord Wemlock,' Father replies to what I realise is a standing joke.

'Julia, a pleasure as always.' He kisses her on the mouth and, to my surprise, she doesn't flinch.

'You, my dear, must be Clarissa.' I fear that he means to kiss me as he did my mother but, instead, he takes my hand and lifts it to his lips. I feel an electric charge and at once understand his attraction to women, independent of his rank and talent. 'Clarissa . . . such a euphonious name! From a saint I presume?'

'No, my parents failed me there,' I say, smiling at them. 'It's from *Clarus*. Latin for bright . . . clear.'

'And illustrious,' Marcus chimes in.

'So, what does your lustre consist of?'

'Precious little, I'm afraid. I make religious programmes for the radio.'

'That's good enough for me. My faithful Grundig is my constant companion in the studio. I take it that you, my chivalrous sir, are the fiancé.'

'Guilty as charged,' Marcus replies, blushing at his own gaucheness.

'And you work at Christie's?'

'Yes, I'm a cataloguer in Mod Brit.'

Despite his visible shudder at the contraction, Seward's smile never wavers. 'Christie's and Sotheby's, the Burke and Hare of the art world! No matter, we won't hold it against you.' He clasps Marcus's slumped shoulder. 'Come on in and meet the clan.'

He escorts us into the parlour, where two women sit opposite each other on Regency sofas, one reading a magazine, the other embroidering. In a corner, two girls, possibly twins, lie on their stomachs playing a board game. The women nod at us; the girls don't deign to look up. To my amazement, Father ignores the lack of ceremony, making straight for the sofas, closely followed by Mother, leaving Marcus and me to hover by the door. Seward moves to the girls, who shriek as he interrupts their game. While Marcus studies a display of family photographs as if they were paintings by Sickert or Seward himself, I survey the room, which is crammed with antiques, collecting dust that dances in the wintry light streaming in from the French windows.

'What are you doing over there?' Seward asks us. 'Why haven't you introduced yourselves? Dora, Valerie, meet St John and Julia's daughter, Clarissa, and her intended, Marcus. How I love that word! When I was a boy, the maids would talk of their *Intendeds*. Which often led – prematurely – to their *Expecteds*. Although I'm sure that there's no danger of that here.' Muffling my irritation, I accompany Marcus to the sofas. 'Trust me, if you wait for invitations in this house, you'll wait till doomsday.' He plants himself beside Dora, the embroiderer, and pats a cushion. 'You, my dear, come here, next to me.' I squeeze into the far corner of the sofa, as Mother sits beside Valerie, and Father and Marcus each take a chair.

'Dora was my model and now she's *me missus*.' Seward utters the words in an accent midway between the Mersey and the Humber. He smiles at the forty-something woman with lightly freckled cheeks, narrow chin and long, limp blond hair, wearing a blue patchwork smock, which, given her concentration on her embroidery, I suspect that she made herself. 'Well, that's not strictly true, but she's definitely mine. I bought her in 1966. You look shocked, my dear,' he says to me. 'Didn't you know that twenty years ago, you could still buy a wife, like in a Hardy novel?' I smile as if at a joke and wait for the punchline. 'Back then a wife was held to belong to her husband. So, when I alienated Dora's affections' – he places the phrase in air quotes – 'Trevor Redway brought a claim against me for compensation. Which he won. She cost me £6250. But I can tell you, I don't regret a single penny. The best money I've ever spent.'

'Trevor was a sad man,' Dora says, in a voice as soft as marshmallow.

'Valerie, on the other hand, came with the house.'

I turn to the stylish woman, whose face (hooded eyes, retroussé nose and high cheekbones), hair (auburn, bobbed), and clothes (silk blouse, cashmere cardigan and tweed skirt) bear all the marks of attention that Dora's lack.

'I live here on Seward's charity,' she says, although her emerald solitaire and coral cameo suggest otherwise.

'Heaven knows, the house is large enough: my grandparents occupied separate wings for more than twenty years without addressing a solitary word to each other. Still, it hasn't stopped tongues wagging. Would they rather I'd committed the sin of Onan?'

Marcus snorts, and Seward turns to him with a grin.

'I see, my young friend, that you labour under the common misapprehension that the sin was the spilling of his seed when, as St John will surely confirm, it was his refusal to impregnate his widowed sister-in-law. I trust that I don't offend you, my dear?'

'Not in the least,' I say, as Mother examines the contents of her handbag. I long for Dora to put down her work and attend to her daughters, who have abandoned their game and are listening closely to the conversation.

'Such obligations apart, I had no intention of dispossessing someone who, singlehandedly and against all the odds, let some light back into the house. The arrangement suits us all.'

'Damn!' Dora lifts up her hoop. Seward looks at her quizzically. 'The thread's snapped.'

'My husband was more in love with his racing cars than he was with me,' Valerie says.

'Your husband was more in love with everything than he was

with you,' Seward adds. 'Our mutual loathing of Hereward was our common bond.'

'*De mortuis nihil nisi bonum*,' Father says.

'It's obvious that you didn't know Hereward. Fortunately, we have two girls. Laurel, Sorrel, come over here and say hello.'

Their age gap, concealed while they lay prone, is revealed as soon as they stand, with Laurel four inches taller and far more developed than her sister. They walk towards us without a trace of shyness. Laurel shakes my hand abruptly. 'Laurel Wemlock, pleased to meet you.'

'Me too,' Sorrel says.

'No, you're Sorrel,' Laurel says, rolling her eyes.

'Well I'm Clarissa and I'm very pleased to meet you both. Such pretty names.'

'You're pretty too,' Sorrel says. 'I expect Seward will want to paint you.' I glimpse Mother grimacing at her *non-Christian* use of his name.

'I doubt that. Besides, I don't have the time. I have a job in London.'

'I'm a quick study,' Seward says, in a tone both sugary and sharp.

'What's more, I'm a terrible fidget. You should paint Marcus. With Radio Three playing one of his favourite composers, he disappears into another world.'

'Seward doesn't paint men,' Laurel says, her voice tinged with disgust.

'Dora, isn't it time for lunch?' Valerie asks pointedly. Barely looking up, Dora rings a handbell.

'A face not without interest,' Seward says, inspecting Marcus, whose flesh tones deepen. 'Handsome but not bland. The first hint of jowls. A fine example of what the French call *un homme moyen sensuel.*'

'Does Sew . . . your father ever paint you?' I ask Laurel, dismayed that my attempt to focus Seward's attention on Marcus has left him exposed.

'I'm his muse,' she replies.

'So am I,' Sorrel interjects.

'You're just his amusement,' Laurel says cuttingly.

'She's only sixteen months older and she thinks she's years cleverer,' Sorrel says, her lower lip quivering.

'I don't think; I know. Can you name all twelve of Jesus's disciples, along with the one who replaced Judas Iscariot? No, I didn't think so.' She reels them off breathlessly.

'Laurel . . . Sorrel, behave when we have guests!' Valerie says, while Dora continues to stitch, as deaf to distractions as a nun at prayer.

'Matthias!' Laurel concludes her list triumphantly. 'Wasn't that right?' she asks Father.

'A gold star,' he replies, his own familiarity with the Twelve lapsing somewhere around James, son of Alphaeus.

The maid appears at the door. 'Luncheon is served, my lord,' she says, neatly sidestepping Dora's equivocal status. We head into the dining room, which, with its stained silk-covered walls, tarnished silver and unpolished furniture, exudes the same air of faded grandeur as the hall and parlour. The rosewood table, large enough for twice the present company, has cracks in its marquetry trim, and the braid on several chairs is torn. I am placed on Seward's left, with my mother on his right, and Marcus at the far end, between Sorrel and Dora. I shrug in commiseration, as Seward circles the table, a bottle in either hand.

'Elderflower or champagne?' he asks my father.

'Now there's a dilemma: do I look after my own health or toast yours? Cheerio!' he says, as Seward anticipates his decision.

'Elderflower or champagne?' he asks me.

'Dora made the elderflower,' Valerie interposes.

'Then I must try it,' I say brightly.

'Please don't feel obliged,' Seward says.

'No, I want to.' I take a sip. 'Delicious,' I say to Dora, who remains as indifferent to compliments as to everything else. Flustered, I seek to draw Seward out. 'We're surrounded by splendid pictures, but no Wemlocks. Why's that?'

'He's too modest,' Valerie replies. 'He won't have any of his paintings on display. Only a few hidden upstairs.'

'As ever, my sister-in-law credits me with the noblest motives, but I'm afraid that the truth is far more mundane. I grew up with my grandfather's racing cups all over the house, not to mention the stuffed corpses of his victims in the trophy room. It would smack of the same self-congratulation.'

'You've often spoken of turning your back on your upbringing,' Marcus interjects, determined not to be left out.

'That's the sort of thing one says rather too freely in interviews,' Seward replies, 'especially when young. To be honest, I felt estranged from my family long before I began to paint. From as far back as I remember, my father regarded me with distaste, which grew more

174

marked as the years went by. The only time he expressed the slightest pride in anything I did was during my National Service, when I was commissioned in the Guards.'

'From what I understand, he spread his contempt widely,' Valerie says. 'I've always felt sorry for your mother.'

'Don't worry, she gave as good as she got. I didn't realise how far apart they'd drifted until the War . . . no, until the American invasion. Father was working in Whitehall. Herry and I came home for the holidays to find a different airman at breakfast every morning.'

'It was Granny's war effort,' Laurel says authoritatively.

'Someone's been listening at keyholes,' Seward says, laughing.

'Not true!' she replies, affronted. 'You were telling the creepy rector.'

'Now now, he's a friend of St John's.' Mother looks askance at the even greater solecism. 'Finally, she found one she wanted to keep. She went to Seattle with him in 1945 and hasn't been back since.'

'Is she still alive?' I ask.

'I believe so,' he replies impassively.

'Do you never go over to see her?'

'Seward won't fly,' Laurel interjects. 'He says that it distorts our relationship with the earth.'

'You see how lucky I am to have my own spokeswoman?'

'I want to go to Disneyland!' Sorrel says.

'Don't be idiotic!' her father replies. 'Where on earth does that come from? You know very well that Disney is banned in this house.'

Sorrel blinks tearfully, casting a chill over the table, which lingers until the maid brings in the soup. She's accompanied by a sullen girl of about Laurel's age. They studiously avoid each other's gaze.

'It's burdock root and ginger, with broccoli, fennel and assorted herbs,' Valerie says, puncturing any illusion that Dora chose the menu.

'Is that an early Blake?' Marcus asks Seward, pointing to a delicate watercolour on the sideboard.

'It is indeed. That's the first picture I ever bought. More than any other artist, he inspired my desire to paint. At Eton I kept my own boat – a little outrigger – and I'd row up river at dawn and sketch. At other times I'd head into South Meadow and draw the Castle. Even my father approved: if he couldn't get me into the saddle, at least I was outdoors. But it came to a sudden end, when the housemaster praised one of my pictures and Herry let slip – he swore, inadvertently – that I'd also painted his daughter, Laura. It swiftly emerged that not only was it a nude but we'd slept together. He was horrified because she was fourteen.'

'So was Juliet,' Laurel says, loyally.

'Thank you. She was my first love. I sometimes think that that's the only true love; all others are tainted by its loss.'

Laura . . . Laurel: the names are too close for coincidence. I glance at Dora, blowing on her soup.

'I was packed off home in disgrace, whereas Hereward, who was twice caught in more conventional public-school amours, was merely rapped on the knuckles. Sorry, Valerie.'

'You're not the one who should apologise.'

'That was my first taste of British hypocrisy. Worse was to come when I joined the Guards. It soon became clear that National Service was less about protecting Queen and Country than keeping healthy young men from fucking.' I look down the table, where Sorrel is swallowing a titter. 'Don't worry, they've heard it before.' I'm not sure that my mother has, at least not at lunch. 'I still remember the chaplain, a babe in the woods, spelling out the dangers of every form of sex, including that with which Onan is erroneously associated. "If you're too weak to control your urges, then you'd best get married, but for Heaven's sake, not to a foreigner." Their pox-ridden flesh evidently posed a greater risk to clean-living Englishmen than the entire Red Army. Most of my friends frequented brothels. They'd come back with stories of saluting senior officers in various states of undress. But it wasn't for me. Don't get me wrong! I'm not knocking brothels. Where would Manet and Munch and Schiele have been without them? But I had a deep-seated belief that sex should stem from mutual affection. I still do.'

The maids clear the soup plates. I can't decide whether the younger one's clatter is down to clumsiness or the need to assert herself in front of Laurel.

'Wasn't it after National Service that you went to Paris?' Marcus asks.

'You are well informed. Does Christie's keep a file on me?'

'No, not at all. I just read—'

'I'm pulling your leg. When you know me better, you'll get used to my warped sense of humour.'

Marcus looks as if nothing would please him more.

'But you're right. Much to the chagrin of my father, who urged me to apply for a regular commission, I moved to Paris, studying with Pierre Le Septier, who'd been a friend and follower of Bonnard. I rented a *chambre de bonne*, with no running water but a large skylight and a spectacular view of Montparnasse. I was determined to rough it: to succeed on my own merits, such as they were. I often think that those two years in Paris were the happiest of my life.'

'Thanks a bunch.'

'Before I had you of course,' he says, smiling at Laurel. 'I frequented the Louvre and the Tuileries. I immersed myself in the work of Redon, Rouault, Moreau and Maurice Denis, the great symbolists and colourists, who taught me everything I know. That is until I came back to the Slade and learnt a new way of drawing.'

Unaware that he'd studied at the Slade, I make a quick calculation, while the main course, mushroom wellington, is served. 'When were you there?'

'Fifty-three to fifty-five. Why?'

'You must have been a contemporary of Thomas Philpotts.'

'We arrived on the same day! As the only two practising Christians in our year, we were thrown together – although he gave no clue that he was thinking of ordination, at least not to me.'

'These days, you'd be hard-pressed to find even one Christian at an art school,' Father says. '1953 was the year of the Queen's coronation, when a third of the population believed that she'd ascended the throne by divine right.'

'The equation of religion with hierarchy might explain the decline. The family chapel was definitely the greatest barrier to my own faith. Yet, somehow, it's survived. My critics maintain that it's a contradiction for someone with my – how shall I put it? – colourful past to profess himself a Christian, but, to my mind, it's wholly consistent. I'm determined to celebrate all the beauty the Good Lord has given us. Wouldn't you agree, St John?'

'So long as you also accept the constraints that He's imposed.'

'And His forgiveness. So long as we accept His absolute forgiveness.' Seward falls silent.

'More champagne, anyone?' Valerie asks. 'Marcus, would you do the honours?' As he opens another bottle, I wait in trepidation for the cork to crack one of the chandelier's dusty prisms, but he eases it out so smoothly that it barely pops. Discharging his buttling duties, he moves around the table, mistaking Laurel's glass for Dora's.

'He's trying to get you drunk,' Sorrel says.

'Be quiet!' Dora says with unexpected severity. 'What nonsense you talk sometimes!'

'Remember you're driving,' Mother says, as Father presents his glass to Marcus.

'You give me little chance to forget,' he replies, signalling Marcus to stop pouring just as he reaches the brim.

'So Philpotts never mentioned his vocation – his clerical vocation, that is?' I ask Seward.

'Clarissa, now's not the time,' Father interposes. 'My daughter has a bee in her bonnet about the man.'

'Not just a bee, an entire hive!'

'Not that I recall, my dear. But, in spite of our shared creed, we were never close. The last time I saw him must have been at the Slade's centennial shindig in seventy-one. He described himself as a priest by day and a painter by night – well, he could hardly call himself a Sunday painter. That combination has been his trump card. Like the singing nun.'

'Except that he's a monster.'

'Clarissa . . .'

'He's obsessed by the so-called threat of women priests,' I say, ignoring Father's admonition. 'His misogyny is so virulent that I wonder what we can have done to him. Did a girlfriend laugh at his penis and scar him for life?'

'The children, Clarissa!' Mother says.

'I've seen a penis,' Sorrel assures her.

'Not that of the Reverend Thomas Philpotts', I trust,' Seward says, with a stilted laugh.

'Such flippancy does you no credit,' Father says to me. 'His concerns may be born of deep conviction.'

'But their expression is obscene.'

'I haven't seen his work for many years,' Seward says. 'It holds little interest for me. It had a certain facility . . . energy . . . edge, but not much going on beneath the surface. Strange to say, not much spirit.'

'Count yourself lucky! It's hard to miss right now. He trades on his notoriety. Endless profiles copiously illustrated with his own pictures. One shows women, naked apart from their clerical collars, advancing on the altar, while a haggard priest keeps them at bay with the cross. In another, a stock lesbian, stole rumpled over her pendulous breasts, drowns a miniature bishop in a font. Or how about the giantesses – naked, naturally – plunging pickaxes through the dome of St Paul's?'

'In person, he's exceedingly courteous. The trouble is he lets his passions run away with him. Which is why I'm so grateful to have an artist of your temperament for the St Peter's project,' Father says to Seward. 'Have you given it any further thought?'

'Of course. Later.'

'May we know where you stand on the issue?' I ask him.

'The decoration of churches?'

'The ordination of women,' I reply, in my driest tones.

'I don't have strong feelings either way; though, in principle, I'm against anything that blurs the distinction between the sexes. My quarrel with the feminists isn't that they demand the same rights as men but that they lay claim to the same emotions. Take the most intimate relationship of all: we're told that women are – or, at least, would be if their true selves were liberated – as voracious as men. Nonsense! In my experience, which is fairly extensive, the maternal impulse is never far from the sexual in women. Their pleasure comes from giving pleasure as much as from receiving it.'

'Maybe your experience, however large, is narrow?'

'I'm always willing to broaden it.'

I glimpse Marcus smiling and wonder whether he'd be so sanguine were Seward not one of his artistic heroes.

'The plain truth is that women are too practical to be priests,' Mother says. 'We keep our feet on the ground. Men are more idealistic . . . more spiritual.'

Father nudges her champagne glass out of reach.

At the end of the meal, we return to the parlour for coffee. The party then disperses, with Dora going upstairs to rest (I stifle my scepticism); the girls retreating to their den; Valerie taking Mother to view the early bluebells; and Seward taking Father, myself and a euphoric Marcus to his studio.

'It's the old game larder. My father must be turning in his grave.'

We head down a drab corridor, past the scullery, where the maids are washing piles of dishes in adjacent cast-iron sinks, and along an overgrown path to a small octagonal building, with a two-tiered lantern, reminiscent of a wayside chapel. On entry, I am struck first by a blast of cold air and then by a thick aroma, both woody and metallic, with a hint of nail varnish. Seward crosses the room, raising the blinds on the eight high windows, which, he explains, have been converted from the ventilation slats. Crisp white light floods in, revealing dozens of paintings on the walls and stacks of canvases in various stages of completion. One, propped on an easel, immediately attracts Marcus's attention, while Father pulls up a paint-splattered chair with a wobbly leg, and plumps himself down to 'soak in the atmosphere'. Although I'm keen to look around, the studio feels so private, so full of Seward, that I wait for his permission. Meanwhile, I stare at the ceiling and am disconcerted by the racks of hooks.

'Don't worry, it doesn't double as a dungeon,' Seward says, noticing my tremor.

'I never supposed—'

'Of course not. My warped sense of humour again. That's where they used to hang the game, all carefully graded by size. I leave them up to remind myself of how far I've come, as well as to support larger canvases, such as the ones required for St Peter's.' He gestures to Father, who's dozing, and although they're almost of an age, puts his finger to his lips, like a schoolboy free from adult tutelage.

'This is magnificent!'

I turn to Marcus, who's standing nearby, enraptured by a painting of a white stag. Drawing closer, I see patches of silvery yellow in the deep purple background, suggestive of will-o'-the-wisp in a night sky, and a snake with iridescent pink-grey skin crushed beneath the stag's hooves.

'Did you do another version of this?' Marcus asks. 'I'm sure I've seen one with an azure background.'

'Four in all. St John would tell you that the stag was a medieval symbol for Christ. Not as prevalent as the fish, but rather more rewarding to paint.'

'Hence the snake,' I say.

'Indeed. You can't keep a good symbol down. Although it demands a level of visual literacy. When I first showed them – oh, a good twenty-five years ago – critics accused me of reverting to type: painting stags when I wasn't shooting them. I'm convinced that at least one of the buyers, an American steel tycoon, thought that he was getting a latter-day *Monarch of the Glen.*'

'Isn't it painful when people misinterpret you?'

'If I minded that much, I'd have given up in the fifties. Although perhaps, without realising, I've made things more explicit. Like this one . . . Where?' He rifles through a stack of canvases. 'Would you be so kind?' he asks Marcus, who, needing no encouragement, helps him to pull out a picture of a camel, crouching beside a needlewoman, on an emerald green bank of shimmering intensity. 'I made some preparatory sketches at Chester Zoo, greatly to the annoyance of a teacher, whose charges were more interested in watching me work than listening to her talk about camels in their desert habitat.'

'Such luminescence! Does it come from using a pink ground?' Marcus asks.

'You have done your homework!'

'Not at all. I only learnt that we were invited here this morning.'

'I'm impressed. Yes, the ground gives the paint an added glow. In my younger days, I thought crepuscular colours better suited to capturing the numinous.' He indicates the stag. 'Now I'm older – or simply more reckless – I use a brighter palette.'

'It's beautiful. But why leave it here for no one to see? And on the floor?' I ask, recalling Marcus's stories of damaged canvases.

'It isn't finished.'

'Really? Is that because, to the artist, no painting is ever truly finished?'

'No, just this one. Feel free to look around. No need to comment,' he adds, the dispensation sounding like an appeal.

I wander round in the opposite direction to Marcus, afraid that my untutored responses will offend him. My eye is drawn to a double portrait of Laurel and Sorrel, posed as for an ethnological study. Each holds a porcelain doll, whose features perfectly replicate her own, but covered in a web of cracks. I take it to depict the death of childhood, nevertheless it's deeply unsettling, as is its neighbour: a reclining nude of Dora, her legs wide open, while her arms, feet and hair blend into a golden background, speckled with butterflies. It's as though, having lived with her for twenty years (or, rather, ten or twelve, since it was evidently painted some time ago), he still finds her as elusive as I did at lunch. I want to ask if it too remains unfinished, but I already know the answer.

'Have you seen enough?' Seward asks. 'Is it time to wake St John?'

'I wasn't asleep. Just resting my eyes,' Father says, refusing as ever to admit to any sign of frailty.

'Let's wind up in here, shall we? I'm starting to feel judged.'

Marcus quickens his pace, loath to waste the opportunity. 'This is a treasure trove,' he says. 'I'd love the chance to come back and take some photographs.'

'Nice try,' Seward replies, patting his shoulder.

'When did you do this one?' he asks, pointing to a picture which, from where I'm standing, looks like the rings of Saturn. 'I thought you abhorred abstraction.'

'I do. And I hang it here to remind myself why. It was all the vogue when I was young. Probably still is, but I'm less susceptible now. Artists and critics alike looked down on those of us who swam against the tide. We were aesthetic, intellectual, even political reactionaries. But just because totalitarian states banned abstraction doesn't make it either radical or profound. I'm sure you know the old joke: "Why is abstract art like masturbation? It's fun while you're doing it, but you're left with an embarrassing mess at the end."'

I join Father in a dutiful chuckle, while Marcus laughs lustily.

'Do you paint every day or only when inspiration strikes?' I ask, happy to show my ignorance if it buys Marcus time to explore.

'My hours are as regular as a bank clerk's. Forget the myth of the impulsive genius – or if you find one, keep him well away from me! Artists are the least spontaneous people I know: less concerned with what is than what we can make of it; valuing representation over reality. Far from living in the moment, the artist lives with one eye on immortality – or perpetuity, if that sounds less grand. But enough of this talk about art! I should leave that to clever young men, like our friend here.' Marcus frowns on being cast in a pedagogic role. 'Why don't you two go back to the house or take a stroll in the garden, if it's not too cold, while I show St John some preliminary ideas I've had for the church?'

'You have some already? Splendid, splendid!'

Marcus looks set to make a bid to stay, but I catch his eye and shake my head. We walk through the garden, where very little of Valerie's handiwork is manifest this early in the year. As we enter an avenue of lime trees, he grabs my arm and leads me to a sundial, confiding his notion of writing Seward's biography. 'It came to me in the studio. He's famously private, but the personal connection could break down his defences. It's a great story: the dysfunctional family; the sex scandal at Eton; the string of women in London; then ending up back here. Although, naturally, my main focus would be the work.'

'Naturally.'

'We could drive up at weekends. I'd interview him while you got to spend time with your parents.'

'Gee, thanks!'

'Your mother would be thrilled. Maybe we could ask your father to suggest it?'

'Best let him sort out the commission first.' Marcus's face falls. 'That shouldn't take long. Meanwhile you can put together a proposal that's impossible to resist.'

We return to the parlour to find Vincent Slater, deep in conversation with Mother and Valerie. He greets me with the familiar lupine smile that makes my skin crawl. Despite his stiff-backed posture, there's something invertebrate about him. No amount of cultural polish can cloak his callowness. As he punctuates his pomposity with girlish giggles, he reminds me of the ordinands at Westcott House, who regarded stealing a nun's wimple as the acme of vice.

'What a gorgeous surprise,' he says, as he stands and gives my hand a feathery shake, like a ghost-train ghoul. 'I didn't know you were coming.'

'Likewise,' I say, at which he looks disappointed, as though it should have been held out as an incentive.

'Clarissa . . . Marcus,' Mother interjects.

'Of course. May I introduce my fiancé, Marcus Derwent? Marcus . . . Father Vincent Slater.'

'So you're the lucky man who has won the heart of *the fairest flower of the north countrie*?'

'You could say that,' Marcus replies, nonplussed.

'Do sit down,' Valerie says. 'Would you like some tea? How about one of Dora's blueberry scones?'

'Just tea for me, thank you,' I say.

'My favourites,' Marcus says, reaching for a scone.

'Father and Seward are poring over some sketches for the church.'

'Vincent wanted to join them, but we held him hostage,' Mother says. 'I see so little of him these days.'

'To my eternal regret,' Vincent says, cutting his scone into doll-size pieces. We engage in desultory chatter, until Seward finally arrives with Father, whereupon Vincent leaps up, genuflects and kisses his ring.

Father pats him distractedly on the head, before wiping his hand on his trousers. 'Vincent, a joy as ever. All well in the parish?' He moves to the tea table. 'Those scones look delicious.'

'Cholesterol, St John,' Mother says.

'I know, I know, but with Lent just around the corner . . .'

'Since you ask, Bishop,' Vincent replies eagerly. 'There've been some local difficulties, indeed, defections to the Free Church, where the worship is lower than a snake's belly.' His further burst of giggles prompts Marcus to choke on his scone. 'I've tried to introduce a dash of colour, a dash of music, a dash of drama, into the services, but all they want is what they had before. Like children asking father for the same bedtime story.'

'I never pictured you in a rural parish,' I say.

'I go where I'm called . . . and where the Bishop sends me. But the path can be a lonely one.' For a moment, his mask slips and I glimpse his desolation.

'What you need is a wife,' Mother says.

'I'm a celibate,' Vincent says, the mask firmly back in place.

'You haven't met the right woman.'

'Sperm retention can be a powerful spiritual tool,' Seward says. 'Look at the Tantric masters. It enables them to attain a higher level of consciousness. I spent several weeks at their sanctuary in New Jersey, but I could never achieve the necessary self-restraint.'

Father, reaching for another dollop of cream, replaces the spoon beside the pot. Vincent looks shamefaced. I suspect that, far from exhibiting such continence, he is a regular dabbler in what I shall henceforth think of as abstract art.

'You're much missed in Chester,' Mother says to him.

'Vincent is the best chaplain I've ever had.'

'You're too kind,' Vincent replies, although he might have been less grateful had Father added, as he once did to me, that such an inveterate gossip was the perfect conduit for all the goings-on in the diocese.

'And we'll be seeing more of you if the St Peter's project goes ahead. Seward's preliminary designs—'

'Sketches. No, not even sketches . . . doodles.'

'Then I'm even more in awe. The paintings will bring glory to the church. In years to come, visitors will flock here as they do to the Giotto chapel in Padua or the Masaccio chapel in Florence.'

'Or the Sistine chapel,' Marcus says.

Even Father, whose ambitions for his legacy are boundless, looks taken aback. 'Why not? And I've had another brainwave. Clarissa must make a feature about it for the radio.'

'Seriously?' I ask. Despite my dislike of being bludgeoned, the idea has an instant appeal. 'I'd be happy to suggest it but, as you know, it's not in my gift.'

'It would certainly be an added incentive for me,' Seward says.

'That's very civil of you. I can but try.'

'Now you must all forgive me,' Seward says. 'The studio beckons. Stay as long as you like. Ask Valerie for anything you need. I doubt you'll see hide or hair of Dora.' He moves to me and clasps my right hand in both of his. Once again, I feel a charge. 'I look forward to meeting you again, my dear. Until then, remember my golden rule: Don't take care . . . take risks!'

Three

Dear Dr Quinn, Thank you for your letter of 27 February. Let me assure you that the BBC has no intention of, in your words, 'sacrificing its core Christian values on the altar of gutless ecumenicism'. I have listened again to the Chief Rabbi's contribution to the *Thought for the Day* in question and can state categorically that he referred to Satan as an 'arch fiend', rather than an 'old friend'.

Dear Miss Harris, Thank you for your letter of 27 February. Please accept my sincere condolences on the death of your mother. Having consulted my colleagues, I regret that we must decline your generous offer of her annotated collection of the *Radio Times* from October 1956 to January of this year. We have no space to store, let alone display, what is clearly a fascinating archive, and I suggest that, instead, you present it to your local library.

Dear Mr Lennox, Thank you for your letter of 1 March and your warning about the forthcoming End Time. The Religious Broadcasting Department takes no part in the choice of guests for *Desert Island Discs*, but I can confirm that, in recent weeks as throughout the programme's history, they have been chosen for their achievements in diverse walks of life and not for membership of the Illuminati.

Dear Mrs Lucas, Thank you for your letter of 1 March. I have examined the files and can only repeat what other producers have told you in the course of a lengthy correspondence, namely that there has been no attempt by the BBC to suppress the story of the Angel Gabriel's visitation to your aunt in May 1981. The Radio Norfolk reporter, who followed up your initial approach, concluded that the anecdotal evidence was insufficient to warrant further investigation. I return the feather, which I trust will remain a treasured family heirloom.

I allow myself a slight flourish as, mirroring Lydia Lucas (Mrs), I sign myself Clarissa Phipps (Ms). We receive more of these green-ink letters than any other department. It's hard to imagine Robert Lennox confiding his fears about an imminent apocalypse to the editor of *The Archers*, or Dr Quinn betraying his anti-Semitism to the Head of Light Entertainment. It's Bruce's proud boast that we treat our listeners with as much respect off-air as on, even if 'the sick and the suffering and the lonely' have been replaced by the prejudiced, the paranoid and the demented. Each producer is allotted a share of the correspondence but, with several having been as castigated for their replies as for the original offences, the burden falls on those of us who aren't as 'lofty' as the Canon, as 'abstruse' as Archie and as 'sloppy' as Terry.

At the thought of Terry, I turn to Jan, who stares back with red-eyed resentment. Once her friend as well as her boss, I long to say something to appease her, but the boundaries breached by my fellow producer have led her to shore up those that remain. She has been *Terried* – the unduly frivolous term employed by the female staff

(PAs, sound recordists, studio managers and, yes, one producer) to describe being groped by Terry Bannister. A briar-bearded, roly-poly man, who favours thick-knit beige cardigans, maroon corduroy trousers and Jesus sandals, he exudes a disarming air of cuddlesome whimsicality. 'Won't you come into my boudoir?' he asked me soon after my arrival, the arcane charm of the phrase vanishing when he pinched my bottom. Reluctant to make a scene, I edged away, which he took as the first step in a courtship dance and lunged again. I slammed his hand hard on the desk; he yelped and gazed at me with the injured expression of a dog that has been smacked for barking.

Quite why an unprepossessing middle-aged man should suppose himself irresistible to young women would be a mystery, were it not that unwanted jokes and innuendoes, passes and pounces, are as much a hazard of Broadcasting House as the antiquated plumbing. His own PA, the long-serving Barbara, is so like an indulgent nanny that I half-expect her to refer to *Master Terry*. Jan was well aware of his reputation, but she credited him with enough regard for her integrity and professionalism to brave the *boudoir*. Her torn sleeve, bruised elbow, and wounded pride proved her wrong.

At her request, I reported him to Bruce, who listened wearily to my account, before questioning the use of the word *assault*, as if it were an ambiguity in the Septuagint. Addressing me with the ill-concealed distaste of a teacher for a sneak, he promised to investigate. Twelve days have gone by and we've heard nothing. At first, Jan blamed the delay on the byzantine bureaucracy, but, ever since I received the green light to make the feature on women deacons for which I've lobbied for months, she has acted as though I've been suborned.

The first women were ordained at Canterbury three weeks ago, with others following across the country, including seventy-one at St Paul's next weekend. Julian's piece for *Sunday* was a textbook example of BBC balance and Anglican fudge, with a champion and opponent of women's ministry, both male, finding common ground in agreeing to differ. Although the title of my feature has yet to be confirmed, it will be subtitled 'a personal quest': the standard safety clause. I'm focussing on two of the new crop of London deacons: Decca Maddox and June Lister, both of whom I met three years ago on a protest march from Westminster Abbey to St Paul's. I'd heard about it from one of my fellow librarians, a bilious, beaky woman, who ostentatiously sprayed air freshener ('at my own expense') around the first-floor music library, where the tramps clustered.

It was her jibe that the 'braless brigade will be out in force', which prompted me to stroll down to Parliament Square after work. Having marched with Marcus in support of the miners only a few weeks earlier, I was dismayed to find that *out in force* referred to no more than thirty women. I watched them assemble, some wearing blue sashes like latter-day Suffragettes; others holding placards with disappointingly rambling slogans: *How long, oh Lord, how long?*; *A Woman's place is at the Altar*; and *God is an equal opportunities employer, how about the Church?* A striking woman of about my age, with spiky red hair and an array of badges like chain mail on her chest, caught my eye, walked over and asked me to help her carry a banner with the more prosaic – and pithy – message of *Ordain Women Now*.

I accepted without demur. As I started to march, keeping step with someone whose name I didn't know but whose most cherished hopes I shared, I felt an extraordinary rush of freedom. Until then, I'd sought to banish my despair at my thwarted vocation by dwelling on my own unworthiness: I was a hypocrite – a fraud – who saw priesthood as a chance to give my life meaning rather than to give myself to God. Which in turn compounded the despair. With characteristic casuistry, Father insisted that to endure rejection was to be one with Christ. He suggested that I seek a post as a non-ordained deaconess. Even Marcus agreed, until I explained that it was as if becoming a castrato were the only way for a man to join a choir.

Now, in the company of two or three dozen women, who couldn't all be the daughters of bishops, charged with both an unhealthy desire to emulate their fathers and a vindictive desire to punish them, I realised that God had another plan for me. I must prove myself worthy of priesthood by fighting for it. We were a small troop but, as we advanced up Whitehall and down the Strand, I felt as powerful as if I were part of a May Day parade in Red Square. Bystanders clapped and cheered; cab drivers sounded their horns; the doorman outside the Strand Palace doffed his hat. Inevitably there were cat-calls, but they were as inconsequential as they were unimaginative. One heckler, spotting the *A Woman's place is at the Altar* placard, shouted 'A woman's place is in the kitchen!' only to slink away when the holder retorted, 'And an ape's is in the zoo!' Another invited us all to 'Sit on my face!' I was as startled as he was when a soberly dressed matron, as far from the *braless* stereotype as could be imagined, yelled back: 'Why, are you a pouf?'

We arrived at St Paul's, congregating on the steps, to the squawky confusion of the pigeons which, with the cathedral shut for the night, had supposed themselves undisturbed. In the gathering dusk, a stout woman, with spectacles that obscured much of her face, lit a candle. Next to her, a white-haired woman sang a hymn from Taizé, which the group picked up with gusto. A small crowd collected beside Queen Anne, among them a posse of press photographers. Discovering that, in spite of the sashes, no one intended to manacle herself to the railings or engage in any other form of civil disobedience, they dispersed, shortly to be followed by the marchers. Although aware that I should head back to the flat, where Marcus would be waiting, I longed for the camaraderie to continue. This it did, when my fellow banner-holder, Decca, whose name I'd learnt during a lull at Ludgate Circus, invited me to join her and her friend, June, for a pizza and a glass of wine.

The two women could not have been more different. Decca is a gay advertising executive ('Don't worry, I use a long spoon!'), while June is married to George Lister, the vicar of St Jude's, Harringay, and has four sons aged between two and eight. Yet they're similarly committed to the struggle, not for natural justice or equal rights (important as those are), but to do the work to which God has called them. We warmed to each other at once, and the following week, they took me to a branch meeting of the ordination movement in Shepherd's Bush. Not knowing what to expect, I pictured a version of the San Francisco cell that Alexander had portrayed so vividly. Instead, I found a group of women, who might have been my mother and her friends organising a whist drive. Their aim was not to damage the Church but to be fully accepted within it, trusting that their very respectability would win them support.

Happy to lend a hand, I proceeded to lobby MPs, picket Synod, draft statements and stuff countless envelopes. When in July 1985, Synod finally voted to ordain us as deacons, I agonised over whether to apply for training. Marcus's initial enthusiasm had waned: in part, because of his own dwindling faith; in part, because of his clashes with Decca, whom he accused – on the most tenuous evidence – of having designs on me; and, in part, I suspect, because a fiancée who worked for the BBC was more glamorous than one on the lowest rung of the ecclesiastical ladder. But it was Kate, who made the decisive case for my staying put, when, over a celebration lunch to mark her promotion from *Woman's Hour* to *The World Tonight*, she asked: 'Why on earth would you move to an institution where male privilege is even more entrenched than at the Beeb?' So here I've remained, chipping away at the glass ceiling and, as my present project shows, slowly achieving results.

Conscious of the time, I pick up my trusty Uher, along with half a dozen spare tapes, and head out of the building. 'That looks heavy, love,' Joyce calls, from her post at the tea urn. 'Can't you get one of the boys to carry it?'

'Shot-putter's shoulders,' I assure her, as I stride past, before transferring the weight from left to right every twenty paces, as I thread my way to Great Titchfield Street and the first of two buses that will take me to Harringay, to interview June.

After swapping gossip, we sit down at her scratched and scrubbed refectory table for a bowl of onion soup and some crusty bread, which she has somehow found time to bake despite the incessant demands of Numbers Three and Four, as she jocularly styles her two youngest children. I ponder whether the shrieks and squalls that punctuate the meal might enhance the interview – an audible demonstration of the obstacles that June has had to overcome on the path to ordination – but fear that they will provide ammunition for critics, who accuse her of maternal neglect. The constant clamour makes me thankful that Marcus and I have chosen to postpone starting a family, and I'm relieved when, lunch ended, she calls the neighbour who has volunteered to take them off her hands.

I begin the questions by asking her to describe her feelings as Sunday approaches. Tears well in her eyes, as she mentions the two-day retreat prior to the service. I'm surprised to learn that it's to be led by the Bishop of London, who recently referred to women priests as 'a virus in the bloodstream of the universal church', a doubly pernicious image given the lethal virus that currently dominates the headlines. Nonetheless, he's prepared to ordain women deacons, and mounts a plausible defence of the distinction, although, to my mind, he's one of those willing to allow us a place at the table, provided that it's below the salt.

'Given that women can now become deacons, are you disturbed or bitter or angry about the forces that remain opposed to our becoming priests?' I ask June.

'Beleaguered, I think,' she replies, after a pause too lengthy for radio. 'Yes, it's hard not to feel beleaguered when, on the one hand, you have the evangelicals, who object to our teaching and preaching and exercising authority, and on the other, the catholics, who object to our presence at the altar. I've even been told that women priests would be a new generation of temple prostitutes. Oh, can I say that on air?'

'Yes, of course.'

I wish that I could be as confident about Decca's typically blunt reply to the same question last week. 'It all comes down to blood. Women with their cursed, bloody bodies aren't worthy to offer up the body and blood of Christ.' I fear that Bruce, who betrayed his squeamishness about menstruation when editing a programme on Jewish ritual baths, will insist that I cut it.

After fifteen minutes, I change the tape and June opens the larder, removing a letter from behind a box of soap powder. 'You can't use this, of course, but you might be interested to see it. George doesn't know I've kept it.'

The letter is charred and I wonder if George put a match to it, until I see that the burns follow a pattern, alongside arcane symbols, some of which I recognise as Satanic. It is written in what I trust is red ink, despite its suspiciously rusty smell. A single glance reveals that the elegant script is in stark contrast to the repugnant sentiments. In swift succession, June is denounced as Eve, Jezebel and the Whore of Babylon, and warned that, if she continues down her damnable path, she will suffer the same fate as her biblical forebears. Then, in case that isn't clear enough, he – I'm assuming that it's *he* – adds that she will be raped, her eyes gouged out and her body chopped into bits.

Trembling, I toss the letter on the table and am amazed that June, to whom its threats are addressed, can remain so calm. 'Have you shown it to the police?'

'No, George begged me not to. I promised him I'd torn it up.' She looks unhappier at having lied to her husband than at the letter itself.

'With respect, George isn't the one being targeted.'

'No, but he's convinced that it must have been sent by a member of the congregation or someone close to them. He's been asking them to pray for me week by week as I prepare for ordination. Apart from family and friends, nobody else knows.'

My admiration for her is greater than ever. With a new tape in place, we resume the interview, although I wish that I'd written out a list of questions, since the letter has so shaken me that I struggle to remember everything I'd intended to ask. Its vileness and violence, however, steel my resolve to be more combative the following lunch-time, when I interview my father at the House of Lords. For all its irregularity, Bruce has agreed that, since this is a personal quest and Father is one of the most high-profile opponents of women priests, it makes good sense – and 'good radio' – for me to question him, rather than some 'rent-a-quote bishop'.

With Bruce's expenses directive in mind, I take a cab to West-minster, joining the queue outside Parliament. I state my business to the security officer who, more exercised by my *Ordain Women Now* badge than any bomb that might be hidden in my Uher, insists I remove it, since 'political or offensive slogans aren't permitted inside the Palace'. Protest is futile and, having acquiesced, I make my way to the statue-strewn, mosaic-clad, gilded and tiled Central Lobby, announce my name at the desk and wait for Father. I'm approached by a middle-aged couple, come to press their MP to vote against the Family Reform Bill, which is designed to protect the rights of children born outside wedlock: in their words, 'a bastards' charter'. Seeing the sticker on my bag, they attempt to enlist the support of the media. Father's timely arrival saves me from having to engage with them.

After a cursory kiss, he shepherds me through the Peers' Lobby and up to the first floor, where he has booked a meeting room. We walk down a corridor, as long and nondescript as any in Broadcasting House, stopping halfway, where Father greets a tall, grizzled man wearing a purple stock, with spectacularly bushy eyebrows. We've never met but, for my part, introductions are superfluous, since I instantly recognise the Bishop of London. Father explains that I've come to interview him about women's ministry for the 'Bee Bee Cee' (elongating each syllable with fastidious disdain). Dr Leonard fixes me with a gaze at once gracious and steely.

'Ah, the Monstrous Regiment,' he says. 'Pray Heaven it remains non-combatant!'

He hurries on, and Father shows me into an airless, windowless room, which lowers the spirits even as it concentrates the mind. I place the machine on a table and roll my shoulders, whereupon he asks me to leave the calisthenics until later. While I set up the tape, we chat about my weekend in Dorset and Mother's root canal treatment. Neither of us has heard anything from Alexander, who is due to arrive on Thursday. He warns me that Mother will be heartbroken if we fail to go up to Chester at the weekend. The words *brother* and *keeper* cross my mind, but I bite them back. Instead, I relay the encouraging news about the Tapley project.

'Bruce is keen on my proposal and we're scheduled to attend an Offer Meeting with CR4—'

'I beg your pardon?'

'The Controller of Radio Four, about my making an hour-long feature to be broadcast in the second quarter of next year.'

To test the level, he reminds me that the last time I interviewed him was fifteen or so years ago at Westcott House, for a school essay competition on *My Father's Job*.

'I remember; I was runner-up to a girl whose father was unemployed.'

With everything in place, I deliver my introduction. 'I'm in the august surroundings of the House of Lords with my father, St John Phipps, Bishop of Chester, one of the principal adversaries of women priests in the Anglican hierarchy.' Father raises an eyebrow at the bald description. 'The Lords is reputed to boast some of the finest lavatories in the land, among them one by Victorian master plumber Thomas Crapper, and another with a set of Art Deco urinals said to be rivalled only by those in the Savoy Hotel.' Father looks bewildered, but he is loath to interrupt the recording. 'Although women have been admitted to the Upper Chamber for almost thirty years, their facilities remain grossly inadequate. Proposals to convert a modest number of urinals into cubicles have been squashed by the conserva-tives ... the traditionalists.' Father's face sets, as he realises where I'm heading. 'While claiming to be sympathetic to women's needs, they argue that it's more important to preserve these WCs – these jewels of sanitation – in their pristine state. It's hard not to discern a similar attitude in the Church. Wouldn't you agree, Bishop?'

'The analogy fails to hold water.' He scowls at my grin. 'Tradi-tion in the Church amounts to far more than custom and practice or, to employ your own tortuous image, decorative splendour. Even those of us vehemently opposed to opening the priesthood to women are in the process of ordaining them as deacons. Why? Because the diaconate is an ancient order, dating from the early Church, which was accessible to both men and women. I trust that you don't reject that tradition.'

'Not at all. But I can think of many more valid reasons for ordaining women deacons than historical precedent. Moreover, the Anglican Church broke with tradition at its very inception. It changed the nature of priesthood by ordaining married men.'

'It broke with Rome: not, as the Creed makes abundantly clear, with the *holy, catholic and apostolic church*. And like the twelve apostles, its priests, whether married or single, have always been men. I don't doubt that women were among Our Lord's close associates. But the very fact that He didn't appoint any of them as His apostles is an even stronger argument against ordaining them as priests.'

'Yet, while His male associates abandoned and denied Him, the women followed Him to both the Cross and the tomb. It was Judas – a man – not Mary, who betrayed Him.'

'She couldn't have done so even if she'd wished, since in Jewish law a woman's testimony was invalid. My intention isn't to devalue women – after all, we have a female prime minister – but rather to celebrate their unique role. When Christ became incarnate, He did so without the involvement of any human father. He was born of a woman alone.'

'So, two thousand years on, in the eyes of the Church, women are nothing but brood-mares?'

'How depressing to hear immutable truths reduced to charges of sexist oppression! I don't believe it was chance that Christ chose to be incarnate in first-century Palestine rather than, say, fifth-century

France or Tang dynasty China. I don't believe it was chance that He chose to minister to the Jews, the people with the most sophisticated theology in the ancient world. I don't believe it was chance that He chose to institute His priesthood at the Last Supper among his male apostles. And I don't believe it's chance that, for two thousand years, He has bestowed His grace on that priesthood, who have all been men.'

'In your judgement then, Christ's gender outweighs His humanity?'

'I most definitely didn't say that.'

'But that's the only conclusion I can draw. Moreover, that a priest's essential quality isn't his heart or his mind or even his spirit, but his scrotum!'

Father looks at me with grim satisfaction. 'I fear, my dear, that you've proved my point. In the last resort, women are governed by their emotions, which is another reason that they are unsuited to being priests.'

I am furious with myself. Interviewing my father may make for good radio, but it has left me exposed. No one else – except perhaps the Reverend Thomas Philpotts – would have goaded me so violently. Pinning my hopes on the editing, I draw the discussion to a close. Father declares himself well pleased and, as if we've been quibbling over a crossword puzzle, tells me that he's booked us into the dining room for lunch. I invent an urgent meeting, which, on my return to Broadcasting House, I find to be the truth, since Bruce has asked to see me at my earliest convenience.

As soon as I enter his office, Marcia, his PA, stands, switches off her typewriter and goes out. I take the seat Bruce offers and wait to hear the nature of my offence, until the news that he has spoken to Terry sets my mind at rest.

'He's as keen as all of us to clear up the misunderstanding.'

'You mean the assault.'

'Please,' he says mildly, 'you of all people should know better: such overstatements devalue the real abuses. Look how cramped this office is – and it's twice the size of Terry's! Marcia and I are constantly tripping over one another.' He gives me time to respond, before pressing on. 'Terry swears that he bumped into Janet inadvertently.'

'Just as he did into me and several of the PAs?'

'He's a big man. Uncoordinated. It wouldn't surprise me if he were in the early stages of Parkinson's.'

He smiles, like a barrister who thinks that he's hit on a winning defence.

'Has he bumped into you inadvertently? Or Julian? Or the Canon?'

His smile turns into a frown at my refusal to play the game. 'Terry's ready to apologise for any hurt he may have inadvertently caused.'

'That word again!'

'Accidentally . . . innocently.' I laugh. 'Unwittingly. He's learnt his lesson.'

'And Jan has learnt hers. When the chips are down, the men stick together.'

'That's not true. First and foremost, I'm thinking of his wife and children. Do you really want to put them through the misery . . . the shame?'

'What if I spoke out?' His shocked face emboldens me. 'Described how he'd tried it on with me?'

'It's not for me to tell you what to do, but I urge you to reflect carefully. You're doing so well here. The last thing you want is a reputation as a troublemaker.'

'Is that a threat?' I ask, open-mouthed.

'I'm a priest, not an intelligence officer! I'll read Terry the Riot Act and guarantee that, from now on, he'll keep his hands to himself.'

'I'll talk to Jan and get back to you.'

I leave the office feeling unsteady, and take a few deep breaths just as the Canon comes out of his door. 'Headmaster's study?' he asks blithely, before sauntering down the corridor. I return to my own office where Jan, no doubt primed by Marcia, observes me eagerly. I give her a selective account of my conversation with Bruce.

'Just as I expected.'

'You can take the complaint further if you wish.'

'What would you do?'

'It has to be your decision.'

'Yes, but what would you advise?'

I replay Bruce's warning and know that I won't rock the boat by accusing Terry. It will be her word against his. In which case, Mary Magdalene won't be the only unreliable witness. 'My advice is to put it behind you: show him that he hasn't got to you.'

'To pretend to be strong by being weak?'

'Does it have to be a pretence?'

'Look at the badge you're wearing – and the marches you go on! What's the point? Why not leave it to the men if you're going to capitulate to them?'

'You're being unjust.'

'Sorry. Justice is so important, isn't it? May I go home now?' She grabs her coat and bag without waiting for an answer. 'I'm feeling sick . . . a headache . . . whatever you like. But don't worry. I'll be back at my desk in the morning.'

I make no attempt to detain her. Her charges ring in my ears, even after I put on my headphones and listen to Father's interview. I note possible cuts but will leave them until after I've recorded the ordination service at St Paul's on Sunday. I'm busy writing my preamble when Marcus calls, telling me to come straight home since Alexander has arrived. I dash down the corridor, briefly slackening my pace in deference to John, one of the wounded ex-servicemen who clump back and forth with our messages, head for the Tube and squeeze into a packed compartment, where, without a protest, I accept the offer of a seat from a man twice my age.

Exiting at Queensway, I jostle through the crowd to reach Orme Court. Pausing only to register the scuffed duffle bag in the hall, I tear off my coat and enter the sitting room, where a phlegmy coughing fit stops me in my tracks. All the inchoate fears of the past few months cohere at the sight of my brother's sallow, sunken face.

'Sis,' he says, managing to articulate the syllable between coughs. I walk towards him, but he holds up his hand, spits into a tissue and takes a sip of water. His breath slowly steadies. 'Sorry, you know what the air's like on the plane. Plus, the guy sitting next to me smoked the entire journey.' I remain dazed. 'You might at least play along with me for now.'

I force my lips into a smile but can't keep back the tears. I hurry over and hug him, dismayed by his unwonted angularity. 'When did you get here? We weren't expecting you till Thursday? Where's Cesar?' I ask, at which Marcus shakes his head.

'I was able to get on an earlier flight. I thought you'd be pleased to have two more days of me. And Cesar isn't coming,' he says with a catch in his voice.

'No *carta blanca*?'

'Something like that.'

'Have you eaten?' I ask, determined not to pry. 'You look . . . you must be starving.'

'My heart bleeds for you, Marcus. She's turning into our mother. Don't fuss! I'm fine.'

'And what are you doing home so soon?' I ask Marcus, before switching back to Alexander: 'Did you ring him rather than me?'

'No, it's sheer serendipity,' Marcus says. 'We – that is the junior cataloguers – were all given the afternoon off.'

'Corruption at the core of the British Establishment,' Alexander wheezes.

'I'm not sure that Christie's is the core,' Marcus replies. 'Something more peripheral . . . the rind?'

'Have you been sacked?' I ask, aghast.

'No, of course not. Not me.'

'His pal, who's named after a skull.'

'Yorick?'

'It's a long story,' Marcus says.

'But one that bears repeating,' Alexander says, sinking into a bean bag. 'Tell all!'

'Yes, go on,' I add, needing time to adjust to my depleted brother.

'You know how works that fail to reach their reserve are kept in the warehouse for a good six months before they're put into another sale,' Marcus says hesitantly.

'If at first you don't succeed,' Alexander interjects.

'With so much stuff coming in every day, it's easy for things to get mislaid. Sometimes the owners themselves forget about them.'

'Did you see where I put my cufflinks, Primula, and what about the Rembrandt that used to hang in the butler's pantry?'

Although I have a thousand questions to ask my brother, I'm happy for Marcus to spin out his story, as the sparkle returns to Alexander's eyes.

'I doubt that anyone would forget about a Rembrandt, but it can – and does – happen with lesser masters, especially when the owner dies. We used to mock Yorick's fascination with the death notices in *The Times*. Now we know why. He was stealing paintings and selling them on.'

'But he never seemed short of money.'

'Oh sis, have all those years of Bible study taught you nothing?'

'The scam came to light last week when the lawyer for some estate or other enquired about a missing Reynolds.'

'Has he been arrested?' I ask, as Alexander coughs or laughs or both.

'What do you think! It's all been hushed up. The directors don't want people fretting that their treasures are unsafe. And the family knows Yorick's uncle or cousin or best friend from school. He was escorted off the premises, and his father's repaying the cash.'

'Alas, poor Yorick!' Alexander says.

'He's having a leaving do at the Punchbowl this evening.'

'What?'

'Just a few drinks,' Marcus says quickly, seeing my expression. 'Tristram felt that we couldn't let him slink away.'

'That's precisely what you should do.'

'Come on, sis. He was doing his bit for the free market.'

'I was in two minds about going, but he's been a good friend, and I don't want to look like a prig. Besides, it'll give you two a chance to catch up.'

'True,' I reply, unconvinced.

'I'll only stay for a couple of drinks, promise. I've already told Alexander that, whenever we have guests, we vacate the bedroom and sleep on the futon. It's good for my back.'

I love him so much. Why complain that he lacks principles, when his principles are simply more accommodating than mine? He kisses me goodbye, and though conscious of my brother's quizzical gaze, I prolong the embrace. He looks surprised, kisses me again and moves away, squeezing Alexander's shoulder, which makes him wince.

'Remember not to slam—' It's too late. I turn to Alexander by way of explanation. 'Our downstairs neighbour has neuralgia.'

'That's what comes of living with a hunk.'

'Stop it!'

'I'm sorry. You, of course, love him for his spiritual qualities alone.'

'Not alone. Anyway, you should approve. He's going through a crisis of faith.'

'That depends on what sort.' He hawks something viscous into his handkerchief.

'Are you sure I can't get you anything? A hot drink? Food? Tissues?'

'If you don't stop fussing, I shall book myself into a hotel.'

'How much are they paying you in Havana? Have you any idea of London prices?'

'Foiled again!' He laughs, with barely veiled desperation. 'You don't usually give up your bedroom to guests, do you?'

'We don't usually have guests.'

'Answer the question!'

'No.'

'You know what's wrong with me, don't you?'

'Yes.'

'It's not so obvious in Cuba, where people are less well-fed. Even Marcus, who's not the brightest crayon in the box—'

'That's not fair.'

'Life's not fair. He saw at once.'

'So what's the real reason Cesar hasn't come?'

'He's in hospital.'

'I'm so sorry. Is it serious?'

'Things could be better, but he's being well looked after.'

'It is a hospital and not an internment camp?'

'Why must you always think the worst?' His voice trails off as he fights for breath, and I realise that I must say nothing to upset him.

'It's just that I've read—'

'I'm sure you have. It's a military hospital in Santiago de Las Vegas, about twenty kilometres from Havana.'

'Why military?' I picture armed guards and barbed wire.

'In Cuba, the majority of cases – of AIDS cases (let's clear the air!) – aren't among gay men but soldiers back from serving in Angola and Mozambique. They've been infected by African sex workers.' I keep silent, as he displays none of the scorn that he did for rich Westerners who exploit poor Cubans, when it's the Cubans themselves who are doing the exploiting. 'So there isn't the stigma that's attached to the disease over here. Cesar wrote that he's been given good food and his own room, with air con and a colour TV. Most Cubans have never known such luxuries. There's a joke doing the rounds that people are trying to get sick so they can enjoy the perks.'

'Some joke!'

'Yes, gallows humour.'

'Why *wrote*? Didn't you see him before you left?'

'Visitors aren't allowed.'

'A colour TV's a high price to pay for the loss of freedom.'

'What you refuse to understand is that there's more than one kind of freedom. What about the freedom to be free of disease? At the station, if you turn up with something relatively minor but contagious – say, pinkeye – you're sent home with a slap on the wrist. The health – the wellbeing – of the community trumps that of the individual. Surely you approve? Isn't that what Christianity's all about?'

His coughing fit spares me the need to respond. I picture Cesar, doe-eyed, generous-hearted Cesar, rumba teacher and mojito maker extraordinaire, with an encyclopaedic knowledge of every Cuban telenovela of the past twenty years. When Alexander denounced the outlandish scenarios, simplistic resolutions and racist casting ('when did you last see a dark-skinned hero?'), Cesar replied quietly: 'I like them, they make me happy, and the guys are hot.' I trust that they still make him happy, as he watches on his government-issue set, without his boyfriend's constant carping. I wonder whether they had the chance to say goodbye or if Cesar were spirited away the moment his condition was diagnosed. Was that the trigger for Alexander's hastily rescheduled flight?

As I contemplate my brother, slumped awkwardly on the beanbag, too tired to move to a more comfortable seat and too proud to ask for help, a new series of questions arises. How much is the cough racking his body due to the chain-smoking passenger and how much to his damaged lungs? If he took off his T-shirt (which is far too flimsy for an English spring), would his chest be a welter of lesions? Has he been given any kind of prognosis, or is the uncertainty as alarming as the disease?

The cough turns into a full-blown spasm. I spring forward and prop him up, which he meekly accepts. 'Jet lag,' he adds, without conviction.

'Of course. Sit over here, while I change the sheets. You'll feel better after a good night's sleep.'

'Yes, Mummy.'

The word sends my mind racing in a new, more painful direction. If I can't bear to envisage a world without Alexander's prickly, provocative, loyal and honourable presence, how will my parents? Will they give him the unconditional love he deserves or treat him with a mixture of pity and disgust? I clasp his hand, as if to protect him from a rejection that is purely speculative.

'The sheets,' I say, striding out.

Four

I am the cynosure of the department. CR4, who professed himself to be a great admirer of Seward Wemlock, has not only approved my feature on the Tapley paintings but suggested that I both produce and present it. Apart from recording in the church, where the acoustics are likely to call for an experienced sound technician, I shall be responsible for the entire programme. The cynic in me suspects it to be a cost-cutting measure. Nevertheless, the prospect is as exhilarating as it is daunting.

I'll be covering the project over the course of a year, from tomorrow, when the St Peter's PCC meets to rule on Seward's designs, to the dedication service, which Father, who takes the faculty for granted, has pencilled in his diary for 19 June 1988. It's a Herculean task, but Marcus, who credits Seward with the stamina as well as the skill of the Renaissance masters, insists that he is equal to it. His assurance is all the more welcome, given Seward's dismissal of his proposed biography. When Father broached the subject on his behalf, during a recent visit to Wemlock Hall, Seward told him that he'd 'rather eat my own faeces'. The euphemism may have been Father's.

The rejection dispirited Marcus, who now prefers to observe the project from afar. I give him a quick call before taking the three o'clock train to Chester, where, with my father debating Disestablishment in Oxford, I'm due to have dinner with my mother and brother. After resisting my request that he visit our parents on his first weekend back, Alexander has spent most of the past two months with them. His health has declined alarmingly. 'This country always did for me,' he declared, with a hint of self-mockery and a rasping cough. It's as though he surrendered to the virus as soon as he was safely home. For all his protests that the military hospital would have been less draconian, he's put himself in Mother's hands, just as he did when we were children and illness was the surest way to gain her attention.

This was not the homecoming that our parents were expecting. To their credit, no word of recrimination has passed their lips, but then neither has the word 'AIDS'. If Alexander, the prophet of plain speaking, sanctions their subterfuge, who am I to object? Each has adopted a characteristic strategy for combating his illness: Father presenting it as an opportunity for prayer and repentance, reflection and transformation; Mother proclaiming the benefits of sleep, fresh air and nutritious food. Despite the national panic over infection, she has taken no additional sanitary measures, although her *cleanliness-is-next-to-godliness* creed has always entailed the rigorous application of bleach. Only once has her mask slipped, when she slapped away my hand, as I reached for a biscuit that Alexander had left half-eaten. 'You've had two already!' she said. But her eyes betrayed a deeper concern than my greed.

I arrive to find Alexander obeying the *fresh air* edict, lounging on a deckchair in the garden. He looks no worse – maybe even a little better – than he did ten days ago, but I'm wary of staring after his offer to buy me a camera.

'Hey there, little sis!' he says, shading his eyes against the watery sun.

'Any good?' I ask, pointing to the book lying face down on the grass.

'Who knows? I've not turned a page all afternoon. I'm becoming one with nature.'

'Now you're really scaring me.'

'I'd forgotten how much I loved this garden.'

'Excuse me! Who was it railed against its "manicured tweeness" when we had to show round visitors on Open Sunday?'

'I was fifteen years old. Half my classmates came to torment me.'

'You got off lightly. Try dressing up as an Anglo-Saxon nun and leading a goose from Eastgate to Northgate, while the cathedral choir sang canticles!'

'You didn't! I would have remembered.'

'I think you'd escaped to London by then.'

'Why a goose?'

'As in St Werburgh, our patron saint, who's said to have resurrected one after it had been cooked and eaten.'

'I always knew that Christians were unhinged but . . .'

'Father had the bright idea of commemorating the miracle. No matter that her feast day falls in February and, on both occasions, it poured! No matter that the goose honked and a group of louts wolf-whistled! No matter that one joker asked if he could have a gander! Don't laugh!'

'I'm wheezing.'

'I'm sorry. I haven't asked you how you are.'

'I'm fine. Don't fuss! This is doing me a power of good. Tell me more.'

'That's it. After two years, even I rebelled. Father couldn't understand why.'

'Sensitivity has never been his strong suit.'

'He does his best.'

'Come on! Remember the thalidomide boy he told to take his hands out of his pockets?'

'He's short-sighted.'

'Yes, and not just optically. Yet he's revered as some sort of higher being. All the bowing and scraping and kissing his ring! Then on Sundays, hundreds – make that, thousands – of worshippers across the diocese pray for St John, our bishop. Give it up, man! You're already in God's good books. Other people need it more.'

I'm intrigued to know whether his rebuke springs from a new-found respect for the power of prayer, but he closes his eyes, curtailing the conversation. I go indoors, returning an hour later to summon him for dinner, where my appetite is ruined and his not improved by Mother's repeated exhortations that he eat more.

In the morning, we window-shop in the Rows, of which Alexander is no more admiring now than in our youth. The chance to disparage their sham medievalism invigorates him, and only the unease registered by passers-by reminds me that he is seriously ill. After lunch and an hour's rest in the garden, I borrow Father's Rover and drive to Tapley, where I'm meeting Seward Wemlock for a tour of the church. I leave in good time and, despite the clanking and rumbling of the ancient engine, arrive with half an hour to spare.

Eager to explore, I open the lychgate, which clatters loudly in the silence, and stroll through the churchyard. The shimmering tower and half-buried graves in the hillocky turf create an air of deep tranquillity. Stepping superstitiously off the path, I translate the mossy inscriptions on the cracked stones into the village Hampdens, mute Miltons and guiltless Cromwells from my *Child's Book of Verse*. Spotting the poignant epitaph on a table tomb, SACRED TO THE MEMORY OF CRISPIN WAINWRIGHT, BELOVED OF FLORENCE, HIS DISCONSOLATE RELICT, AND THOMAS, THE SON HE NEVER KNEW, I ruminate first on the relict, whose fate is encapsulated in the word (no chance there of a modifying *Merry*), and then on the fatherless son.

Anxious not to keep Seward waiting, I walk to the church, pausing only to study two gryphon-like gargoyles on the guttering and a blocked Norman doorway. Passing the tower, I see from the diamond-shaped clocks that I'm still five minutes early, so I crane my neck to view the spire.

'Penny for them!'

I start, as Seward emerges from the porch, the sunlight haloing his hair. For a moment – inexplicably – I think of Mary Magdalene mistaking the risen Christ for a gardener. 'I was just examining the tower.'

'Impressive, isn't it? One of the few bits of the original church that my ancestors didn't demolish. They built things to last in the fifteenth century. It's survived two lightning strikes since the War. Though the spire's Victorian.'

'That figures.'

'We have a peal of six bells. The two oldest date from the Restoration. St Peter's has a proud tradition of ringing, often passed down from father to son—'

'Not daughter?'

'Not as yet. The current tower captain, the village postman, has just brought his teenage son into the band.' He looks at me closely. 'I don't see any tape recorder.'

'It's in the car. I'm hoping that for now you'll give me a sense of where the paintings are to be placed. I'll start recording at the PCC.'

'Understood. Shall we go inside?'

We enter the porch where, to my surprise, he dips his fingers in the holy water stoup and makes the sign of the cross.

'I don't know how much you know about Gothic architecture,' he says, holding open the church door.

'More than you might suppose. It's one of my father's passions. I knew my Perp from my Dec almost before my left from my right.'

'Good for you, my dear. As you see, St Peter's is predominantly Perp, built in the late fourteenth and early fifteenth centuries. It suffered minor damage during the Reformation and far worse during the Civil War. Fairfax's troops were billeted here before the Battle of Nantwich. They systematically smashed all the stained glass in the aisle and clerestory windows – and, though I blush to admit it, the extra light will be a blessing for me. It's a toss-up as to whether they were bigger vandals than my great-grandfather, Hereward. During his so-called improvements in the 1860s, he rebuilt the nave and removed the box pews, extended the chancel and widened the north aisle. Just about the only parts he left untouched were the tower and the two chancel chapels, the Lady Chapel to your left and the Wemlock chapel to your right.'

'You actually have a family chapel! When you mentioned it at lunch, I assumed it was a metaphor.'

'No, it's all too real. Though I suppose it might be a metaphor for the feudal attitudes that survived well into my youth. The rich man in his chapel; the poor man in the nave. At least the War wiped that out. Would you care to look inside?'

'Absolutely.'

We step up to the chancel, stopping beside an exquisitely carved parclose with a canopy of cherubs.

'As a boy, I used to cringe with embarrassment when we took our seats on a Sunday, sometimes arriving so late that we collided with the choir. My Great-Aunt Beatrice, whose eccentricities were spuriously imputed to a fall from her pram rather than anything in the Wemlock genes, would wave to the congregation as if she were Queen Mary, whom half the time she thought she was. This elicited ridicule and resentment in equal measure.' He shakes his head as though to dislodge the memory.

'We really don't need to go inside if—'

'Nonsense. I'm no longer six years old.'

We pass through the parclose and, although it may be fanciful, the air feels damper than it did in the body of the church. He switches on a dim light, revealing a large double tomb and a score of memorial plaques. I approach the tomb, which is that of the first Lord and Lady Wemlock, loyal supporters of Henry VII, whose deaths *of the sweating sickness* in 1491 allowed them little time to enjoy their enno-blement. Conscious of Seward's discomfort, I glance at the wall of plaques, noting only a simple bronze tablet eulogising the virtues of Ophelia Wemlock, who drowned in the lake on the eve of her wedding. The name alone is enough to cast doubt on the *cruel mishap* that the epitaph relates.

'You must stay as long as you like, but I'm finding it hard to breathe,' Seward says, retreating to the chancel. I follow to find him bent double, his hands on his thighs like a winded sprinter.

'Are you all right? It was very humid in there.'

'It's nothing. Let's take a pew.' He leads me into the choir stalls. 'That's better. What were we . . .? Ah yes. I'm profoundly grateful to your father for proposing the decorative scheme. Of course, I'm delighted it's for St Peter's but, most of all, that it gives me the chance to express my faith openly, not in a gallery but in a church.'

Safely outside the chapel but still close to his past, I ask about the origin of his faith. 'Were your parents religious?'

'Not to speak of. My father regarded his role as patron of the living much as he did that of chairman of the bench. My mother enjoyed the sentimental side of Christmas. Nanny oversaw our bedtime prayers, ignoring the chafing of the nursery floor on our knees. It was a childhood with little affection, but I comforted myself with the thought that there was one person who truly loved me: Jesus. Then when I was eight, I was given proof of that in the most extraor-dinary – the most miraculous – way.' He looks at me fixedly. 'I feel that I can tell you, but you must understand, my dear, that this isn't for public consumption.'

'Yes, of course,' I reply, wondering whether 'public' includes Marcus.

'We lived in Richmond until I was ten, when we moved to the Hall. Before then, we came here for regular holidays, which I dreaded on account of my grandfather. He favoured Hereward, who would one day inherit, forever giving him tips such as "There are only two requirements of a rector: that he supports field sports and delivers a sermon in under ten minutes." He abhorred my grandmother, despised my father, and affected not to remember my mother's name. He hated the fact that I was small, which he equated with effeminacy, and ruled that I needed to be toughened up, so as to hold my own against bullies – although the greatest bully I've ever encountered was him. One afternoon, with no one about but the servants, he took – or rather dragged – me up to the roof and ordered me to walk around the parapet. He knew that I was terrified of heights. "Go on, boy! What are you waiting for? You'll be fine so long as you don't look down."'

'He should have been certified.'

'He was, two years later. But that's another story.'

'What did you do?'

'I decided to jump. I told myself I'd be dead by the time I reached the ground and it would all be over. The next moment, I felt an overwhelming strength . . . a warmth . . . a radiance beside me. I can't put it into words; I can't put it into paint, however hard I've tried. Even fifty years on, I find it ineffably moving. It was Christ, who took hold of my hand . . . but not just of my hand, of my entire being. "Follow me," He said, and I understood Him perfectly, although He wasn't speaking English. I felt totally secure as I trotted around the parapet. When I got back to my grandfather, he was green. He pressed a half-crown in my palm and told me that what had happened must remain our secret. For a moment I fancied that he'd seen Christ too, but the only thing in his eyes was fear. I knew then that Christ had saved me. It's the one mystical experience of my life.'

He notices the look of wonder on my face and changes his tone.

'At least the only one that I can't attribute to drugs or gonorrhoea. Come on!' he adds, as if afraid of having disclosed too much. 'You wanted to see where the paintings were to go. We're wasting time.' He grabs my arm and steers me into the transept. 'The whole church will be an image of paradise.' He gestures to the back of the nave. 'On the west wall, conveniently bare except for those hymnbook stands, will be Adam and Eve in Eden.'

'Before or after the Fall?'

'Neither. The only Fall I acknowledge wasn't initiated by them but imposed on them by prurient scribes and exegetists.'

'How do you plan to convey that?'

'You'll see from the drawing. I don't want to intellectualise.' I trust that he'll be more forthcoming with the PCC. Patron or not, he needs them to endorse the scheme. 'In each of the spandrels above the arcade, an angel will be leading a villager to Heaven.'

'The gathering of the faithful?'

'The gathering of everyone, faithful or not. If there were an infamous Tapley axe-murderer – don't worry, there isn't – he'd be my first choice for inclusion.'

'Are you saying that you don't believe in Hell?'

'How can I when I believe in God? My apologies to Lennon – or was it McCartney? – but "Everyone was saved".' He looks at me as intently as if I were sitting for him. 'Have I shocked you?'

'Not a bit. You've made me think. I wish I had your certitude. But surely there are some crimes that even God is unable to forgive?'

'You mean gas chambers and gulags?'

'For a start. But also individual ones, like serial killings and child abuse.'

He ponders the question for longer than I expect. '*Tout comprendre, c'est tout pardonner* is to me the essence of Christianity – more so even than *Love God and love your neighbour as yourself.* And if it's true for us, how much more so must it be for an all-comprehending God? One of the books that has spoken to me most powerfully over the years is St John's *Visible, Invisible, Indivisible.*'

'Really? Do tell him. He'll be thrilled.'

'I have done. Remember how he defines the Trinity as Love, Creativity and Moral Responsibility? Well I believe that it's the loving, creative and moral aspects of each and every one of us that will be reunited with God. "What? Even Hitler?" my elder daughter asked – she's *doing* the Nazis at school. I told her that even Hitler had a loving side, if only in his affection for his dog, and a creative side, in that he was a frustrated artist, which, of course, she used against me . . . although I admit that I'd find it hard to credit him with a moral side. We accept that matter can be neither created nor destroyed. The same applies to spirit.'

'It's a very consoling thought.'

'More importantly, it's the truth.' He turns back towards the chancel and I follow his gaze. 'Above the arch will be the figure of Christ, arms open to welcome the eight souls to Heaven and the congregation into the sanctuary . . . That's another of my bugbears. I appointed Vincent on your father's say-so and, while I'd never seek to interfere, I deplore his churchmanship. He spends half the service facing the altar as if engaged in a cosy chat with God, to which the rest of us are incidental, if not downright intrusive. You might call it masturbatory—'

'I might not!'

'I've made it my life's work – oh dear, that sounds pompous – to tear down barriers. And here they are: going up in my own backyard.'

I need time to reflect on his remarks, which both stimulate and disturb me, and readily agree when he suggests that we head to the church hall to inspect his drawings, on display prior to the PCC meeting. I propose to fetch my Uher and meet him there, but he insists on accompanying me to the car and carrying the machine.

The hall door is opened by a plump young woman with a pretty face and shy manner. 'My lord,' she says, stepping aside as Seward leads me into a fusty, nondescript room. An assortment of chairs is set out in front of a low stage, hung with black drapes and furnished with a battered upright piano, opposite which are three screens pinned with what I take to be the drawings.

'Clarissa, may I introduce Shirley Redwood, our new parish secretary?'

'Pleased to meet you,' I say, smiling at Shirley who, regarding me suspiciously, tucks her hands in the pockets of her tightly buttoned cardigan and stretches it over her thighs.

'I'm trying to persuade Shirley to pose for me.'

'Who'd want to look at me?' she asks, twisting her arms and pockets across her stomach.

'When I've had my way with you, you'll be the toast of Tapley,' he replies, in a voice at once seductive and sinister. 'But Shirley has eyes for only one man. Isn't that right?'

'I don't know what you mean,' she says, reddening.

'Our good rector.'

'That's a wicked lie!' she says, although her pursed lips and puckered brow betray her. 'I can't stand here all day talking drivel. I've got work to do.' She sniffs and sidles out.

'You shouldn't tease her.'

'I know.' He raps himself on the knuckles. 'But it's irresistible. Vincent told me himself that, whenever he looks up from his desk, he sees her staring dewy-eyed at him.'

'No one can be that naive!'

'This is Tapley.'

'Let's hope some nice young man steps in and sweeps her off her feet.'

I set up the tape and microphone and follow Seward to the screens, on each of which is a large charcoal drawing, along with several smaller sketches. The first, for one of the spandrels, is of an angel raising an elderly man to Heaven. The sketches are of additional figures, both male and female.

'I intend to use eight representative villagers as models.'

'Won't that provoke jealousy?'

'Given all the stories circulating about me, I suspect that the problem will be finding enough people to pose . . . I'd rather you didn't use that.'

'Of course,' I say, gritting my teeth.

We turn to the second screen, featuring the design for the chancel arch, of a youthful Christ between an equally youthful couple, whom I take to be St John and the Virgin but who, he explains, are Adam and Eve.

'Are you bent on courting controversy?'

'Not at all, although it seems to seek me out. See, I have Scripture on my side.' He points to a sketch of a banner with a verse from St John's Gospel: *And I, if I be lifted up from the earth, will draw all peoples to Myself.*

I read it out for the benefit of the listeners. 'Will you be putting the wording under the figures?'

'Under or over. I've yet to decide. Shall we move on?'

We stand before the third screen, with by far the most intricate drawing. A fresh-faced Adam and Eve cling to each other in front of a luxuriant tree, their naked bodies positioned for maximum discretion. Behind them, wolves and lambs cavort on a carpet of wild flowers. In the background, a heavily bearded man sits, writing on a parchment scroll, out of which a serpent is sliding. Beneath are detailed sketches of fruit-laden branches, the scroll, and the serpent. I describe the elements of the drawing but need Seward to elucidate them, as much for myself as for the listeners.

'Adam and Eve look very young. Is that deliberate, or is it just an effect of the sketch?'

'Definitely deliberate. It may be unfashionable in a post-Freudian world, but I still see the young as innocent.'

'And the man holding the quill: is he Moses?'

'That depends on whether you think that Moses wrote Genesis.'

'So, the serpent is introduced by the scribe rather than intrinsic to the story?'

'I hope that everyone who views the finished painting will be as discerning as you, my dear. In eating the fruit, Adam and Eve didn't engender a universal Fall. They were the scapegoats – if you like, the *fall guys* – for subsequent sinners. Remember what it says in Genesis. The couple ate of the tree of the knowledge of good and evil and *knew that they were naked*. How? Why? Is nakedness inherently evil? Little children feel no shame about being naked. It's adults who instil it in them when they make them wear pants. Likewise, the biblical writers instilled their own sense of shame into Adam and Eve when they made them wear fig leaves. That shame has been passed down through the centuries to us.'

'Critics might accuse you of promoting shamelessness.'

'They might,' he replies, with a mock bow, which is wasted on the microphone. 'But not guiltlessness.' His features harden. 'Shame is learnt; guilt is innate.'

'Are they mutually exclusive?'

'No, not necessarily, although they're far too often confused. And by no one more than St Augustine. Having abandoned the mother of his son in order to marry a ten-year-old heiress, he became the prime proponent of genital depravity. He turned his own guilt into universal shame or, as it's commonly known, Original Sin.'

'So, do you reject the concept of the Fall?' I ask, mindful that the listeners were not privy to his earlier comments in the church.

'I reject the Fall, but how can I reject the concept when it's everywhere around us?' He speaks directly into the microphone, as if determined that not a single word should be lost. 'I don't believe that the Fall damned mankind, but I do believe that the concept of the Fall irreparably damaged it.'

'That's a serious charge.'

'Just look at the evidence. It implanted the notion that we come closest to God by denying the flesh. Even as a boy, I failed to understand why, having given us bodies, He should wish us to mortify them. Now I'd go further: if sexual shame is at the heart of the Original Sin that separates us from God, then surely to make love without shame is to find our way back to Him?'

For a painter, he makes an impressive theologian. Who'd have thought that I would find his words as compelling as his work? They bear the stamp both of deep thought and hard-won experience. I'm keen to question him further, but the church clock strikes six, and Shirley emerges from her office so promptly that I half-expect her to cry *Cuckoo*. She assures us that the meeting will start soon, since Father Vincent demands strict punctuality. Within minutes, the council members, eight women and two men, enter the hall. They greet one another warmly, Seward deferentially, and me with reserve. As they talk among themselves, Seward, evincing a previously hidden hauteur, mutters about having to 'pander to people who regard a green Chinese Girl as art'.

Vincent flings open the door. Shirley, eyes sparkling, hurries towards him, but he brushes her aside like an importunate child. Fawning as ever, he treats Seward to a tortuous explanation for his delay, which further holds up proceedings. 'Ready when you are, Ms de Mille,' he says, turning to me with a phrase that sounds practised. 'Is that all the equipment you've brought?' he adds, gazing at the Uher as if he'd envisaged an outside broadcast vehicle.

'It does the trick. As I explained on the phone, I'll record the full discussion, although I doubt that more than a couple of minutes will make it into the final cut.'

'Whatever . . . whatever. They've all been primed. Shall we take our seats, ladies and gentlemen?' He calls to the members who, apart from one old lady, busily knitting, are milling around the screens. 'Come along now, you've had three days to appraise the designs!' They move to the chairs, although, rather than arranging them into a companionable circle, they fill up the first two rows facing the stage. 'Are we all here?'

'We're missing Dickon.'

'And Daisy Quantock.'

Vincent groans. 'Our new headmistress, the cross I have to bear,' he whispers conspiratorially. 'If that's not impious.'

As if on cue, a woman whom I take to be Daisy sweeps in. Her auburn hair stands out against the prevailing pewter, as does her jade-green suit from the mouse-coloured anoraks, gilets and tweeds.

'Oh dear, am I late?' she asks, disingenuously. 'Roland Broady bit Miss Perrin so I kept him behind after school.'

'Indeed,' Vincent replies, as if his main regret were Roland's choice of victim. 'Now that our headmistress has seen fit to join us, we won't wait for Dickon.' He conducts Seward and myself to two chairs on his right. Then, asking us all to stand, he opens the meeting with a prayer.

He visibly relaxes, as he turns from God to Seward. 'For today's meeting, I trust that you'll forgive me if I ask Miss Redwood to postpone reading the minutes until later, so as not to impose on our guests. Lord Wemlock needs no introduction to anyone in this village or, for that matter, to art lovers throughout the world.'

'Not to mention, readers of the *Daily Mail*,' Seward says, to an awkward silence.

'No, indeed,' Vincent says, with a studied laugh. 'Clarissa Phipps, the daughter of our own Bishop St John, has come from the BBC to make a programme about the decoration—'

'Provided we approve it,' Daisy interjects.

'That goes without saying.'

'And the Diocesan Advisory Committee recommends the granting of the faculty.'

'That too.'

'It's a pleasure to be here. Thank you so much for inviting me.' I stare out on a sea of indifference. 'If you'll allow me to take a quick sound check...' I switch on the tape. 'I should just say, to assuage any fears, that no one will be identified.'

'Some of us are quite happy to stand up and be counted,' Daisy says tartly, and I wonder what I have done to offend her.

'The Wemlock family has served St Peter's for more than four centuries, but never before has one of them offered such personal support. Lord Wemlock is an artist of international repute.' I sense

Seward's shoulders tense, although I can't tell whether it's from exasperation or embarrassment. 'The decoration . . . the proposed decoration' – Vincent smiles waspishly at Daisy – 'will not only greatly enhance our worship but will put Tapley on the map.'

The door bangs open and I take the chance to play back a few seconds of the tape, which has recorded perfectly. A bald, snub-nosed man lurches in. 'I'm sorry, Father,' he says, with a thick Cheshire burr, before turning to Seward and proving, to my amazement, that *tugging one's forelock* is no mere figure of speech. 'I got stuck in Meadow Lane behind Will Prentice, who was taking his cows for milking.'

'No harm done, Dickon,' Seward says.

'The rector was just telling us that Lord Wemlock's paintings would put Tapley on the map,' Daisy says.

'Isn't it on the map already?' Dickon asks, in puzzlement. 'A mile and a half off Burland and three mile off Nantwich.'

At the sound of a snigger, Daisy looks contrite and pats the chair beside her. 'Come and sit here, Dickon.'

'Right then, to return to our muttons!' Vincent says, watching Dickon shuffle to his seat. 'Or, in Dickon's case, should that be cows?' His joke falls as flat as Seward's. 'We've discussed the scheme exten- sively over the past few weeks and I, for one, rejoice at the drawings Lord Wemlock has provided. He has most graciously agreed to join us this evening to answer any questions – even if, to my mind, the outcome isn't in doubt.'

A long silence follows, during which Seward taps a tattoo on his chair, until I point to the tape recorder. Finally, a man with a high forehead clears his throat.

'My lord,' he says.

'Please, I'm Seward when I paint.'

'Indeed, yes . . . yes, indeed. These drawings are all very well – very well indeed – on paper, but who's to say that they'll look the same on the walls? The begonias I planted in March have come up a completely different colour from the catalogue.'

'That must be very frustrating. But in this case, the man who produced the catalogue will also be tending the bulbs.'

'What about the disruption?' asks a woman with a pronounced goitre. 'Where will we worship while you're at work? We've all seen *The Agony and the Ecstasy.*'

'We've been into this,' Vincent interjects, but Seward holds up his hand to silence him.

'I'm not Michelangelo, more's the pity! So I shan't be painting directly on the walls, but rather on canvases that will be fixed in place.'

'I'm no art expert,' Daisy says smugly, 'but I know my Bible. In your design for the chancel arch, is that Christ standing between the Virgin and saint?'

'It is indeed,' he replies, glossing over the secondary figures.

'I couldn't be certain, without a beard.'

'I'm no biblical expert,' he says wickedly. 'It's true that most first-century Jews would have been bearded, but I've taken my inspiration from the earliest Christian images, in the Roman catacombs.'

Daisy looks unconvinced, but then a smooth-cheeked Christ is a challenge to those who see Him more as judge than advocate.

'I mustn't monopolise the floor. I'm sure that the rest of you have equally strong misgivings.' Daisy peers round, but no one stirs. 'Very well then, let me ask about Eden. Firstly, your serpent is separated from the sinful couple. If he's tempting anyone, it's the scribe with the scroll.'

'Yes, that's a neat way of putting it.'

'Putting what?'

'The sin, if that's what you wish to call it, is in the interpretation of the act, rather than the act itself.'

'That's in blatant contradiction of Scripture. Should Adam and Eve not be punished for their disobedience?'

'Possibly, but a short sharp punishment, not one with cataclysmic repercussions until the end of time. It's hard to make out from the sketch, but the forbidden fruit is a quince. I don't need to remind anyone here that the actual fruit is never specified.' From their baffled expressions, it appears that he does. 'So I've followed the scholarly consensus that it was a quince. A taste of its tart flesh would be punishment enough.'

He parries a question from the woman with the goitre about Adam and Eve's youthful looks with a blithe 'the world was young', and a rebuke from the begonia planter that 'quinces and meadow flowers wouldn't be in season at the same time', with an imperious 'in paradise, all seasons are one'.

Vincent, sensing his growing impatience, draws the discussion to a close. 'Thank you, Lord Wemlock, for giving us such cogent answers. Now we must let you escape, while we conclude our deliberations.'

Seward scrambles to his feet. 'If I were my grandfather,' he says, 'this is the moment when I'd point out that the beer is on me in the Wem. But things are done differently these days, so I'll slip away and trust you to reach the right decision.' Turning to me, he murmurs: 'Will you come to the pub and bring me news?'

'Can't you ask Vincent? I have to drive back to Chester.'

'Just five minutes. Put me out of my misery.'

'In that case . . .'

Nodding briskly to left and right, he goes out, whereupon the tension eases, that is until Daisy starts to speak.

'If he thinks he can bribe us with beer . . .'

'It was a joke, Mrs Quantock,' Vincent says, scarcely veiling his disdain.

'Or was it a double bluff? Never mind. I hope that everyone took note of what he said – all that blather about "the interpretation of the act" and quinces . . . did you know that you had an Adam's quince, Dickon?'

He looks alarmed.

'Don't worry, you don't! You may call it artistic licence, Rector. I call it unchristian.'

'Unorthodox I grant, but—'

'I'm well aware that, in the Middle Ages, church paintings were "the Poor Man's Bible". These days it will just be another distraction from God's word.'

'You've raised your objections, and I'm sure that Shirley has minuted them.'

'Oh yes, Father.' She holds up her pad. 'Mrs Quantock doesn't want to return to the Middle Ages.'

I follow Vincent's weary glance at the heavens.

'I've no wish to sound a sour note,' a soft-spoken woman says.

'But between ourselves' – she gazes nervously at the tape recorder – 'are we sure that Lord Wemlock is the right man for the job? I have nothing against his paintings. But for the rest . . . there's been so much talk. His wife or rather not his wife . . . Then there's his sister-in-law. My neighbour's niece helps out with the laundry at the Hall. I'm not one to gossip—'

'Then don't!' Daisy interjects, to my surprise. 'This village is far too prone to tittle-tattle.'

'But he gets his name in the papers,' the woman with the goitre says. 'We all know it broke his father's heart.'

'Artists don't always lead the exemplary lives of members of the WI,' Vincent says acidly. 'I know for a fact that Lord Wemlock is an admirer of Blake, whose great hymn you sing at every meeting. Yet, given Blake and his wife's predilection for reciting *Paradise Lost* in the nude, I'd have thought twice before paying them a pastoral visit . . . Time's moving on. Shall we take a vote?'

'Pardon me, I must just . . .' Dickon stands irresolutely, before making for a door marked WC.

'Can't it wait, Dickon?' Vincent asks.

'Best not. You go ahead. These things can't be rushed.' He disappears through the door.

'Every time we come to a vote, it's the same story,' Vincent says to me. 'Very well. We'll repeat it if there's a tie.'

The safeguard proves to be unnecessary, since there's a clear majority in favour of the scheme, with only Daisy and the woman with the goitre voting against it. A beaming Vincent declares that he will submit a proposal to the DAC.

'Take it from me, you'll live to regret it,' Daisy says. 'It'll bring nothing but trouble.'

'Thank you, Mrs Quantock, your reservations have been noted. Now, to the rest of the agenda . . .'

'Which is my cue to leave,' I say, switching off the tape and picking up the machine. 'I'd like to thank you all once more for allowing me to sit in on your deliberations. I'll be back when the faculty is granted.'

'If the faculty is granted,' Daisy says dourly, as I walk out.

'Who's she again?' the elderly knitter asks, only to be loudly shushed by her neighbour.

I make my way to the car, where I deposit the Uher, and then on to the pub. Ducking to avoid a low beam, I take in the polished brasses, *Wanted for Highway Robbery* posters, and exclusively male clientele. Seward breaks off his conversation with the barmaid and heads towards me.

'So what's the verdict?'

'Seven to two in favour.'

'Who were the dissenters? I want names. Their rents will be raised, tenancies revoked. They'll be turfed out of their tied cottages.'

'No, you can't!'

'What sort of monster do you think I am?'

I feel myself blush.

'You're so susceptible,' he says.

'I'm sorry.'

'Don't be! It's one of your most – one of your many – attractive qualities.'

'That's enough!'

'Let me buy you dinner to celebrate.'

'What's on the menu? Pork scratchings?'

'Not here. There's a halfway-decent restaurant in Nantwich.'

He gives me a beguiling smile. I realise with dismay that I'm starting to succumb.

'I've told you already; I have to get back. My train leaves at the crack of dawn. Besides,' I add archly, 'you have two women waiting for you at home.'

'Four.'

'Four?'

'You're forgetting my daughters.'

'Yes, of course,' I reply, feeling foolish. 'Goodbye then. I'll come again after the DAC meeting.'

'You've disappointed me.'

'What? How?'

'You've ignored the advice I gave you. Take risks!'

Five

'We are not pregnant,' I say firmly to Marcus, 'I am.'

The last thing I want is to dampen his enthusiasm, but he's not the one with the permanent headache. He's not the one whose nipples are tender and stomach tight. He's not the one forever worrying about whether there's a loo within reach. Yesterday, I was forced to fake a hangover during a departmental meeting. The drone of the Canon's voice, combined with a flickering fluorescent light and the metallic taste in my mouth, made me so queasy that I fled the room. I returned to explain to my startled colleagues that I'd spent the evening at a friend's birthday party, preferring them to deplore my youthful intemperance than to discover the truth.

Marcus and I have agreed that, until the end of the first trimester, we'll tell no one, including our parents, with the exception of Alexander: not, I insist, for fear that he won't be around to make his niece or nephew's acquaintance, but to lift his spirits. For the past two weeks, he's been the first and only AIDS patient in the Countess of Chester hospital. Given the barrier nursing and the grim sideward, I suspect that the Santiago sanatorium would have been a cheerier option. Mother visits every day, never staying longer than fifteen minutes, so as 'not to tire him' and, by his account, keeps up a relentless stream of chatter. Father visits, albeit less frequently; but having promised to avoid anything contentious, he finds that, after the standard health, food and comfort enquiries, he has nothing to say.

'I close my eyes after five minutes, as a kindness to us both,' Alexander tells me.

I drive up to visit at the weekends. When I kiss him, his eyes fill with tears and he explains that I'm the first person to touch him, without a protective layer of latex, since he was admitted. In a voice that would once have rung with rancour but is now slurred, he relates how, even masked and gloved, the nurses shun him. Rather than the constant medical hubbub he was expecting, he feels as if he is the only patient left behind after a fire.

I sponge the sweat oozing off him, not shrinking from his groin. 'Did we ever play doctors and nurses?' he asks, more, I fancy, to spare my blushes than his own.

'I should hope not. You're five years older.'

'Just as well.'

Unprepared for the cluster of bulbous lesions on his thighs, I move to moisten the cloth at the basin where, with my back towards him, I silently heave, forgetting my reflection in the mirror.

'Is anything wrong?'

'Morning sickness,' I reply, grateful for the silver lining.

'Snap!' he says. Then with a veteran's sang-froid, he rattles off a string of ailments, illustrating why AIDS is a syndrome, not a disease. He has thrush, which I'd thought unique to women, although his is in the throat, making it hard for him to swallow, even without the cryptosporidiosis that makes him gag at the sight of food. He has cytomegalovirus in his eyes, which has so far affected his reading but will ultimately render him blind; and toxoplasmosis in his brain, which has so far caused violent headaches but will ultimately lead to dementia – although he assures me that the prospect doesn't alarm him, since either TB or pneumonia will have finished him off first. He has herpes, shingles and chronic diarrhoea. 'But the saving grace, my final gift to Mother, is that the Kaposi's sarcoma, which triggered your morning sickness, is so far confined to my legs.'

To my surprise, he has shown a keen interest in the preparations for my wedding, which we've brought forward to 21 August. He's thrilled that his illness has provided a pretext for the switch since, while chary of announcing the pregnancy, I've said from the start that, with Father presiding, I want Alexander to walk me down the aisle, which, with a reduced congregation, will now take place in the Lady Chapel. Watching him totter from his bed to the loo, I fear that, even in five weeks' time, the effort will be too great. Although, were we to wait until the autumn, it would surely be impossible.

'I assume that you won't be marrying in white,' he says wryly.

'With all the trimmings,' I reply.

Given his predictable contempt for the institution of marriage ('and who wants to live in an institution?'), I'm at a loss as to why he's so eager for mine. His stock answer is that, as my older brother, he has a responsibility to see me settled. He even suggested that my two-year engagement sprang from doubts about Marcus, which I swore couldn't have been further from the truth.

'Yes, there are times when he can be offhand or pompous – usually, after a client dinner – but there are a hundred others when he's sensitive, generous, funny, charming and gloriously romantic. Who else would have taken Valentine's Day off work to cook an entirely pink dinner: chilled beet soup, poached salmon and raspberry fool, washed down with pink champagne? In fact, the soup was more puce than pink, but it passed.'

'Hmmm,' he says, spitting phlegm into a tissue. 'Don't get me wrong, I like Marcus. If fit and fleshy's your bag, you could do worse. Trouble is you've no one to compare him with.' Once again, I regret my rashness in trusting him with my most intimate secrets. 'That doesn't have to be a problem. In my experience, good sex is either with someone you know very well or barely at all. It's the in-betweens who disappoint.'

'I'll bear that in mind.'

'I'm not suggesting orgies. But as I see it, morality lies in how we treat our partners, rather than how many we have.'

'Or even sticking to one?'

'You're not going all *Wages of Sin* on me, are you? Talk about hitting a man when he's down!'

His mock outrage sparks a coughing fit. I pour him a glass of water, which he sips before slumping on the pillow.

'You'll exhaust yourself. We'll speak later.'

'Have a heart, sis! My brain's all that's left to exercise. And who knows how long till the parasites gnaw it away?'

'Don't!'

'I know what you're thinking.'

'I doubt it,' I reply, banishing the image of Seward's Great-Aunt Beatrice.

241

'He's only thirty years old; he could have achieved so much. But I don't regard my life as wasted. Of course I wish that I hadn't contracted the virus. But I was never heading for a pipe-and-slippers old age, bouncing grandchildren on my knee. Though I admit a couple of nephews and nieces would have been nice.' He grins and immediately winces. 'My five years in Cuba have brought me more happiness than I ever believed possible.'

'I'm very glad.'

'Ever since I was in my teens, I've been searching for somewhere I could find myself . . . where I could be myself. At first I thought it was San Francisco, but that was an illusion – a false Eden, if you like. So I could buy my dill and my dildo at the same store in the Castro! Great! So I could find a club catering to the most rarefied fantasy or fetish! Doubly great! But it was soulless – and I'm not talking about God.'

He rasps and points to the glass of water, which I hand him.

'Tell me another time. You need to rest,' I say, as he replaces the glass on the locker, so feebly that it almost falls.

'What? Just when we're coming to the good bit. Hang on a moment!' He holds up his hand and catches his breath. 'I found it at last in Cuba. My Eden, Nirvana and the Promised Land, all rolled into one. Of course, much of that was down to the system. Granted, it has its faults, but Eden wasn't built in a day . . . though I suppose it was in seven.'

'Six.'

'Six, of course. Silly me! And while I moved there on account of the system, I stayed on account of the people: their openness, their generosity, their spirit, and their passion . . . above all else, their passion. It's in the very air you breathe. A scent as intoxicating as the galan de noche, the night-blooming jasmine, the unofficial emblem of those of us who flower after dark.'

I blanch at the memory of walking through Havana, reeling from the stench of exhaust fumes and rotting refuse. 'And Cesar?' I ask softly. 'Have you heard from him?' Tears well in his eyes, which he swiftly shuts. 'Would you like me to write to him? Alexander, I'm not Father; I know that you're awake.'

As his breathing stills, I'm no longer so sure. Planting a kiss on his forehead, I return home, where Mother asks how I found him, as breezily as if he had the flu. 'It does him good to get a break from me while you're here. I'll pop in again on Monday.'

'He feels very alone,' I say awkwardly. 'I think what he misses most is being touched.'

'Yes, well we all miss that,' she replies, taking me aback.

'Maybe if you could hold his hand . . .'

'I'm well aware what you're implying,' she says irritably. 'But the doctors made it quite clear that I should keep my distance. For the past two weeks I've had a head cold. The last thing we want is for him to catch it.'

I spend the evening, trying – and failing – to detect a sniff.

On Sunday morning I drive to Tapley. In an unexpected turn of events, it was Father who granted the St Peter's faculty. The DAC endorsed the scheme after Seward, remonstrating bitterly, replaced the scribe and scroll in the Eden drawing with a rocky landscape. The change failed to appease Daisy Quantock who, despite the lack of signatures on her protest petition, launched a formal objection with the

243

backing of the Protestant Truth Society. The case reached the consistory court where, after hearing representations from both sides, the chancellor caused consternation by withholding judgement. He declared himself torn, acknowledging the weight of opinion in favour of the paintings and their undoubted artistic merit, while sharing the concern of those who considered them ill-suited to a parish church. The only solution was for Father to invoke ancient precedent and pass judgement himself.

The week after the ruling, I visited Seward in his studio, where he was working on the first of the spandrels. As I'd anticipated, he'd had a surfeit of candidates, whom he'd whittled down to eight: five men and three women. His model that morning was Stanley Furness, the headmaster of Tapley grammar school, which was under threat of closure. Unlike Daisy's, the petition demanding its reprieve had attracted the signature of every villager (and the mark of one brave father, willing to risk ignominy for the sake of his children's education). While Seward, an improbable traditionalist, railed against the blighting of rural communities, the headmaster drew placidly on his pipe.

Speaking into the machine, I described Seward standing in front of a large canvas on which the triangular shape of the spandrel was neatly delineated, before asking how he felt as he started to paint.

'Seeing the blank canvas is always the most exciting moment. Faced with the infinite possibilities, the artist feels like God. Then from the first brushstroke, you realise that you're all too human.'

'Yet you persevere.'

'I must be a glutton for punishment.'

I watched, as he guided his model into a recumbent position, which he promptly adjusted when the headmaster's arthritic shoulder prevented his leaning back. He returned to the easel, switched on the radio and, within ten minutes, he'd roughed out the figure in charcoal.

'Do you always have the radio on while you work?' I asked.

'Always.'

'It doesn't distract you?'

'The only thing that distracts me is talk,' he replied pointedly. 'I leave the choice of station to the model. Stanley wanted Radio Three.'

'A luxury on a weekday,' the headmaster interjected.

'But I watch. I watch as the model listens; I watch how he listens. Animation is all.'

I waited until he stood back from the canvas to ask whether he would switch off the radio while I was recording. With a sigh that mixed exasperation with regret that he'd ever agreed to take part, he obliged. He poured water into a rectangular box, before squeezing in some white paint.

'That's an unusual palette,' I said tentatively.

'The paint's acrylic. The water stops it drying out.'

'Will you be using it throughout the church?'

'That's the plan. Sir William Coldstream would turn in his grave ... which is unfortunate given that it's not six months since I attended his funeral.'

'He was your teacher at the Slade,' I said, for the benefit of the listeners.

'Yes, and my mentor for many years afterwards. Acrylic for him was the devil's brainchild. But I've learnt to value it. Not just for speed, which is key on a project this size, but for clarity and consistency.'

He lit a cigarette and the headmaster took the opportunity to tamp down the tobacco in his pipe. After switching the radio back on, Seward returned to the canvas and began painting the headmaster's mouth, complete with the stem of his pipe. No doubt I have a jigsaw mentality, but I'd expected him to start with the contours of the face. Assuming my most winning smile, I repeated my request that he switch off the radio. As he hit the knob so hard that the table shook, I realised that the flirtatiousness he encouraged elsewhere was taboo in the studio.

'Is it because of the pipe that you're starting with the mouth?' I asked, refusing to be intimidated.

'No, it's the same with any model. I have to get it right before I can go further. Ask a hundred people to name the most expressive facial feature and ninety-nine will say the eyes. But they'd be wrong; it's the mouth. We breathe through it, speak through it, eat through it. We use it to kiss and to receive communion.'

'And smoke,' the headmaster added.

'Stanley asked if he could take his pipe to Heaven. It would have been barbarous of me – to say nothing of his guardian angel – to deny him.'

Lighting another cigarette, Seward chain-smoked as he painted, taking only a few puffs of each before stubbing it out and lighting the next. As sweat beaded his brow, I thought better of interrupting him again.

To accommodate his models, he's working on several pictures

concurrently. Until term ends in a fortnight's time, he spends his weekends in Eden with his daughter Laurel and fifteen-year-old Andrew Leaves. Eager to discover what they make of the experience, I've arranged to interview them in the studio. A paint-speckled Seward ushers me inside, where a large canvas is hung from a meat hook and clamped to the floor, opposite a makeshift dais. Laurel sits at the front swinging her legs, while, behind her, a tall, curly-haired boy stands, munching a bar of chocolate, which he crams into his mouth at my approach.

'Don't be shy, my dear. Come on in and meet the miscreants.' The word jars, even in jest. 'Laurel you know, of course. This is Andrew Leaves, my Adam. I call him SB.'

'Which stands for?'

'Strange boy,' Laurel interjects. 'Because he's a very strange boy.'

Andrew smiles, as though grateful for any form of recognition. He's strikingly good-looking, with an open face, full lips, wide grey-green eyes and, above all, an exceptionally clear skin. With his mop of dark brown curls, he presents a sharp contrast to Laurel, who not only has the same freckly, heart-shaped face as her mother but even wears her long blond hair in the same loose style.

'How are things going?' I ask.

'Early days,' Seward says, with a shrug.

'It's been great,' Andrew says.

'I bet,' Laurel says. 'Staring at my tits for hours on end.'

'Must you be so uncouth, daughter of mine?'

'I looked where I was told,' Andrew says, sounding hurt.

'If only all my models were as compliant as SB. I have Vincent to thank for him. He told me he was the most beautiful boy in Tapley. Don't scowl! It's a compliment.'

'Not for a bloke!'

'Why not? Why should girls be the only ones who suffer?'

'Desist, Laurel!' Seward says. 'SB was keen as mustard to pose. The hard job was persuading his mother.'

'I don't have a dad, see. He was killed.'

'I'm sorry to hear it,' I reply, discomposed.

'Well you have Vincent . . . Father Vincent, who takes a paternal interest,' Seward says, complacently. 'His mother was convinced that the Hall was a latter-day Bluebeard's Castle, but she has complete faith in Vincent, who drove her up here to see how boringly respectable we all are.'

'Speak for yourself,' Laurel says.

'True, daughter dear. No one would ever accuse you of being boring. SB tells me that he wants to be a painter,' Seward says, prompting Laurel to snort.

'That was a secret!' Andrew says.

'And will remain so. I catch him watching me . . . picking up tips. I'll have to look to my laurels,' Seward says, winking at his daughter. His mocking tone suggests that his much-vaunted egalitarianism stops short of his own profession.

'Have you seen any of his work?'

'Soon.'

'I've brought some drawings . . . just a few. They're no good really. But Lord Wemlock's been busy.'

'I need time to give them my full attention.'

Sensing his reluctance, I move to the canvas. 'May I take a look? Or don't you like to show work in progress?'

'As you wish. It is what it is. But please, not a single word, however flattering.'

I examine the painting which, the quince-laden tree apart, consists solely of the two focal figures, and then only their faces, torsos and Adam's arms around Eve's back. There's no sign of either the animals gambolling in the meadow or the serpent crawling over the crag. It's hard to equate the intimacy of the primal couple with the antagonism of the models, the one aimlessly picking his cuticles and the other studying the nude portrait of her mother with disconcerting detachment. I admire the richness of the flesh tones and wonder whether the pair have spent the morning clinging together, chest to chest, or if he allowed him to wear a vest and her a training bra. Either way, were their feelings as innocent as those he attributes to Adam and Eve, both before and after they tasted the fruit, or were they prone to the same carnal urges as other adolescents?

'I know that you want to talk to Laurel and SB in private,' Seward says. 'So I'll absent myself for ten minutes.'

'Are you sure? We can go elsewhere. I'd hate to think I was driving you out of your studio.'

'Not at all. They're due for a break, and I could do with some air.'

He goes out and I set up the tape recorder. Andrew regards it as warily as Native Americans once did the camera. Having explained the programme and confirmed that they're happy to be interviewed (Andrew's assent appears to depend on deflecting Laurel's scorn), I ask them to move closer to the microphone and begin the questioning.

249

'What's it like for young people like yourselves to sit for one of the country's leading artists?'

'He's painted me heaps of times,' Laurel replies. 'My ma used to be his muse. Now I am.'

Andrew's gaze strays to the portrait of Dora. Meeting mine, he turns swiftly away.

'That's the privilege of being one of the family. But it must be very different for you, Andrew.'

'It's the best, the most exciting thing that's ever happened to me . . . Just to watch the way he works. The canvas is so big that he can't look at it and us at the same time. So he moves in and out, like he's fixing our pictures in his head. Yesterday, he walked backwards and banged into the table, knocking the water jug and the paintbox-thingy on the floor—'

'It's called a palette,' Laurel interjects.

'I know that! "Why didn't you warn me?" he shouted. But he'd told us not to speak to him.'

'You're scared of him,' Laurel says.

'No, I'm not.'

'You are so! Like this morning, when he came towards you pointing his brush, and you ducked, like he was going to poke you in the eye.'

'I did not!'

'He calls him SB for scared boy.'

'We're getting sidetracked,' I say, with a growing sense of unease.

'And smelly boy. All boys smell, but you're the worst.'

'To return to the painting,' I say, forestalling Andrew's retort. 'What does it mean to you to be a part of the Eden story?'

'We're already part of it. It's like Father Vincent explained in confirmation class. Adam represents all men and the way we disobey God. But Eve tempted him. Which is why women are especially cursed.'

'Cursed, really?' Laurel says, as I bite back my anger. 'Tell her how you thought that women's monthlies were magazines!'

'I did not!'

'What about when I had cramps last week?'

Their bickering, which might be pertinent to a *File on 4* survey of today's teenagers, is an unwelcome distraction. 'So what does the Eden story mean to you, Laurel?' I ask, steering the discussion back on course.

'Not much. It's like Seward says; it was written to make us feel ashamed of our bodies. Besides, it doesn't hold up. God tells Adam that, if he eats from the tree of knowledge of good and evil, then he'll die. The very same day! But he doesn't. All that happens is that he and Eve realise they're naked. So was God wrong? Or is being naked as bad as being dead? But how can it be when they were made in God's image? You'd think that, after three thousand years, people would have seen through it. But no! Things aren't that different now. At least that's what Seward says,' she adds, as if afraid of having spoken out of turn. 'He can paint my ma like that.' She points to the nude of Dora, a gesture that will need clarification in the edit. 'But not if it's in church. In church, he says, there are still bits of God's image that must be covered up. So, I have to kneel beside SB, with his sweaty hands and his grubby thoughts and his prick poking me in the stomach.'

'Liar!'

'I think I have all I need,' I interject.

'Yesterday, he got an erection when we were posing. He went bright pink. That's why Seward gave us a break. Or he'd have had to repaint his face.'

'You're a dirty liar!'

'He thought it was the best joke.'

'He did not!'

'He did so. He told me afterwards.'

I switch off the tape.

'You're evil, you are,' he says. 'My mum was right when she said you're a tart.' Grabbing a denim jacket and large satchel, he storms out.

'He'll be back,' Laurel says. 'Like he told you, nothing exciting's ever happened to him. He thinks I'm his girlfriend. But Seward explained that girls mature long before boys, so I shan't go out with anyone under thirty.'

'The difference isn't that extreme,' I say, perturbed. 'I'd better try to find him. Your father will want to start again soon.'

Having promised to fit in with Seward's schedule, I fear that I may have disrupted it. Convinced that Andrew has too much invested in the work to have gone far, I leave the studio and search the estate. As I pass the kitchen garden, I spot Sorrel who, rather than say whether she has seen him, picks up an ancient gramophone horn and sputters through it: 'SB, SB, come out wherever you are!'

Moments later, Dora steps through the gate with a basket of greenery. 'Sorrel, what on earth are you're doing? Your father needs quiet.'

'He didn't hear when the treehouse collapsed. And that was loads louder.'

'Hello,' Dora says to me. 'Haven't we met before?'

'Indeed.' More amused than piqued, I won't embarrass her by adding that it's the third time. 'Clarissa Phipps, St John and Julia's daughter. From the BBC.'

'You must forgive me. I'm such a scatterbrain.'

'Seward says she's away with the fairies.'

'I'm sure he's here somewhere.' She looks about her, as though he might be hiding in a bush.

'It's Andrew I'm trying to find . . . the boy who's posing with Laurel. They've had a falling-out.'

'Lovers' tiff.'

'Don't talk nonsense, Sorrel.'

'It's true. Laurel's told me everything. They're sexing. But he squirts too quickly. Not like a proper man.'

'Go to your room! Now!' Dora's face suffuses with rage. 'I won't have you making up vicious stories. And put back that . . . thing. It's a valuable antique.' Eyes blazing, Sorrel stomps towards the house, stubbing her toe as she kicks a stone. Even in the bohemian atmosphere of the Hall, I'm shocked to hear a thirteen-year-old girl being so outspoken, but I know better than to remark on it to her mother.

'Pay no attention,' Dora says. 'She's jealous. There's only sixteen months between them and she's growing up too fast. Seward isn't concerned. When I said that it was important to preserve the girls' childhoods for as long as possible, he said it was more important to preserve their childlike sense of wonder . . . or was it innocence . . .

no, it was wonder. Is it any surprise he loses patience with me? I'm babbling.'

'Not at all,' I reply, distracted by the thought of how long Marcus and I should wait before trying for a second child.

'I'm sorry, but I have to go inside. The herbs lose their potency as soon as they're cut. Weren't you looking for someone?'

'Andrew, Seward's model.'

'Then he'll be in the studio. Take the path to your left. It's a small round building. You can't miss it.'

She wanders off and, following my instincts, I continue towards the copse. Sure enough, as I pass the old stable block, I come across Andrew perched on an alarmingly rickety gate.

'I'm allowed,' he says, before I utter a word. 'Just as much as Laurel. Lord Wemlock gave me permission to go anywhere I like in the grounds.'

'No one's disputing that.'

'It's not right, is it, to laugh at someone whose dad is dead?'

'Or at anyone else, for that matter. Did he die recently?'

'No, when I was a kid. There was an accident in the mine at Bickerton. A freak accident. But he wasn't a freak.'

'Of course not. There's no connection.'

'She thinks I am, just because I'm a boy. She wants to do things – private things – every bit as much as me. Then afterwards, she calls me names.'

'Girls can be complicated. I should know; I was one.'

He fails to echo my laugh. 'Boys can be complicated too. She thinks because her dad's rich and he's a famous artist, that she's special. But I'm an artist too. And one day I'll be more rich and more famous.'

'I'd love to see some of your work. Would you show me if I came to your house later?'

'You're just saying that so I'll talk on your programme.'

'Not at all. I mean it.'

'Really?'

'Really.'

'I've got stuff here.' He jumps down from the gate and picks up his satchel. 'I bring them every time just in case. But he says *not yet*, cos he's afraid they'll change how he sees me. That's how a true artist thinks.' He opens the satchel and takes out a plastic folder. He leafs through the contents before handing it to me. 'You'll think they're no good. You won't say so, but you'll think it, I know.'

I study the first drawing, an intricate depiction of a tree stump, covered in lichen and crawling with lice. Earthworms, slugs and beetles complete the picture, as they do several of the others. While larger creatures, such as rabbits, stoats, foxes and crows, feature in some of the drawings, they're mostly dead and in the later stages of decay and devourment. I relish the draughtsmanship and eye for detail, even as I shrink from the subject matter, which I trust it's not facile to ascribe to the trauma of his father's death.

'These are really excellent.'

'You're just saying that.'

'Not at all. They're so vibrant, so beautifully observed. You have a genuine feel for nature.'

'I could do indoors too. But my mum gets narked if I spend

too long in my room and she won't let me do anything messy downstairs.'

'You can try some interiors later,' I say, taking an instant dislike to his mother. 'In the meantime, you have boundless material in the woods.'

'You honestly think they're good? You're not just saying it?'

'I promise.'

'You swear?'

'I swear.'

Tears glisten in his eyes, which he furtively wipes while blowing his nose.

'My mum thinks I'm wasting my time. She says you have to be rich to be an artist, like Lord Wemlock.'

'Quite the opposite. Seward's an exception. Ask him to explain one day. Although perhaps you should leave it till he's finished the painting and looked at your portfolio.'

'My what?'

'Your collection of drawings. And I've had another idea. Why don't you show them to my fiancé? He works at Christie's, the auction house, but he's been offered a job at the Tate.'

'The museum?'

'Yes.'

'Why do you say that? Now I know you're laughing at me. They won't want them.'

'No, I didn't mean . . . I just thought he might give you some advice.'

'I got to go. Lord Wemlock will be waiting.' He grabs the folder from me and thrusts it into his satchel, not stopping to fasten the straps but clutching it clumsily as he strides away.

Marcus isn't alone in seeking change. Life at the BBC has not been the same since Jan's departure and her stinging attack on what she saw as my lack of support, which seems to have offended her almost as much as Terry's assault. Moreover, an oversight during the recent election campaign has brought me into disfavour. *The Daily Service* on 10 June, the eve of the polls, included a reading from 1 Kings 25, with the verse *The dogs shall eat Jezebel by the walls of Jezreel*, which Conservative Central Office took to be a coded reference to Mrs Thatcher. Quite why they're so keen to cast their leader as an idolater, blasphemer, murderess and expropriator of a poor man's property is not for me to say. They lodged a formal complaint and, despite apologies from CR4 and the DG himself, remain unappeased, threatening ever closer scrutiny of our output. With the Canon's position inviolable, the humble producer-presenter has been left to shoulder the blame.

Away from Broadcasting House, my desire for change has been strengthened by Jane and Decca's accounts of serving their titles. Although neither is enamoured of her vicar (Jane's a sleek Old Harrovian, with a drawl she derides as 'irritable vowel syndrome'; Decca's a former prison chaplain, with a biker beard and pepper-and-salt pony tail), both are devoted to their parishioners, no matter how exacting, cantankerous and, in the case of one of Decca's most devout families, criminal. Hearing them talk, I realised that I'd been overhasty – if not downright arrogant – in disdaining the diaconate. While Marcus, fresh from reading *Pregnancy for Men*, worries that I'm being swayed by my emotions (he had the tact to avoid 'hormones'), I've weighed up the arguments for ordination and am convinced that I can fulfil my vocation in the subsidiary role.

My parish priest, Duncan Leveret, referred me to the Diocesan Director of Ordinands, an elderly deaconess, whose support I mistakenly took for granted. Had she been a man, I might not have disclosed my pregnancy. Given the February due date, the baby would be seven months old by the time I commenced training, and I was confident that I could juggle coursework with childcare, especially given Duncan's assurance that I'd already covered much of the theory at Cambridge. It soon became clear, however, that my private life affronted the deaconess who, having been denied ordination herself, was only prepared to recommend postulants in her own image. Her refusal to put me forward for a selection conference outraged Duncan, who wrote a blistering letter of protest and promised to find me a different assessor next year. I, on the other hand, though disappointed and hurt, am more sanguine. An unplanned pregnancy is a powerful lesson in *What will be, will be*.

I've no time to fret since, for the next fortnight, I'm producing the *Sunday* programme. Other than a visit to Tapley on Monday week (technically, my day off), I won't have a chance to go up to Chester. Mother grumbles that she has been left to supervise all the wedding arrangements, while dismissing my offer to contact the various suppliers by phone. At least the tight schedule hasn't kept me from visiting Alexander, who's now in London. Faced with his raft of opportunistic infections, the doctors at the Countess of Chester decided that he needed specialist treatment, so Marcus and I drove him down to the Middlesex, where he's been given a bed on the country's only designated AIDS ward, opened by the Princess of Wales two months ago. I don't know whether to be dismayed or comforted by his claim that for the first time since his return to England he feels at home.

The staff on the ward have done away with visiting hours which, though not an auspicious sign, enables me to drop in whenever I'm free: the walk between Portland Place and Mortimer Street taking a mere seven minutes. Entering a room of prematurely aged young men, I feel embarrassed by my own good health. Alexander is more robust than most and, on several occasions, I've arrived to find him dragging his drip towards one of the bedridden patients. He has introduced me to them all and, with none as yet having been discharged, I've come to know them and even their regular visitors, chiefly other young men, who gaze at the waxy, wasted bodies as into a crystal ball.

Alexander's bed is at the far end of the ward, which affords us a measure of privacy. Depending on his fatigue, he wants either to talk or listen or just to lie still, holding my hand. This afternoon, his eyes swollen and face slick with sweat, he tells me about a recurring dream.

'It always starts the same way. I'm having dinner, though each time with different people: once with you and the parents; once with Cesar and his family; once with a group of disco bunnies; and once – don't laugh – with Castro and the Pope. Then in the middle of chatting and joshing, or arguing with Father, I'm sucked out of my chair and up to the ceiling. I soar above you all in a nightshirt, which I struggle to tuck in so as not to expose myself to Mother or the Pope.'

'When have you ever worn a—'

'It's a dream, sis! And sometimes a reverie since I'm half-awake. Then I fly towards the brightest light ever.'

'Do you feel at peace?'

'I feel euphoric. But don't get too excited. It's all drug-induced. The strange thing is that I'm having the same dreams of flying, when I'm about to die, as I did when I was three or four.' I open my mouth to protest against the fatalism but think better of it. 'Mother told me then that it was because I'd been an angel before I was born. She wouldn't say that now.'

'Of course not. You're thirty.'

'You know what I mean.' He sinks into a stupor, but just when I'm wondering whether to slip away, he pipes up: 'A fallen angel perhaps? Poor woman! Whenever she maddens me, I try to imagine what it must have been like being married to Father all these years.'

'She loves him.'

'That's no excuse. Once when I stood up for her after he'd been particularly high-handed, she turned on me in fury. There was the usual guff about him being a great man. Then she held me tight – at least she does in my memory – and told me I'd learn as I grew older that just because people didn't say what we wanted them to say didn't mean that they didn't feel what we wanted them to feel.'

'Still waters.'

'Another time – or it may have been the same time, who knows? – she told me that the biggest mistake people made in life was to wait for the echo. No one could say "I love you" without expecting to hear it back. She'd said it to Father, who'd simply replied "Ditto". Ditto!' He laughs and then yelps.

'Is it very bad?'

'Yes. The lesions you affect not to notice aren't just on my skin.'

'Why not ask the doctors for stronger painkillers? Maybe morphine?'

'Over my dead body. Ha! My brain will be mush soon enough.'

After watching helplessly while he retches, I wipe the phlegm from his chin.

'You should rest now.'

'Yes, Mummy.' He says it so solemnly that, for one terrifying moment, I fear that his mind is already disintegrating. Then he laughs, gags again, and reaches for my hand. 'The first thing she said when I told her I was gay was: "You're going to be so lonely in your old age." That from a woman who had to be content with "Ditto"! "You're going to be so lonely in your old age." Well, she doesn't need to worry about that any more.' He lies back. 'Now I'll rest.'

I hold his hand and listen to his scratchy breathing, until the ward sister arrives to dress his ulcerated lesions. Beneath the banter about 'favourite patient' and 'if only I were straight', I discern a deep mutual respect. As she draws the curtain round his bed, I cross the floor to chat to Cloud, a former West End chorus boy, who despairs at my ignorance of musical theatre.

'What have you been listening to?' I ask, pointing to the Walkman on his pillow.

'See for yourself,' he says, handing me the machine. After a fleeting hesitation, which shames me, I insert the earphones, to be greeted by Ella Fitzgerald singing 'The Way You Look Tonight'.

'Smart choice! Even I know this one.'

'I'm putting together the music for my funeral. I don't know whether it should be Ella or Fred Astaire with "You Were Never Lovelier", as the pallbearers bring in the coffin.'

I gently suggest that both songs might be open to misinterpretation, only for him to explain that that's precisely the plan. 'Those that love me will laugh their tits off. The rest can go fu . . . hang themselves!'

His shriek of laughter turns abruptly into a stream of tears. I clasp his hand in confusion, as the sister draws back the curtain round Alexander's bed. 'I'd better go. My brother's ready.'

'I hope he appreciates you,' Cloud says, refusing to relinquish my hand. 'A couple of years back, I was queer-bashed and all my sister could bring herself to say was, "Don't talk to me about discrimination! You should try being a smoker these days."'

I return to Alexander who lies supine, eyes closed and mouth gaping. As I glimpse his blistery purple tonsils and white-coated tongue, I vow never again to press him to eat. I stroke his cheek, and his eyes slowly open.

'Where have you been?'

'Here. Waiting.' I resolve to use Cloud's playlist as a pretext for a discussion that, however painful, we can no longer put off. 'I was killing time with Cloud, who's working on the music for his funeral.'

'Don't tell me: "There's No Business Like Show Business"!'

'Not far wrong. If it were me, I'd want Holst's "The Evening Watch" in the Gents recording, with Marcus singing tenor solo. How about you? Have you given it any thought?'

'Subtle as ever!' he replies, with a grin that twists into a grimace.

'Why should it concern me? Half this lot act as if they're going to leap out of their coffins, yelling "Surprise!" For all I care, you can grind me up and use me as bone meal. Although, knowing Father, I suspect it will be the full ashes-to-ashes routine.'

'I wish I could give you some of my faith.'

'You give me faith in faith, if that makes any sense.'

'A little. But it isn't enough.'

'Besides, I do have faith – but in this world, not the next. That's just a comfort blanket. In spite of all the ignorance and greed and cruelty and violence and . . . my mind's too shot to spell it out, I have faith in humanity. Why do we have to search for answers outside ourselves? It's nothing but arrogance. Take Father. You can't have forgotten: "The best book on humility is mine." What he and all the rest of you are saying is: "How can anyone as remarkable as me be the product of pure chance?" But why not? Why do we need an all-powerful creator to give us life and then tell us how to use it? Would you behave differently if you knew there was no God?'

'But there is.'

'That's not what I'm asking.'

'No,' I reply, pondering the question. 'My morality comes from being human.'

'There you are.'

'But my humanity comes from the Divine.'

He says nothing, and while in normal circumstances I'd be glad to have the final word, his silence scares me. I squeeze his hand.

'I'm whacked, little sis,' he croaks. 'I'm going to close my eyes.'

They're already closed, and I kiss him on both lids before leaving. I return at least once a day for the rest of the week, but he's too drowsy to sustain a conversation. He spends more and more of each visit asleep, and I'm torn between gratitude that he isn't in pain and regret that he's losing what little time he has left. I ring my parents with a report every evening but, no matter which of them answers, the response is the same: "Give him our love and let him know that we're praying for him." I've emphasised the urgency of their coming down to see him, so far without success, and although Marcus tells me that I'm being unjust, I can't decide whether his illness is too painful or merely too embarrassing for them to contemplate.

I worry about going up to Chester for the weekend, but the nurses assure me that he's stable. Meanwhile, I've promised Father to attend the annual civic service and Mother to meet the caterers and florists and 'take some responsibility' for my wedding. Though, having abandoned all hope of Alexander's walking me down the aisle, I now fear that the ceremony itself will have to be postponed.

Marcus and I drive up on Saturday morning, arriving in time for the service at noon. As we take our seats in the cathedral quire beside Mother in a pink picture hat, I raise a rare smile when Marcus, pointing to the mayoral chains and assorted medals dotted about the nave, expresses a wish that Father's sermon will be on the theme of *All that glisters is not gold*. In the event, he takes his text from Jeremiah: *And seek the peace of the city*. At the end of the service, the twenty Cestrian worthies Mother has invited to lunch gather in the cloisters. As well as the Lord Mayor and Lady Mayoress in full regalia, I recognise my former headmistress, showing far more cleavage in her navy polka-dot dress than she would ever have permitted her pupils; the Lord Lieutenant, a sprightly widower with wandering hands; and our local MP, a recently promoted junior minister who, rumour has it, makes the Whips' Office a source of legitimate innuendo.

At lunch, I am seated between Unilever's regional director and the university's vice-chancellor. The former regales me with tales of the Territorial Army; the latter takes me to task for the BBC's rejection of his six-part history of midsummer festivals and treats me to an exhaustive account of his researches. I listen meekly to the one during the vichyssoise and the other during the baked cod, exchanging rueful glances with Marcus, who is similarly trapped by the headmistress. The distant ring of the telephone holds out the prospect of escape, but Mother's glare frustrates it. As I resign myself to a lengthy description of a 1560s Chester Midsummer Watch Parade, a caterer enters with a whispered message for Mother, who excuses herself and follows him out. I turn back to the vice-chancellor, who expounds on a Puritan mayor's prohibition of the 1600 parade, during which Mother shuffles tipsily back to the table.

The headmistress is the last of the guests to leave, having secured Marcus's promise to appraise her Munnings on his next visit. 'At least it's not her etchings,' he says, after we see her out. Bone-weary, I head upstairs and collapse on the bed. The next thing I know is that Marcus is sitting beside me, stroking my face. I mumble my thanks, until the strokes become more emphatic and he urges me to wake up.

'I'm afraid I have some bad news.'

'Don't tell me. Mother's insisting that we go to the florists this afternoon.'

'No, really bad.'

One look at his anguished expression tells me everything. 'When?' I ask, acknowledging the superfluity of *what*.

'The hospital rang to say that Alexander has died.'

'When?' I repeat, although I know that it shouldn't matter.

'I'm not sure. I didn't ask.'

'He had no one with him.'

'There were doctors . . . nurses. You said yourself that, when you saw him yesterday, he was fast asleep. I don't think he ever woke.'

'I should have been there.' He sits down on the bed and takes me in his arms, but if he feels anything, it can't be me since I'm an emptiness . . . an abyss. 'The nurses told me he was stable.'

'Stable's good. Stable means that he didn't suffer. He just slipped – ebbed – away.'

'How do you know?' I ask, wanting to wrest the words from his mouth. 'I should have been there.' He clasps my face tight to his chest. 'How long have I been asleep?' I break away and look at my watch. 'Ten minutes. When did they ring?'

'Your mother took the call at lunch.'

'What?'

'Or so I gather.' He looks worried. 'I may be wrong.'

'And she came back in, for the pudding and coffee. She carried on as if nothing had happened.'

'Don't upset yourself . . . I mean not about that.'

'Talking and laughing with the Mayor and that odious MP.' I press ahead, rage filling the void inside me.

'I didn't hear her laugh.'

'Where is she?' I ask.

'Downstairs, in the drawing room with your father.'

I stand up, wincing from a spasm at the base of my spine.

'What is it?'

'Just a cramp.' The spasms increase, but I shrug them off and head downstairs. I enter the drawing room, where my parents sit on either side of the fireplace, their faces grey with grief.

'Clarissa . . .' Father says, opening his arms and half-rising from his chair, before sinking heavily back.

Ignoring him, I turn to Mother. 'How could you?'

'What?' she asks, bewildered.

'Alexander died, and you came back to the dining room as if the call were a wrong number. He'd died.'

'Not now, Clarissa please!' Father says. Marcus moves towards me, but I push him aside.

'He'd died. There was nothing more I could do for him. I had a responsibility to your father . . . to our guests.'

'Your son was dead!'

'*My* son, yes,' she replies. 'And I loved him. And I mourn him, as I have done every day for months. When you have a child of your own, you'll understand.'

I feel a stab of pain so sharp that I wet myself. With shame now added to grief, horror and burning fury, I ask Marcus to help me upstairs. Once there, I shut myself in the bathroom and tear off my pants to discover that the discharge isn't urine but blood. While Marcus pleads to be let in, I drag myself to the loo, where I'm racked with cramps far too violent for something the size of my fingernail.

They finally cease and I flush away what remains of my child, vanished as if making common cause with his or her uncle.

After cleaning myself as best I can, I crawl to open the door for Marcus, who grasps the situation in an instant. He kneels beside me, holding me close, kissing me on the lips, cheeks and hair and whispering words of comfort, as if the loss were mine alone. He draws me a bath and helps me into it, sitting on the side, tears pouring down his face, while I lie sweating in the water, resolutely dry-eyed. Having raided the linen cupboard for one of Mother's good bath towels, he wraps me inside it and leads me to the bed. He goes down to the kitchen to make me a pot of camomile tea, after which I sleep until the early evening, waking for a moment of blissful disorientation, until the pain both seeps through and shoots up me.

I'm determined to go straight back to London, and Marcus makes no attempt to dissuade me. While he packs our bags, I sit silently in the drawing room, sensing both parents' resentment, not just at my unconscionable outburst but at my selfishness in abandoning them. A part of me wants to tell Mother that her callousness has cost her her grandchild, but that would make me no better than her and, besides, for all my outrage, I can't be sure that it's true: the shock of Alexander's death might have brought on the miscarriage, even if I'd been at his bedside.

Clearing his throat as if in warning, Father asks whether he left any instructions for his funeral. 'Quite the opposite,' I reply, biting back the 'bone meal'.

'I'd like to hold it in the cathedral.'

'Well we've booked the Lady Chapel for a fortnight's time. Half the congregation will be the same. No point in wasting the slot.' I catch his injured glance at Mother and feel contrite.

Returning to the flat, we go straight to the bedroom, where Marcus unpacks the bags, among them the blood-smeared towel.

'How sick is this?' I yell. 'Are you keeping a memento?'

'I was worried . . . your parents. I didn't think you'd want them to know.'

I lay my head on his shoulder, and the tears that have so far eluded me drench my cheeks. 'I'm sorry. That was so thoughtful. I love you with all my heart. And I want to be with you . . . married to you forever. Nobody else but you.'

'And you shall be, my dearest darling.'

The BBC grants me a week's compassionate leave. 'Under the circumstances,' I tell Marcus, 'I should have asked for two.' More sensitive to my loss than to my tone, he takes the comment seriously.

With my pregnancy never made public, his own loss goes unacknowledged, except by Father Duncan, in whom I confide at the midweek Communion. He visits us that evening and, after commiserating on the double bereavement, insists that there's a reason that God has gathered both souls at once, however hard it may be to comprehend. I baulk at his use of *soul* in respect of an eight-week-old foetus, which, for all my grief, I regard as damaged tissue. Growing expansive as Marcus refills his glass, Duncan assures us that we have every right to feel angry with God and looks cheated by our failure to exercise it, beating our breasts – or, at the very least, our cushions. But I remain adamant that to blame God for either death would make us guilty of the very arrogance with which Alexander charged

Father. 'How can anyone as remarkable as me be subject to natural law?'

At the end of the week, I return to Broadcasting House, where Bruce, eager not to overtax me, asks me to put together a ten-minute filler on church organists. Left to my own devices, I have no trouble slipping out the following afternoon to buy champagne and cakes, which I take to the Middlesex as a farewell gift for Alexander's friends. After a painful round of thanks and condolences, I head back to my desk, where I make a further attempt to reach Cesar in Cuba. With the help of one of Kate's *World Tonight* contacts, I finally get through to the Santiago sanatorium, which denies any knowledge of a Cesar Montero, past or present. I can only assume that he's dead and, for tactical reasons, they've been ordered to downplay the mortality rate.

My sardonic suggestion of reusing our slot in the Lady Chapel or, as Marcus put it, 'furnishing the wedding-baked meats at the funeral table', has been taken up. So, at 7 a.m. on 21 August, we leave for Chester. Our sombre mood is compounded by the news that a further victim of Thursday's massacre in Hungerford has died overnight, taking the death toll to sixteen. 'Seventeen,' I say, quietly correcting the newsreader, before responding to Marcus's quizzical look. 'Don't forget the killer, the victim of his own demons, long before he loaded his gun.'

We arrive at Bishop's House shortly before ten. Although I've been in regular touch with Father about the arrangements, I've barely spoken to Mother since Alexander's death, but my fears of further discord prove to be misplaced. I enter the hall, where she greets me with the single word 'Friends?', smiling gratefully at the echo. She kisses me on the cheek, and almost as an afterthought, presses me to her bosom, enveloping me in the orange-blossom scent of childhood. Dressed in black, with a single string of pearls, she looks drawn, although I have to admit that mourning suits her complexion better than the mother-of-the-bride turquoise she was set to wear. She leads me into the dining room, where the coffin rests, ready for the pall-bearers. We stand in silence, lost in memories of the brother and son, cruelly crated in front of us. Then, seeking relief in practicalities, we head into the cathedral to inspect the flowers.

The ceremony, although modest, isn't the furtive affair I'd dreaded. Among the congregation, I make out the dean and precentor; a smattering of relatives, both Latimers and Phippses; Alexander's former headmaster, and two of his King's School contemporaries, their presence all the more moving given his rebuff of his old friends. Defying my terror of breaking down, I read Neruda's 'And How Long', its pertinence enhanced by the Latin American connection. There's no eulogy, but in his prayers Father commends to God's safe keeping all those who suffer prejudice and persecution on account of their sexuality, which makes me both tearful and proud. After the final hymn, the choir sings a four-part harmony version of 'Where Have All the Flowers Gone?' which isn't listed on the service sheet. I turn to Mother in surprise.

'I thought he'd like it,' she whispers.

'He'd love it!' I reply.

I drive north again three days later, this time straight to Wemlock Hall, where Seward welcomes me with a mixture of irritation and bemusement as if he'd forgotten the appointment we confirmed only yesterday. Expecting to find Laurel and Andrew, I'm surprised when he introduces me to Patsy, a moon-faced girl of twelve or thirteen with a flat, boyish figure, who is posing for one of the angels. She wears a chaplet of white peonies and a white taffeta robe above pink wellingtons, which are either a curious homespun touch or else an indication that the angel won't be seen below the knee.

She's accompanied by her mother, who sits in a corner poring over *The Bumper Book of Puzzles*. 'She watches me like a dowager at a debutante's ball,' Seward says, with a mirthless grin.

'What an idea!' the mother replies. 'Patsy was that keen to be in the painting, especially now she's missed out on being a bridesmaid at her gran's wedding. But I couldn't let her walk three miles through the wetland alone, now could I?'

'I've offered to let you wait inside the house.'

'Oh, I couldn't do that,' she says cryptically. 'It wouldn't be right.'

Whatever the reasons for her vigilance, her presence shields her fidgety daughter from the full force of Seward's wrath. When she lowers her outstretched arm, he asks with withering scorn whether she's leading Mrs Fenn to Heaven or Hell.

She gives it a moment's thought. 'Well, our dad says she's a real scrubber. Perhaps . . .'

'No!' he shouts, causing the mother to choke on the pencil she's chewing. 'No,' he repeats, moderating his tone. 'I think we can trust Our Lord to be the judge of that. Or not, in His infinite mercy.'

The girl resumes her pose, only to flag after a few minutes, casting agitated glances at her mother, who's preoccupied with her puzzle.

Finally, she pleads that she needs 'to go', prompting a disgruntled Seward to hurl down his brush and propose that they take a break.

'I'm sure you know your way to the lavatory by now. Then if you ask in the kitchen, Mrs Lennon will give you some cordial and biscuits.' As Patsy and her mother exit, Seward vents his frustration. 'Never work with children and animals: isn't that what actors say? Trust me, they're not the only ones.'

I turn to Eden, which has been rolled up and raised aloft, leaving only half the canvas visible. He has painted the tree trunk in a range of mauves and reds, and the quince skins appear to have ripened, but Adam and Eve remain spectral below the waist. 'Is Andrew not around?' I ask.

'Not for the past ten days! He and Laurel have had a blazing row. She refuses point blank to tell me what it's about, but knowing my daughter, I suspect that she's been leading him on. Thoroughly unprincipled I grant, but I wish she'd kept it up until I'd finished with him! As a rule, once I've outlined the figures and blocked in the canvas, I'd paint them separately, which I'm doing with the angels and the saved souls. But given the intimacy of the pose, it wouldn't have worked.'

'Have you spoken to him?'

'I've tried. I went round to see him. His mother invited me into the front room – it felt like a morgue. She said he was out, but I could hear footsteps overhead. So, unless she has a secret lover . . . Since then I've rung three times, but he won't come to the phone. I'm far enough advanced that, if need be, I can carry on without him. And I've decided to use an older couple for Adam and Eve on the chancel arch. But I'm still hoping that they'll patch things up and he'll be back.'

'They were at loggerheads when I interviewed them. Even so, it makes no sense. He was so excited about posing – and especially watching you at work. I can't see him dropping out, whatever his problem with Laurel. Shall I try to find out more?'

'Best not to bother. You never know with teenagers. He may have got hold of the wrong end of the stick.'

'It's no bother. I'm due at the rectory, but not until three. And it concerns me as well. Laurel and Andrew are key voices in the feature.'

With ninety minutes to spare until my meeting with Vincent, who has agreed to record a potted history of St Peter's for the top of the programme, I resolve to visit Andrew. As an outsider, I may be better placed than Seward to heal his breach with Laurel. Moreover, I'm determined to persuade him to show his drawings to Marcus. While I'm convinced that he has talent, I'm not confident enough of my own judgement to encourage him down a path that may lead nowhere. I know too much about thwarted vocations for that.

Having neglected to ask Seward for the address, I call in at the village shop, where the woman behind the till tells me that, 'though I wouldn't call us friends exactly', she knows Andrew's mother, Lily, from the WI. She not only gives me the address but draws a map on a paper bag.

Durance Lane is a row of identical terraced houses, at the less scenic end of Tapley. My knock at number 11 is answered by a middle-aged woman, with the round face and ample hips of a comfort eater. After eyeing me suspiciously, she invites me in, turning the doorknob to the front room as if it were the dial on a safe. The atmosphere is every bit as dismal as Seward described. The heavy furniture appears not to have been used since her husband's wake. I decline her offer of tea but, rather than fetch Andrew, she plumps down opposite me and explains that she'd been against his posing from the start.

'You hear such stories. Not that I pay them any heed, mind. And Mrs Quantock – she was the boy's headmistress in year five and six – she's a very persuasive woman. She's been to see everyone – not just me – and warned us not to get involved.'

'I can well believe that.'

'But Andrew had his heart set on it. It hasn't been easy for him. Without his father.'

'He told me. Please accept my condolences.'

She looks at me in surprise. 'Good riddance is what I say.' Now it's my turn for surprise. 'He says he wants to be an artist – to his form teacher, not to me. He knows well enough what I think about it. Father Vincent said it'd help him see that it's not all about drawing pretty pictures. So I went along with it.'

'But he's given it up.'

'Don't ask me why! He tells me nothing. Lord Wemlock came here himself – in person – and he wouldn't speak to him, not even when I clipped him round the ear. Though I know one thing and that's for sure, it's to do with that minx, Laura Wemlock. Born on the wrong side of the blanket.'

'I'm rather pressed for time,' I say coldly. 'So if you'd be kind enough to call Andrew . . .'

Wheezing, she stands and moves to the door. 'I'll do my best, but don't blame me if he says no. If he wouldn't talk to Lord Wemlock, why will he talk to you?'

She clomps up the stairs and opens a door without any audible knock. Perturbed by the raised voices, I examine the mantlepiece, adorned with a single ornament – a porcelain shepherdess with a glazed smile – and two photographs: one of a 1940s bride and groom, presumably Lily's or her husband's parents, and the other of Andrew, aged nine or ten, on the barred-and-netted viewing platform of the Eiffel Tower. I pick it up, as he enters the room.

'Was this taken on a trip to Paris?' I ask.

'Blackpool.'

'My mistake! I should have recognised the clouds.'

'If you're here to get me to go back, you're wasting your time,' he replies, ignoring my attempt at levity.

'That's a pity. Most of your work for the picture is done.'

'So?'

'I thought you of all people would want to see how it developed.'

'Why?'

'To study Seward's techniques. Aren't you hoping to be an artist?'

'Artists are sick. And he's the sickest of all. He calls me SB, but the real SB is him. Sick beast. SSB. Sick sick beast.'

The thought strikes me – smack in the solar plexus – that Seward, so susceptible to female beauty, may also be attracted by adolescent boys.

'I realise that this may be hard for you to talk about, especially given your admiration for Seward Wemlock's work.'

'It's a load of crap.'

'Have you ever sat for him alone?' I ask, refusing to be deterred. 'Without Laurel.'

'Twice, yeah. So what?'

'Did he ever touch you?'

'What?'

'When you were posing. Did he put his hand inappropriately . . . unintentionally—'

'No! Laurel!'

'I see.' I brim with relief. 'But you can't blame Seward for that.'

'Who else?'

'It's for you and Laurel to settle your differences. You're both young adults,' I add, having hitherto classed them as children.

'Not me and Laurel – him and Laurel! Don't you understand anything?'

I understand the words but not the sentence. 'Are you saying that Seward is . . .?'

'Fucking his daughter? Yes.'

'That isn't . . . that can't be . . . you're mistaken.'

All at once, she's a child again. Moreover, she's his child.

'She told me herself. She and me . . . we were . . . Then she said it had to end. That I was no good, just a boy. She knew what it was like with a proper man. Then she told me who the proper man was. She said artists are special. They live by different rules from the rest of us. That's why she's so stuck up. But they're wrong rules. Sick rules! And they're going to put his pictures in the church!'

His face and chest crumple and he punches the back of a chair. I step forward to put an arm around him, but he thrusts me away.

'Fuck off!' He moves to the door, flings it open and runs out of the house. His mother's irate shout betrays her presence in the hall and, although there's no keyhole, I wonder how much she has overheard.

'That's him away for the day now. I told you you'd get nothing out of him,' she says, with a strange satisfaction. 'Run off to the woods, to be sure. Then he'll slink back, all grubby. Grubby and muddy. I tell him: "You're not too old for me to put you in the bath and give you a good scrub."'

She can't have heard anything or else she'd be concerned about a more sinister sort of dirt. I'd like to ask about her son's veracity but suspect that she's of the opinion that all boys are born liars. So I take my leave and sit stunned at the wheel of my car until, spotting a twitching curtain, I start the engine and drive back through the village, stopping at the churchyard. Although the weather is cooler than on my previous visit, it's still warm enough to be outside and, leaning against CRISPIN WAINWRIGHT, I drink in the calm. As the sky clouds over, I gaze at the church and reflect on Seward's Eden. Has he used his beliefs to validate his actions? Or have his actions determined his beliefs? Rather than creating an image of universal salvation, should he have kept to a traditional Doom painting: a warning to those who break both God's and Nature's laws?

At ten to three, I fetch the Uher from the car and walk to the rectory, a few yards down the road from the church whose design it mirrors. Its mock-Gothic facade is a monument to Victorian self-confidence, while the arched stone lintel, dated 1859, shows that the religious doubts, rife in metropolitan circles, had yet to penetrate the shires. With its two upper floors built to accommodate the children, whom the rector's wife was expected to produce at regular intervals, it's far too large for Vincent, an avowed celibate, who lives alone.

I rap the ridged oak door and Vincent appears, exuding his familiar scent of talcum powder and spoiled milk. He has laid out tea in the sitting room, the sugar bowl furnished with a pair of apostle tongues. He goes out to the kitchen and returns with a teapot in a country-cottage cosy.

'I think you'll like this. It's Bollands' Imperial Afternoon.'

Sensing his hunger to impress, I assure him that I can savour the bergamot, even though my taste buds, along with the rest of me, are numb. While he reflects on Alexander's funeral, which he found 'most moving under the circumstances', I wrestle with how to broach the subject that consumes me. Flustered, I blurt out Andrew's charge.

'What arrant wickedness! You should be ashamed of yourself for repeating it.'

'If you'd seen him—'

'I don't need to. This is Lord Wemlock you're accusing—'

'I'm not accusing anyone, just reporting what I was told.'

'Whatever can have possessed Andrew? I've always thought the idea of an adolescent Adam was a mistake. No teenage boy is in a state of grace. This proves it.'

'It appears that he and Laurel have been having some kind of affair.'

'Surely not?' He sounds as disgusted as by the alleged incest.

'I've no idea how far it went. But when she broke it off, she accused him of not being half the man that Seward is.'

'There you have it. Guilt! It's all guilt, which he's trying to deflect on to someone else.'

'But why should he feel guilty? There was no coercion.'

'You don't know his mother. I'm saying nothing against her. A mainstay of the church – although she polishes the brasses as if she's trying to purge the world of sin . . . a stalwart of the WI – although I doubt that her quiver is filled with arrows of desire. But she's a lonely, embittered woman, obsessed by her husband's desertion. She's poured all her frustration on to Andrew.'

'Desertion? He told me that his father had been killed in the mine at Bickerton.'

'What? How? It's been shut for the past eighty years. To the best of my knowledge, Len Leaves is living in Colwyn Bay with his second wife and children.'

'No wonder she looked so startled when I offered her my condolences.'

'The boy's clearly disturbed. He tells lies . . . tales, if you're being generous. But I can't be. It's one thing to lie about his father, quite another to lie about Lord Wemlock!'

'But it was Laurel who told him. Why would she fabricate something so vile?'

'The mysteries of the female mind . . . who can say? By your own account, they'd quarrelled. She picked on something that she knew he'd find most hurtful. Perhaps, in some perverse way, she thought it would make her seem more grown-up?'

'Perverse in the extreme!'

'And who says she did tell him? Only Andrew. Think for a moment. She's an intelligent girl, much more so than him. If her father were sleeping with her – that is purely for the sake of argument – would she be so rash as to boast about it, given the very grave implications?'

'What if it were a cry for help?'

'To Andrew Leaves?' His incredulity chastens me. 'If that were the case, she'd have told her mother or her aunt or the police or me. But not Andrew Leaves.'

'I admit that what you say rings true.'

'Because it so evidently is.'

'And yet . . .'

'Yet what? We can't let the delusions of a damaged boy threaten a project in which we've all invested so much. In his rancour against Laurel, Andrew seems ready to trample on everything she holds dear.'

'Yes, you're right. Of course. You don't know how much you've eased my mind. Thank you.'

I should have realised from the start that the charge was absurd. This is Seward, who chose Laurel as his Eve expressly to equate youth and innocence: how could he defile both? This is Seward, a man of acute sensibility and profound faith: how could he deny both? This is Seward, a man whose mystical encounter with Christ has defined his life: how could he destroy everything that Christ represents? I shouldn't have needed Vincent to convince me, but now that he has, I'm eager to seek his help. 'Please, would you speak to Andrew? He's utterly wretched and I'm afraid that he may do something to hurt himself, as well as spreading more calumnies.'

'Yes of course. I'll put it at the top of my list. I'll ask him round for a heart-to-heart, away from dear, misguided Lily. But what about you? You look exhausted. Are you sure you want to go ahead with the recording? I'm happy to reschedule.'

'Thank you, no.'

His saccharine smile makes me recoil anew.

'I'm here now. I need to get back on track.'

'Understood. Let me go and refresh the pot before we begin. And do try a Chocolate Oliver. I bought them specially.' He smacks his lips. 'So good that they shouldn't be legal.'

THREE

2019

One

'So, the scribes and the Pharisees bring the woman taken in adultery to Jesus. He gives his spiel: "Let him who is without sin cast the first stone." The crowd falls silent, followed by a shriek, as a stone flies through the air and grazes the woman's ear. Jesus turns round. "Mother," He says, "I told you to stay at home."'

Marcus beamed at the appreciative laughter, while Clarissa felt so dizzy that she feared she might faint. Had she been standing next to someone less elegant, she would have grabbed her arm. It was so far from his nature to mock her, let alone to wish to hurt her, that she had the sickening suspicion that Marcus had told the joke, with its painful associations, in an attempt to put her at her ease. She would have preferred his cruelty to his incomprehension.

She'd joined a group of eight VIPs, whom Marcus was conducting round a preview of the William Blake exhibition. Their names had meant nothing to her, but her surmise that they were either sponsors or donors was confirmed in at least one case, when they stopped beside a watercolour of *The Woman Taken in Adultery*, lent by the Boston Museum, whose Director of Collections commended its hanging.

She braced herself to confront the image, conscious that, despite the horror of Brian's funeral, she couldn't ignore one of the foremost Gospel stories indefinitely. In Blake's portrayal, Christ, bent double, was writing on the ground, with the arraigned woman facing him, breast exposed and hair tangled, as if she'd been dragged straight from the illicit bed, while behind them her accusers fled, confounded by Christ's countercharge. The mystery was why, contrary to the Gospel, He was writing after the crowd had turned tail. Was He reiterating what He'd already written, or was it a private message to the woman – not the *Go, and sin no more*, which scholars held to be a later addition to the text, but, true to what she knew of both Christ and Blake, an expression of support?

Hanging back as the group moved on, she was roused from her reflection by a familiar voice.

'There you are! I've been looking everywhere.'

'Helen, hello!'

Clarissa was always at a loss as to how to greet her husband's mistress. A kiss felt too intimate, a hug too pastoral, and a handshake too formal. The problem was compounded by the picture before them. So smiling brightly, she took a step towards her and trusted that that would suffice.

'It's years since we've seen you at one of these shindigs.'

'Yes. I don't know where the time goes. There aren't enough hours in the day.' What was it about Helen that reduced her to platitudes? 'But recent events in the parish have taken their toll. Marcus insisted that, once I'd made it through Holy Week, I should come down for a break.'

'Yes, I heard about what happened. It must have been awful for you.'

At least she had the grace to leave the 'from Marcus' unspoken. Did he report back to her after every visit to Tapley, or only the exceptional ones? Was that the difference between a wife and a mistress: that she wanted to know as little as possible about his life with Helen, which even now had the power to wound, whereas Helen enjoyed learning about his life with her, which was safely remote? Or was that too simplistic? A quick flick through the history books would show that there were as many different kinds of mistresses as of wives. While reluctant to flatter Marcus's vanity, she thought of Madame de Maintenon: the mistress as conscience. Yet, had that been what he'd wanted, he need never have strayed.

She listened politely as Helen praised Marcus and Perry's curation of the show. 'They've quite won me round to Blake's vision. I've always admired his poetry but, for the rest, I've regarded him as more of an illustrator than a painter.'

'Marcus introduced me to his work in Cambridge,' Clarissa replied, playing her trump card. 'Over the years, I thought I'd seen pretty much all of it. But this is a new one on me.' With nearly two hundred pictures in the exhibition, there had to be a reason that fate had thrown them together in front of the adulteress. 'I'm fascinated by the way he's identified Christ with the woman. Look how they're both dressed in white, while the accusers' robes are coloured. They've got the same reddish-gold hair, the same aquiline nose and, most importantly, the same serenity.'

'I'm sure you're right. Though I still find his faces inexpressive.'

'What with this and the Seward Wemlock exhibition, the Tate is making a strong case for the religious strain in British art.'

'Not everyone approves.' Helen pointed to a knot of people standing beside two of Blake's *Job* engravings, among them Marcus's friend and fellow curator, Otto Markham, and a striking young woman, in a white crepe midi dress, blue denim jeans and gold ankle boots, with a mass of strawberry-blonde curls piled on one side of her head, while the other side was shaved.

'Is that . . .?'

'Yes, Herm Merriott, the thorn in Marcus's flesh – or is that blasphemous?'

'Not at all. Why?'

'The crown of thorns.'

'Different thorns. Though the phrase does come from the Bible . . . St Paul,' Clarissa said, irked by the thought that Helen was trying to put her at her ease.

'I gather there are plans to devote an entire gallery in the Wemlock show to a replica of your church. Are you ready for all the publicity?'

'Whatever it is, it'll be preferable to the publicity we've had of late.'

'No doubt you'll be called upon to advise. Meanwhile, I'm looking forward to making Xan's acquaintance at the end of May.'

'Yes, of course,' Clarissa replied, nonplussed.

'I'm touched that he's so eager to meet me. I was afraid he'd see me as the wicked witch of the south.'

As she struggled to assimilate the news, Clarissa had no intention of challenging the description. 'He's very excited about the trip.'

'I must let you go. I'm supposed to be on duty, and you'll want to catch up with Marcus.'

'I'll follow in a moment. I don't want to make him self-conscious. I know how nervous he gets at these events.'

'Don't you believe it! He loves every minute. He says it's the closest he comes to the buzz of his singing days.' Making a wry face, as if remembering who it was that she'd corrected, Helen moved away. 'Catch you later!'

Clarissa cast her eye over the gallery in which clusters of people were chatting, several with their backs to the pictures. Her sporadic ventures into Marcus's world made her own seem so small – parochial in both senses. As she exchanged smiles with Otto, his expression switched from respect for her calm acceptance of her marital situation to disdain for her misplaced forbearance. She blushed before realising that it was her confidence, not his smile, which had wavered. A vicar's son himself, he would have seen his mother cut threadbare bedsheets sides-to-middle, while less frugal women discarded them.

With two dry kisses and the scent of sandalwood, Otto chided her for standing alone, before introducing her to 'our most dynamic young curator, Hermione ... um ... Herm Merriott.'

'I've heard a lot about you,' Clarissa said. 'I'm sorry, I know that's a conversation stopper.'

'Not necessarily. I like being talked about. I trust that my name is never far from Otto's lips,' Herm said teasingly.

'I'll leave you two ladies – persons – together. I must ... there's someone I must ...'

289

'Blessings!' Clarissa called after the departing figure. 'Dear Otto, he hasn't changed in twenty years.'

'And that's a good thing?'

'Not necessarily,' Clarissa replied, picking up Herm's phrase. 'But it's a comfort in an ever-changing world.'

'Young fogey becomes old fogey. It's a pose – a ploy – to stop the rest of us making demands on him, leaving him free to write his seminal study of ruffs in Jacobean portraiture, or whatever.'

'Isn't that rather cruel?'

'I am cruel. Whereas you're contractually obliged to turn the other cheek.'

'Oh, I allow myself the odd *eye for an eye*.'

'I'm glad to hear it. Your husband would readily pluck mine out.'

'Nonsense,' Clarissa said, alarmed by the suggestion of violence. 'He's set in his ways . . . no, that's unjust: he has deeply held views about art. You threaten them.'

'Really? In a gallery founded by men, reeking of hierarchical male values, where, even now, women and genderqueer artists are criminally underrepresented, Marcus feels threatened by me?' Clarissa strove to distinguish the pain from the scorn. 'Surely, as a woman working in an even more chauvinistic organisation – if such a thing is possible – you share my frustration? Or are you so inured to the *Our Father* ethos that you blindly follow the rules?'

'Not at all. But I believe in amending them, not breaking them.'

'In other words, anything for a quiet life.'

As Herm held forth, Clarissa found herself respecting them

more and liking them less. 'Are you an admirer of Blake?' she asked placatingly.

'Another Dead White Male, who married an illiterate girl in order to mould her mind?'

'I thought that, as artists' marriages go, it was one of the better ones. A professional as well as a personal partnership. Didn't she become an accomplished engraver and colourist in her own right?'

'I don't see her name on any monographs. "I have very little of Mr Blake's company. He is always in paradise." What was her tone when she said that? I know that paradise is your bag. No doubt you hear esteem, even awe. But I hear the plaint of a neglected, put-upon woman.'

'We all have our flaws. Artists are no exception. Marcus once claimed – I'm not saying I agree with him – that the greater the artist, the greater the flaws.'

'Yes, the get-out-of-jail-free card! We hand out a lot of those here. For a different perspective, you'll have to come to my Luciana Calderón exhibition next spring.'

'I'm afraid I don't know her. Is she Spanish?'

'Colombian. A conceptual artist. Something your husband delights in calling a contradiction in terms. At one planning meeting, he pointed out that I'd confused *oxymoron* and *tautology*, differentiating them with brio: "A conceptual artist is an oxymoron. A fraudulent conceptual artist is a tautology."'

'As I said: deeply held views.'

'One series of her photographs will particularly interest you. Twelve staged tableaux from the life of a female Christ. The most controversial will be Christ locked in a lesbian embrace with Mary Magdalene.'

The odd tabloid headline apart, Clarissa suspected that she'd be disappointed. If her aim were to create a scandal, Calderón should have chosen Mohammed. A female Christ – even a gay one – felt both dated and jejune. As a priest who stood *in the person of Christ*, she was living proof that that person was universal. It encompassed men, women and, indeed, non-gendered. She would have explained the precept to Herm but was wary of being accused of proselytising.

'It's been a pleasure talking to you,' she said, 'but I must go and find Marcus. I look forward to seeing the exhibition.'

'I'll hold you to that.'

'Blessings!'

Giving the startled Herm a hug, Clarissa hurried through the remaining rooms, finding Marcus among a small circle of well-wishers at the exit. She hovered, increasingly piqued at his failure to introduce her, until he led her out, whispering that he'd forgotten half their names. They made their way to the Grand Saloon where, after a cursory greeting, the director dragged Marcus off to meet 'an American Maecenas', the Latinism failing to cloak his cupidity. She strode through the crush of guests with an air of purpose, which didn't deter an elderly man from accosting her. He was dressed as eccentrically as Herm, in a puce velvet jacket, mustard waistcoat, red plaid trousers, and with a pink spotted handkerchief in his breast pocket. 'Are you a wife, a floozie or an artist?' he asked, with a foamy grin. It might have been the result of her recent encounter with Helen but, far from taking offence, she felt a frisson of excitement that anyone – even an octogenarian – should place her in the second category.

'That's for me to know and you to find out,' she said skittishly, before slipping back into the crowd lest he should take her at her word.

After protracted goodbyes, Marcus hailed a cab to drive them to Marylebone. She added her congratulations to the many he'd received, at which he clasped her hand and lifted it to his lips. With Tapley never far from her thoughts, she switched on her phone and scrolled through her messages, three of which gave cause for concern. The first was from Pamela, announcing that the date of Susan's tribunal had been set for a fortnight's time. The second was from Shirley, with a request for *more incest for the rabble*, which she finally deciphered as *more incense for the thurible*. The third was from Xan complaining that his grandmother had banned him from texting.

She shared it with Marcus, who warned her not to submit to emotional blackmail. That was easier said than done. Although her presence did nothing but provoke him, Xan had been enraged to learn that, in addition to spending a week in London, she had asked his grandmother to look after him. 'How old am I? Four?' he'd spluttered, before reeling off the names of classmates, who'd allegedly been left on their own while their parents went away. 'You don't give a toss what's best for me. All you care about is what people think of you,' he'd yelled, before sinking into such a prolonged sulk that any guilt she'd felt about abandoning him vanished.

Nevertheless, her heart ached for him. In the aftermath of Brian's death, he'd lost – or, rather, disowned – one of his best friends, while the other was preoccupied with his new girlfriend. Hayley Seagrove had barely waited for the funeral before pursuing Matthew. 'Bereavement has its compensations,' Pamela remarked mordantly, adding that nothing was more attractive to a teenage girl than an air of tragedy. For all her fears that the fickle Hayley (the word *floozie* flashed through Clarissa's mind) would rapidly tire of him, leaving him more hurt and confused than ever, Pamela was grateful that, for the time being, Matthew had been taken out of himself.

Thoughts of Xan conjured up her conversation with Helen and, without wishing to dampen Marcus's mood, Clarissa was determined to confront him. 'Helen told me how pleased she was to be meeting Xan at half-term.'

Marcus's face flushed crimson, until she realised that it was a reflection of the traffic lights. 'After his bombshell at the lunch table,' he said, 'we had a long heart-to-heart. I filled him in on my relationship with Helen.'

'It might have helped if you'd mentioned it to me.'

'You had more important matters on your mind. Pamela had just turned up with the news of Brian's arrest.'

'More urgent perhaps, not more important.'

'It wasn't easy – and the boy's only fourteen – but I tried to explain both the joys and constraints of a long marriage: how you and I still love one another; that, over time, our wants changed, but the bedrock remained strong; that, like it or not, his mum and dad would be together till death do us part; meanwhile, we do our best to accommodate our differences.'

'Admirably put,' Clarissa said, feeling that the reality was somewhat messier. 'You might try being equally conciliatory to your colleagues.'

'In what way?'

'I talked to Herm.'

'I'm so sorry. I saw her prowling around – how could I not have? To be honest, I'm surprised she came. It wasn't a three-line whip.'

'I liked her. Obviously, it was just a quick chat, but she reminded me of the more impassioned women in the ordination movement. Not always the easiest allies or the most effective strategists, but their energy was life-enhancing.'

'I'll bear that in mind.'

'And she's so extraordinary-looking. Something of an exhibition in herself.'

'Make that *exhibitionist*. The other day, a group of us were having lunch in the Grosvenor. She insisted on recounting her latest dream, in which she was – wait for it! – a man searching for a penis. For reasons best known to herself, she wanted a modest, snail-size one, but all she could find was a huge one, as thick as a ram's horn. "What does that say about men?" she asked.'

'I'd have thought it said more about her.'

'I held my peace. Of course, Helen lapped it up. She's fascinated by dreams. The first thing she does each morning is look up the symbolism of the night's offering in the dream dictionary she keeps by the bed.'

'Really?' Clarissa asked, trying not to picture it.

'I'm a constant disappointment to her since I never remember my dreams . . . Correction, I "repress" them. Forgive me. You don't want to hear all this.'

'It's fine,' Clarissa said, turning aside.

After a blessedly (and, no doubt, suspiciously) dreamless sleep, she spent the morning in the West End, before heading to Putney for lunch with some of her former parishioners. As they shared news, she gave thanks for the Christmas round robins, which had kept her in touch with the births, marriages, deaths, cruises and kitchen extensions in the congregation. She in turn gave a selective report of life in Tapley – or Great Snoring, as it had been dubbed by Esther Blair, her long-time churchwarden, still aggrieved at her taking the 'easy option' of a rural parish. After animated accounts of the changes instituted by her successor ('not improvements, of course, although attendance has shot up'), she left amid a flurry of her warmest hugs, to remind them of what they were missing.

She took the tube from Putney to Acton, where she was to have tea with Julian Wotton, the closest of her erstwhile BBC colleagues. Now in his early eighties and paralysed with MS, he depended for day-to-day care on his formidable housekeeper, Margaret, who ushered Clarissa into the kitchen the moment she stepped through the door. Though impatient to greet her friend, she listened sympathetically as Margaret listed her complaints, ranging from Julian's refusal to take his pills, do his exercises and 'go easy on the hard stuff', to the council's reduced refuse collection.

'Have they no thought for those of us with two weeks' supply of dirty nappies?'

Clarissa's initial amazement turned to dismay, as she realised that the nappies in question were Julian's. She escaped to the sitting room, where he was drumming the arm of his rise-and-recline chair. Knowing his horror of being infantilised, she resisted the urge to kiss his balding pate, with its poignant resemblance to her father's, instead squatting to reach his cheek. They exchanged pleasantries, until Margaret wheeled in the tea trolley.

After setting out the crockery with proprietary deliberation, she handed Clarissa a thin slice of date-and-walnut cake. 'None for Father,' she said, mouthing 'diabetes' as though it were 'gonorrhoea'.

'I'm sure he's sweet enough already,' Clarissa said, with an apologetic smile at Julian.

'I could tell you stories,' Margaret replied, pouring the tea – milk first – and passing them each a cup. 'I'll leave you to your chitchat. If you need me, I'll be in the kitchen.'

'Make sure you are,' Julian said. 'No eavesdropping in the hall.'

'You can moan about me all you want. I'd like to see anyone else put up with you; I really would.' With a martyred expression Margaret moved to the door, closing it firmly behind her.

'Never grow old, Clarissa. Or at least, never grow helpless.'

'You have the cake,' she said, seeking to salve his bruised pride. 'I've had a large lunch.'

'She's a bloodhound. She'd smell it on my breath.'

'I thought you were fond of her.'

'Stockholm Syndrome. But I shan't let her spoil your visit. I want to hear all about you and Marcus and Xan.'

Just as at yesterday's tea with Decca in Willesden and today's lunch in Fulham, she outlined life in Tapley but, this time, there was little reciprocity. Julian declared that he had nothing in his life but his books and the 'meeja' (she was unsure whether the pronunciation sprang from dental problems or disdain). So debilitating had his condition become that, on some Sundays, even the cab to church was too taxing for him, though the vicar would always give him communion at home. With so few current points of contact, they fell to reminiscing about Broadcasting House.

'My former PA, Jan, goes from strength to strength.'

'I'm afraid I haven't read any of her novels.'

'You're not exactly her target audience. Xan lapped them up as a boy. I wrote to congratulate her, but she never replied.'

'Happy days.' As he spoke wistfully of Bruce's 'meeting to define the concept of a meeting', it was clear that retrospect had cast a rosy glow over even the most arcane departmental practices. By contrast, he was virulent in his censure of present-day religious broadcasting. 'Radio is bad enough, but television is an outrage. They can't film a pilgrimage to Lourdes unless it's fronted by a nineties pop star, a former game show host, an ageing soap actress and a disgraced politician. And they can't feature a vicar unless he – or she – is suitably toothsome and inclined to strip off at the first opportunity, like that chap who immersed himself in all the holy wells of Wales. What hope for the culture when it sinks to the level of the magazines women read at the hairdresser's – worse, that are read by their stylists?'

'That's a question for another time,' Clarissa said, as she stood up to leave, although she'd no doubt hear it in a different form from Marcus, long before her next visit to Acton.

She returned to Marylebone where, with Marcus still at work, she took the occasion to snoop around the flat. She neither knew nor wanted to know his weekday schedule: whether Helen spent Monday and Tuesday here and he spent Wednesday and Thursday in Highgate, or whether they preferred an element of spontaneity, but she was grateful that one of them – presumably Helen – had had the tact to remove any tangible traces of her presence. But if her reading of detective stories had taught her anything, it was that even the most painstaking criminals slipped up, and as she opened the grocery cupboard, she chanced on a box of muesli. Holding it between finger and thumb, she pictured herself in the witness box, appealing tearfully to the judge. 'It couldn't be my husband's, milord. For years, his breakfast cereal has been All-Bran.' By turns amused and depressed by her investment in the fantasy, she entered the bedroom and lay down, alert for any unfamiliar hollows. Sensing that this was an investigation too far, she drew a bath and, after luxuriating in it for half an hour (it was a holiday of sorts), she dried herself and dressed.

Marcus returned as she was brushing her hair. 'You always look good in black,' he said, kissing the nape of her neck.

'Most women do,' she replied, as she clipped on her amethyst drop earrings, a teenage reward for not piercing her ears. The thought prompted her to ring her mother, who answered, while a hoover hummed in the background.

'Is Maureen still there?' Clarissa asked, fearing that she'd been held hostage until she'd cleaned up every last speck of dust.

'No, it's Xan.'

'Xan's hoovering?' she screeched so loudly that Marcus, fresh from the shower, put his head round the bathroom door.

'Of course. He walked in without wiping his shoes and left a trail of mud through the hall and up the stairs. I asked him to clear it up. He said that you never bothered. I told him I could well believe it, but while he was under my roof, he'd observe the proprieties. "Actually," he said, "you're under my roof." Which was hurtful, but we both know where he gets it from.'

Envisaging the torrent of abuse that would greet her, Clarissa decided not to speak to Xan until her return. 'I won't disturb him. Give him my love and tell him that I'm looking forward to seeing him on Friday.'

'You do him no favours by pampering him,' Julia said. 'He won't have women waiting on him hand and foot for the rest of his life.'

It took all her resolve to choke back: 'You mean unless he becomes vicar of All Saints', Harpenden, principal of Westcott House, Cambridge, and Bishop of Chester?' Instead, she thanked her mother for her help, switched off her phone, and headed into the sitting room, while Marcus finished dressing. Five minutes later, he called her to put on her coat, since the cab was due to arrive.

For all that she regarded black tie as pretentious for a private dinner party, she had to admit that Marcus looked particularly handsome, even with his cummerbund doubling as a corset. 'What should I know about our hosts?' she asked, as they settled into their seats.

'Victor and Sybil Milford are joint owners of the Cockaigne fashion group. More to the point, they're serious collectors of Seward. They've offered us anything we like for the show, although we've yet to agree on what.'

'How very generous!'

'Yes, but not entirely altruistic, since the exposure will increase the value. We're also hoping that their foundation will be a major sponsor. But there are still several hurdles to overcome.'

'The size of their name on the posters?' Clarissa asked, having been privy to such negotiations in the past.

'The hurdles are more at our end than theirs. Some of the staff are kicking up rough after reports that Cockaigne's suppliers run sweat-shops. Worse, they're in Bradford, not Bangladesh.'

'What does it matter where they are?'

'Not to me . . . I mean they're equally unacceptable. But after all the protests over the BP connection and those clowns from Liberate Tate pouring oil over one another in the 1840 room, it's been harder to attract sponsors.'

'A publicly funded gallery needs to be squeaky clean.'

'Were the Medici squeaky clean – the greatest patrons in history? And what about the medieval Church?'

Or the modern Church, Clarissa thought, recalling Daisy Quantock's fury at her father's recourse to an archaic privilege, in order to unravel the legal tangle over the St Peter's faculty. 'Though neither of them were in receipt of public funds,' she said.

'Taxes . . . tithes: what's the difference?'

'So the end justifies the means?'

'No, but the art does.'

The car pulled up outside Albany. Worried that they were late, he jumped out, giving Clarissa only a moment to straighten his tie. He led her down a covered walkway to the Milfords' set, informing her casually that it had once belonged to Graham Greene. To her horror, Sybil, who opened the door herself, greeted her as Helen. How typical of Marcus not to have told their hosts of the change of plan! How typical of him not to have told her of the original one! Glimpsing his doleful expression, she kept silent as Sybil introduced her as Helen to Victor and their four fellow guests.

A cawed 'Clarissa!' from the shadows of the room shattered the pretence. 'Mrs Hamilton-Brooke,' she said, turning in astonishment to the wizened creature tucked in the corner of a wingback sofa.

'Clarissa Derwent!' Phipps, Clarissa breathed at the second misnomer. 'Let me look at you! It's been years.'

'Five at least . . . since before we moved to Tapley.' She bent to take her hand.

'No, no touching! My tenosynovitis is agony. Come here, next to me.'

Clarissa sat down, as terrified of stumbling as when she'd lain the newborn Xan in her bed.

'Clarissa?' Sybil said to Marcus. 'I thought your wife's name was Helen.'

Mrs Hamilton-Brooke cackled.

'No, that's my colleague, Helen Leslie. She sometimes accompanies me on Tate business.'

'Business?' Sybil sounded affronted.

'Work-related pleasure.' Clarissa felt no qualms about enjoying his discomfort. 'I should have explained, but I didn't want to cause embarrassment. As they say in the bankruptcy courts, there was no intention to deceive.' His laugh drew no response. 'Clarissa's a priest.'

'Really?' a man with a gravelly voice interjected. 'We had one of them in Henley, but she didn't stay the course. Ran a self-defence class in the crypt. Rum do!'

Clarissa smiled wanly.

'Is no one going to give the poor woman some champagne?' Sybil asked, gesturing to the waiter. 'Or don't you drink?'

'Champagne would be lovely.'

The waiter handed Clarissa a glass. Marcus followed her to the sofa, hovering uneasily as, in a show of disapproval, Mrs Hamilton-Brooke failed to invite him to sit down. Clarissa took slow sips as she stealthily studied the milky-eyed lady who, by any calculation, had to be approaching her century.

'What a wonderful surprise! Marcus didn't tell me you'd be here.'

'He didn't know. At my age, it's wiser not to announce one's plans. I'm ninety-eight, though I keep that to myself,' she said, with a snort of derision. 'I've been widowed for more than half my life, which is immensely satisfying. But my energy's not what it was. I wasn't sure I'd be able to come tonight, after yesterday's private view.'

'You were there? I didn't see you.'

'Just for an hour. I can't stand for longer. I'm a martyr to bunions.' Clarissa glanced in alarm at her court shoes. 'I spotted you talking to that vexing young woman, Hermione Merriott.'

'You know her?' Marcus asked.

'I knew her grandmother. The family owns half of Shropshire.'

'She's kept that quiet.'

'My cousin Reggie went on to marry Vernon Merriott's second – or was it third? – wife. Thick moustache. But then he'd developed a taste for hirsute women after learning to dance, cheek to cheek, with a mop at Stowe.' She chortled. 'Hermione's been trouble ever since an overzealous tutor told her that the family fortune was founded on sugar cane.'

'You mean slavery?' Marcus said. 'But that's wonderful.'

'It is?' Clarissa asked.

'Don't you see? It accounts for her attacks on Henry Tate. It's displacement.'

'Isn't that a bit glib?'

'You haven't had to listen to her. Lettice, I could kiss you.'

'Please don't,' she said. 'I have raging neuralgia. I take it that you and Hermione don't see eye to eye.'

'It's Herm now,' Clarissa said.

'She's far too old for diminutives.'

'No one would deny the evil of slavery – certainly no one at the Tate,' Marcus said. 'Which makes it all the more important to acknowledge that some beauty emerged indirectly – I stress *indirectly* – from its profits.' The art justified the means, Clarissa told herself. 'She was incensed when my colleague Perry Chapman asked if she would ban the Harlem Gospel Choir from singing "Amazing Grace", given that it was written by a slaver.'

'Who turned abolitionist,' Clarissa interposed.

'Yes, but not until years after writing the hymn. I know that there's more joy in Heaven over one penitent sinner and all that, but it doesn't alter the facts.'

'Surely one can disown one's background out of idealism as much as guilt?' Clarissa said.

'Are you thinking of yourself or Herm?' Marcus asked.

'Sorry to butt in,' Sybil said, heading towards them. 'Dinner is served. Lettice, do you need a hand?'

'I need new legs, but I take what I can get. Marcus, you know the drill.'

He stood in front of her and levered her up by the elbows. To Clarissa's surprise, she didn't uncross her ankles until she was bolt upright when, after struggling to steady herself, she hobbled out and into the dining room, leaning heavily on Marcus. Clarissa followed with Sybil, who led her to a long ebony table gleaming with candlelit silver. Prominent on the opposite wall were two full-length Van Dyck portraits of a sumptuously dressed Caroline couple.

'Ancestors?' Clarissa asked.

'Sotheby's,' Sybil replied. 'Our ancestors would have been pulling their ploughs. Victor's recipe for a contented life: old masters and a young mistress,' she said lightly. 'He has both.'

Clarissa noted with amusement that her place card bore evidence of haste, lacking the elegant calligraphy of its neighbours, *Henry Struthers* and *Francis Fontayne*. She took her seat and was immediately addressed by Henry, who turned out to be a member of the Bach Choir. The meal was less of a trial than she'd feared. Conversation was as palatable as the food and as mellow as the wine. If this was new money, it was a marked improvement on the old. She still shuddered at the memory of accompanying Marcus to cheerless country houses, where he tried to charm the owners into lending their pictures for some exhibition or other. They called themselves custodians of the nation's heritage, yet the works were not just badly but dangerously displayed. At one breakfast, she'd feared that Marcus was ready to leap up and rescue a Gainsborough, hanging directly above a hotplate.

There was no such danger here. The Milfords and their guests knew and respected their art, listening attentively as Marcus detailed his plans for the Wemlock retrospective.

'There's not a shadow of doubt in my mind that he was one of the four or five greatest English painters of the second half of the twentieth century, but he has yet to gain full recognition. In part, that's down to his choice of overtly Christian subject matter and imagery. Rothko's non-specific "spirituality" or Chagall's Hasidic mysticism would have served him better with the critics. Then of course, there was his private life. Even twenty years on, he remained, to the public at large, the playboy of the sixties and seventies. So, his work was regarded as somehow frivolous – a rich man's fancy – which, as my wife can testify, was very far from the truth.'

'Were you close?' Francis asked Clarissa.

'I got to know him a little in the late eighties after interviewing him for the radio.'

'Pity. I thought that you might have been one of his *rosebuds* – isn't that what he called his girlfriends?'

'That's hardly my style.'

'I apologise for my husband,' Francis's wife, Tilly, exclaimed from across the table. 'I do it so often, I should have cards printed.'

Marcus forced a smile as he waited for the laughter to fade. 'Most damaging to his reputation has been his upper-class roots. Even when he referenced Stanley Spencer, a painter he much admired, in his use of an elevated viewpoint, he was accused of looking down on us lesser mortals.'

'Your exhibition aims to change that?' Tilly asked.

'I trust so. It's the most comprehensive survey of his career to-date. We have a couple of watercolours of Windsor Castle he painted at Eton, plus a highly accomplished if somewhat academic early nude, entitled simply *Portrait of a Girl*. We've tracked down several apprentice works from his time in Paris: Rouault-like still lifes and panoramas of Montparnasse.'

'How long was he in Paris?' Henry's wife asked.

'About eighteen months. He came back to study at the Slade. It's been fascinating to discover the work from that period. With the paint more thinly applied than in his mature style, the figures in several of the portraits are almost evanescent. I wouldn't wish to make too much of it, but I think we can directly connect it to what he later said about his difficulties forming relationships in his youth . . . "People always seemed to be escaping from me." Of course, the heart of the show will be those more mature works, which is why I'm so grateful to Victor and Sybil for agreeing to loan us the cream of their collection.'

'What about the widow?' Henry asked. 'Is she on board?'

'We've corresponded. She was always private, but I gather that in recent years she's become very withdrawn. I'm due to visit her to report on progress and see how much of his work she's kept.'

'Is she actually his widow?' Sybil asked. 'Did they ever marry?'

'I can vouch for that,' Clarissa said, 'since it was my father who officiated. Not long before Seward's death.'

'She was considerably younger than him,' Marcus said. 'She's only just turned eighty.'

'A spring chicken,' Mrs Hamilton-Brooke said drily.

Citing her glaucoma, she remained at the table, while the rest of the guests followed Victor and Sybil into the master bedroom, where the two 'London Wemlocks' were hung. Clarissa stopped short at the sight of the first, a half-length portrait of Dora and Valerie, naked to the waist, the latter pinching the former's nipple, which was explicitly modelled on *Gabrielle d'Estrées and One of Her Sisters* in the Louvre.

'Racy,' Henry said. 'I see why you keep it in here.'

'Don't you find it intimidating to face them night after night?' Tilly asked Sybil.

'But I'm not invited in here night after night. Once a month if I'm lucky,' she replied with a cryptic smile.

'Now Sybil, don't give away all our secrets,' Victor said darkly.

'But it isn't a secret, darling; everybody knows.' She turned to Clarissa. 'It's not that my husband likes younger women; he just doesn't like older ones.'

At any other time, Clarissa would have acknowledged the hurt in her voice, but for now her focus was the portrait. She was one of the few people – perhaps the only one apart from the principals – who was privy to its full meaning. Maybe in three or four centuries, an art historian would seek to explain it to his girlfriend, as Marcus had explained the original to her on their first trip to Paris. He'd described how Gabrielle was Henry IV's mistress and, though no one could be certain, the nipple-pinching was thought to be an affectionate allusion to her pregnancy. For all she knew, the sister herself might have borne several children; Valerie, however, had none. She was smiling broadly and must have complied with the pose. Yet despite the caressing flesh tones, it struck Clarissa as unconscionably cruel.

'Do you think it's because of what he said about the lion lying down with the lamb?'

'I beg your pardon,' she replied, as Tilly's voice cut into her musings.

'Isaiah.'

She moved to the second painting, entitled *Homage to Isaiah*. It showed a lion mating with a stag and, according to Victor, was also closely modelled on a well-known original: Stubbs' *A Lion Attacking a Stag*.

'I suppose it must be, though I'm not sure that this is quite the lying down he had in mind.'

'The stag is an ancient symbol of Christ,' Marcus interjected.

'Yes, but so's the lion, so it doesn't get us much further. And we mustn't ignore the broken cross in the background. I don't want to encroach on Marcus's turf, but Seward did expound his beliefs to me at considerable length. He held that the flesh and the spirit were one, and the attempt to separate them was the source of both human misery and human wickedness. He extolled the libertarian strand of Christianity, which, though driven underground and persecuted, has been present from its earliest days. He was especially keen on the Ranters, dissenters at the time of Cromwell, who maintained that nothing in God's creation could be sinful and therefore everything was permitted.'

'Sounds like anarchy,' Tilly said, with a sniff.

'Though it might get people back into the pews,' Victor said.

'Not in Henley,' Henry replied.

'Fascinating,' Sybil said, bringing the conversation to a close. 'I'm sure you're all ready for coffee, if not something stronger.'

They returned to the drawing room for coffee and brandy. Shortly afterwards, Mrs Hamilton-Brooke summoned her chauffeur, and the party broke up. As she watched her wrap herself in a mink-lined gabardine, Clarissa finally ventured to compliment the old lady on looking so well.

'At my age, my dear,' she replied, 'well is simply a euphemism for alive.'

After a round of goodbyes and the unnerving claim from Henry's wife, Charlotte, with whom she'd scarcely exchanged a word all evening, that 'it's been so lovely talking to you,' Clarissa followed Marcus to a cab.

'I hope that I didn't disgrace you,' she said, as they made their way down Piccadilly.

'You were a triumph. Everyone loved you.'

'More than Helen?'

'Mea culpa. I so hate going to these things on my own. The wives flirt shamelessly in the hope that their husbands will notice.'

'So Helen's merely your wingman?'

'She could never have explained the Isaiah picture so brilliantly. I'd no idea that you and Seward had had such intense discussions. If I ever write that biography, you'll be my first port of call.'

'I'm still not sure whether he was trying to shock me or seduce me.'

'Probably both.'

'Well, he didn't succeed in either. Looking back, I'd say that, after my father, he – or at least his doctrine of universal salvation – has been the single greatest influence on my own faith. Then again, I was young and overawed. As well as being a celebrated artist—'

'And *Lord* Wemlock.'

'And Lord Wemlock, I grant – he was a force of nature. I found it hard to challenge him. It can't be a coincidence that all the heretical sects he admired belonged safely to the past. He read widely and must have known about the Children of God—'

'Aren't we all?'

'No . . . I mean yes, of course, but they were a specific American movement, which grew out of the free love and flower power of the sixties and seventies and, by the late eighties, were known to practise rape, paedophilia and incest. The founder (or so-called prophet), a man called Berg, was denounced by one of his daughters.'

'There's a fine line between Blake's *Everything that lives is holy* and Crowley's *Do what thou wilt shall be the whole of the law.*'

'How can we be sure not to cross it?'

'I suppose that's where moral responsibility – the third and, to my mind, toughest part of your father's holy trinity – comes into play.'

'Do you think that it did so for Brian?'

'Please stop beating yourself up over that! What's done is done. You told me yourself that you had no choice.'

'No, the Church told me that I had no choice. So many lives have been ruined – one lost – because of my intervention. I'm in no doubt that, in every other respect, Brian was a thoroughly moral man. So was it just one fatal lapse, when he was blinded by passion, or was he consciously setting his own moral code above society's laws?'

'I can't answer that, any more than you can.'

'Maybe Seward can.'

'He'd have a job.'

'No, you idiot,' she said, unable to resist a smile. 'There were two other sects he used to cite – at least two that I recall. Both Russian. One was the Khlysts – Rasputin was alleged to have been a member – who practised ecstatic rituals and unbridled sex as a pathway to God. The other was the Skoptsy, their polar opposites, who believed in abstinence, self-mutilation and castration. Which do you think God favoured?'

'Are you asking me?'

'No, Seward was asking me.'

'I don't want to go all C of E on you, but might there not be a middle course?' He let his arm fall easily around her shoulder and she felt her anxieties fade. 'You heard what Sybil said about being lucky to sleep with Victor once a month.'

'Yes,' she replied hesitantly.

'Will you make me lucky, as well as extremely happy, tonight?'

Two

Clarissa never thought she'd say it, even to herself, but it would have saved a great deal of trouble if the Victorians had left the lath-and-plaster ceiling in place. The Puritans, who erected it, had been as affronted by the richness and colour of the hammerbeam roof as by the stained glass and wall paintings. Yet tearing it down would have jeopardised the entire building, so they chose instead to conceal the offending masonry. Thus it had remained for two centuries, until Seward's great-grandfather, fired by Puginesque zeal, exposed the medieval timbers and foliate bosses, one of which had fallen so inopportunely during Brian's funeral.

The last quinquennial inspection sixteen months earlier had revealed no trace of the deathwatch beetle, now known to be present in the ancient oak. Joseph Sturges, the investigating architect, had explained that, even if the infestation were confined to a small portion of the chancel, its eradication would be time-consuming and costly. Advising against the use of external sprays, he recommended that they inject insecticide through small holes bored in the wood. Clarissa had conveyed his findings to a sombre meeting of the PCC, where her proposal that the new lighting system be placed on hold came as an evident relief to several council members, until she mentioned that the money saved on the initial consultation would be a fraction of the cost of the roof repairs. After a spate of fundraising suggestions, including sponsored walks, treasure hunts, trivia nights, raffles and sales of local produce, she voiced her frustration out loud.

'That's all well and good and please don't think I don't appreciate Alec's quiz questions and Hetty's cakes and jams, but they won't get us very far. What we really need is a substantial legacy.'

Her remark triggered alarm among some of the older members, which was compounded by Wendy's joke. 'You've been looking peaky, Katy. What's your poison, strychnine or cyanide?'

As Katy's eyes widened, Daisy Quantock asked with steely calm whether Clarissa had any particular benefactor in mind.

'I was speaking hypothetically.'

'There's been far too much of that here lately. I move that, from now on, we stick to the facts. Before we get bogged down in the details of the repairs, let's remember when and how the damage occurred.'

'The architect's report made it clear that the erosion was impossible to foresee,' said Lewis who, following Pamela's resignation, was Clarissa's chief ally on the council. 'You may be able to spot beetle faeces forty foot up; I know I can't.'

Daisy gave him a look of utter disgust, as though she suspected him of being familiar with faeces in all its forms. 'I'm not talking about the damage to the roof alone,' she said, notwithstanding her insistence on sticking to the facts. 'Why should the boss have fallen at the very moment that the rector uttered those words?'

'It was a sheer coincidence,' Lewis said, refusing to be cowed.

'There are no coincidences in church.'

'Then we should be grateful that it fell on the coffin, where it did no harm ... that is except to the lid,' Wendy interposed. 'It could have fallen on one of the pallbearers or Clarissa herself.'

Daisy's silence spoke volumes.

'It doesn't bear thinking about,' Alec said, 'what with the compensation and increased premiums.'

'We're straying from the point,' Daisy said. *'He who is without sin among you, let him throw a stone at her first.* And what happens? A stone, or the next best thing, crashes down from the roof. It's as if the church itself was asserting its purity.'

'I thought you held that it was impure: that the presence of Seward Wemlock's paintings polluted it,' Clarissa said.

'Quite,' Daisy replied, with an air of triumph. 'It wasn't a lump of plaster from the chancel arch or the spandrels, let alone the west wall, that broke off, but a boss from the roof, part of the original masonry, a relic of a more righteous age.'

Clarissa couldn't blame Daisy for seeking a mystical explanation, when her own collapse had lent it credence. But the following day, as she stood in the nave to survey the scaffolding, she reminded herself that the destruction had been wreaked by a colony – and not a plague – of beetles. As Sturges' report spelt out, the saturation of the wood after the recent theft of lead had created ideal conditions for the pest to thrive. The shattering of the boss had been 'an accident waiting to happen'. The key question was how far the infestation had spread. Hoping for an answer, she intercepted the structural engineer, whose strident whistle filled the church as he arrived for work. After a bootless exchange in which he refused to anticipate his conclusions, she left him to climb the tower, while she made her way to the school for her regular Thursday morning assembly.

She walked through the churchyard, assailed by a deep sense of unease on realising that this would be her first assembly since Susan Leaves' reinstatement. Although the tribunal judge had declared that he was ruling, not on the merits of her petition but solely on whether, by posting it online, Susan had breached the terms of her contract, he'd nonetheless expressed surprise that she'd been dismissed for affirming Christian values in a church school. Furthermore, he'd ruled that, along with the right to return, she had the right to have her concerns addressed, leaving Pamela no option but to remove the relationships classes from the curriculum. The governors, who'd approved their introduction, had been summoned to a meeting with the bishop. But Clarissa's immediate objective was to prevent Pamela fulfilling her threat to resign.

She paused outside the almshouses for a word with Major Millington, whose complaints about the 'hideous' metal roofing had led to a delay in the replacement of the stolen lead and indirectly to the accident. So if she were looking for someone to blame . . . which she wasn't, she reminded herself, as she hurried down the High Street. She arrived at the school, where Miss Nixon, the sparrow-like secretary, stood alone in the yard.

'Jake's busy in the boiler room, so I'm on guard duty,' she said shyly. Clarissa trusted that the security measures, introduced during Susan's protest, could now be relaxed, not least since Miss Nixon, whom she'd once encountered in the administration block oblivious of the *Miss Nickers* pinned to her back, would win no prizes for vigilance.

Entering the assembly hall, she saw no sign of Susan among the twenty or so staff lining the platform. Might it be that, faced with her colleagues' hostility and secure in her legal – and, to her mind, moral – victory, she'd no sooner returned than she resigned? Curbing her curiosity, she stood by the door and, at Pamela's nod, strode to the platform, where she greeted the children, before pulling a torch out of her bag and announcing that, this week, she'd be talking to them about living in the light of God. As usual, the prop sparked a buzz of anticipation, followed by squeaks, squeals and one loud wail, when she asked a teaching assistant to lower the blinds, while she was still fumbling with the torch. She switched it on, shone it at the serried ranks, and called for a volunteer. A forest of hands shot up and she chose a girl with ragged plaits, who grew instantly coy, wrinkling her nose and shaking her head. Seizing his chance, the boy beside her jumped up and climbed on to the platform, ignoring Clarissa's entreaties to stand still, until Pamela's flinty *Liam!* brought him to a halt.

'I'm going to ask Liam to walk slowly away from me. Slowly, Liam!' Clarissa said. 'Can everyone at the back see?'

'We don't need to, Miss,' said a husky-voiced boy, a definite year six. 'You showed it us before. You showed how his shadow—'

'Yes, thank you. Let's not spoil it for everyone else!' Clarissa said, feeling a trickle of shame, as if she'd been caught recycling a sermon. 'Carry on walking across the platform slowly . . . slowly, Liam! Can you see, children, how Liam's shadow grows bigger the further he is from the light?'

'Yes, Reverend Clarissa,' came the stuttered response.

'It's the same for us all when we move away from the light of God. Would you walk back please, Liam?' Ever more confident, he began to goosestep. 'Now see how his shadow grows smaller and smaller, until it almost disappears. That's enough,' she said when, egged on by his friends, he pressed his face against the torch. She signalled to the assistant to raise the blinds. 'Thank you, Liam, you can sit down.'

He returned reluctantly to his seat, where his neighbour hugged him with affecting tenderness. She thought of Xan, so afraid of being labelled gay that he'd cut off all contact with David Leaves, and prayed that these five-year-olds' intimacies would outlast their milk teeth.

She asked them to join her in the Lord's Prayer, stumbling over *Give us this day our Daily Bread*, as she had done ever since Herm's remark about tautologies. The children filed out, and she followed Pamela to her office.

'Will instant do?' Pamela asked, switching on the kettle.

'Yes, of course,' Clarissa replied, with a plaintive glance at the Nespresso machine. 'Is it on the blink?'

'I forgot to order the pods. You have my permission to leave.'

'Don't be ridiculous!' Clarissa said, removing three wooden bricks from a chair and sitting down. 'No Susan? Is it too much to hope that, having made her point, she's handed in her notice?'

'Much too much! She has some family crisis meeting with officials and care workers. I didn't ask but expect it's to do with . . . her son. She should be back this afternoon. I'm sure she'll be sorry to have missed you.' They laughed companionably. 'Credit where it's due, she's avoided triumphalism.'

'Then she can't be her mother's daughter.'

'The first thing she said when she came back was that right had been done by the children, and she hoped we could put our differences behind us. Then she asked how I'd been coping since Brian's death and told me she'd been praying for me.'

'That's good of her.'

'Is it?' Pamela asked. 'She's made it clear that, in her world of predators and victims, I'm one of the latter. At least it makes a change from some in the village, who see me as Rose to Brian's Fred West.'

'You're imagining things.'

'Did I imagine the poison-pen letter, pieced together from scraps of newsprint?'

'Saying what?' Clarissa asked, with trepidation.

'It wasn't what you'd call literate, but pretty much what I've just described. I'm a monster who should never be allowed near a school.'

'Have you shown it to the police?'

'Of course.'

'Though I suppose that without means of identification . . .'

'Oh, she identified herself quite clearly: Daphne Redwood.'

'Shirley's mother?'

'I knew you'd be upset. That's why I haven't mentioned it. She went to all that trouble, cutting the words out of various papers, and then wrote her address on the back of the envelope.'

'She spends three days a week on dialysis,' Clarissa said feebly, presuming that, having missed the 'drama' of the funeral, Mrs Redwood had decided to create some herself. 'Not that that's any excuse.'

'They let her off with a caution. She just expressed what everyone else was thinking: how could I not have known what Brian was like? Or worse, was I in cahoots with him: giving him the run of the school? Oh fuck! I really can't take any more.'

The kettle boiled, giving her a moment to compose herself. She made the coffee, handing a cup to Clarissa.

'Thank you. Trust me, I'm not minimising it. But as soon as there's another' – she refused to say *scandal* but could think of no alternative – 'it'll all be forgotten.'

'The way that Maureen Thring's affair with the African student has been forgotten? Or Bob Goodfellow's flooding of Maynard's field? I know you advised me to wait before making any big decisions. I wasn't going to say anything, but I've applied for the deputy headship of the Ark Beatrix Potter academy in Keswick. I've put you down as a referee.'

'Keswick?'

'It's a bigger school, so I'm under no illusions about my chances. But I've always loved the Lakes. Len and Josie have a caravan there. Who'd have thought it but, with everything that's happened, I feel more protective of them than I do of my own parents! They're living in a dream world. Len's determined that Brian should have a plaque in the ringing chamber, like all the tower captains before him. I've begged him to let it drop, but he won't budge.'

'I know. He's written to the PCC.'

'So soon? What do you intend to do?'

'I'll start by sitting on it till August, when we're barely quorate and you know who is on holiday.'

'Can't you sit on it until the children and I have moved away?'

'Have you discussed it with them – the move that is, not the plaque?'

'I've told them it's on the cards. Margaret's all for it, in so far as she can think of anything beyond her GCSEs. Matthew accuses me of setting out to destroy his life (no mention of his father having done that already!). He's refusing to leave Tapley: swears he'll camp out on the wetland . . . even ask to be put into care.'

'Xan was the same when we left Fulham.'

'I doubt it was for the same reason. On Monday evening, after the governors' meeting, I came home to find a used condom floating in the loo. I don't know whether he'd left it there as a provocation or it had simply failed to flush.'

'Hayley?'

'Living up to her reputation. I suppose I should just be grateful that he's wearing one. Brian said he'd given him "the talk", but the RSE lessons must have helped.'

'Up to a point. Xan told us the teacher demonstrated by pulling one over his fist. After meeting him at parents' evening, Marcus said that his little finger would have been more fitting.'

'They begin relationships classes aged five at the Academy, but then it's not a faith school. Listen to me, acting as if I'm a shoo-in when I've not yet been called for interview.'

'They couldn't hope for a better candidate,' Clarissa said, swallowing her dismay at her friend's departure.

'Even after the Susan debacle? They're bound to know.'

'You did what you thought – we all thought – was right. So, it didn't work out—'

'I couldn't give a damn for myself. What hurts is that I've failed the children. Only last week, I was standing at the window during break and I heard a gang of boys yelling "tranny" at Lee Belben from year three. When I spoke to his teacher, she explained that they'd found out his older brother, Michael or, as she now is, Michelle, is taking puberty blockers and they've been taunting Lee that he's also going to turn into a girl.'

'Are they serious?'

'Who knows? If ever there were a case for relationships classes . . . Remember the polar bear book to which Susan took such exception? Well, I've done some research and there are several types of fish that change gender naturally. How great would it be to have a book about them to read with the children? I've even dreamt of writing one. Mine would be clownfish, and not just because their yellow-and-gold markings would make splendid illustrations. It'd have a powerful secondary theme. A school of clownfish is always led by a female; when she dies, the dominant male changes sex and takes her place.'

'Transgenderism, feminism and the double meaning of "school": Susan would have a seizure.'

'As it is, we're muzzled by the judge's ruling. All we can do is tell a class of misinformed seven-year-olds that it's wrong to call one another names.'

Clarissa left, promising to write her a 'killer reference'. She walked to her office, where Shirley was tinkering with her pedometer. After Doctor Workman's warnings about her blood pressure, she'd started to count her daily steps. It had taken all Clarissa's powers of persuasion to convince her that rolling her chair from desk to filing cabinet wouldn't register on the display. Nevertheless, she blamed her consistently low scores on its faulty mechanism.

Unsure how much she knew about her mother's letter, Clarissa greeted her with reserve. With no overnight crises or urgent requests, she left promptly for the weekly Eucharist at Wemlock Hall. To avoid painful parallels, she preferred to hold it on a different day from the school assembly, but Friday's rescheduled chapter meeting had given her no choice.

'Will you ring Gillian Mainwaring and confirm that I'll call round at three to discuss her husband's funeral?' she asked Shirley. 'With all she's going through, it may have slipped her mind.' It would be the first funeral in the church since Brian's, and she was afraid that the scaffolding tower would be a grim reminder, as well as an eyesore.

'So sad! He was one of Titus's special friends, wasn't he, boy?' The drowsy dog pricked up his ears. 'So much for him to sniff on those ratty old cords. We used to see Peter on a Friday night in the Wem. Mother likes to pop in for her weekly tipple. He called it Gin and Sin, which made us laugh. The last couple of times, Titus wouldn't go near him. That's how I could tell he wasn't long for this world. Dogs have a way of knowing.'

Glancing sceptically at the canine seer, Clarissa headed for the car. She took the familiar road out of the village, stopping when she spotted a heavyset woman tramping past the bowls club.

'Can I give you a lift?' she asked, gulping as she recognised her prospective passenger.

'It's fine, thank you,' Susan replied, looking equally uncomfortable.

'Where are you heading?'

'Wemlock Hall.'

'Same here! Hop in and I'll take you.'

After a slight hesitation, which Clarissa affected not to notice, Susan opened the door. Other than a chance encounter in the village shop, they hadn't spoken since the tribunal, and Clarissa was keen to grasp the nettle.

'I was sorry not to see you at assembly this morning,' she said, setting off as soon as Susan had fastened her belt.

'I squared it with Pamela,' Susan replied defensively. 'I have a meeting at the Hall about Lily.'

'Is anything wrong . . . silly question . . . anything out of the ordinary?' Clarissa asked, relieved that the family crisis didn't involve David.

'The last thing I need is more gossip about the Leaves. But seeing as it's you . . . Yes, she's made another of those wild accusations. A man in the night, coming in and . . .'

'It's part of her illness. You mustn't take it to heart.'

'But this time it's different. She specified a big black man. And there's only one of those . . . I mean at the Hall. Worse, Elaine Perkins overheard her. It was her husband whose room Lily broke into last year and . . . well, tried to do the things she's accused the rest of them of doing to her. You'd think she'd be the last person to credit Lily's fairy tales. But no, she's a great one for speaking up for those who aren't able to speak for themselves! She's demanded a full investigation and threatened to lodge a formal complaint with the council. It's Benjamin I feel sorry for. He doesn't deserve it. Such a dear man! He's a regular at our church.'

'I know,' Clarissa said, acutely aware of his defection after only a single visit to St Peter's. Since then, he'd kept her at a distance, as though he'd abandoned her at the altar rather than simply chosen to worship elsewhere.

'He reads the lesson so beautifully, and in an accent that reminds us that God's Word is for everyone. There's no way that such a decent young man and with Lily a bag of bones . . .'

'I don't think it works like that.'

'I know,' Susan said crisply. 'I wasn't born yesterday. Dr Workman examined her.'

'Couldn't they have found a woman?'

'Lily wouldn't have known the difference.'

'Given what's happened, that's demonstrably untrue.'

'Anyway, it's too late now. He said that there was chafing . . . down there, but it could be explained by the incontinence pads. And I'm absolutely sure that's the case. But then you read – did you read? – about the home in Northampton, where the owners were convicted of making pornographic films?'

'An old people's home?' Clarissa asked incredulously.

'Yes, but with young men brought in . . . It was in the paper.'

'I must have missed it. I can't say that I'm sorry.'

'What kind of pervert would watch those films, with women like my mother-in-law who've no idea who they are, much less what they're doing? And the owner – he was Polish too; no, I don't mean *too*! – was unrepentant. At his trial, he claimed that the money he made from the films was the only way he could manage to keep the home open. What's more, he said that the women enjoyed it: it was the first time that some of them had been touched in years. It doesn't bear thinking about.' She twisted the handles of her bag. 'We have to protect the young and vulnerable, of course, but what about the old and vulnerable? Who's looking out for them?'

'You're right; we must all be vigilant. But that's an isolated case and an appallingly extreme one. I'm quite certain nothing like that has occurred here.' Clarissa's voice rang with conviction. 'As you said, Benjamin is an honourable, churchgoing man and Lily has made false allegations in the past.'

'That may be so, but if paedophiles can worm their way into children's homes, why wouldn't – I don't know the word, but there must be one – men who are attracted to frail old women do the same in care homes? I have these pictures in my head all day long. If it's not David and Brian Salmon, it's Benjamin and Lily. I just want the world to go back to how it was.'

She took a tissue from a bag and blew her nose. Clarissa considered pulling over but decided that, given their history, the kindest thing was to drive straight to the Hall. She pressed down on the accelerator, only to brake sharply when she turned into Meadow Lane and found herself behind Danny Prentice's tractor. Resigned to a lengthy delay, she turned to Susan.

'What time's your appointment? You might do better to walk.'

'Mr Kovačić will wait. To be honest, I'm dreading it. I'm sure he's going to ask us to move Lily.'

'Is Andrew meeting you there?'

'No, he's old-fashioned in his way.' No surprise there, Clarissa thought. 'He holds that family problems are women's business.

Besides, he isn't close to his mother. I shouldn't say it, I know, but I think a part of him feels that she's getting her comeuppance. He didn't have a happy childhood. He won't talk about it, even to me, so I've had to piece it together, best I can. He blames Lily for his dad's leaving them. If it wasn't for my mother, I'd have gone through life supposing he'd been killed in the mine. When the kids asked about their granddad's grave, he told them he was buried beneath the rubble. Even now, pushing fifty, he sticks to the story, until I wonder if he's come to believe it himself. What's more, it was a Wemlock mine, which gives him another reason for his grudge against the family. I've never understood why he stayed in Tapley,' she added, while Clarissa sounded the horn, as much for a moment's respite as to alert Danny. 'Of course, I'm glad he did, or we'd never have married. Though I say it myself, he was a catch. Girls were lining up for him from here to Crewe. But once we'd gone out a couple of times, that was it. It's the same as how he joined Clifton's the week he left school and has worked there ever since. My mother – it's no secret that she's not his biggest fan – she says he was a real live wire back in year six. But then he fizzled out. She blames it on posing for Lord Wemlock. I don't need to tell you about that. I've even wondered . . . but no, it couldn't happen twice, not to both him and David.'

Clarissa sounded the horn more forcibly. 'He had such talent.'

'Lord Wemlock?'

'No. Well yes, obviously, but Andrew. His drawings were really special. I advised him to apply to art school.'

'Andrew?'

'Yes.'

327

'My Andrew?'

'I'm sorry. I'd have thought . . . has he never told you?'

'But he hates art! He wouldn't even come to see the *Mona Lisa* when we took the kids to Paris. Andrew . . .? You're having me on.'

'He showed me the drawings when I was making the programme.' To her relief, the tractor turned into a field. 'I did my best to encourage him.'

'He's never had a kind word to say about you, but I thought that was to do with the church. I can't get my head round . . . Andrew wanted to be an artist?'

The question hung in the air as Clarissa drew up at the Hall gates and stated her name into the intercom. Susan, sunk in contemplation, rallied as they jounced over the ruts. 'I feel like someone in a book who finds out that she has a different father.'

'At last!' Clarissa parked alongside the Kovačićs' Lexus. Having disappointed Ozren in the past by her lack of interest in its luxury features, she wondered for the first time how he'd been able to afford it. Burying the thought, she headed into the vestibule where Mirna was waiting. As usual, her welcome was less effusive than Ozren's, rousing Clarissa's suspicions that, despite her prominent crucifix, she regarded the weekly Eucharist as a disruption to the well-regulated routine.

'My husband expects you in the office,' she said to Susan, who thanked Clarissa for the lift and disappeared down the corridor.

'I'm sorry to hear about the problem with Mrs Leaves,' Clarissa said. 'It must be wretched for you.'

'It would not happen in my country,' Mirna replied, with rancour.

'You Brits, you leave us your elders and ask us to clean up their dirt. We clean up the dirt that comes from their backsides, that is our job. But now you want us to clean up the dirt that comes from their mouths. This is too much. It is not correct.'

'You do a wonderful job,' Clarissa said weakly. 'I'm in awe.'

'It is not me who does this job,' Mirna said. 'It is my staff. Poor Benjamin, now he is afraid that he will be sent back to Nigeria.'

Mirna led the way into the day room. 'Here is the Reverend, come to say Mass,' she said, drawing no response other than a splutter from a new arrival, hunched over a glass of lurid orange squash. 'I leave you to it,' Mirna said, as though she'd instructed her to scrub the floor.

Clarissa observed the residents, with their bleats and moans, their jabber and babble, and equally impenetrable silences. How ironic, given the propensity to madness that Seward had identified in his grandfather and aunt, and which later resurfaced in Sorrel, that these should be the inheritors of his ancestral home!

She circled the room, making one-sided conversation, wishing, here as nowhere else, that she were a man, whose presence might trigger a childhood memory, rather than a woman, whose clericals could never be more to them than fancy dress. She moved to the newcomer, who sat stupefied, while Blessing introduced her as if she were filling in a form.

'Her name's Marjorie. She lived on her own with her dog. She let it sleep on her bed, with all its nasty fleas.' She shuddered. 'One night the dog passed, and she couldn't lift it off her leg. She lay there, trapped, until the binmen called the police. They don't know how long it took, but from the smell, they think it must have been a week.'

'What university did Wilf go to?' Marjorie piped up.

'I'm afraid I don't know,' Clarissa replied eagerly. 'Is Wilf your son?'

'Wilf's her dog,' Blessing interposed.

'How rude!' Marjorie said, as Clarissa stood, bewildered. 'Why are you staring at me? I'm not a television.'

Clarissa prepared for the Eucharist, thankful for the doctrine, learnt at her father's knee, that the grace of the sacrament did not depend on the disposition of the recipient. Even those who no longer had ears to hear or minds to comprehend had mouths to accept, and as she distributed the bread and wine, they opened them as instinctually as fledglings.

'You naughty girl!' Blessing said, when Marjorie regurgitated the wafer. 'The body of the Lord all over your nice clean dress. Fresh on today!' As she continued to chide her, it was hard to tell whether she were more concerned about the sacrilege or the laundry.

Failing to find either the Kovačićs or Susan, who she presumed were still in conference, Clarissa drove back to the rectory, where she made an abortive phone call to Angela Wilcox, who was adamant that, 'God-given talent or not', James was quitting the choir, followed by a more fruitful one to Wendy Plowright, interim leader of the Holiday Fun Club, who proposed Major Millington as a suitable candidate to 'step into Brian's shoes . . . that is, the breach'.

'Excellent idea!' Clarissa said. 'Judging by the barrage of complaints he fires off at me, he has plenty of time on his hands. Just so long as he doesn't turn it into the Holiday Boot Camp.'

After finishing up the previous night's cauliflower cheese, she moved to the chapel and prayed the Daily Office, adding petitions for Benjamin and Lily, as well as both the victims and perpetrators of the Northampton pornography outrage. Replenished, she headed to the Mainwarings' where, to her relief, Peggy, Gillian's supercilious daughter, deferred to her mother on the order of service, confining her dissent to a deep sigh at the choice of the theme tune from *Match of the Day* ('your dad's favourite') at the exit.

Returning home for an hour of the downtime that the rural dean had advocated after his recent sabbatical, Clarissa lay on the sofa with *The Best of Aretha Franklin*. She was so absorbed in listening to (and, occasionally, accompanying) 'A Natural Woman' that she failed to hear Xan come in.

'What's all this, Mum? Tapley's answer to *Britain's Got Talent*?'

'I was unwinding. Aretha Franklin, the Queen of Soul.'

'Oh well. So long as it's soul, it's allowed.'

She switched off the record, as alert to Xan's *Mum* as Marcus to the slightest scratch on the vinyl. Moreover, he'd entered the sitting room of his own accord, rather than stomping straight upstairs.

'Busy day?' she asked, avoiding the contentious 'good'.

'Double maths. French test. Pervy Mr Lennox explaining that Shakespeare's girls are best played by boys. Ringo Lewis and Warren Matthews having a set-to at lunch. Oh yes, and the Head rounding up the whole of year nine in the hall and telling us why we shouldn't kill ourselves.'

'Was there any particular reason for it?' she asked, wondering if she'd missed World Suicide Prevention Day.

'Yeah, Ruth Taylor tried to hang herself in the bog.'

'No! How terrible! Why? She must have been in a very bad way.'

'What do you think it was like for the girls who found her?'

'I take it that the school has systems in place.'

'Yeah, the children can talk or, better still, sign up for counselling. It's all pants!'

'Ruth Taylor . . . don't I know that name? Did she go on the skiing trip?'

'No way! Her parents don't allow her to join in any after-school activities. Except their church or fellowship or whatever.'

'Yes, of course. I remember now.' Ruth was the Seventh Day Adventist: the girl whose half-naked photograph Xan had forwarded to a friend.

'So I suppose you think it's my fault?'

'What? Not at all. Why?'

'Go on say it! If Matt and I hadn't sprayed *Slag* on her locker, she'd be fine.'

'That was months ago.' She remembered an issue with tampons. 'From what you told us, she had a very disturbed home life. Let's pray she'll now get the help that she needs.'

'The way I see it, we'd all be better off topping ourselves. That paedo Brian had the right idea.'

'Don't you dare say that!'

'What: *paedo* or *right idea*?'

'Both. As you know better than most, Brian was in a very dark place. I've witnessed the pain that his death has caused the whole family, including Matthew, however much he may deny it.'

'He's loving it! A paedo for a father or Hayley for a girlfriend? Do the maths!'

332

'Won't you sit down? You look so uncomfortable hovering there.'

'I'm OK.'

'Then you're making me uncomfortable.'

'Oh well, I'll go up to my room.'

'No! Stand, sit, whatever you prefer,' she said, grateful that he made no attempt to leave. 'It hurts me so much to see you like this.'

'I'm very sorry, but this is the real me: the one you pretend to love.'

'There's no pretend about it.'

'No, I forgot. You may not always *like* me, but you'll always *love* me. Did I get that right?'

'Definitely the second part.'

'You wouldn't love me – you really wouldn't – if you knew what was inside my head.'

'I'm quite sure it's no worse than what's inside my head or Dad's head or any of your friends' heads.'

'That's easy to say. What if I turn out to be a rapist and mass murderer, like the Yorkshire Ripper? It'd be better for everyone if I killed myself now.'

'You're not a rapist or a murderer and you're not going to kill yourself.' She refrained from jumping up and hugging him: the surest way to send him scuttling upstairs. 'Your life is supremely precious, not just to me and to everyone who knows you, but to . . .'

'Go on, say it! You don't usually hold back.'

'God . . . to God. You may not want to hear it, but He created each and every one of us.'

'Then He created far too many of us. Overpopulation; global

warming; famine; billionaires being cryogenically frozen so they can come back to life and guzzle even more of the planet's resources. Why stick around for that?'

'To try to fight it . . . to make the world a better place. And it's your generation that must take the lead.'

'Yeah, right. Throw the children a bone. Make them feel worthwhile. But nothing we do makes any difference. Don't you remember your lesbo friend saying that every breath we take contains the atoms of everyone who's ever lived?'

'Her name's Decca and, yes, I do. It may not be in every breath, but it's certainly over the course of every day. Why should that depress you? Just imagine: Gandhi and Shakespeare and Marie Curie . . . and Jesus.' Without thinking, she inhaled deeply. 'It's the most wonderful connection, a communion even for those who never go to church.'

'And Hitler and Stalin and Attila the Hun. Yeah wonderful! It shows that no matter what we do, we stay the same.'

'But we're more than just atoms. We're consciousness and spirit.'

'I wondered when we'd get round to that. I'm going upstairs.' This time he edged to the door.

'Please wait a minute.'

'I've got geography homework.'

'We have so few opportunities to talk.' Taking a calculated risk, she stood up, clasped his arm and guided him towards the sofa. He broke away and flopped into one of the armchairs.

'What's the use when you never listen?'

'I'm listening now.'

'But are you hearing me? You say that there has to be a God behind the universe. Like, even if they find out what happened before the Big Bang, there had to be something before that, and then before that, and so on. And I agree. See, I think about these things, whatever you may suppose.' Clarissa willed herself not to interrupt. 'But who says He has to be a loving God? What if He's actually the Devil, and His best trick has been to fool your lot for thousands of years? If He really cared about us, why did He create so much evil?'

'God didn't create evil.'

'Then He couldn't have created the world. You can't have it both ways.'

'I'm not trying. Evil is the inevitable consequence of living in a world that isn't God . . . a world of time, rather than eternity. The creation can never be as perfect as the Creator or else it would *be* the Creator. And all the faults in human nature, like those in nature itself, whether it's violence and greed and cruelty, or an earthquake, a drought and a tidal wave, stem from that.'

'Is this in the Bible?'

'Not exactly. It was your grandfather who explained it to me. With a little help from Seward Wemlock.'

'The bloke who painted your church?'

'Our church.'

'Not mine. Defo!'

'It's the parish church and you live in the parish, like it or not.' She noted the slight puckering of his lips as if he were suppressing a smile. 'Seward loathed the story of Adam and Eve—'

'Then why did he paint it?'

'I should have said he loathed the way it's been interpreted down the ages . . . the notion that we're innately sinful and that Jesus came to save us. He maintained that Jesus assumed our flesh not to redeem it, but to validate it: to show that we were one with God and innately good.'

'Do you agree?'

'Defo.' This time he had to smile. 'Some people thought he was self-serving, but I believe that he was sincere.'

'I didn't ask for a sermon,' he said truculently.

'You're not getting one. But it is my field of expertise. If I were a doctor and you had a rash, wouldn't you want me to look at it?'

'Depends where it was.'

'Point taken. All I ask is that, if you ever feel desperate or futile or' – she couldn't bring herself to say *suicidal* – 'you talk to somebody. Do you remember when we used to read the Narnia books together?'

'I'm not six!'

'I know,' she replied, stifling the unworthy wish that he still were. 'I can't remember which one it was in, but there was a character called Mr Puddleglum. When the witch – only she wasn't called the witch – held the children captive in the Underland and tried to convince them that there was no Narnia—'

'She was the Lady of the Green Kirtle.'

'That's right! Mr Puddleglum declares that he's going to live as a Narnian even if Narnia doesn't exist.'

'You mean he's a wally, living in cloud cuckoo land.'

'Or a wise man, asserting the value of faith.' Xan shook his head, but so gently that Clarissa felt a glimmer of hope. 'Now I'd better let you go and do your homework, or you'll blame me if you do badly. We won't be eating till seven. Would you like me to bring you up some toast?'

'I'm not hungry. Can I stay down here and listen to the record?'

'Really?' she asked, dumbfounded. 'You want to listen to my music?'

'It's not yours, it's Aretha Franklin's.'

'How can I say no?' She moved to switch on the record player and picked up the album cover. 'Which track should I choose? How about "Say A Little Prayer"?'

'No way!'

'Or "You Make Me Feel Like A Natural Woman"?'

'I'm out of here,' he said, without making a move.

'I know. "Bridge Over Troubled Water." That should suit us both.'

Three

'Can't you put your foot down?' Marcus asked. 'There are no hidden cameras in the hedgerows.'

'Don't be so sure. The last thing we need is for me to be booked. Sit back and enjoy the view.'

Marcus, whose sensibilities were more attuned to art than nature, sulked. Clarissa, meanwhile, relished the patchwork of grass-green and leaf-green and moss-green and every other shade of green, dotted with the dappled skins of grazing cattle and the grey-browns of field barns and drystone walls. The Nidderdale valley unfolded before her like an illustration in a children's storybook, one that even Susan Leaves would approve.

They were visiting Dora Wemlock. Marcus, never the most relaxed of passengers, had been given a six-month driving ban in June. Since he didn't use the car in London, he'd amassed the penalty points during his weekly trips to Tapley, for which he'd somehow contrived to blame Clarissa. Reluctantly, she'd agreed to ferry him to and from Crewe station, adding that elsewhere, he'd have to fend for himself. But when he wheedled and pleaded with her to take him to Yorkshire, she relented. With the Wemlock retrospective due to open in spring 2021, it would soon be time to make a final selection of the work. After a fitful correspondence, Dora had offered to loan him anything in her possession, while neglecting to specify what that might be. She'd cancelled three previous meetings, the most recent on spraining her ankle in May, and Marcus was starting to doubt her good faith. To complicate matters, she wasn't on email. While appreciating his frustration, Clarissa couldn't resist a smile on hearing the high priest of tradition denounce her as a Luddite.

Marcus insisted that he wanted her with him for more than her clean licence. Long experience of artists' widows had taught him the importance of gaining their trust, and who better to do so than an old friend? Clarissa was more doubtful, her relationship with the taciturn Dora having never been close. Besides, she felt guilty at not having written to her after learning of Laurel's death. Since her days at the hospice, she'd supported scores of bereaved parents, several of whom had suffered the additional blow of suicide, but no one whose daughter had killed herself so brutally. For months, she'd brooded over Laurel's choice of method. Had drinking bleach been, in some subliminal way, an attempt to cleanse herself?

Despite Marcus's complaints, Clarissa was relieved that Dora shunned the internet. After Father Vincent broke the news, she'd searched online for information. Along with brief reports in the *Norwich Evening News* and *Eastern Daily Press*, she found a raft of conspiracy theories, which might have been posted by Andrew Leaves himself, had he used the pseudonyms Tellithowitis or Buzzcat99. She had no idea how allegations that she'd thought known only to her had seeped into the public domain, but, whatever else, she acknowledged that she'd been remiss in failing to investigate them at the time. Regardless of any embarrassment, she should have confronted Seward, not least to give him the opportunity to defend himself. She could picture his wry smile as he explained, with complete conviction, how Andrew had misconstrued this innocent remark or that innocuous gesture. And in the event – however inconceivable – that the allegations were true, wouldn't he have welcomed the chance to unburden himself as well as to protect Laurel? She'd attached too much weight to Father Vincent's assurances. Then again, it was unjust to blame him, when they'd been what she'd wanted to hear.

'Nervous?' she asked, shrugging off her own concerns and turning to her disgruntled husband.

'Of course. She was always odd. The last time I saw her was Seward's funeral in ninety-three. She holds the key to so much. What happened to all the paintings in his studio? They've none of them come on the market. Has she sold them privately to some Russian or Chinese billionaire? And how about all his notebooks and drawings and letters? Do you think he kept a diary?'

'Are you asking for the exhibition or the biography?'

'Both. Well, the exhibition first, of course. There are several works I remember from our visits that I'd like to include. That wonderful crouching camel, if we can't get the Houston version, and the reclining nude of Dora herself. Who knows whether she'll want it to be seen? Maybe she's become religious.'

'Seward was religious.'

'All right then, religiose. And, yes, if she's happy with the show, it can't hurt my chances for the book. She's turned every other request down flat.'

'As Seward did yours.'

'That was thirty-odd years ago. She knows it's time, especially after that hack Hayden Bennett's cut-and-paste job. Trotting out all the old clichés.'

'Perhaps she should be grateful he was so slapdash.'

'Whatever do you mean?'

'Too idle to conduct any in-depth research.'

'You do say the strangest things. Of course, she shouldn't be. Though I have to admit I am. She's recognised the need for an authoritative life. It's early days yet. But when I made my pitch, she sounded keen.'

'It's a big commitment. Will the Tate give you leave of absence?'

'They're itching to give it me permanently. A grand send-off: more crocodile tears than in the reptile house at the zoo.'

'You exaggerate. Everyone was singing your praises at the Blake.'

'My last hurrah. I don't fit the corporate image. Diversity's the watchword, as much for the staff as for the collection. What would you say was the most important attribute of a curator?'

'I don't know,' she replied, afraid he was going to suggest black skin or gender fluidity. 'Expertise?'

'Integrity. And it's in ever shorter supply. I may be old-fashioned – old hat, in the eyes of some of my colleagues – but I believe in an artistic canon. And, yes, I believe that Berthe Morisot and Angelica Kauffman and Georgia O'Keefe are part of it. I don't believe that Artemisia Gentileschi was as great a painter as her father; I do believe that Gwen John was a greater painter than her brother. I judge a work of art on its merits, nothing else. Bollocks to the latest ism!'

'We've arrived,' Clarissa announced, spotting the long, low, rough-hewn building with its mottled, clay-tiled roof, which the satnav had identified as their destination. 'The Old Byre! Well, it certainly lives up to its name,' she said, parking on a strip of waste ground in front of a rusty gate.

'What an extraordinary place for her to have fetched up!' Marcus said. 'He must have left her a pretty penny, unless there were mountains of debts or an extremely well-endowed cats' home.'

'Something for the final chapter of the biography?'

'It's all very well on a day like this, but it must be bleak in the middle of winter. Or do you suppose that she goes south? I can't picture her taking the air in Madeira.'

'Shush,' Clarissa said, as, with the tinkle of wind chimes, the front door opened and a giant dog of indeterminate breed bounded out. As it ran barking through the wild, windswept garden, Clarissa hoped that Dora didn't allow it to sleep on her bed. With no other houses in the vicinity, she doubted that the binmen paid regular visits.

Dora appeared in the shadow of the doorway, and it felt as if they were transported back thirty years. She stood straight and slim, with long, lank hair, and wearing one of the distinctive calf-length smocks, which, to St John and Julia's horror, she'd also worn to Seward's funeral. As they walked down the weed-infested path, she came into sharper focus: her blonde hair flecked with grey; her pale face wrinkled, with sagging jowls and drooping eyelids. The effect was disconcerting, as if a fifty-year-old actress had been made up as an octogenarian.

'Quiet, Robin!' Dora said, to her overexcited dog. 'We have so few visitors. Please come inside.' She led the way through a dusty hall into a spacious sitting room, with low-hanging beams and exposed stone walls, the furniture draped in richly coloured throws and scattered with needlepoint cushions. Standing in front of the open fireplace, she gestured to the chairs. 'Do sit down. Apologies for the mess. Fling everything on to the floor.' Clarissa sat gingerly on the sofa, scratching herself on a crochet hook, obscured by a patchwork square. Marcus, taking their hostess at her word, heaved three hefty tomes off a chair. '*Flora Britannica*,' she informed him.

'What a delightful room!' Clarissa said.

'It's the old milking parlour. Once home to forty cows. Now only me.'

Clarissa smiled hesitantly. Never having heard her make a joke, she was unsure whether this one were intentional.

'Did you convert it yourself?' Marcus asked.

'Heavens no! It was done years ago, but I told the agent that I'd rather not know any dates. After Wemlock Hall, I wanted somewhere without a history . . . I've prepared tea. I just have to boil the kettle.'

She walked out, her steady gait showing little sign of the recent sprain. Marcus leapt up to examine the pictures, all of which, to Clarissa's unpractised eye, were by Seward. The large canvas of a white stag trampling on a snake, which hung over the fireplace, had been in his studio. The rest were either landscapes or animal studies, without a single figure even in the background. Moreover, while every surface in the room was covered with crystals and ammonites, shells and fir cones, driftwood sculptures and snow globes, there wasn't a single photograph.

343

'Seward would have hated this,' Dora said, as she wheeled in the tea trolley. 'He'd have told me that I wasn't running a boarding house. He never came here, but I still feel his presence all around.'

'In a way it is,' Marcus said, pointing to a picture of the Tapley wetland, bathed in an ethereal glow.

'I suppose so,' she replied, 'though by now they've become part of the furniture.' Marcus bit his lip. 'Tea? I should warn you it's herbal.'

'Perfect!' Marcus said, a touch too brightly.

'And my own blend. Would you like some cake? Courgette and raisin.'

'Sounds delicious,' Clarissa said.

'Just a small slice for me,' Marcus said, patting the stomach that he usually pulled in. 'Doctor's orders.'

'Have you lived here long?' Clarissa asked, as Dora handed her a plate.

'Hard to credit, but it's nearly twenty years. When Seward died and the Hall was sold, I moved to Norwich, but things didn't work out. I needed some time to rebalance. I came to a soul-coaching centre up here and fell in love with the Dales.'

'A far cry from Tapley.'

'There's the motorway. Oh, I see what you mean.' It may have been the setting, but her low laugh resembled a moo. 'I needed somewhere just for myself. Please don't get me wrong, it was a privilege to be at Wemlock. But I'd never lived anywhere with more than three bedrooms before. I come from a very different world to Seward.'

'Most of us do.'

'When I think of all the things I'd have missed if I hadn't modelled for him! I used to be so square. At first, when I refused to sleep with him, he presumed I was playing hard to get, holding out for clothes or jewellery or whatever else he'd given his former girlfriends: the *rosebuds*, as he called them. I called them the *thorns*. Even though my marriage was more or less dead, I wouldn't cheat on Trevor. But Seward finally convinced me that the person I was really cheating was myself.'

'I can imagine,' Clarissa said drily.

'What's more, I was cheating Trevor by not giving him the chance to move on. Which, I'm happy to say, he did.' She pressed her bosom. 'All that matters is your heart.'

'Hear that darling?' Marcus said to Clarissa. 'Food for thought.'

'Another slice of cake?' Dora asked him.

'I won't say no,' he replied. 'I'll count it towards my five a day. Is it your own recipe?'

'Mine and Mrs Edwards' – the cook at Wemlock. It was Valerie's favourite. I used to bake it for her while she could still swallow.'

'Did she live here with you?' Clarissa asked.

'Heavens no! She moved to Bexhill-on-Sea. Not that she saw much of the sea after her stroke. But I took the train down there every couple of months. She'd been a good friend to me. People expected me to resent her, but without her, I'd never have survived at Wemlock. And it wasn't as though she set out to betray me. I didn't know it till later, but she and Seward had been sleeping together for years, long before Hereward died. It was painful at the start, but I came to see that that was how their world worked. Better to keep it in the family.' Clarissa took a gulp of tea. 'The one thing I'd never do was join them, if you see what I mean.'

'Yes,' Clarissa replied, anxious to be spared the details, however useful they might prove to the prospective biographer. 'I think of her whenever I'm in the Wemlock chapel. Such a beautiful plaque.'

'Strange to think of you there. I'm not a churchgoer – down in the village they take me for some sort of witch—'

'A sibyl, surely?' Marcus said.

'No, a witch. But if I were . . . a churchgoer, that is, I'd prefer to have a woman in charge. Still, who'd have thought you'd end up in Tapley? Was that your father's doing?'

'Not at all. He was dead by then. Besides, he was bitterly antagonistic to women priests. No, there were reasons for me to leave London.' She peeked at Marcus, who stared at his plate. 'I knew the parish, and the wardens knew me from having made the radio feature. They were receptive to the idea of a woman rector after Father Vincent, who became increasingly eccentric in his later years.'

'He used to give me the jitters.'

'On top of which, I wanted to be nearer my mother.'

'Lord knows why!' Marcus interposed. 'It's a battle royal.'

'True. But she's getting on. Like it or not, I'm all she has.'

'I'm sure she appreciates how lucky she is to have such a devoted daughter.'

Rather than demur, Clarissa took the opportunity to offer her condolences on Laurel's death.

'You heard about it?'

'I'm sorry. I should have written, but I was swamped with problems in the parish.'

'I didn't hear from many people, but then I hadn't seen Laurel since Seward's death. She broke off all contact. The only news I had of her came from my sister, Karen. She made strenuous efforts to keep in touch with Laurel after she married. She said it was for my sake.' She shook her head. 'We've never got on.'

'At least you had news,' Clarissa said, refusing even to contemplate losing touch with Xan.

'She'd become a Catholic, which makes what she did still harder to explain.'

'Not necessarily. My son recently asked me why, given the state of the world, we didn't all kill ourselves.'

'When was that?' Marcus asked.

'You weren't there. I know the orthodox view is that suicide stems from despair, and, with my clerical hat (or collar) on, I ought to echo it. But I realise that for some people, it may seem less like a rejection of the God-given world than an exercise of God-given reason.'

'Only if that reason were hopelessly muddled,' Marcus said. 'You should have told me about Xan.'

'It was just teenage angst . . . I'm thinking of people who believe that their deaths will make life easier for those they leave behind. If they're terminally ill or have committed some heinous crime.' The muffled toll of the tenor bell rang in her ears. 'I'm not saying that it's the right decision, but it may be a rational one. Which is why I would never judge them.'

'But you're a priest,' Dora said.

'Precisely.'

'Do you have any idea of Laurel's reasons?' Marcus asked. 'Was there a note?'

'Not that I know of. But unless she'd laid all the blame at my door, I doubt Karen would have told me.'

'And it was one of her daughters who found her?'

'Ann . . . she's seventeen now. Jane's fifteen. I've never met either of them . . . not even seen a picture. I thought of buying a computer so I could follow them on their sites. But it would hurt too much.'

Clarissa surveyed the room, the absence of photographs starting to make sense.

'You're their grandmother,' Marcus said. 'Surely you have a right to see them?'

'We mustn't pry, Marcus,' Clarissa said, while discreetly trying to shake off the priapic Robin.

'He'll have no choice if he wishes to write Seward's biography,' Dora said. 'Is anything wrong?' she asked Clarissa.

'Your dog seems to have taken a fancy to my leg.'

Dora grabbed Robin by the scruff and tapped his nose. 'I should have had him neutered, but Seward would never have forgiven me. Just behave!' she said, clutching the dog, who appeared none the worse for his chastisement.

'I'm prying again,' Marcus said, with a look at Clarissa, 'but did Laurel give you any explanation for cutting off ties?'

'No, but then she didn't need to. She'd always accused me of putting Seward first. And she was right. But I owed him so much. I was nothing before I met him. Did you know he painted more pictures of me than of everyone else combined?'

'We have several already promised for the exhibition,' Marcus said. 'I was wondering if you had any others. To complete the picture, as it were.'

'At first it was because I was so still,' she continued, as though she hadn't heard him. 'He said he'd never known a model who could hold a pose for so long. It was no effort: simply being in the studio with him put me in a kind of trance. Over time, he said he saw more and more possibilities in me. What's more, he made me see them too – and not just on canvas. I'd never been with any man but Trevor. He wasn't very passionate – or, at any rate, imaginative. Seward was everything he wasn't. Sleeping with him was like Christmas Day and VE day and sweets coming off the ration all at once.'

'I almost feel sorry to have missed the War,' Marcus said, with a laugh.

'I hope this won't offend you, but the first time he went down on me – you know what I mean?'

'She certainly does,' Marcus said.

'Well, I was shocked. He came straight up to kiss me and, without thinking, I asked him to wipe his mouth. He was outraged. He told me that he couldn't make love to a woman so full of self-disgust. I never made that mistake again. I never needed to. He taught me to love my body as much as he did himself.'

'That love shines through every brushstroke.'

'With hindsight, perhaps I deferred to him too easily.' She frowned and let go of Robin, who looked up at her and yawned. 'But he was so much older than me, so much cleverer and more cultured. He had theories where I just had thoughts. One was that children should be given the same freedoms as adults. You remember how

349

he revered Blake?' Marcus nodded. 'Well, that was where he broke with him. He insisted that innocence should be juxtaposed with ignorance, rather than experience. Without experience, we'd never grow. So against my better judgement (or, as he put it, my suburban upbringing), I allowed him to bring the girls into the bedroom to watch us making love. I know it sounds strange,' she said to Clarissa, who struggled to conceal her consternation. 'It did to me, and they were my daughters.'

'How old?' Clarissa asked.

'I don't recall exactly. Six and seven? Seven and eight? The same age as Seward when Hereward took him to see a ram tupping a ewe. He was so revolted by the perfunctory, mechanical motions that, for a while, he decided to become a monk.'

'But they were animals.'

'Quite. He wanted the girls to see how different it was for a man and woman who loved each other. He didn't want them to grow up like him, horrified by the thought of his parents having sex. They needed to know that they were born of something beautiful and joyous. Was I wrong to go along with it? Might it have harmed them? When you think of what happened to Sorrel . . .'

'Their father was a great artist,' Marcus said. 'Their childhood was bound to be unconventional.'

'That's true,' Dora said gratefully. 'And it was a happy one. With such a small age gap, they were practically twins. They did everything together. Even when we moved to Wemlock, they opted to share a room. I dressed them alike, much to Seward's annoyance, but then he'd been in the army. Everything changed when Laurel hit

puberty. She demanded her own room, which was perfectly reason-
able, except that she retreated from Valerie and me as well as Sorrel.
At the same time, she grew closer to Seward, which only made Sorrel
more jealous, especially when he picked Laurel as his Eve, while she
was just to be one of the angels.'

'Higher up the celestial hierarchy,' Marcus said.

'But less prominent and, of course, sexless – I think I'm right?'
She looked at Clarissa.

'That was certainly Christ's view.'

'And traditionally depicted as male,' Marcus added.

'It was as if she felt her femininity was being rejected at the very
moment that her body was starting to bloom. And in return, she
rejected her body. She refused to wash. I warned her that she was
starting to smell, but she replied that she liked it. She wore baggy
clothes, fusty fur coats which she'd found in the attic, and when I
protested, she appealed to Seward, who said that she was old enough
to make her own sartorial choices, and I should respect them. But for
all his sympathy, he was a man: unable to comprehend the ordeal that
puberty could be for a sensitive girl like Sorrel. Laurel was far more
resilient. She'd relished her first moon party, whereas Sorrel would
have none of it. I was at my wit's end. I wanted her to see a doctor, but
Seward forbade it. He said that she'd blame all Sorrel's quirks on our
way of life. And as it turned out, he was right.'

'He paid a heavy price for it,' Marcus said. 'If she'd received
medical help, she might never have tried to stab herself, and he
wouldn't have been injured.'

Dora looked first at him and then at Clarissa, as if deciding what to say. 'I've never spoken about this before and – who knows? – at my age, I may never have the chance again, but the truth should be acknowledged. She didn't try to stab herself.'

'But Father Vincent . . .' Clarissa said.

'Father Vincent wasn't there. He was the first person on the scene, but he wasn't there.'

'Then what did she do?' Marcus asked.

'She lashed out at Seward. Laurel, who *was* there, told me everything on the day of his funeral, the same day she told me that she never wanted to see or speak to me again.'

'But why would Sorrel attack her father?' Marcus asked.

'Why would Father Vincent lie?' Clarissa asked.

'Her behaviour had become more and more erratic. The week before the attack, she chopped the hair off all her dolls. I should have recognised the signs. I mean, is that a normal response to puberty? But it was easier to go on pretending than to accept that there was a strain of madness in Seward's family, which our darling girl had inherited. As for Vincent, he was trying to help. He thought that, by saying she'd turned the knife on herself, she'd be treated more leniently. In the event . . .'

'Seward was widely praised for intervening,' Marcus said.

'In most quarters, yes. Even the tabloids that had previously vilified him. But there were some dissenting voices, which grew louder over the years. One, in particular – a bitter rival – maintained that Sorrel's aim hadn't been accidental and that, by stabbing him in the groin, she'd destroyed the source of his potency. He claimed that that was why he produced so little after the attack, when the truth was that, from then on, he never knew a day free of suffering. And the only pills that brought any relief made his hands shake. In his words, he had to choose between 'pain and painting'.

'So he gave up work?' Marcus asked, his voice thick with disappointment.

'Heavens no! He was an artist to his marrow. I never admired him more than I did then. Days after returning from hospital, he was back in the studio, determined to finish the final spandrel: the rector being led by an angel, who should have been Sorrel but had become an amalgam of her and Laurel.'

'How odd! I've always found it the least convincing of the eight. I presumed it was on account of Father Vincent.'

'But, if you don't mind my asking, why should Laurel blame any of this on you?' Marcus said.

'Because I allowed her sister to be sent away. What's more, I was the one who signed the papers. Looking back, I wonder now whether, had we kept her at Wemlock with a nurse like Seward's aunt, she might have recovered.'

'The aunt didn't, did she?' Clarissa asked.

'No, but times had changed . . . treatments had changed. What Laurel forgets . . . forgot – it's hard! – is that she was the one who pressed for her to go. She insisted that she'd be better cared for in a clinic but, to be honest, I think that she found her an embarrassment. She wouldn't speak for days and then she'd babble for hours, a mixture of gibberish and filth. She'd spew out her food at table and pee – and worse – wherever she happened to be standing. She'd pound on the door of Seward's studio and, while he was amazingly

– disturbingly – indulgent, Laurel was afraid that she'd drive him away. And for all her grown-up airs, she was terrified of losing her father.'

'What about Seward?' Clarissa asked. 'Surely he had some say in the matter?'

'For the first and last time in his life, he left the decision to me. He found it too distressing. Bear in mind she'd tried to kill him.'

'And the doctors? You must have taken expert advice?'

'Of course. Valerie's uncle was a professor of neurology. He recommended a clinic, where they'd had remarkable results with a drug that induced convulsions. But something went wrong. The dose they gave her was too high; the convulsion too long or too strong . . . I forget. Whatever it was, it left her irreparably brain-damaged.'

'Is she still there?' Marcus asked.

'At the clinic?' He nodded. 'No, it was shut down shortly afterwards. She's spent the past twenty years in a private hospital. She's safe, well looked after and as content as she ever can be. There's a gazebo, where she sits in all weathers, contemplating the world . . . although *contemplating* may be the wrong word.'

Her voice cracked, and Clarissa reached for her hand, which remained limp. 'Do you visit?' she asked.

'Not any more. The director said that seeing me disturbed her. I think he was trying to be kind. Karen told me that Laurel went three days before she . . . I can't help wondering if that played a part. Guilt, of course, but maybe fear that she'd end up the same way . . . Now there are two more sisters whose lives have been blighted.'

She shook off Clarissa's hand and stroked the dog.

'If he went on working, against all the odds, how come he produced so little?' Marcus asked, returning to the point at issue.

'He destroyed most of it. It tortured me to see how his confidence faded. You must remember?' she said to Clarissa.

'I only saw him twice, maybe three times, after the broadcast. He joked about needing a stick and that he'd solved the riddle of the Sphinx. Then I'm afraid we lost touch.'

The truth was that, after her acceptance for ordination (or, rather, her parents' opposition to it), she'd curtailed her trips to Chester and hence to Wemlock. Moreover, try as she might, she'd never fully discounted Andrew Leaves' allegations.

'He buried himself away, scarcely even going into the village. It wasn't only the pain. He was convinced that people were talking about him.'

'Saying what?' Clarissa asked, feeling a flutter in her breast.

'That he was also mad. And the more he vanished from view, the more the rumours proliferated. One man in particular was behind them. A contemporary of Seward's at the Slade. You may know him; he's also a priest. Though, at ninety, he's long since retired.'

'Philpotts!'

'You do know him?'

'Not personally, I'm glad to say.'

'For years, he was Clarissa's bête noire,' Marcus said.

'I'm with you there. They were friends as students, but he grew ever more jealous of Seward's success in what he considered to be his exclusive preserve.'

'Religion?' Marcus asked.

'Quite. He lost no opportunity to snipe at him. You'd think that a priest would have been more generous, but Seward said he would have even cast aspersions on St Luke. They hadn't met for decades, but he wrote that he was coming to see the paintings in St Peter's, and Seward felt obliged to invite him and his "catamite" to lunch. It was a disaster. Philpotts complimented Seward on the work, but so extravagantly that he seemed to be mocking him. Seward, who was in excruciating pain from what Philpotts insisted on calling his "psychic wound", retaliated by attacking his guest's "kindergarten cartoons". And though, as you know, he was no feminist, he asked him how he could object to women priests when, as a practising bugger, he regularly flouted the tenets of the Church.'

'Ouch!' Marcus interjected.

'Philpotts retorted that Seward had no idea what he practised, and he wouldn't be preached at by a man who engaged in incest – at which his friend, a harmless enough young man, had the hiccups.'

'Incest?' Clarissa asked.

'Valerie.'

'Oh, I see.'

'Although it wasn't strictly true, since she was only his sister-in-law. They then had an acrimonious exchange, which I remember unusually well, given that I was busy rubbing the young man's neck. Seward, who associated homosexuality with Hereward, declared that the two prohibitions were very different. Homosexuality broke the law of nature, whereas incest merely broke that of man. In support, he cited the Bible, where Abraham, who married his half-sister, and

Moses' father, who married his aunt, stood high in God's favour, whereas God reduced Sodom to ash.'

'I don't think we should read too much into the Old Testament,' Clarissa said. 'Incest features heavily in all ancient mythologies.'

'That was Seward's point. Why would Oedipus, a man in the flower of his youth, have fallen for a woman old enough to be his mother (since, of course, he didn't know she was his mother), except for a powerful natural affinity? He added that it would be the same for us all if it weren't for the laws that compelled us to repress it.'

'But why did Seward trouble to refute Philpotts' charge when, as you say, it didn't apply to him?'

'Who knows? He enjoyed playing Devil's Advocate, as you may remember from his discussions with your father.'

'Did Philpotts answer back?' Clarissa asked.

'Not as far as I recall. By the way I trust that you won't be approaching him to lend pictures.'

'Does he have any?' Marcus replied evasively.

'Oh yes, he boasted of having bought several at Seward's early shows. I wouldn't want anything of mine to hang alongside his.'

'You have my word,' Marcus replied, as Clarissa envisaged him replacing *Rev. Thomas Philpotts* with *Private Collection* on the labels.

'As I said in my letter, you're welcome to anything I have. Most of it's in storage in Barnard Castle. I'll arrange for you to be given access.'

'Have you kept any of the sketches he made for the church?' Clarissa asked, wondering whether she might be willing to donate them to the roof fund.

'There may be some in the store. He gave others to Father Vincent.'

'Really?'

'I know! I always thought he despised him. "Unctuous" is the word that springs to mind. But then he never ceased to surprise me. I have one painting that I'm certain will interest you. The only major canvas he completed during those final years. Would you like to see it?'

'Need you ask?' Marcus replied.

'Come this way!' She headed into the hall, with Robin at her heels. 'Watch out!' she said, as Marcus brushed against the overhanging ceiling. Clarissa followed him up the narrow staircase, where he paused to look at the pen-and-ink drawings lining the walls. It was a series of nudes of Dora: lying; kneeling; curled up; and on all fours; in some of which she was openly pleasuring herself.

'Sensational!' Marcus said. 'So tender and erotic. Such mastery of line and form. We must include them. Or are they too intimate?'

'Heavens no! They're so old now that they might as well be my mother. You said you intend to cover the whole range of his work. These are part of it.'

'Absolutely.'

'Though I wouldn't want any of them to be sold as postcards,' she said, opening her bedroom door.

Clarissa entered the room, turning to the large picture that dominated the adjacent wall. On an iron bed, the bottom sheet rucked up to expose a square of mattress, Seward stretched out, naked, between his two teenage daughters. His head was thrown back, with his eyes wide open, while his mouth gaped . . . in what: anguish, horror, or even fulfilment, given his flaccid (or detumescent) penis at the centre of the canvas? The girls, identically dressed, lay in his arms, their heads resting on his chest and their knees pressed against his thighs. To the left of the bed, in muted tones and at an oblique angle, Dora's torso emerged from a block of marble. As she gazed aghast at the thinly veiled confessional, Clarissa realised that she'd never before seen a self-portrait of Seward, let alone a nude.

'I'm speechless,' Marcus said, before launching into a panegyric. 'It's so strong, so courageous, so full of compassion . . . I'm gabbling. The way he defies expectations . . . overturns conventions. The fear in the man's eyes as he clings to the girls, protecting them from whatever lurks beneath the tilted bed or in the unseen corners of the room, although he's the one who's naked while they're fully clothed. The pain in the woman's eyes—'

'And the tears!' Dora said. 'So delicately done.'

'Absolutely. And who is she, alone in her monochrome world: a ghost or a monument, helpless to save her family from their fate?'

'I see something different in it every time I look,' Dora said.

Except for the obvious, Clarissa thought, as she recast the block of marble as a pillar of salt. The story of Lot might not be as familiar as that of Noah or Joseph, but the connection must surely have occurred to someone who'd lived with the picture for twenty years.

'Does it have a title?' she asked.

'*The Power,*' Dora said.

'*The Power?*' Clarissa repeated, as Marcus gave her a warning look.

'Enigmatic, I know, but I take him to be questioning which of them has it – the power, that is. Sometimes I think it's the mother, who's sacrificed her life for her family – though perhaps I shouldn't say so, given that he modelled her on me. Sometimes I think it's the daughters, secure in their own dream world. And sometimes I think it's the father, keeping vigil over them.'

'But he's naked,' Clarissa said.

'Yes, though don't forget that Seward painted it after Sorrel's committal, when he'd been helpless to save her from the family curse. By rights, there should be a huge, disfiguring scar across his groin.'

'Positively Wagnerian,' Marcus said.

'It makes me think of Gandhi.'

'Was he scarred?' Marcus asked.

'No. At least not that I know of. But he slept naked next to young virgins, to show that he had the strength to resist temptation. Seward, who was so often accused of decadence, was doing the same.'

'But they're his daughters,' Clarissa said, no longer able to contain herself.

'What do you mean?'

'Not virgins . . . that is, not strangers.'

'It's open to a wealth of interpretation,' Marcus said quickly. 'Everyone who sees it will make up his own mind. And no one else has seen it so far?'

'No one, apart from the occasional cleaner. He made me promise never to display it without the girls' permission. But now that Laurel is dead and Sorrel . . .'

'It will be the centrepiece of the final room: the crowning glory of the exhibition. Thank you so much for entrusting it to us. May I take some photographs?'

'Of course.'

That done, they returned downstairs and took their leave. With Robin marking their departure as boisterously as their arrival, Dora escorted them to the car. Waving them off, she expressed her delight at meeting 'two fellow guardians of Seward's flame'.

They drove for several miles in silence. Finally, Clarissa spoke. 'How much do you think she knows? Is she as naive as she seems or is it all an elaborate front?'

'Could she really be that disingenuous?'

'You tell me. I certainly underestimated her. All those visits to Wemlock, when we thought she was as dull-witted as she was dull, and it turns out that she was quietly taking everything in.'

'She may not have heard of Lot. I doubt I would have if I hadn't read history of art. Seward called it *The Power* and, unless one of those cleaners was a lay preacher, who was to tell her otherwise?'

'How about her own curiosity? If my husband portrayed me as a lump of rock while he slept with our daughters, I'd definitely want to find out more.'

'You're overthinking it. If she were worried about how we'd react, why did she show us the picture?'

'Perhaps she was conflicted. She said something earlier about the truth needing to be acknowledged. She may need you to acknowledge what she can't herself.'

'I must say I'm disappointed in Seward.'

'Disappointed!'

'Look out!' He grabbed the wheel as she swerved.

'Don't you mean disgusted?'

'I've always admired his courage, but to call it *The Power* is so mealy-mouthed. A man who can paint that extraordinary, emotive, mysterious, unsettling picture should be able to stand up and give it its true title, *Lot and His Daughters*.'

'The first place he'd be standing up in is a court of law, where artistic merit would be no defence.'

'It's a painting: a work of the imagination, not a record of his life. Given his remarks to your friend Philpotts about the innate attraction between family members, maybe he's showing – symbolically – that his power to resist was even stronger than Gandhi's.'

'Two damaged daughters and their mother lying to herself, if not to us, strikes me as fairly conclusive evidence.'

'Circumstantial. And didn't you see the expression on the girls' faces as they nestled against his chest? Pure adoration.'

'Don't forget who painted that adoration.'

'And don't you forget that, in Genesis, it's the daughters who seduce Lot.'

'That proves nothing. Look at how he put his own stamp on Eden.'

'Whether it's *Lot and His Daughters*, *The Power*, or *At Home with the Wemlocks*, Seward is doing what all good – not to say, great – artists do, challenging our most cherished assumptions through his unique vision and creative brilliance.'

'I'm sorry, I can't talk. I have to concentrate on the road.'

Four

Clarissa had misjudged the weather. It was too warm for a jacket, and she expected her mother to make a pointed allusion to her 'colour'. Dabbing her forehead as she walked up the drive, she resolved not to rise to it. She followed the faded instructions to push the bell hard, which her mother insisted was due to the faintness of the chime, rather than her loss of hearing.

Julia opened the door, kissed her distractedly, and ushered her inside. 'Leave your work bag on the table. I don't want to feel like one of your charity cases.' No, Clarissa thought, that was reserved for the African children jumping for joy on the Christian Aid collection box, which the bag now obscured. At least it was an improvement on the Spastics Society box, which had stood in the hallways of both the All Saints' vicarage and Westcott House: the little blonde girl, clutching a teddy bear and wearing callipers, who, bearing a sinister resemblance to Clarissa herself, had clomped through her childhood nightmares.

She followed her mother into the kitchen. 'What a delicious smell!' she said, her hopes of a cold meal shattered.

'It's an experiment. Rafaela has been teaching me to make tortilla.

She may have a mind of her own, but there's an upside to having a Spanish cleaner.'

Clarissa moved to the window. 'It's such a lovely day. Shall we eat in the garden?'

'And spend half the meal scratching? I'm a magnet for midges.' She opened the oven door, removed a dish and poured in the beaten eggs. 'We have to leave it to bake for twenty minutes.'

'There's no rush,' Clarissa said, selecting cutlery and crockery for the table. 'Drinks?'

'I've put a bottle of white in the fridge.'

'Perfect!' She reached for the wine glasses. 'We've time for a good catch-up.'

'I suppose I should be grateful that your tea with Vincent makes it worth your while to come here first.'

'It isn't a social call. I'm hoping he'll donate some of the drawings Seward Wemlock gave him to the church roof fund.'

'Where are you meeting? The cathedral?'

'His house.'

'You are honoured. He likes to meet me in the refectory café.'

'That was the original plan. Then he had an attack of gout. He tried to put me off, but I stood firm.'

'Poor Vincent. I must ring him. I get the feeling he doesn't have much support. The new bishop's all very well, but as he admitted to me himself, he spends half his life on committees. He has little enough time for active clergy, let alone retired ones. Your father was the opposite. Regardless of how busy he was, his door remained open.

There wasn't an alcoholic or adulterous priest in the diocese, who didn't receive his full attention.'

'A pity that his children couldn't say the same.'

'You didn't want his attention; you wanted his approval.'

'Not for what we did, Mother, just for who we were.'

'As I said, times have changed. Your father belonged to a different generation.'

'Parents usually do.'

Julia moved to the fridge and took out a lettuce, some rocket, spring onions and garlic. Turning her back to Clarissa, she washed the leaves and placed them in the salad spinner, rotating it furiously.

'May I help you with that?' Clarissa asked, in a conciliatory tone.

'Just sit quietly. You don't always have to be helping someone,' Julia replied, crushing a clove of garlic.

'Marcus and I drove to the Dales last week to visit Dora Wemlock.'

'Gracious! Is she still alive?'

'She's younger than . . . your age.'

'Such a wet weekend of a woman! Your father and I could never understand what Seward saw in her.'

'Her daughter, Laurel, took her own life last autumn.'

'No? How dreadful!' She put down the garlic press. 'I remember now, didn't she have mental problems?'

'No . . . well, perhaps. But you're thinking of her sister, Sorrel.'

'It goes to show that money can't buy happiness.'

With the moral neatly packaged, she turned to chopping the onion.

'How close was Father to Seward?'

'What an odd question!'

'Maybe, but it's a critical one. I could never work out whether they were sparring partners or genuine friends.'

'A bit of both, if you ask me. Your father admired him enormously as a painter. There again, who didn't? But he also respected him as a thinker: one of the few with whom he'd debate theological niceties.'

'So if Father had suspected anything amiss about his private life, he wouldn't have turned a blind eye?'

'What is this? Did Dora say something?'

'No, quite the reverse.'

'Naturally, he disapproved of the *rosebuds*. Although they were largely in the past by the time Seward moved back to Wemlock. But he was an artist – a bohemian – so St John made allowances. Nothing more.'

She looked up, with glistening eyes.

'I didn't mean to upset you.'

'What?'

'You're crying.'

'It's the onion!' She transferred all the salad ingredients to a bowl. 'Why must you always think the worst of your father?'

'I don't . . . I don't know. Perhaps because you always think the best.'

'He was my life. You make great play of your vocation, yet you've always refused to acknowledge mine.'

'At least your parents didn't reject yours.'

'Is that so? You don't know the first thing about it.' Julia pulled back a chair and sat opposite Clarissa at the table. 'Both of them were deeply hostile to the marriage. My father because St John had no money and, seemingly, no prospects. My mother because she believed that clergy should be celibate and St John's proposal betrayed a lack of commitment.'

'But they came round.'

'They came round to you and Alexander. I'm not sure that they ever came round to us. And they weren't the only ones who put obstacles in our path. We got engaged when St John was at West-cott. But we were only allowed to meet for half an hour a week, after Sunday Mass. The reasoning was that the sacrament would keep our bodily urges in check. His, I should say; I wasn't deemed to have any. When he returned there as principal, I made him promise to extend the time that women were permitted on the premises.'

'I remember. It earned him an unwarranted reputation as a liberal.'

'Why bring all this up now? Your father's been dead for twelve years.'

'Not to hurt you, I swear. Nor to discredit him. But we need to face up to the truth.'

The mysteries in Seward's past had impelled her to resolve as many as possible in her own.

'What do you want me to say? For all his outward assurance, he was a troubled man. I did my best to keep it from you children.'

'We weren't blind! Mealtimes are stamped on my memory. Sitting around this very table.' She faltered, as she realised that, were she to crawl beneath it, she would find her twelve-year-old brother's crudely carved FUCK. 'Father castigating Alexander or me for some fault, real or imagined, before blaming you for your failure as a mother.

Then one of us – you or me, never Alexander – would burst into tears and, in a twinkling, he'd be as sweet as pie.'

'He had his demons; he fought against them.'

'And against us,' Clarissa replied, choking back *you*.

'He hit me,' Julia said, as if reading her mind. 'I know that's what you want me to admit. As if it were all-important.'

'Isn't it?'

'No! It happened once or twice . . . three times at most. You were very young, which is why it made such an impression. I'm sorry.'

'It's not for you to apologise.'

'I know it offends you that I won't play the victim. But we were man and wife: one flesh. When he hit me, he was hitting himself.'

She took a tissue from her sleeve and wiped her eyes. Clarissa marvelled at how she'd rationalised as love what the women on the Chapel Hill estate knew as abuse. She stood up and moved to her, crouching by her chair and putting her arms around her shoulders.

'No,' Julia said, pushing her away. 'A hug's not the answer to everything.' She walked to the oven and looked inside. 'A few more minutes. Rafaela says that it should be golden brown.' She fetched bottles of olive oil and balsamic vinegar from the cupboard. 'The person I feel for is Marcus.'

'You've made that patently clear.'

'What husband wants to hear that the happiest day of his wife's life was the day she was ordained.'

'You're the one who raised the subject.'

'From then on, he knew that you were never going to put him first.'

'It was the same for you with Father.'

'Women expect it; we are able to deal with it.'

'Not everyone's prepared to sacrifice herself on the altar of a man's ego.' She winced, as the words hit home. 'Besides, as you well know, you can never see inside someone else's marriage.'

'Yet you think you can see inside mine.'

'I was living in yours!' She stood and prowled round the kitchen.

'Pass me the mustard, will you?' Julia said. 'On the middle shelf. No, the Dijon. Thank you. Would you rather have watercress or parsley in the dressing?'

'Parsley,' Clarissa said, knowing that 'whichever is easier' would be seen as a sign of indifference.

'You talk of speaking the truth about things that happened thirty . . . forty . . . fifty years ago. Perhaps you should look closer to home. You said nothing to Xan about Marcus's lady friend.'

'No, we left that to you.'

'I never intended . . . I'm sorry. But he's no fool. He knew that there was something wrong and was frightened that his father would leave.'

'Would that be such a bad thing?'

'What?'

'Nothing. Just thinking aloud.' Was she to admit to her mother what she'd barely admitted to herself? 'But you're right about one thing. Whatever the case with Marcus, I shall always put my son first.'

'Is that remark directed at me?'

'No,' Clarissa replied, equivocally.

'Alexander's been dead for thirty years.'

'7 August 1987.'

'Yet you still blame me for not being at his bedside.'

'Not only that,' Clarissa muttered.

'What did you say?'

'Nothing.'

'You see! You can't let it go. I know you'd like me to have walked back in from that phone call, tears streaming down my face, and asking everyone to leave – that is if I'd been in a fit state to walk at all. But I was in shock! What's more, I'd have had to deal with twenty guests: their shock; their condolences; their meaningless, well-meant kindnesses.'

Their questions, Clarissa thought, with a pang of shame.

'How would that have helped Alexander? How would that have helped anyone?'

Clarissa instinctually touched her stomach. She wasn't proud of her relationship with her mother and the deep resentment that decades of prayer had failed to expunge. But the one thing for which she gave herself credit was that she'd never revealed her miscarriage nor the part she believed that her mother had played in it, even when, only hours after Alexander's funeral, she'd been fretting about her missing towel.

'Shall we open the wine, Mother? I could do with a glass.'

'You go ahead. The corkscrew's in the drawer. I must just powder my nose. And would you switch the oven to Warm?'

Although the corkscrew should have been a clue, Clarissa was surprised to find a bottle of 2015 Sancerre, with a label that she recognised from regular Christmas, Easter and 'pick-me-up' presents.

She was touched to think that Julia must have consulted Lewis after a visit to Tapley. Pouring herself a glass, she moved to the window and admired the display of sweet peas and delphiniums. A lavatory flushed and, moments later, Julia returned, her glowing cheeks a sign that the powder had been no mere euphemism.

'I've put your glass on the table. This wine's truly excellent. Lewis has done you proud.'

'Who's Lewis? Richard sent me a case of six bottles after he came to dinner. I think it was a hint.'

'Yes, of course,' Clarissa replied, deflated. She resumed her seat, as Julia served the tortilla. 'This is delicious,' she said, after the first mouthful.

'It's a little dry.'

'It seems just right to me.'

'You don't need to humour me. It's not a parish supper.'

'Good,' she replied, exasperated. 'Then you won't mind my asking another question about Father.'

'Oh no, Clarissa! Aren't I allowed to eat my meal in peace?'

'Now you even sound like him! You called him a troubled man.'

'He was a thinking man, so it was inevitable.'

'I knew of course that he had doubts . . . spiritual doubts, compounded by Alexander's death, although he wouldn't discuss them with me.'

'You were the last person he could confide in. At first, because you admired him so much. Later, because he was afraid that you'd use anything he said against him.'

'What?'

371

'In pursuit of your own agenda.'

'That's not fair . . . never mind. Whatever else, Father was an honourable man. If he'd lost faith, why didn't he resign?'

'Precisely because he was honourable. He felt that he owed it to the hundreds of men he'd trained for the ministry and the hundreds of clergy in the diocese. Besides, it wasn't as simple as losing faith. The older he got, the harder he found it to believe in God, but he never stopped believing in the idea of God. Paradoxes puzzle me, but I remember him saying that the concept of a creative, loving, moral God was humanity's greatest achievement. The finest minds had attempted to explain the mystery at the heart of the universe; the finest imaginations had celebrated it. He may have abandoned faith itself, but he always treasured its expression: the poetry; the music; the architecture; and, above all, the art. Which was why he set so much store by Seward Wemlock's work in Tapley. He saw it as a new direction for the Church.'

'All this makes his objections to my priesthood even more unpardonable.'

'But surely you see how they went far beyond the doctrinal concerns he voiced in public, real though those were? All he had left of the Church was its traditions, which he feared that you and your friends would destroy.'

'What about you, Mother? At the moment I most needed your support, you joined the arch-conservatives. Was that of your own volition or did you do it to please Father?'

'How can I make you understand that there was no distinction?'

'You said earlier that I described the day I was ordained as the happiest of my life. I grant it was tactless, though in my defence I'll point out that it was in response to your claim that your wedding day was yours, and that Marcus took it in good part. As I recall, it was a day of immense joy, tinged with apprehension that, even with God's blessing, I wouldn't be equal to the task ahead. But it was also a day of sadness: that you and Father weren't there to share it with me.'

Julia held her gaze for several seconds before replying. 'Wait here! I won't be long.'

Bemused, Clarissa drew the wine bottle towards her, pushed it away, and then drew it back, pouring herself half a glass. She was finishing her tortilla when Julia returned and handed her a book. 'Here!'

'You're giving me a copy of Mrs Beeton?'

'Look inside!' Clarissa picked up the book, which fell open in the middle to reveal a pressed rose. 'Do you remember sending me this?'

Clarissa blinked. Without warning, her eyes filled with tears. It was the single rose, which she'd sent to her mother on the day of her ordination, when, in her absence, she'd been unable to present her with the customary bunch of flowers.

'You kept it.'

'As you see.'

'Thank you.' She lifted the rose, which was dry and powdery, several of its petals having broken off and the rest faded, leaving a red stain on the page. Whoever it was who'd said *A rose is a rose is a rose* could have had no inkling of its full significance. Her father may have gone to his grave regarding her as an interloper, but here was proof that her mother valued her vocation, even if she'd chosen to conceal it in the one book that she could be sure he would never read.

373

By tacit agreement, they stuck to small talk for the remainder of the meal and, on her departure after two cups of black coffee, even the prospect of visiting Father Vincent appeared less bleak. No sooner had she driven to Granby Close, however, than she revised her opinion. It was a brute fact that many clergy were obliged to move into inferior housing when they retired, but she'd never known such a sharp decline as that from the Tapley rectory to this pokey terrace. As she parked outside number 8, her eye was drawn to the trio of gnomes on the parched lawn at number 6, one of which had been fitted out with a clerical collar and cassock. She speculated on the dispute (noise, mess or sheer personality?) that had prompted such a brazen assault on Vincent's values.

Assuming a smile, she walked up the path and rang the bell, which was answered by a large, balding woman with no bottom teeth and an apron emblazoned with the slogan *World's Best Cook*.

'Good afternoon. It's Clarissa Phipps, here to see Father Vincent.'

'Oh yes, he's expecting you,' the woman replied, in a thick Lancashire accent. 'Frieda ... I'd shake your hand but it's greasy. Mine that is, not yours,' she added, snorting with laughter. 'You've caught me on the hop. Come through. His lordship's in the lounge.'

Startled by her irreverence, Clarissa entered what its occupant must, at the very least, have designated his *living room*. He was sitting, right leg outstretched on a stool. 'Forgive me for not rising,' he said. 'Gout.'

'Stuff and nonsense,' the housekeeper interposed. 'It's a bunion. Painful for sure, but not so posh. Isn't that right, Vince?'

'I suppose you know better than the doctor?'

'Not as a rule, no. But after forty years in home care, I know a bunion when I see one.'

'Then maybe you can draw on that vast experience to make us some tea.'

'Once a bully, always a bully.'

'Have you known each other long?' Clarissa asked in confusion.

'I should say so. We slept top to tail for ten year.'

'Just go! And put your teeth in. It's indecent.'

'I'm going,' she said, with a shrug at Clarissa. 'Receding gums. Receding hairline. What's next, I wonder?'

She went out, and Vincent threw his head back in the chair. 'Now you know why I didn't want to subject you to that.'

'Not at all. I'm delighted to meet your sister,' Clarissa said, marvelling at how thoroughly he'd gentrified his past.

'We can't all be children of the manse,' he replied bitterly. 'Slater the slattern: that's what they called her at school. But she had nowhere else to go, so what choice did I have?'

'She's clearly quite a character.'

'If you enjoy horror stories! Last week, I went to pour myself a glass of water and found a full set of false teeth, like a death's head, on the draining board.'

'Still, it's company,' Clarissa said. 'You must—' She was interrupted by a furious barking.

'It's more than flesh and blood can stand,' Vincent said, hammering his temples with alarming force.

'The neighbours?' she asked.

'No, the people who live next door!'

Hence the gnomes, she thought.

'Grub's up!' Frieda entered with a toothy grin, as if to show that she'd obeyed orders. She deposited the heavily laden tray on a side table, before passing Clarissa a crazed plate and a napkin embroidered with Vincent's initials. 'Shall I be mother?' Vincent groaned. 'How do you like your tea, dear?'

'As it comes. Thank you.'

'Like life, I always say. Strong or weak, what counts is how sweet you make it. Sugar?'

'None for me, thank you,' Clarissa replied, afraid that she was letting the side down.

'A biscuit then?'

'Just the one. I had a large lunch.' As she accepted a custard cream and took a sip of the breakfast tea, Clarissa reflected on the change from the last time Vincent had given her tea, at the rectory.

'Leave that to me,' Vincent said, as Frieda not only heaped three spoonfuls of sugar in his cup – the tongs having disappeared, along with the exotic blend and fancy biscuits – but stirred it for him.

'Don't worry, I know when I'm not wanted. I can see you're having a good old chinwag. You're the one who took over Vince's parish.'

'That's right.'

'He wouldn't have liked that.'

'I don't think he did.'

'There are many things I don't like, which I'm forced to endure.'

'Such a pretty church! We only went there – ma and me – twice in all those years. Vince felt it would be a distraction for his parishioners.'

'Some priests prefer to preserve their mystique,' Clarissa replied, feeling for Frieda's rebuff more than her brother's discomfiture.

'But I'll never forget those paintings all over the walls. Like being abroad. And there was Vince himself above an arch. "Trust our lad," ma said. "Already booked his ticket to the pearly gates."'

'Have you quite finished?'

'Righty-ho, crosspatch!' She headed out. 'I'll be in the kitchen if you need me.'

'Knows when she's not wanted, does she? If she did, she'd pack her bags today.'

'She's your sister.'

'As if I hadn't suffered enough feeble-minded old maids in the parish, the Almighty has chosen to saddle me with her! Do you have any idea what it's like to live with somebody you despise?'

'Thankfully not.' She'd resented Marcus – sometimes bitterly – but never despised him.

'It corrodes the soul. And you know the thing I despise most about her? Her devotion to me. I could plunge a knife into her heart and she'd look up and smile at me: a toothless, witless smile, but a smile nonetheless. But you didn't come here to sample the horrors of my domestic life. Tell me, how are things at St Peter's! Any more buggery in the belfry?'

'It wasn't buggery. Rather what used to be called heavy petting.'

'I trust that such fine distinctions satisfy Petunia Wyatt and Alec Whittle and dear old Daisy Quantock. Although I'm sure you've won them round through the warmth of your personality. I gather that, at the Peace, they queue up for your hugs. You have them osculating in the aisles. Whereas I wouldn't even permit them a handshake.'

'*Autre temps, autre moeurs.*'

'At least we had some *moeurs*. And we knew the danger of abandoning them. One of the most odious crimes of our brave, new, feminised Church – and please don't think I lay the fault solely at the feet of women; your male apologists are equally culpable – is that you downplay the concept of sin and, in consequence, Hell. You sanitise it with phrases like *the absence of God* – and what terror does that hold for people with only the barest conception of Him? Teach them that it's Dante . . . it's Bosch: with snakes curling around their ankles and flames leaping up to their armpits, and they might learn to do what's right.'

'I've never understood why you remained an Anglican. Given how strongly you feel, you could have taken the compensation and laughed all the way to Rome.'

'Because Canterbury is still my spiritual home. Although now we have bishops in bitch collars; how long until we have a woman on St Augustine's chair?'

'Then perhaps it's time to accept the status quo,' Clarissa said, refusing to let herself be ruffled.

'This is the state of souls!' he replied, thumping the table.

She rearranged her cup to give him a moment to compose himself.

'But to business! You said that you'd been to visit the Widow Wemlock.'

'Yes,' she said, shrinking from the epithet. 'My husband needed to consult her about the forthcoming retrospective.'

'I'm looking forward to it.'

'As I said on the phone, she mentioned that Seward gave you some preparatory drawings for the St Peter's paintings.'

'Yes. Eight of them.'

'I thought that you'd have them on display,' she said, looking to see if she'd missed any among the sombre prints.

'No, it wouldn't be appropriate.'

'I trust you won't think me presumptuous.' She shivered at his brittle smile. 'But I'm sure you know of our infestation issue. We prayed that it would be confined to the chancel ceiling, but it's spread throughout the church.'

'Some might see that as symbolic.'

'Some saw the fallen boss as divine retribution, but they were wrong. The cost of treating the wood will run into six figures. We're raising money by any means possible. I was hoping I might persuade you to donate a drawing or two to a sale.'

'Why don't you ask the widow herself? She must be sitting on a fortune.'

'She lives very modestly.'

'She wouldn't know any other way,' he said, disparagingly.

'I don't want to complicate matters for Marcus, who's negotiating to borrow her pictures.'

'So you come to me? You reorder my church; you discard my liturgies; yet you expect my help.'

'I didn't mean to offend you. I thought you might wish to contribute. I'll go.' She picked her bag off the floor.

'I didn't say that I wouldn't. Though the drawings may not

be quite what you anticipate. I have them ready for you. Be my guest.'

He handed her a large cardboard folder, which she opened to find eight drawings of the fifteen-year-old Andrew Leaves. Full-length nudes, they bore no relation to the kneeling Adam in the church. Neither the artist's gaze nor the model's pose evinced any of the eroticism she'd seen in the studies of Dora. The approach was clinical, using simple, unbroken lines and minimal shading, apart from the hair stippled on his head and groin. With Xan in mind, she saw how perfectly Seward had caught the sinewy awkwardness of a boy on the cusp of adulthood.

'Do they shock you, Rectoress?'

'The drawings, no. That you should have them, yes, a little.'

'Rumours were rife in the village about questionable goings-on at the Hall.'

'I heard nothing on any of my visits.'

'Of course not. People closed ranks, afraid that a scandal would reflect badly on them. The rumours reached Lily and she threatened to stop Andrew posing. I promised to investigate.'

'How?'

'I spoke to Seward, who invited me to watch him at work: to see for myself that there was nothing untoward.'

'Was that an invitation to all his sessions?'

'Any that I chose. But knowing me better than I realised, he suggested I'd find those with Andrew and Laurel of most interest.'

'And they had no misgivings?'

'I was their rector. Above suspicion. I sat in a corner of the studio,

380

as still as one of the portraits on the walls. After a while, they forgot I was there.'

'You watched?'

'I contemplated the beauty of creation.' She searched in vain for a hint of irony. 'Nothing had prepared me for the glory of the unclad Adam.'

'Andrew!' Clarissa said, refusing to let him lose sight of the actual boy.

'He had the palest, most flawless skin I'd ever seen, even though he spent half his life out of doors,' he continued, heedless of her interruption. 'The drawings, exquisite as they are, don't begin to do him justice. Every so often, Seward would stop and alter his pose, fingering his shoulders and chest and even his stomach. I knew of course that he was doing it for my benefit. He was aware of my weakness. He corrupted me with my own corruption.'

Clarissa listened in bewilderment, wondering whether Father Vincent, who had restored sacramental confession to St Peter's after four hundred years, himself wished to confess. If so, why had he chosen her, a woman whose orders he refused to recognise? Or was that part of his penance?

'Were you just a voyeur, or did you ever . . . touch him yourself?' she asked shyly, wondering whether Andrew's hatred of the church and all its works sprang as much from Vincent's violation of him as from Seward's of Laurel.

'How you love to label things!' he replied. 'I expect every pan in your kitchen has its appointed hook. Is *touch* all that matters to you? So long as I receive my DBS clearance, everything's fine?' He turned to her with a tortured expression. 'What about Christ's stricture on those who commit adultery in their hearts? Don't worry, I never touched him. For sixty years I've curbed – no, conquered – my deepest desires. I've confined them to my head and, sometimes, my hands, but I've never imposed them on anyone.'

'Surely you'd have been happier if you'd found a friend . . . lived together discreetly?'

'Oh my dear Rectoress, you really believe that my desires are the same as yours, but with an added twist of transgression. My *sixty years* was no approximation. I was fifteen the last time I touched another set of genitals. We were on a school camping trip in Snowdonia. My best friend Billy and I refused to join in our classmates' nocturnal contests. They pounced on us and ordered us to put worms down each other's shorts. Billy resisted, but I agreed, with the regulation show of reluctance. I can still feel the worms squishing around his penis, until I couldn't tell which was which. The gang cheered, while I squeezed, and Billy squealed. He never spoke to me again, but it was worth it. You look pale. Are you all right?'

'My throat's a little dry. May I have some more tea?'

'Of course. I'll call Frieda.'

'No need. I don't mind if it's cold.' She poured herself another cup and took a gulp. 'I'm sorry, I should have asked you.' She held out the pot; he shook his head. 'Did Andrew Leaves know of your feelings for him?'

'At first, I'm sure he thought I cared for nothing but his well-being: his test results; his wickets and goals or whatever meagre triumph Lily pressed him to boast about when she asked me to *tea*

– by which I mean supper. But later, about the time of the painting, when he became aware of his body as an object of interest, if not of desire, then he knew. He looked at me with such contempt, even when he was kneeling at the altar rail. Which, as you may now have grasped, thrilled me all the more. But everything changed after his breach with Laurel and refusal to sit again for Seward.'

'I told you—'

'Yes, that – forgive me – cock and bull story. I tackled him about it, as I promised you I would. He insisted that it was true. He offered to swear on the Bible, as though we were in some third-rate melo-drama. I warned him that Seward was a very powerful man, and if he repeated what he'd told me – what he'd told you – to anybody else, he'd find himself in serious trouble. His whole life would be ruined.'

'His whole life was ruined.'

'Poppycock!'

'He had the makings of a fine artist.'

'A gifted amateur at best.'

'Doesn't it worry you that he lost his faith?'

'What more could I have done?' His raised voice and cough brought Frieda to the door.

'Did someone call?' she asked.

'Yes, but not for you. Go and ruin another recipe.'

'Water off a duck's back,' she said, retreating with a smile.

'Confronted Seward,' Clarissa said. Vincent looked at her, per-plexed. 'You asked what more you could have done.'

'That's just what I couldn't do.'

'Why? Because he was your patron.'

'No, because I'd lowered my guard. He knew how I felt about Andrew.'

'Even after Sorrel attacked him, you never re-examined Andrew's story?'

'No, never. In any case, Sorrel didn't attack him. She had some sort of fit, picked up one of his palette knives and tried to stab herself. Seward was wounded when he intervened. I saw it all.'

'No, you didn't,' she said steadily. 'Dora told me what Laurel admitted to her before Seward's funeral. You were simply the first person to reach them.'

'What is this? A trap to elicit a confession? I denied your right to the priesthood, so you've waited until now to exact your revenge?'

'Of course not. I'm just trying to ascertain the truth.'

'Seward and Laurel are dead, and Sorrel is locked in a world of her own. How can we ever know the truth?'

'We can start by acknowledging the lies.'

'You asked for some of the drawings. Here! Take them all and go.' He slid them back into the folder so roughly that Clarissa was afraid they might rip. 'I don't want them. Sell them. Burn them for all I care. Just go.'

'Oh no!' she said, feeling nauseated. 'Did Seward give them to you to buy your silence?'

'What?' He gaped at her in disbelief. 'Not even you could think that badly of me!'

'I'm sorry,' she replied, both ashamed and relieved.

'Except to ask about his health – which was awkward, given the location of the wound – I never spoke to Seward about what happened that day. It was Laurel who told me what I should say, first, to the police and, then, to the reporters and the world at large. I arrived to find the studio in uproar. Seward was howling in agony and Sorrel was screaming and shaking, but Laurel had kept her head. Once I'd rung for an ambulance, and her mother – or was it her aunt? – was calming Sorrel, she took me aside. She said that Sorrel, who'd long been jealous of her closeness to their father, had burst in on them while she was posing for him and tried to slash the canvas. In the ensuing scuffle, Seward had been hurt – trust me, there was no mention of her having lunged at him. Laurel insisted that, with me as witness, no one would question the attempted suicide but, without my testimony, there'd be an official investigation: Seward would once again be pilloried in the press; he'd be too despondent to work and, therefore, to finish the St Peter's paintings. The family would be torn apart, and the person who'd suffer most would be Sorrel, sent to a high-security hospital, along with the likes of Myra Hindley.'

'And you believed her?'

'Not the Hindley part, obviously. But the rest, yes. Why wouldn't I?'

'Because it didn't add up. Because of what Andrew had told you. Because Sorrel would have seen her sister pose many times before. Because Laurel was unduly desperate to avoid an investigation. Because of Seward himself, so wayward and forbidding in spite of his charm.'

'It was more than thirty years ago. Why rake it up now? Are you saying that Seward abused both his daughters? What evidence do you have?'

'The evidence of his own hand. One last painting: the only one, according to Dora, that he completed after the attack. It's a family portrait based on the story of Lot. He depicts himself lying naked between his two daughters, with Dora to one side, transmuted into a pillar of salt.'

'Where did you see it?'

'In Dora's cottage. He left it to her, with strict instructions as to when and how it could be shown. Believe it or not, she's hung it in her bedroom.'

'And is it good?'

'Define *good*! If you're asking: "Is it audacious, well painted and powerful?", the answer's an unqualified yes. But if you're asking about the impulse behind it, I'm not so sure.'

'Why on earth would he lay himself open like that? He must have known what people would read into it.'

'Maybe he couldn't help himself, like a criminal returning to the scene of the crime. Or maybe he needed to make a final confession.'

'Or to have the last laugh?' Vincent said, his face brightening. 'He was a lifelong provocateur. He loved to shock people, myself included. The day before your father came for the dedication, we were in the church, checking for any last-minute snags, and he told me that he'd stirred menstrual blood and semen into some of the paint.'

'How puerile!' Clarissa said, filled with revulsion.

'I'm inclined to agree. But perhaps it stemmed from his belief that everything in God's world is holy and therefore has a place in God's house.'

'Whose blood?'

'What?'

'Was it Dora's or Valerie's or one of his daughters'?'

Indeed, might Seward's use of her blood have triggered Sorrel's derangement?

'How should I know? I didn't ask.'

'So once again you did nothing?'

'What could I do? Order him to repaint the offending sections overnight?'

Clarissa pondered the irony that a man, whose prime objection to her priesthood was that she might contaminate Christ's blood by the flow of her own, should have presided over a church that was itself contaminated. 'Do you think that he was telling the truth?'

'As I've said already, how can we ever know?'

'Dora is authorising Marcus to write his biography. Maybe he'll find a clue among his papers.'

'Surely only teenage boys keep a record of their emissions? Besides, as you well know, facts aren't the same as truth.'

'So he remains an enigma?'

'But a surprisingly straightforward one. He was a man in whom light and darkness were inextricably mixed. He had a deep faith, yet he chose to challenge the Almighty as much as to celebrate Him: as though to discover whether his accomplishments would outweigh his misdeeds.'

'I could have saved him the trouble. The answer is no.'

'Your answer is no. I would never make so bold. So please take the drawings.' He handed her the folder once again. 'Seward gave them to me on the day of the dedication. It was a bittersweet gift, as well he knew. How better to use them than to preserve the church which houses some of his greatest work!'

'So the paintings have a place in the church, even though the painter is unworthy?'

'If we excluded all unworthy people from the church, there'd be no one at the altar, let alone in the pews. And who knows? Maybe Seward's unworthiness makes his work that much more precious. It's clear that our differences extend far beyond the nature of priesthood. I believe that people are inherently sinful, so I admire Seward for making something profound and beautiful out of his sin. You believe that people are inherently good, so the revelation of their wickedness dismays you.'

'Thank you,' she said, standing to leave.

'For the drawings or the distinction?'

'Both.'

Five

The paper-strewn table jogged Clarissa's memory. Marcus had told her that Hugo Treves, one of the assistant curators, was driving him back from Barnard Castle, before spending the night with his parents in Warwick. Seeing his jacket draped over one chair, his briefcase open on another, and his laptop charging by the kettle, she considered putting up a sign: *Guests are politely requested to keep the common parts tidy.* Her smile faded with the realisation that she'd have to rethink dinner, in case the pizza she'd intended for Xan and herself be used against her in a future custody battle (it helped to make a joke of it). Rummaging in the freezer, she found three fillets of plaice, looking like frozen footprints, and put them in the microwave to thaw.

She wandered over to the table and idly picked up a drawing of a mossy cliff with a giant hand reaching into a crevice. She studied it further before dropping it, as if it were on fire. 'Marcus!' she shouted. 'Marcus!' she repeated, trying to rid her voice of reproof.

'Two seconds!' he replied, entering and brushing his lips against her cheek. 'Hello, darling. Forgive the mess! I've had the most incredible day. That storeroom: it's an Aladdin's cave . . . no, that's far too

389

tame. It's the horn of Amalthea. There were sixteen paintings, including two I'd never seen before: a jewel-like Crucifixion in a blood-red landscape, and a flight of herons, rose-pink, against an azure sky, which I swear is one of his most transcendent nature scenes. There are half a dozen trunks crammed with papers that I only had time to glance at, along with sketchbooks and drawings. I've brought a couple of them with me.'

'So I see,' she said, brandishing the one that had shocked her.

'For Heaven's sake, take care! Which is . . .? Oh yes, isn't it witty?'

'That's not the adjective I'd have chosen.'

'You may not get the references. The cunt comes straight from Courbet's *Origin of the World* and the arm from Michelangelo's *Creation of Adam*. Hence the title *The Creation of the World*. You're sure your hands are clean?'

'They may be a little fishy.'

'Please!' He seized the drawing from her and held it to his nose. 'Nothing I can smell.'

'So why have you singled out this one?'

'He doesn't usually go in for visual puns. I want to scan it and put it out there, to discover if anyone knows anything. Is it the preliminary drawing for a painting he sold privately, or a one-off jeu d'esprit?'

'How can you be so irresponsible?' she asked, his excitement annoying her further. 'You left it here, where Xan could see it.'

'Come on! I'm sure he's seen a lot worse. For all we know, he's up there as we speak, clicking on some adult website.'

'*Adult* being the operative word! And we ought to know; we have the software.'

'I've told you before. I'm not prepared to spy on my son.'

'Even to protect him? What if he came downstairs now and told us that, next summer, he wants to go trekking through Kurdistan?'

'I'd ask him where he expects to find the money.'

'I'm serious!' she replied, refusing to be deflected. 'Yet we allow him to take equal risks every time he goes online.'

'Don't you think you may be overreacting? I know you've had a rotten few months, but don't take it out on Xan. Try cutting him some slack.'

'I have. And look where it got me! That poor girl.'

'Laurel?' he asked, perplexedly.

'No . . . no, it can't be!' Snatching the drawing from the table, she was reassured by the thicket of hair. 'I meant Xan's classmate, the Seventh Day Adventist who tried to kill herself, the girl he and Matthew branded a slut.'

'Slag,' he replied, at which she clenched her teeth. 'You're the one who preaches free will. So, give Xan a chance to exercise his. If anyone's been taught the difference between right and wrong, he has. But if you're truly afraid that the drawing might corrupt him, we can try the Schiele test.'

'The what?'

'Egon Schiele, trailblazing Austrian artist, fearless scourge of the bourgeoisie.'

'Thank you,' she said drily.

'In his field, he was as radical as Freud. Some would say more so, since Freud allegedly downplayed childhood sexual activity, banishing it to the realm of fantasy, for fear of alienating (not to say, incriminating) his wealthy patrons. Schiele, however, was unsparing in depicting the sexuality of his adolescent models and, what's more, depicting them not as victims but as individuals with their own agency. One of them, a thirteen-year-old girl whose name escapes me, stultified by living in a small town with her small-minded parents, begged Schiele to help her flee to her grandmother in Vienna. He duly obliged, whereupon the girl's father – a general or admiral or some such – had him arraigned for kidnap and statutory rape. The charges were soon dropped – a timely reminder, by the way, that not every artist who portrays illicit sexuality engages in it! So instead, they convicted him of offending public morality, namely (and this I can quote verbatim) *failing to keep his erotic nudes in a sufficiently safe place.*' He moved to the door. 'Xan!' he shouted. 'Now let's see whether I'm to be condemned on a similar count.'

'No, not in my house! I forbid it.'

'I'm sorry?' He looked at her darkly. 'I was under the impression that this was our house.'

'Yes, of course. All I meant was that it's benefice property.'

She remembered the folder of drawings locked in her desk. She'd planned to ask his advice on placing them, either with a dealer or at auction. Would that now smack of hypocrisy?

'Xan!' Marcus was still calling his name when he appeared at the door, as ever more alert to his father's voice than to hers or, she preferred to think, more afraid of ignoring it. 'We need you to settle an argument.'

'No way!' he replied. 'Leave the child out of it.'

'You *are* it. All we want is for you to take a look at a drawing and give us your opinion.'

'Do I get a prize?'

'Our everlasting gratitude.'

'Not mine,' Clarissa said, withdrawing from the table, as Xan picked up the drawing and examined it. The paper trembled in his hand.

'It's sick.'

'Is that good sick or bad sick?' Marcus asked.

'Both. He's stuck his finger right on her clit.'

'All right darling, you don't need to go into details,' Clarissa said.

Xan looked away, a blush suffusing his cheeks, although she couldn't tell whether it were from seeing what he shouldn't have seen or having done so in her presence.

'What are you doing with it?' Xan asked Marcus.

'It's for the Seward Wemlock exhibition I'm curating.'

'The bloke who painted David's dad bare-arsed?'

'Yes.'

'Was he some kind of perv?'

'Yes,' Clarissa said.

'Your mother has her own slant on it. What I want to know is what, if anything, the drawing makes you feel? Shocked? Disgusted? Threatened? Aroused?'

'For real?'

'Yes, of course.'

'That she ought to get a Brazilian.'

Marcus turned to Clarissa, unable to conceal a note of triumph. 'I rest my case.'

'But seriously, Dad, you won't leave it out when Hayley comes round after supper?'

'Don't worry,' Clarissa interjected. 'We'll have to clear the table before we eat anyway.'

'Who's Hayley? This is the first I've heard of her. Do I detect a girlfriend?'

'Dad please!' Xan said, with a mixture of diffidence and pride.

'Hayley was Matthew's girlfriend. Now that the Salmons have moved to Keswick, she and Xan are just "hanging".' Clarissa repeated the explanation Xan had given her, in the hope that he might expand on it.

'That's great, son,' Marcus said, with a smile that resembled a wink.

'Dad please!' Xan reiterated, stretching out the syllables, before opening the fridge and taking a carton of milk.

'Glass!' Clarissa reminded him, before turning to Marcus. 'You win! You haven't corrupted our son.' She'd have felt happier, nonetheless, if he hadn't identified the image so fast. 'But where your test falls down is with the artists themselves. Schiele was acquitted of raping his teenage models; Seward abused his.'

Xan snorted milk on his shirt. 'Shit! Sorry.' He grabbed a tea towel and wiped it roughly across his chest.

'Which is why we must remove his paintings from the church,' Clarissa said, convinced that anything else would be to endorse what Father Vincent had described as his challenge to God.

'Even if you're right about the man – and I grant the evidence is strong – is that any reason for rejecting the work?'

'Absolutely, when it breaks the contract between artist and viewer: the moral contract that binds us all.'

'Really? I don't remember signing anything.'

'None of us do. We were too young. It's the cord that binds us to our mothers at birth.'

'I'm out of here. This is way too heavy for me.' Xan headed for the door. 'Pizza tonight?'

'Of course not,' she replied quickly. 'Baked plaice.'

'See you later,' Marcus said. 'And I promise I won't disgrace you with your ... sorry, Matthew's girlfriend.'

'Fat chance,' Xan said, with a smile.

'When did you become so hard-hearted?' Marcus asked, as Xan's footsteps receded. 'Remember what you said about Brian: that we shouldn't allow one wicked act to define a person's life?'

'That hasn't changed. But there'll always be exceptions: when the act – the wickedness – is too great.'

'Please don't get the idea that I'm trying to justify him. I'm honestly not. But Laurel may have been as eager to sleep with Seward as David was with Brian.'

'That's neither here nor there,' she replied, blanking out Vincent's assertion that it was Laurel who'd concocted his alibi. 'He betrayed her trust, not to mention his duty as her father. You mentioned Freud; didn't he say that the incest taboo was the prerequisite of a civilised society?'

'Did he? I'm no expert. My point is, given that the damage has already been done, shouldn't we try to salvage what we can? I can't think of many artists whose private lives merit the *Good Housekeeping* Seal of Approval.'

'The difference in this case is the church. The seal carries that much more weight.'

'Not all of the Pietas and Madonnas in Florence were painted by Fra Angelico! You should read Vasari. Which, by the way, would have stood those E. M. Forster ladies in far better stead than their *Baedekers*.'

'I'm not responsible for the entire corpus of ecclesiastical art, just one tiny part of it.'

'What about the traditional belief that, on the Day of Reckoning, we'll be judged not by our actions but by their consequences after our deaths?'

'What belief? Who told you that?'

'Your father, one St John Phipps. It's another reason that conventional moral judgements don't apply to artists, whose work endures to delight and inspire future generations.'

'The posthumous consequences of Seward's actions include one daughter's suicide and the other's catatonic madness. To me, that outweighs any benefits that a latter-day Lucy Honeychurch might gain from seeing his pictures.'

'I envy your certainty.'

'You used to call it faith.'

'To my mind, the world's foremost religious painter, bar none, is Caravaggio. I'll take his *Death of the Virgin*, prostitute model and all, over even the greatest *Assumption* by Titian, Poussin or El Greco. Yet as we know, he was a braggart, a bully, a ruffian, a lecher and, ultimately, a murderer. Would his *Denial of St Peter* be half so powerful if it weren't steeped in his own guilt? And how many people down the ages have drawn comfort – even courage – from the image: the expression of a common humanity, which enables us to transcend our individual failings?'

'I wouldn't argue with that. And I'm not proposing that we chop Seward's paintings up for firewood, like Fairfax's soldiers taking pot-shots at the stained glass. The decision doesn't rest with me, but if, in the fullness of time, the diocese grants us a faculty to dispose of them, I'd be happy to donate them to the Tate.'

'And we'd be more than happy to accept. Nevertheless, it's my firm conviction that works made for a particular setting should remain there.'

'Even when the work and the setting are at odds? When it's an Eden that was made, not to justify the ways of God to man, but the ways of Seward to God?'

Marcus walked up to her, put his hands on her shoulders and rubbed his forehead against hers. 'Think for a moment of the damage you'd do if you went ahead. I'm not talking about damage to the paintings,' he added quickly, 'but to all the old dears, whose only brush with incest has been in some bodice-ripper about the Borgias.'

'Don't you see? We have the perfect pretext.' She tried not to sound smug. 'The deathwatch beetle. We'd be removing the pictures for their own protection.'

'And once the roof has been treated?'

'We can always find some excuse for not putting them back: the effects of damp . . . the prohibitive cost of insurance.'

'I see you've worked it all out.'

'My head's splitting. Can we leave this for now? I need to think

397

about dinner.' She opened the vegetable drawer to reveal three sprouted potatoes and a bunch of wrinkled carrots. 'I'll have to pop down to the shop.'

'Take away the pictures and you take away the tourists! You won't be very popular with the Chabras, or Jayne in the café. I'd say the whole village would be up in arms. Questions are bound to be asked.'

'What about the questions that will be asked if the truth about Seward comes out?'

'How? Everyone involved is either dead or Sorrel.'

'Andrew Leaves is very much alive. He might still speak out. And not just about Seward and Laurel, but about his warnings to Father Vincent and me.'

'If that were the case, wouldn't he have done so by now? Why stir things up after all this time?'

'Because it's open season on weak ... myopic ... complicit clergy. And given what happened between Brian and David, he has more reason than ever to hate us.'

'It sounds rather far-fetched.'

'Then there's whatever you might divulge in the biography,' she said, fixing him with a look.

'Come on! I've yet to sign the contract.'

'You said that there were trunk-loads of documents: letters and diaries.'

'I only opened two of them. One was filled with leases and ledgers from the seventeen hundreds.'

'And the other?'

'It'll take me weeks to sift through everything.'

'Suppose for a moment – keeping to your analogy – that it's as much Pandora's Box as Amalthea's Horn and that somewhere in the hoard of papers are intimate, incriminating disclosures about Seward's private life. I'm willing to strike a deal. I'll abandon any attempt to remove the paintings if you promise not to publish anything untoward about Seward and his daughters, the sort of salacious details that would guarantee you a bestseller but compromise the church.'

'You are joking, of course,' Marcus said, with a nervous laugh. 'You can't expect any writer to agree to conditions like that. I'd be betraying my charge.'

'Likewise.'

'Besides, even if I presented irrefutable proof of an incestuous relationship, I fail to see why it should discredit the paintings. On the contrary, it would show how, at his most dissolute, he was still striving to reach God.'

'Strange! Vincent said much the same, but he didn't convince me either. Do you remember an evening at Cambridge, when a group of us were having one of those intense, meaning-of-life discussions?'

'We had so many.'

'True, but this one sticks in my mind. Someone or other posed a conundrum. If a building were on fire and you could rescue either a child or the first folio of Shakespeare, which would it be? Without hesitation, we all opted for the child. The questioner then upped the ante: what if it were the only copy of Shakespeare's works in existence? There was an uneasy silence. Someone asked if a hidden copy might be unearthed in a hundred years' time. Someone else suggested that the child might grow up to be another Hitler. And it became clear that everyone in the room would save the Shakespeare, but no one was prepared to admit it. So I said, "On the other hand, the child might grow up to be another Shakespeare, a superior Shakespeare," before casting my vote for the child.'

'Shakespeare in this case being Seward?' Marcus asked. She nodded. 'And the child the church?'

'With a capital C.'

'Writing the biography will take years. But if you were to jetison the paintings and the story leaked out, it would put paid to the exhibition.'

'Why? You're a gallery; you follow different rules.'

'You've no idea how sensitive these issues have become. You didn't see the recent Gaugin show, which was plastered with reminders that the artist exploited his status as a rich European and entered into inappropriate relationships with underage girls, just in case any of us should be seduced by the gorgeous images into setting sail for Tahiti and infecting the islanders with syphilis! I'm genuinely afraid that, in twenty years' time, his work will be banned from the world's great museums and only available in some bleak repository, under the eye of a censorious guard.'

'I'm very sorry, but I can't trim my conscience to fit your aesthetics.'

Marcus walked to the window and stared out, seemingly blind to his angry reflection in the glass.

'I should warn you that, were you to rip out the paintings, I'd find it hard, if not impossible, to come to Tapley.'

'I didn't realise that they were the main attraction,' she replied, instinctively trying to lighten the mood, even though he'd given her the opening she required.

'Don't be absurd! But how could I live with someone who'd committed such vandalism?'

'And how could I live with someone willing to ignore such iniquity?'

'So what is this?' he asked, turning slowly to face her. 'An impasse?'

'Or the chance of a new beginning?' she replied softly.

'I'd be interested to know how you make that out.'

'I love you, Marcus, and I always will, but we can't pretend that this arrangement – never mind marriage – is working.' She raised her hand to check any interruption. 'I'm not blaming you. I entered into it freely. It suited me as much as it did you . . . perhaps more so. But not now. I find myself resenting you – not envying Helen, resenting you. I have a dread of growing old and bitter.'

'I don't see any danger of that.'

'That's just it: you don't see me at all.'

'So what are you saying? That we should split up?'

The words sounded so irrevocable that she was tempted to backtrack. 'Be honest,' she said, to herself as much as to him. 'Aren't we there already?'

'What about your parishioners?' he asked, pulling out a chair and plumping down at the table.

'I may be fooling myself, but I don't think it would be a problem. They'd be saddened rather than shocked. Of course, there'd be exceptions.' Inevitably, Daisy Quantock crossed her mind. 'But they've come to accept me for who I am. The roof won't fall in – or if it does, it will be because of the beetle, not me.'

'I see,' he said, failing to return her smile. 'I take it this is something you've thought about for a while.'

'Felt at first . . . thought about for the last few months.'

'I took us to be chugging along quite happily.'

'We were,' she said, anxious neither to hurt him nor to be won round. 'But maybe it's time for a change, not a chug.'

He let out a hollow laugh. 'And what about Xan?'

'Xan's fourteen. You're the one who said that we have to trust him. He's old enough to take the train to London on his own.' She dispelled the image of him, abducted on the Euston concourse. 'It will be a new chapter for him too.'

'I feel dazed.'

'I didn't mean to spring it on you,' she said, moving towards him and stopping abruptly, lest her resolve appear to be wavering. 'Think about it. I'm not asking you to decide straight away.'

'I remember saying the very same thing to you the first time I asked you to sleep with me.'

'I remember it too.'

'Forty years!'

'In March.'

'Forty-one since you came up to me after evensong.'

'It took me weeks to pluck up the courage.'

'I'm awfully glad that you did.'

'So am I.'

'This should have knocked me for six. But, like your parishioners,

I think I'm saddened rather than shocked. I'm not sure what to say.'

'Then say nothing for now. Especially not to Xan. It's only the second time that Hayley's visited.'

'So "hanging" does mean something more?'

'I can't speak for Hayley, whose track record doesn't inspire confidence. But yes, I think it does for Xan.'

'First love! I don't know whether he's to be envied or pitied.' He shook himself vigorously. 'I need a drink. The ten-year Glenfiddich, or would that strike the wrong note?'

'I'll leave it to you,' she replied, heartened by his composure. 'I'd better go and buy the veg. Any preferences?'

'Whatever looks good. I can do it if you'd rather.'

'No, I could use the air. I shan't be long.'

She left the house in a state of elation, although she knew better than to mistake the relief of having made a decision for the assurance of having made the right one. She thought of the many women who'd come to her over the years, complaining that their husbands had changed, as if to absolve themselves of their marital failure. If the bishop's visitor were to ask her to account for her own break-up, she'd be obliged to say the opposite: Marcus had remained utterly himself. But his faith in art, which had hitherto complemented her faith in God, now challenged it. She'd accepted Helen and a marriage without passion, but she could no longer accept the schism in their beliefs. Would *spiritual and artistic differences* be grounds for divorce?

Her mood shifted as she approached the church and the need to make another momentous decision. Was Marcus right to suggest that she'd cause more harm by taking down the pictures than by leaving them up? Would future generations revile her as a twenty-first-century Puritan? As well as denuding the building, she'd be betraying her father: both destroying his legacy and denying his belief in the bond between human and divine creation. Yet for all Seward's gifts, he'd been singularly lacking in the love, let alone moral responsibility, that were the other two elements in St John's Holy Trinity. In the final analysis, was it a choice of which to whitewash: the artist or the walls?

Trusting that a fresh look at the paintings would help to concentrate her mind, she made a detour into the church, only to find herself more conflicted than ever. She stood at the back of the nave and studied the chancel arch. Although Seward had cited ancient precedents for his clean-shaven Christ, she suspected that he'd had another, more private reason. It was as if that very smoothness would make Him more forgiving, not just of the primal couple to His left and right, but of the artist himself. This compassionate, clement, almost feminine Christ was one with whom she found it easy to identify. But if she were truly to 'stand in His person', she must also be the judge: *Christ Pantocrator*, whose heavily bearded face stared down implacably from every Orthodox apse.

She turned to the even more contentious image of Adam and Eve in Eden. As a young woman, she'd been profoundly influenced by Seward's rejection of Original Sin, along with his censure of St Augustine for a creed as self-serving as the one which she now imputed to him. But while renouncing the doctrine of the Fall, she'd never disputed the human capacity for evil, whether in despite of

404

God, in despair of God or, in Seward's case, in defiance of God. It was abundantly clear that, for all its beauty, Seward's Eden was a snare. His counter myth was as treacherous as the traditional one. The serpent in his garden wasn't slithering out of a cleft in the rock, or even from the scribe's scroll, but rather from the artist's own palette. He himself was the serpent who tempted Eve.

Hearing a rustle, she turned to see David Leaves silhouetted against the open doorway. With his shorn hair and dressed in a plain white T-shirt and jeans, he resembled an army cadet, but one who was unlikely to survive basic training.

'David, what are you doing here?'

'The door was open. It's a church.'

'There's no service. I just popped in for . . .' She barely stopped herself saying *vegetables*.

'I often come by in the evening, but it's always shut.'

'Why?'

'It's allowed, isn't it?' He moved forward, as if to assert his rights.

'Yes, but . . .' A thought struck her. 'You're not meeting somebody, are you?'

'No. Who?' His horrified voice chastened her. 'I come to be with Brian. Not like a ghost or something . . . I'm not mental. But in my head.'

'I understand. I didn't mean to doubt you. You caught me by surprise.'

'I go over and over what I did wrong the night you found us. If I'd tucked my shirt in quicker . . . if I hadn't opened my big mouth, Brian might still be alive.'

'Perhaps,' she said gently. 'Or perhaps it would simply have delayed the inevitable.'

'No, he was going to get us a place. Not to live, obviously. But where we could be together and . . . things.'

'He told you that?'

'And he would have!' he said defiantly. 'But now he's dead and Matt's left Tapley and Xan won't speak to me.'

'I can't rewrite the past. But I can talk to Xan. I know he misses you too.'

'Only because Matt's left.'

'Much more than that. You've been friends for years.'

'Really? That'd be great. I mean I don't expect him to change his mind, but great . . . really great.'

Touched by his eagerness, she moved a pace towards him. 'Would you like a hug?'

He took a moment to consider. 'Maybe a quick one.'

She put her arms around him, hoping that it was just the flimsy T-shirt that made him feel so frail.

'He was fit, my dad.' She broke away, to find him contemplating Adam.

'You might be twins.'

'Don't say things like that!'

'It's a compliment.'

'Mrs Miller, in biology, says that kids look like their dads to protect their genes: so that their dads won't think their mums have been screwing around and reject them. Course, she didn't say *screwing*,' he added, with a shy smile.

'You amaze me!'

'But with my dad, it's the other way round. It's like he rejects me *because* I look like him.'

'If that were true (and I'm not for a moment saying it is), perhaps it's because he's afraid he can't protect you.' She struggled to find words to reassure him, without revealing any secrets. 'Perhaps seeing you reminds him of things – unpleasant things – that happened when he was a boy.'

'Nothing happened to him. I know about the Skull – sorry, Father Vincent – fancying him. That's why my gran hates him so much . . . Father Vincent, I mean. Not that she's that fond of Dad either. But he never did anything. The real sicko was Lord Wemlock. With his own daughter!'

'Your father told you that?'

'The night before Brian's funeral. He came to my room for a chat (of course, I know it was Mum's idea). He even knocked, though he still wouldn't sit on the bed. He explained why he hated coming here. It's not what Gran says about being ashamed to see himself like that.' He pointed to the naked Adam. 'But he was ashamed for the girl. Then he told me why. He said I must never repeat it to anyone, not even Mum.'

'But you've repeated it to me.'

'You already know.' His expression hardened. 'He said he'd begged you to help and you did nothing.'

'Next to nothing, I confess,' she replied. 'I was culpably naive. I refused to believe that a man who could paint something so beautiful could do anything so wicked.'

'Do you think that's why he painted them this young? So he could get her to take her kit off?'

'It's possible, though I doubt he'd have needed the pretext. Eden is timeless, so Adam and Eve might be any age. As I understand it, he wanted to emphasise their innocence: to show them enjoying their nakedness even if, in the Bible, they're not conscious of it until they eat the fruit. Which is why Adam holds it, intact, in his hand.'

'Is it a Golden Delicious?'

'No, a quince. But let's not go into that now.'

'Who'd have thought the picture had so many meanings?'

'Talk to my husband . . . Xan's father, and you'll discover several more.'

'Is that why Father Vincent hung a curtain over it?'

'You'd have to ask him, but I think he considered it inappropriate for certain services.'

'Kids say he used to come here at night, open the curtain and . . .' He fell silent.

'That's not fair,' she said, wishing it could be *not true*. 'You of all people should know better than to listen to scurrilous rumours.'

'You pulled the curtain down,' he continued, ignoring the rebuke. 'Gran was furious.'

'I may have been overhasty,' she replied, wondering whether Daisy might prove to be her principal ally.

'The rail's still there. Look! You could always put it back.'

'The cloth was cut up and recycled in the church hall. Besides, I'm thinking of proposing that the painting – all the paintings – be taken down permanently.'

'For real?' He stared at her in astonishment.

'It's not going to happen overnight . . . that's if it happens at all. But knowing what I do about Seward Wemlock's life, I can't see how we can leave them up. What about you?'

'Me?'

'Yes. You have more right to an opinion than anyone: what with your father . . . and Brian.'

'No one ever asks what I think.' He sounded faintly annoyed at the imposition.

'They do now. What's more, you can speak from the heart. You don't have to worry about offending the authorities or losing revenue.'

'Can I have a moment? I'm afraid of getting it wrong.'

'There is no *wrong*. All I want is an honest answer. Given your own story and what you know of Seward Wemlock's, do you think that the paintings have a place in the church? I can't promise to act on your decision, any more than that the PCC will act on mine, but it'll help me enormously to make up my mind.'

David cast a guarded gaze over Eden.

'So,' Clarissa asked, 'what do you say?'

Acknowledgements

For help and advice on matters great and small, I would like to thank Sally Barnes, Revd Georgiana Bell, Julia Bicknell, Revd Marjorie Brown, Martin Butlin, Mark Cazalet, William Chubb, Roger Clarke, Penny Gold, Nicholas Granger-Taylor, Canon William Gulliford, Bishop Richard Harries, Lady Selina Hastings, Bruce Hunter, Dickon Love, Rosamund Mason, Joseph Mutti, Canon Mark Oakley, Sue Reid, Revd Katherine Rumens, Canon Angela Tilby, Olivia Timbs, Revd Claire Wilson, Revd Joanna Yates and Linsey Young. I owe especial thanks to Luke Brown and Hilary Sage for their assistance with the text and to Katharina Bielenberg, Paul Engles, Rita Winter, Corinna Zifko and all at Arcadia.